The La

Book 1 in the Spellsinger Series

Amy Sumida

More Books by Amy Sumida

The Godhunter Series(in order)

Godhunter
Of Gods and Wolves
Oathbreaker
Marked by Death
Green Tea and Black Death
A Taste for Blood
The Tainted Web

Series Split:
These books can be read together or separately
Harvest of the Gods and A Fey Harvest
Into the Void and Out of the Darkness

Perchance to Die
Tracing Thunder
Light as a Feather
Rain or Monkeyshine
Blood Bound
Eye of Re
My Soul to Take
As the Crow Flies
Cry Werewolf

Beyond the Godhunter
A Darker Element
Out of the Blue

The Twilight Court Series
Fairy-Struck
Pixie-Led
Raven-Mocking

Here there be Dragons
Witchbane
Elf-Shot

The Spellsinger Series
(The Last Lullaby)

Sign up for Amy's Newsletter and get a free gift:
http://google.us11.list-manage.com/subscribe?
u=398603e0fc6b3876340e37356&id=3abd32edce

Dive further into the worlds of the Godhunter,
Twilight Court, and Spellsinger, at Amy's website:
AmySumida.com

Acknowledgments

I want to thank Kara Dempsey for her suggestion of using Angels Rock Bar in Baltimore for one of my scenes, and for being an inspiration to kick ass women everywhere. Karmen Simmel is also owed a huge thank you for all of his work on countless trailers and promotion pieces for me. And finally, thank you to my editor, Michelle Hoffman, whose help has been priceless.

Pronunciation Guide/ Character List

Adam MacLaine: Human client

Arnet: Are-net, Knight of Fluorite

Ava: A-vah, Queen of Sapphire

Banning: Ban-ing, Gheara of the Kansas Gura

Barret: Bare-it, Commande

Branna: Bra-nah, Duchess of Jade

Carrick: Care-ick, Knight of Onyx

Cerberus: Ser-bur-us, Demi-god dog-shifter

Declan: Deck-lan, King of Alexandrite

Edmond: King of Jet

Eileen: I-lean, Queen of Copper

Elaria: Eh-lar-ee-ah, Spellsinger

Finbar: Fin-bar, Duke of Sapphire

Galen: Gay-lin, King of Sapphire

Gerard: Jare-rod, Knight of Onyx

Hugh: Hew, Knight of Onyx

Isandra: I-san-dra, Queen of Diamond

Jack Armstrong: Loup

Jameson: Jay-meh-son, Knight of Fluorite

Jarlath: Jar-leth, King of Diamond

Jonah Malone: Human gangster

Kean: Key-in, Knight of Howlite

Lorcan: Lore-can, King of Copper

Moirin: Moy-rin, Queen of Tiger's Eye

Mrs Chadwick: Adam MacLaine's housekeeper

Niall, Nigh-all, King of Citrine

Odran: O-drawn, King of Howlite

Oonagh: Oooh-nah, Queen of Snowflake Obsidian

Parthalon: Par-tha-lawn, King of Jade

Quinlan: Kwin-lahn, Alchemist

Riona: Ree-oh-nah, Queen of Malachite

Sara: Sare-rah, Pink tourmaline fey.

Sean: Shah-n, King of Turquoise

Teagan: Tee-gan, Queen of Jet

Tír na nÓg: Tier-nah-n'awhg, Realm of the Fairies, the Land of Youth

Torin: Tore-in, King of Onyx

The Last Lullaby references several songs. If you'd like to listen to them, in order of their appearance in the book, please check out The Last Lullaby playlist on Spotify:

https://open.spotify.com/user/ashstarte/playlist/53JpzskA89bFtkSA pbTvWu

Chapter One

I hunched my shoulders in an attempt to lift my coat collar a little higher around my ears. The weather in Seattle was dismal in December. Hell, in my opinion it was dismal during most times of the year. I longed for the kinder climate of my home, where even the rain was warm. But I couldn't go back to Hawaii yet, I still hadn't met with my client, and the payday for this job promised to be worth a little discomfort.

I finally made it to the top of the ridiculously long driveway, my eyes scanning the area surreptitiously from within the cashmere confines of my coat. I'd had the taxi drop me off a little ways down the street so I could do a bit of surveillance on my approach. Even in the gray, grim weather, there were at least eight guards spaced around the front of the house. One of them moved to intercept me, and I acted as if I hadn't seen him.

"Hold on, Miss. This is private property." The overly muscled man in combat pants held a gloved palm out to me in the traditional "stop" gesture. I saw the gun on his hip, but he hadn't drawn it. That was mistake number one. I was in the driveway already, which made me a threat.

Bad guard, no biscuit.

"I'm expected." I could have announced myself right then, but I wanted to test Adam MacLaine's security team.

That was my client, MacLaine—or he would be soon. If this guy was an accurate representation of MacLaine's security, it was a wonder the man wasn't dead already.

"Do we have a guest arriving today?" Mr. Combat Pants

asked a little microphone clipped to his shirt.

He had to open his leather jacket to access the mic, giving me a flash of the knife he had secured to an inner pocket. Damn this guy was dumb. He even turned away from me to talk into his comm. Like he couldn't conceive of a woman being a threat. I could have killed him three times already. I suppose I should have berated him for his bad habits, but I hated doing other people's jobs. And it was definitely someone else's job to whip this guy into shape. The mere thought exhausted me. I do not suffer fools.

"Name?"

"What?" I asked, completely distracted by his ineptitude.

And the spaghetti stain on his shirt. It was nearly invisible from a distance, but now that I was up close and personal, I could clearly see the crusty red mark on the black fabric. So, a fool and a slob. Definitely not the type of man I'd have chosen to protect me.

"What's your name, Miss?" the slob asked.

"Tanager," I said, whispering to see if he would make the mistake of coming in closer to hear me.

"What was that?" He sure did. He leaned in close enough for me to stab him in the throat.

Of course I would never deign to dirty my hands in such a manner. My mother raised me better than that. I killed like a lady.

"The name is Tanager," I said more clearly. "And I'm cold."

Whoever was on the other side of the microphone heard me, and must have barked something into the muscle-head's ear. He flinched, then straightened.

"Sorry, Ms. Tanager," he stammered and gestured to the looming house. "My team wasn't notified. Go on in. Someone will meet you at the door."

2

"Thank you, Mr. . . ?" I drew it out into a question.

"Uh, you can call me Jake, Ms. Tanager," he stammered.

"Thank you, Jake." I walked off, striding quickly to the beckoning warmth of the open front door.

A woman stood within the golden light of the doorway, her features as stern as her severe bun, and her eyes razor sharp. She nodded to me, and shut the door behind me after I entered.

"May I take your coat, Ms Tanager?"

"Yes, thank you." I slid out of it and sighed.

I had worn my usual getup to greet clients–pencil skirt and modest blouse. But instead of heels, I'd chosen knee-high boots. It was just too cold outside to go without something covering my calves. The woman looked over my prim outfit, and nodded in approval. With my long, dark curls pinned up, I looked very professional.

"I am Mrs. Chadwick," the woman introduced herself as she hung up my coat. "Mr. MacLaine is waiting for you in his office. I'll take you there now."

I followed Mrs. Chadwick down a corridor much too wide to be called a hallway. It was lined with expensive artwork, and the sounds of our footsteps were muffled by a silk carpet runner that looked as if it had taken years to weave. It was nice, but I'd seen all of this before. Done better, to tell the truth. My clients were the wealthiest people in the world. They had to be in order to afford me.

"Mr. MacLaine, she's here," Mrs. Chadwick said as she walked through an open door.

"Thank God," a man's voice groaned.

It was a pleasant voice, and it matched the office I entered.

3

Not nearly as pretentious as the rest of the house, this room was more personal. It held framed family photos, an old chair that must have come from a time when MacLaine wasn't so wealthy, a wide desk made for function instead of form, and several sitting areas; one before the desk, one before a picture window to the right of the desk, and one in front of a modest fireplace. That's where MacLaine had been, at the fireplace enjoying its comfort instead of working at his desk. In the crowd I normally contracted with, that said a lot.

Adam MacLaine was around forty, with a trim build that suggested he didn't spend all of his time making money. His oak-brown hair was lightly sprinkled with white at the temples, and his skin had a healthy tan, but not the sunbed tan so prevalent in Seattle. His skin had seen real sun. Blue eyes crinkled as he smiled in relief, and came to meet me halfway across the room, hand extended.

"Thank you for coming, Ms Tanager." He shook my hand firmly. "Could you close the door on your way out, Mrs. Chadwick?"

"Of course, sir." She smiled a little, showing a hint of affection for her employer. That said a lot too.

"Would you like something to drink?" MacLaine offered as his hand swept to a sideboard where several bottles waited. Not decanters, mind you, he had straight up liquor bottles out on display. The social elite would be shocked.

"No, thank you."

"All right then." He looked unnerved by my refusal. "Would you care to have a seat?"

"Yes." I slid into the chair across from his, and he relaxed a little, coming over to join me.

"I don't know how–" he started to stammer, but I held up a

4

hand.

"Mr. MacLaine, who wants you dead?" I cut through the pussyfooting.

"I believe it's a man named Jonah Malone." He sighed, and sank back into his chair. "His company was failing, and I bought it at a . . . well, for a song, really."

"Uh-huh." I chuckled at the song reference.

With the exception of his ironic wording, my clients's stories were always so similar. Someone got the better end of a business deal. Or they were cheating on their spouse. Or cheating on their mistress. Or cheating on their taxes. No, that last one doesn't require my intervention. Not usually. But the issue was often about someone screwing someone else in some form or another.

"I assume you've compiled a dossier on him?"

"Oh, yes," MacLaine fumbled with something on the floor beside him, and then handed me a manila folder.

"What exactly do you want me to do to Mr. Malone?" This was the line I asked all of my clients. I needed to be very clear with them. A lot of them assumed I was purely an assassin, but that wasn't the case. I thought of myself more as a fixer. I could kill when necessary, but death was the most extreme result I offered.

"I . . ." He gaped at me. "What are my options?"

Just as I'd thought. Cer hadn't told him. My old friend was having a laugh at my expense right about now. MacLaine had doubtless been referred to me by one of his friends, but he'd had to go through *my* friend, Cerberus Skylos, before he could arrange a meeting with me. Cerberus made sure the client was someone I'd want to work with before he passed on the info. And he usually did me the courtesy of explaining who I was, or at least, what I could do, to my potential customers.

"Do you know what I am, Mr. MacLaine?" I asked gently.

"An assassin," he whispered, as if he might be overheard.

"No," I shook my head. "I have killed people, but that's not who I am. Or *what* I am."

"Uh." He started to look confused. "Are you a vampire?"

"Good guess," I chuckled, "but no."

The mere fact that I was sitting there, facing him, meant that Adam MacLaine knew about the supernatural world that existed in the shadows of the human one. "The Beneath."– or just plain "Beneath." is what we, the denizens of said community, called it. So, MacLaine knew of it, but it was very doubtful that he knew the scope of the situation. He hadn't even known the correct term for a vampire–blooder. The wrong titles give away ignorance in a heartbeat.

Humans who were aware of the Beneath usually knew about the forerunners of paranormal society, the obvious races; loups (don't call them werewolves, they hate that), other shapeshifters, and blooders. Sometimes they knew about fairies, but the Shining Ones were really good at covering their tracks, so that was rare. What was even more rare was when humans were acquainted with the other races; gods, witches, demons, dragons, angels, and so forth. Things that went bump in the night, and did a fair amount of rabble rousing during the day as well. We just knew how to hide our supernatural gifts better than the shifters and blooders.

"A friend of mine told me about you. He said you were the best. That you never failed," MacLaine's face started to fall into the sharp lines that always preceded my revelation of the Beneath. It was like they could sense I was about to tell them something that would change their entire life. Or at least their ability to sleep through the night.

"That's true," I agreed. "So you know about vampires. What else do you know?"

"What else?" He scowled. "The shapeshifters, of course."

"And that's it?"

"There's *more*?" MacLaine's eyes widened.

"Oh yes," I smirked. "There's quite a bit more. But that's not for me to reveal. I only have the right to tell you about my own kind. Now, do you know what a siren is, Mr. MacLaine?"

"Like in the *Odyssey*?"

"Yes, exactly," I smiled, relieved that I wouldn't have to explain everything. "My mother's people are considered to be a class of god. They were minor deities, more like an entourage to the more powerful gods, but still considered a divine race."

"Are you seriously telling me you're descended from gods?" He started to stand.

I quickly sang the lyrics from Hollow Point Heroes' "Sit Down Shut Up."

I had a whole arsenal of quick-draw lyrics just like this one, ready to be shot out like a bullet when necessary. I didn't even need the song to say exactly what I wanted to accomplish. All that I needed was one word to work with–sit, dance, die. You know, the usual. And then I could visualize, and direct the magic from there. This particular lyric just happened to work really well. And you'd be surprised how often I employed it.

MacLaine froze, his eyes going wide with horror as his body disobeyed him, and plopped back into the chair. He leaned forward onto his forearms, and regarded me intently. Giving me his full attention, just as I'd commanded.

7

"Good." I pushed down the power that rose whenever I began to sing. "Now, don't look at me like that. You're perfectly safe. I simply needed to demonstrate what I could do before you wrote me off as insane. I put no permanence into the spell so the effects will wear off momentarily."

"What did you just do to me?" Adam strained to push his words past the weakening magic.

"I'm getting to that," I smiled. It wasn't often that I got a chance to talk about my heritage. "As I was saying, my ancestors were minor deities, companions of the goddess, Persephone. You do know who Persephone is?"

"Yes." He sighed deeply as the effects of my spell wore off. "I didn't think she was real, but yeah, I'm familiar with her myths."

"Oh, she's very real." I laughed to think of what Persephone's reaction to his disbelief would have been.

She just couldn't accept that people didn't believe in the gods anymore. I told her she was in denial, and she told me there were several rivers in the Underworld, but the Nile was not one of them. The Greek goddess has a silly sense of humor.

"When Hades did his little abduction routine, Persephone's mother, Demeter, enlisted the aid of my family to find her daughter," I said. "She gave them wings, and bade them to search the world for Persephone."

"I've never heard that part of the story." He was relaxing more and more now that it was apparent that I wasn't going to attack him. "They never found her, I imagine."

"No, Persephone wasn't in the world. She was with Hades, in his domain. So my ancestors failed," I confirmed, "and Demeter cursed them for it. They were turned into sirens–women who sing eternally to their missing mistress, begging for her to return home."

8

"I thought the sirens were mermaids who lured men to their deaths."

"They're closer to birds than mermaids, but they do lure men to their deaths," I said. "Their song is so beautiful, few can resist its pull, but it's also tragic. And tragedy can only create more tragedy."

"Are you saying that you're a siren?" MacLaine cocked his head at me, fascinated, when really, he should have been afraid.

"No, only part," I shook my head. "The other part of me is witch."

"What? Like a Wiccan?"

I burst into laughter, and he scowled at me.

"No, Mr. MacLaine," I got my humor under control. "Real witches are nothing like those tree-hugging, circle dancers. They're a separate race entirely, grisly and powerful. People you should hope to never encounter. My mother lured one of them to her, but he was strong enough to withstand the pull of death in her voice. In fact, he decided he quite liked her, and her music. He married her."

"You're the child of a warlock and a siren?" MacLaine's voice rose in shock.

"The word 'warlock' means liar. Oathbreaker, from the Saxon waerloga. Male witches are still called witches."

"Oh."

"Yes."

"So you're the daughter of a siren and a witch?"

"Yes."

"Oh. Um." He chewed at his lower lip a bit. "What does

9

that mean exactly? What does that make you?"

"It makes me rare, Mr. MacLaine," I smiled slowly. "Very rare."

"And you can sing people to death?"

"I can do much more than that," I decided to put him out of his misery. "My kind, though rare, have been born before. We are called spellsingers. We can transform songs into enchantment, bring lyrics to life."

"Like how you made me sit down," he whispered.

"And shut up, yes," I laughed. "There are a lot of races living among humans. Spellsingers are only one variety, though we are, admittedly, one of the most dangerous."

"Other races?" MacLaine looked as if he couldn't take much more, so I took pity on him once more.

"Don't worry about that right now," I waved a hand. "They aren't the ones who want you dead."

"Jonah," MacLaine growled. "I can't believe he's taken it this far."

"Mr. MacLaine," I said carefully, "my kind have toppled kingdoms, burned cities, changed the history of the world. I can do anything to Jonah Malone that you wish... for the right price."

"So, from conqueror to mercenary, eh?" MacLaine chuckled.

"I have no desire to destroy monarchies or watch Rome burn–that was my Grand Aunt Adelaide's thing," I rolled my eyes.

"Wait– the burning of Rome, where Nero supposedly fiddled . . ." He exhaled roughly. "A relative of yours did that?"

"Nero didn't own a fiddle," I grimaced. "That instrument wasn't invented till much later. He played a cithara."

"A what?"

"It looks kind of like a lute . . . never mind that." I was terrible with tangents once I got talking. "Nero wasn't in Rome at the time of the burning. He hired Adelaide, just as you're hiring me. Someone else played music for her while she set Rome ablaze."

"Someone else . . . you can start fires with your song?"

"I told you," I huffed. "I can do anything the words permit me to do. If I sing about fire, stuff burns. If I sing about water, someone drowns. Sometimes, a whole continent," I shook my head. I wouldn't tell him about Uncle Eilener and Atlantis. He still got flack over that fiasco.

"So you're . . . wait. Nero hired someone to burn Rome?"

"Sure." I shrugged. "Everyone hated him. After Rome burned, Nero came in with food and supplies, opening his own gardens to house people. He polished up his image while secretly deciding on a spot to build his new golden palace. It was good PR, and smart property management."

"What a bastard," MacLaine winced.

"Yeah, Aunt Adelaide regretted working with Nero. That's why I'm a bit more choosy with my clients," I smirked. "But what do *you* want, Mr. MacLaine? What result would you like, concerning Jonah Malone?"

"I'd like for him to just back off," he huffed. "But I don't see how . . ." He trailed off as he saw me smiling. "You can do that? Just make him change his mind? Permanently?"

"Absolutely," I inclined my head. "And it's even cheaper

11

than killing him. Only two and a half million."

"Two and a half *million*?" MacLaine huffed. "That's more than I paid for the company."

"Your acquaintances did warn you about my price, correct?"

"Yes, but," he frowned, "that's when my life was in danger."

"Your life is *still* in danger," I stood. "I haven't agreed to take your case yet."

He gaped at me for two seconds before standing, and offering me his hand again. "Two point five million is just fine, Ms. Tanager."

"Wonderful, then we have an agreement." I shook his hand, then started heading for the door. "And just a suggestion." I stopped–halfway there–and looked back at him. "Fire your security team and get some professionals. Even without my magic, I could have killed them all within ten minutes. Especially the one called Jake."

"You . . . what . . ." He blinked, and then recovered. "Alright. I'll do that today."

"Smart man." I smiled. Maybe he would live long enough to pay me. After all, he hadn't hired me to do his–

"How much for you to head my security?"

"No." I shook my head. "I don't have time for that, and you don't have enough money to pay me." His face fell. "However"–I pulled a card from the pocket of my skirt and handed it to him– "this man will help you."

"Cerberus Security," MacLaine read, and then looked up at me. "This is the guy I called to arrange our meeting."

I nodded.

His eyes went wide, "Please tell me this isn't the same Cerberus who . . ."

"Guarded the Greek Underworld?" I laughed. "That was a giant dog, Mr. MacLaine. With three heads, I believe."

"Oh." He laughed, but it sounded strained. "Just a reference to the protection skills then?"

"Yes, exactly." I smiled. Nope, I wouldn't tell him that he had guessed correctly.

Cerberus was actually a shapeshifting god with a fondness for practical jokes and dangerous women. I'm unsure which had cost him his job. I've known him for centuries, and he still hasn't told me. I know that Hades personally kicked his old, guard dog out of the Greek Underworld. Gave him the fiery boot. So now, Cerberus watched over humans. Humans who could pay him enough to soothe his wounded, puppy pride. Cer was damn good at what he did, but he was better at defense. He lacked the subtlety for a proper offense. If you told Cer to kill someone, he would probably just punch them in the face, really hard. I doubt he'd even stop to ask if the guy needed killing to begin with. So he kept to the security side of the business, and he called me for anything beyond that. Conversely, when my clients had a bunch of buffoons guarding them, I sent them to Cerberus.

"Ms. Tanager?" MacLaine stopped me again.

"Call me Elaria." I smiled at him.

"That's lovely." He grinned. "You must call me Adam then. I was just wondering . . . isn't a tanager a type of bird?"

"Why, yes, it is, Adam." I was still smiling as I left. It was always nice when someone appreciated the subtleties.

Chapter Two

Jonah Malone was a gangster. Or a mobster. Probably a whole lot of words that ended in "er." He had clawed his way to the top, and then discovered that he didn't actually have a head for business. All of his enterprises were failing, not just the one MacLaine had purchased, and Jonah was reverting to his old thug ways to handle the frustration.

It had been a simple thing to schedule an appointment to see him. I simply sang to the receptionist over the phone, and she found a spot for me that very day. Then I walked into Jonah Malone's office, closed the door, and sang to him. In five minutes, he had completely forgotten why he wanted to kill MacLaine. He also decided to sell off his remaining businesses, and get out while he could. Perhaps meditate more. I figured why not help improve the guy while I'm messing with his head?

I walked out feeling relaxed, and satisfied with a job well done. I had video taped Jonah's "change of heart", and sent it to Cer, who would pass it along to MacLaine as confirmation. Within ten minutes, MacLaine had transferred my payment into my account. I could finally go home. Maybe I'd have a Mai Tai on the plane as a special treat. Hell, maybe I'd have two.

I was on the way to the airport, when Cerberus called.

"Got another one for you, El." Cerberus didn't bother with a greeting.

"I'm tired and cold, Cer." I sighed. "Give it to someone else. I'm going home."

"No one else can handle this. It's bad."

"How bad?"

"Blooder army bad."

"That's pretty fucking bad." I made a face at the phone.

"Yes."

"Fuck."

"Yes."

"Whose army?" I asked.

"Some guy named Lincoln." Cerberus's voice had a shrug in it.

"Like the president?"

"Yep." He didn't offer anymore info.

"Where is this army going? What do they want? Who's the client?" I huffed. "You wanna give me anything without me pulling your fucking canines to get it?"

"Whoa, easy now," Cer chuckled. "You're turning me on, Elaria, sweetheart. You wanna stop in Denver and make good on some of your promises? We can fly to Kansas together after your failed attempts at pulling my pearly whites."

"Kansas!" I nearly screeched, causing my driver to look back at me in concern. "It's fine. I'm fine," I told the driver. To Cer, I said, "I'm not going to Kansas. Who do you think I am? Dorothy?"

"You'd look cute in a little gingham dress," he offered.

"The only way you'd get me in gingham is if you put on a collar and let me call you Toto," I shot back.

"For you, baby? Anytime."

15

"Great." I rolled my eyes. "Now we have our next couple's costume planned."

"No, really." I could hear Cerberus smirk. "I look good in a collar."

Cerberus and I had been playing this mating game since we met, back when I was sixteen, and we'd never concluded it. Part of me wanted to see if he was as good as he implied, but the other part of me knew our friendship was worth too much to risk it. Plus, we did business together, and everyone knows that saying about mixing business with Percocet. Or something like that.

"Look." Cerberus got serious. "The guy is an old friend of mine. He's a blooder, a gheara, but he keeps his people in line, and they don't cause any trouble. He's one of the good ones."

"I don't know about a blooder being good, but I'll believe the bit about him keeping his people in line." I chuckled. "It's not like you hear a lot of vampire stories originating in Kansas. I didn't even know that Kansas had a Beneath. I thought they'd all flown away to Oz."

"Banning's a tough one. He fought his way out of Europe, and now the fuckers are coming for him." Cerberus didn't even acknowledge my jokes on the Beneath, aka the paranormal community. Which he knew irritated me. I put effort into my comedy; the least he could do was acknowledge it.

"Lincoln doesn't sound European," I noted dryly.

"He's not." Cer finally laughed. "He's a local hire. Mercenary."

"Ah," now that I could relate to. "So the guy is just doing a job. I can't hold that against him."

"Yeah, but he contracts with the Falca all the time. Those elitist bastards wouldn't even bother to come to America, and kill

16

Banning themselves," Cer huffed. "Lincoln, what kind of stupid merc name is that?"

"So what do you want me to do?" I rolled my eyes, something I did a lot when I talked to Cer. He had a thing about names, especially professional ones, and was always going on about them. And the fact that I didn't have one.

"Ma'am? We're here," the cabby called back to me.

"Hold on, Cer." I stuffed my phone into my purse and pulled out some cash for the driver. I hurried out of the cab and over to a semi-secluded bench, then pulled out the phone again. "You there?"

"Why do you always shove your phone in your purse when you put me on hold?" Cerberus grumbled. "Just press the fucking hold button. You think I like listening to all your lady loot knocking against the mic?"

"I'm going to hang up," I threatened.

"Fine," he growled. "I can get you ten million for the job."

I nearly dropped the phone. Ten million was twice my assassination fee. But then I thought about it. An assassination was one person, and Cerberus was asking me to kill . . . Wait, how many blooders *was* he asking me to kill?

"How big is this army?" I asked.

"I'm not sure," he muttered.

"How big, Cer?"

"Big enough that a gheara blooder can't handle it with his entire gura backing him," Cerberus snapped.

Blooder, as I mentioned before, is the correct appellation for a vampire. Kind of obvious, I know, but that's how those names usually came about. I mean look at my race, the spellsingers. Well– duh. But the word gheara was a little more interesting. It was Romanian for "fang," and it indicated that this particular blooder was a big deal, akin to a king, maybe even bigger than that. There were usually hundreds of blooders in a single gura–that's the group of vampires who kiss the gheara's pale patootie. In fact, most people call them a kiss, but the blooders don't like that. Probably because of the ass-kissing thing. The polite term is gura, which is yet another Romanian word, meaning "mouth". Then there was the Falca, which were the elite blooders who controlled everything in the blooder world. Falca meant "jaw" in Romanian. Yeah, I guess all the names were obvious; they just sounded less so in another language.

Anyway, if this guy had an entire gura looking after him, and Cerberus still couldn't help him without me, then there must be a whole lot of mercenary blooders coming after Cer's friend. Crowds were tough; it was much easier to weave a spell around a single mind. To alter the free will of thousands of people at once was nearly impossible. So I would probably have to go another route. I could sing a spell to affect the environment, and attack them physically, leaving them their free wills. Or I could enchant a few of them at a time, and force those to attack the others. Possibly even a combination of both. It would be exhausting, and probably take me multiple songs to complete. I wasn't even sure I could do it.

"Ten million per song," I said to Cerberus.

"What?" Cer shouted into the phone.

"An assassination usually takes a few lines, half a song at most." I explained my reasoning. I never arbitrarily picked a price. "And I charge five mil for a kill. So ten million for an entire song is a bargain, especially when you'll be wanting me to kill hundreds, possibly even thousands, of blooders. You know I'll need to sing more than one song to take out an army, so your friend can pay per song. If it gets too expensive, he can tell me to stop singing, and handle the survivors with his gura."

"Gods damn you, Elaria," Cerberus snarled. "You have the mind of Archimedes and the cold calculation of Hades himself."

"Thank you," I said primly. "But you know as well as I that you were trying to dick me over on this one, Cerberus, and I'm not happy about that."

"He's a friend, El," he sighed.

"Yeah, that's why I'm letting you slide," I acknowledged.

You'd think immortals would end up having tons of friends, what with our extensive lifetimes. But it's actually the opposite. When you live as long as we do, you end up breaking most bonds. Family is usually the exception, but even they can drive you crazy enough to make you avoid them for a few decades. When you form a friendship that lasts, like mine and Cer's, it means something.

"So, are you meeting me in Kansas?" I finally asked him.

"You'll do it?" Cerberus asked with a measure of surprise.

"Of course I'll do it." I rolled my eyes. Again. "Any friend of yours, and all that heroine bullshit."

"Thanks, El," he said sincerely.

"Of course," I said just as sincerely. "Now, where in Kansas am I going?"

"Head to Lawrence," Cer said. "Check into the Springhill Suites–it's one of the nicer hotels there. A Marriott."

"Well, as long as I can stay at a Marriott," I teased.

"I'll book a room for you," he promised. "Under your usual alias."

"Florence Nightingale," I agreed. "Perfect."

"And I'll come and get you after I arrive."

"Alright," I agreed. "See you in Kansas, Toto."

"Bring your sexy red heels, Dorothy. I'll pack my collar." Cer laughed as he hung up.

Chapter Three

Ah, Kansas. It was actually kind of pretty. Lawrence was a bustling town, but not quite as busy as Seattle, and not nearly as cold. It was November, so there was a nip in the air, but something about that breeze coming off the water in Seattle, made things so much colder there. Lawrence was more mellow with its chill, like Seattle's hippie sibling. Autumn had painted the city in its vibrant colors, and there was the smell of the season on the breeze–dry leaves and cooling earth. I breathed deeply of it as my cabby drove me out to the Springhill Suites.

As promised, I found a room already booked, and paid for, under my alias. I showed the surprised clerk my Florence Nightingale ID, and he handed me the keys with a twitching smile. I gave him the standard line: my folks had thought it was a great joke to name me Florence, what with our last name being Nightingale and all. The clerk let his lip twitching take the shape of a proper smile.

I went up to my room, threw my bag on the bed, and started digging around for a change of clothes. I needed a hot shower, and something more comfortable than my secretary get-up. I found a pair of jeans and a cotton blouse with bell sleeves. Perfect to relax in, and maybe go grab some dinner. Then I headed to the bathroom. When I came out, dressed but still rubbing at my damp hair, my phone was ringing. I snatched it up and answered.

"There's no time for me to meet you," Cerberus said urgently. "Get over to the Crouching Lion Country Club now." He rattled off an address.

"What?" I glanced out of my picture window at the night

sky. It was still early; the stars hadn't even brightened yet.

"Now, Elaria!" Cerberus roared. "They're here!"

"Fine," I snapped and disconnected him, muttering to myself, "Crouching Lion. What is it, a kung fu country club?"

I grabbed the essentials and rushed out of the room. When I got to the street, I paused, not really knowing what I was going to do. I didn't have time to call a cab, and I couldn't exactly show up at a blooder battle with an innocent human in tow. So I needed to grab some wheels of my own. I scanned the road, where a steady stream of cars drove by. I was considering running out to flag one down, when a red sports car pulled away from the pack and screeched up to the hotel. A smarmy guy got out of the car, and I smiled at him.

"Excuse me." I ran over before the valet could reach him, and then leaned in close.

"Hello, pretty lady." He leaned closer.

I began to sing, and his face went blank.

"Here." He handed me his keys. "I think you need to borrow my car. I'll be at the bar when you get back." Then he walked past the stunned valet, and into the hotel.

"Some people are so nice," I gave the valet a sweet smile before I climbed in the . . . what the hell was it? Oh damn! A Ferrari. Talk about luck.

I squealed away from the hotel and hit the convenient GPS on the dash. Within minutes, I was pulling up the tree-lined, private road of the Crouching Lion Country Club. As I approached, the night brightened until finally, florescent flood-lights illuminated the outskirts of a blooder horde. They considerately stayed off the road, too intent on crossing the massive golf course to bother getting in my way. It was the straightest path to their goal.

22

A line of blooders stood before the main building of the country club. They posed in the aggressive manner employed by determined defenders throughout history. There were quite a lot of them, all armed despite the fact that they were blooders, and could have been considered weapons themselves. But I suppose when you faced an army of your own kind, your talents, no matter how impressive, negated themselves.

At the head of this fierce flock stood Cerberus, towering over Banning's gura. His massive muscles looked a little too He-Man next to the more mundane physiques of the previously human blooders. Cer's long, dark hair was pulled back in a no-nonsense ponytail, and his even darker eyes were narrowed on the oncoming army. Until he saw me.

Cerberus smiled, an altogether chilling thing to see since it showcased a set of prominent canines that were a little thicker than your average blooder's. He let out a triumphant howl, and the line of mercenaries paused to look around at what had excited the shifter god. When they saw only me, a woman in a sports car, they went back into attack mode. Obviously I wasn't a threat.

A guy at the center of the horde paused a little longer than the others, watching me carefully as I sped past him. I had my chosen playlist on pause, my iPod hooked up to the car's stereo, and I hit the button as I raced alongside the golf course. Music blared: Fall Out Boy's "My Songs Know What You Did in the Dark" going into its long intro. I shot up the drive before the club, and pulled the car to a screeching stop right in front of Cerberus.

The door slammed open with my violent shove, and I leapt out. Music blasted out of the vehicle as I jumped on the hood. I could feel the beat of it in my bones, vibrating through the metal beneath my feet. I glanced back at Cerberus and winked, my eyes briefly catching the shocked expression of the man beside him. He was blond and a blooder. Had to be Cer's friend, Banning. Not that it mattered. I turned back around just as the lyrics began pelting my ears.

23

I started singing absently as I thought out my battle strategy. I knew I'd have to rein in these mercenaries as fast as possible so that they didn't make a run for it before I could get to them all. I couldn't leave any alive to make a second attempt. That's just sloppy work.

Fire would be perfect for forming a blooder-proof barrier. But I had to work up to it, wait for the words in the lyrics that would magnify my intent. So I started with the poor sods in front. My hand lifted to them as words shot from my mouth like bullets. Aggression blaring in my ears. Tension coiling in my thighs. The stuttering strength of the song cut through the cold air. Every blooder I pointed to exploded as if I'd blown their heads off with a missile launcher.

The crowd behind me started muttering as Cerberus chortled.

"Isn't she wonderful?" Cerberus sauntered up to lean over the top of the car and watch me work. "An artist. A true artist." He laid his chin in his palm.

I continued to slam out the vicious verses, ignoring Cer. The song was filling me, becoming a part of my being, and the strength of the spell was rushing around me. A tornado of charged molecules clambering for motivation. Waiting for me to give them a direction. An objective. I felt glorious, powerful enough to make all those mercenaries mine. And I did, I snatched up their minds. Their will. Then I used the next line to vent the brewing musical malice. The blooders before me turned on their companions, and started tearing them to pieces.

"Holy fucking hellfire." The blonde man moved up beside Cer.

I sensed him there, felt his intense stare on me, but didn't have the time to look at him. Still, his face flashed in my mind–a picture of aloof male beauty. Strong jaw, regal nose, eyes glowing

24

green in the shadows. Nice.

"I told you!" Cerberus laughed harder as I continued to pour my lyrical rage over the mercenaries. "She's worth every penny."

The chorus came, giving me what I needed to manifest fire. I angled my hand flat, bringing it down like a blade with every sharp word. Each slice brought a line of flames surging up around the faltering army, causing many of them to shriek in terror and stumble back into their companions. The hand motions were more for me than the magic, like a conductor directing his symphony. This symphony didn't need me to conduct it. All the magic required was for me to picture the result I desired, and sing. That was it. So I let my arms fall limply to my sides as I screamed the cataclysmic conclusion to the chorus, and my fiery prison penned the blooders in. The ring closed, and the magic surged through me, responding to the triumph I felt.

"Oh my god, I think I'm in love," I heard one of the blooders behind me groan.

"Of course you are," Cerberus called back to him. "For fuck's sake, I'm rock hard right now."

The blooder who had watched my approach more carefully than the others rushed forward. He snaked through the terrified mass, but he wasn't trying to calm them; he was simply trying to reach me. I was obviously his biggest threat, and he was obviously a take-action sort of guy. It had to be Lincoln, coming to kill me before I could slaughter his entire army. It was a smart move, probably the best option available to him. Cut the head off and all that.

Too bad it was useless.

The song turned truly tragic, as if sensing my need. I looked right at Lincoln, directing the destruction at him alone. The merc leader flared up like a torch, blooders pulling back from him

25

in horror. But the bonfire didn't last long. It burned so hot, so intensely, that it turned Lincoln into cinders within seconds. He exploded into sooty snowflakes, swirling down over his army. Blooders cringed away from the remains, hardened soldiers turning into bawling babies.

The song surged on, and I spread my arms out in welcome to it. It was a confession now. A baring of what I had been born. A show of the hand that life had dealt me, and what I had done with it. What I had become. A creature of nightmares. A sorceress of songs. The villain no one could escape. The lyrics couldn't be more perfect for me. It was a declaration of pride in my own monstrosity, and a deep, secret fear of it. I let them see me.

And that's when the real screaming started.

It went on for another two songs, during which I killed every mercenary there in various lyrical ways. The blooders behind me were cheering, some of them singing along with me, and some even mimicked the motions I made. I had blooder backup dancers. Maybe we could take this act to Vegas. A song, a dance, and some magic. We were perfect for Sin City.

By the time I ended the third song, I was trembling, on the verge of passing out. But it was okay; the threat had been eliminated. My fire-oriented playlist had kept the heat up, ensuring that no one escaped, and those within the ring were dead or dying. I let the flames die down as well, until the only illumination originated from the building behind me and the scattered lampposts. The soft glow gently lit a field of corpses, slowly turning into the ash of the undead. One thing good about killing blooders; there was very little clean up involved.

The next song started to play. My shoulders fell in exhaustion. I turned to Cerberus and held my arms out to him like a little girl. Even with me standing on the hood of the car, he was still nearly as tall as I was, and he easily picked up my five-foot-four frame. Cer set me down on the road, but held onto me long enough to make sure I could stand on my own. He gave me a concerned look, blocking my shaking body from the cheering crowd. We never let others see our weaknesses. I nodded that I was all right.

Cerberus gave me a kiss on the cheek, and backed away. "Thanks for coming, El."

"No problem, honey." I smirked, then looked at the blond.

"I'm Banning Dalca." The blooder held his hand out to me.

"Nice to meet you." I went to shake his hand, but he did that suave, old-school vamp thing and kissed my hand in a way that was so much more sensual than a human could make it.

"Thank you for your assistance, Ms. Tanager." Banning smiled slowly at me, his eyes lingering over my face.

"Just make sure my payment goes through by tonight," I said abruptly as I pulled away.

Banning's eyes widened, and he looked as if he was going to say something more. But I was too tired to deal with him. I needed to get out of there before I passed out.

"I gotta run." I looked back at Cerberus. "I'll wait for you at the place, babe." I spoke vaguely on purpose. The last thing I needed was for an entire gura to know where I was crashing for the night.

"Of course," Cer said with a smirk, as if we were an item.

I smiled back; it was our routine when some client flirted with me. Cer acted like I was his, and the guy usually backed off. This guy didn't buy it, nor did he back off. As I slid into the front seat, and turned down the music, Banning Dalca followed me. He leaned in, his eyes fading to mint under the car's interior light, and gave me a very unsettling look.

"Please don't leave, Ms. Tanager," he whispered. "I'd dearly like to speak with you."

This seemed way past some mere flirtation. It was weird, and it sent chills racing down my spine. The guy was hot, but I didn't sleep with clients, and I especially didn't sleep with blooders. Blooders were bad news.

"Maybe another time." I tried to reach past him for the door handle, but he didn't budge.

"Please," he said again.

"Get away from the car, Mr. Dalca," I said in a dangerous tone.

"Ban," Cerberus growled. "What the fuck, man?"

"Five minutes of your time." Banning tried once more.

"No," I snapped. "Now are you going to back away or do I have to make you?"

"All right, Ms. Tanager," he sighed, but produced a business card, and stuffed it into my hand. "Please call me after you've rested. I promise you, I have the most honorable of intentions."

"Uh-huh." I slid the card into my bra. "Thanks; I got it."

Banning sighed again, then eased away, shutting the door for me. I gunned the engine and yanked the car about, but I couldn't help looking back at Banning as I drove off. He stared after me like I was breaking his little, undead heart. But the strangeness didn't stop there.

Just as I hit the border of golf course turning into forest, I saw a movement in the shadows. A flash of skin. I was instantly alert, despite my exhaustion, and angled the car enough to shine the headlights into the area. There he was, a gods-damned fairy.

28

One of the fucking Shining Ones was standing in the trees of Lawrence, Kansas, watching me like some otherworldly peeping tom. Instead of hiding when my lights hit him, he held up a hand in greeting.

I nearly drove off the road.

I didn't though. I veered back onto the asphalt and kept going. If a fairy waves at you from the forest, you don't stop for him. Heading over for a little chat is a great way to get yourself abducted. The Fey were generally considered to be the perverts of the paranormal world. They'd fuck anything, anywhere, anytime. A fairy's interest wasn't flattering; it simply meant you had a heartbeat and were within reach.

Okay, so maybe that was a bit of an exaggeration. The lesser fey–pixies, leprechauns, trolls, goblins, those sorts–would mount you in a heartbeat if you let them. Most would try even if you didn't let them. However, the elite sidhe, those who were known as the Shining Ones, were a bit more discriminating in their choices of bed partner. That didn't make them any less terrifying. In fact, the Shining Ones had all sorts of seductive spells on their side. They might not technically be rapists, but with that kind of magic, the technicalities blurred. And once they got you, they tended to keep you until you were completely used up. I've heard stories of all manner of debaucheries going on in Tír na nÓg. So it didn't really matter, lesser or greater, fairies were freaks.

It was that whole hedonism thing. No one did it better than the Shining Ones. They lived every moment of their immortality to the fullest, believing that they shouldn't do anything they didn't want to, and conversely, they should do everything, and every*one*, that they did want to do. They ate the best food, drank the finest wine, and wore the most luxurious clothes. They loved to mix it up too. They didn't care who created an item; if it was the best, they wanted it. Several of them lived this side of the Veil for that very reason, the luxury.

The Veil is what we call the border between worlds. Planes of Existence. Realms. Again, take your pick. These places were laid on top of each other, separated by an invisible sheet of magic. If you were sensitive enough, you could feel the magic, and in some places the Veil was thick enough that even people who weren't so sensitive could feel it. But to cross it, you had to either be magically powerful or know someone powerful enough to take you through. Which meant that the fairy dude standing in the forest, waving at me like it was just another casual night in Kansas, was powerful. And very pale.

I have good eyesight, okay? I caught a lot in that glimpse of flashing headlights. Though I didn't really need my advanced perception. The guy was really white. His hair was white. His skin was white. I couldn't see the color of his eyes, besides them being pale, so maybe they were white too. His delicate features and slim figure nearly hid the fact that he was a guy, but that he was definitely masculine.

Not that his looks mattered. What mattered was what he was doing in those woods. Had he been watching me? Listening to me sing? Or had he been there for Banning? Maybe he'd been the blooders's backup, something more subtle to go in afterward on the off chance that the army of blooders didn't succeed. I almost turned around, but I knew I was too exhausted to be of any help. So I kept driving, and left the Shining One to Cerberus. If the dog-god couldn't handle one fairy, he might as well give up protecting people for good.

Chapter Four

I was so drained, I barely made it up to my hotel room. I passed out on the bed fully clothed, and didn't wake until Cerberus pounded on my door like a battering ram. I lifted my head, looked around in confusion, and slowly realized who was the cause of that racket. A glance at the bedside clock told me it was 3:00 AM. Cer must have partied it up some with the blooders before stopping by. No biggie. In fact, I was glad he'd given me some time to rest.

I stumbled to my feet and ran a hand over my face. The pounding came again.

"Stop that!" I snapped at him as I yanked the door open. "You're going to get me in trouble with hotel security."

"So what?" Cer chuckled as he came in. "Like they're going to say anything when I open the door."

"Yeah, they'll just turn around and call the police." I went back to the bed and flopped across it.

"That was a hell of a thing, El." Cerberus closed the door, and locked it before coming over to sit on the bed beside me. "Three in a row, and heavy fucking magic too. You were right: ten mil a song was a steal. And Banning paid you, by the way. I watched him do it."

"I'm paid?" I muttered, and then gave a tired, "Yay."

"Yeah, he sent it immediately after you left." Cerberus paused, and the silence dragged on long enough for me to open my eyes and sit up.

"What?" I narrowed my gaze on him. "Is it about that conversation he wants to have with me?"

"Yeah." Cerberus looked embarrassed.

That was a first.

"What the hell, Cer?" I punched his arm lightly.

"He says . . ." Cerberus shook his head, and huffed. "No, I promised I wouldn't tell you. He wants to be the one to explain it."

"Explain what?"

"It's fucking bizarre, Ellie-girl," Cerberus sighed. "But it's not like we don't live in the bizarre. It could be true, and I don't think Banning would lie to me about it. He didn't smell like he was lying."

"About what?" I growled.

"Can't tell you," he said. "But I promised Banning I'd try to get you to talk to him. It's that serious. And who knows? Maybe it will be a good thing."

"Cerberus, I'm going to kick your ass if you don't tell me what the fuck you're talking about right now!"

"I can't, Elaria." He shrugged. "Just believe me when I say you need to hear him out."

"Get out." I flopped back down. "I'm too tired for this bullshit."

"Come on, kid." He pushed at my leg.

Cerberus loved to call me "kid" since he was like this ancient god, and I was only 257 years old.

"What's with the country club, by the way?" I tried to get

off the subject since it didn't look as if he was leaving anytime soon.

"What's wrong with the club?" Cer asked. "It's a good cover. It makes Banning money, and only attracts a certain type of human."

"What? Rich and stupid?"

"Rich and docile, mostly," he shrugged. "Not a lot of riots started at country clubs."

"Yeah, all right." I chuckled. "Is that where he lives too?"

"The whole gura lives there." Cer nodded. "There are five subterranean levels beneath the club."

"Holy hellhounds," I swore, and Cerberus scowled. That curse was a particularly irritating one for him. Which was of course why I used it often.

"Banning has a bunch of businesses all over America, but the Crouching Lion is his stronghold." Cerberus tried to ignore my smirk. "He's a good businessman. I think he'd expand to the other realms if he could."

"That reminds me," I said. "Did you see a fairy in the woods outside the country club?"

Cerberus went silent again. I opened my eyes and stared. Hard.

"Cerberus."

"You weren't supposed to see him," he huffed. "Fucking fairy–I thought they were good at blending in with nature."

"The guy waved at me," I said dryly. "And he's a walking snowman. How did you expect him to hide in the dark?"

"He *waved*?" Cerberus was horrified.

"Well, he didn't wave exactly." I sat up again. "He did that thing where they just hold up their palm and stare at you, like some kind of Native American cliché."

"Did he say 'how'?" Cerberus chuckled.

"I think it's pronounced– howgh." I drew the word out. "With a 'GH' at the end."

"Really?" Cer frowned. "Howgh did I not know that?"

"Cerberus!"

"Oh! Yeah, um, he's your next client."

"He's my what?"

"He wanted to see you in action, so I told him to stop by." Cerberus shrugged.

"A potential client, who also happens to be one of the Shining Ones, contacted you to contract my services, and you told him to just stop by and check out the mass slaughter of a blooder army?"

"Yeah."

"Yeah, okay." I deflated. Then I got up to search the mini bar for tiny bottles of alcohol. I held up a bottle of vodka triumphantly as Cerberus continued to watch me. "What?" I asked just before I downed the contents.

"The job is in Tír na nÓg," Cerberus said.

"No."

"But it pays"

"No." I cut him off. "I don't go there. Nobody with any

sense goes there voluntarily. Unless they happen to be a Shining One."

Tír na nÓg was the world of the Shining Ones, fairy central, and going there was akin to going to hell, any of the hells. Not the looks part–Tír na nÓg was supposedly awesomely beautiful. No, it was the torture part, and the no-escape part, that was similar to being sent to hell.

"You'd have a diplomatic charm," he went on anyway.

"A what now?" I grabbed a miniature bottle of Jack.

What the hell, vodka was like Russian water. In fact, its name stemmed from the Russian word for "water". I could surely mix some Jack Daniels with it. Jack went with everything, just like water. He was very fey that way.

"A diplomatic charm," Cerberus explained, "is a spell placed upon you before you enter Tír na nÓg. It guarantees you safe passage. You can't be held against your will or harmed, unless you offer harm first."

"If I'm going there for work, I'll most likely be offering someone harm." I grimaced.

"Yeah." He gave me a guilty look. "They want you to kill a king."

"A *fairy* king?" I gaped at him.

"No, a troll king," he huffed. "Of course a fairy king."

"I'd get my ass handed to me." I swallowed hard. "In pieces. And possibly shoved down my throat."

I was pretty bad-ass, if I do say so myself. But my mama used to warn me that no matter how powerful I got, there would always be someone better than me. I was raised to fit my britches, thank you. I knew my limitations. Fairy kings didn't get to rule because they ate sugarplums and danced around trees all day with flowers in their hair. They were the most powerful magic users in all of Tír na nÓg, and Tír na nÓg was the most magical plane of existence there was. Which meant that fairy kings–and queens, let's not be sexist–were the baddest motherfuckers in all the worlds. No one went up against Shining Royalty. No one sane at least.

"It pays fifty million dollars," Cerberus said.

"Money is meaningless to a dead woman," I downed the Jack. "Plus, I just made thirty mil–what the fuck do I care for another fifty?"

"How many times do I have to tell you?"

"I know, I know." I rolled my eyes. "Eternity is a really long time, and that makes it really expensive."

"Fifty million would be a nice nest egg." He smiled encouragingly.

"First you want me to have some weird conversation with your blond, blooder friend, then you want me to traipse off to Tír na nÓg holding hands with some fairy revolutionary while I sing 'Ding-Dong the King is dead'?"

"I don't think those are the right words to that song," Cerberus said dryly. "And he's not dead yet."

"I can improvise when needed," I stared blankly at him. "You know that."

"One convo and one king." Cerberus shrugged. "What's that to the Slayer of Armies?"

"That's an awful name; I don't like it," I said dryly.

"The Conqueror of Crouching Lion?"

"Dumb."

"The Berserker of Blooders?"

"That makes me sound like one of them." I shook my head. "Will you please stop trying to come up with a scary assassin name for me?"

"The Last Lullaby?" Cer asked hopefully.

"That's not half bad, actually." I frowned, and he let out an excited whoop.

"The Last Lullaby it is! Oh, El, that alias will shoot up business like crazy."

"I don't think you said that right." I frowned deeper. "Why don't you just call me 'L' for short?"

"I already call you 'El'." He grimaced. "It sounds exactly the same."

"Well, I never agreed to the name; I just said it sounded okay."

"Too late," he snickered. "You have been dubbed Lady Last Lullaby."

"And now you're dumb again."

Chapter Five

I had gone back to sleep after Cerberus left, but it wasn't long before I was awakened again. It was like coming out of a dream into a nightmare, one of my personal hells. The thing all spellsingers feared had been done to me while I slept. I was gagged.

It was a professional gag too. Or maybe that's the wrong term. It wasn't just some bit of cloth tied around my face. This was a piece of leather with a plastic bit that had been shoved into my mouth. The leather was strapped around my head and buckled into place. And all of that was done in the seconds it took for me to wake up. Which meant that my attacker had some super speed. Supernatural speed. In the seconds that I reeled under the knowledge of my vulnerability, my limbs were bound. I was stretched across the mattress, the blankets yanked down to the foot of the bed, so the ropes could be tied around the bed frame.

I came to in a panic, flailing and squinting in the darkness to try and find my attacker. Spellsingers may seem pretty powerful, almost god-like, but we have a very big weakness. Our voices. Plugging your ears wouldn't work. Proximity was more important. It came down to the range of my spell, not someone's ability to hear it. But if you stopped me from singing altogether, I was powerless. I didn't even have much physical strength. I was the equivalent of an average human woman. And whoever had invaded my hotel room, knew that.

The bedside lamp switched on, and I blinked against the sudden illumination. A gentle hand pushed my hair out of my face, and I looked up into the stunning features of Banning Dalca. I inhaled sharply and looked down my body. I had only worn an oversize T-shirt to bed. One of my favorites, Labyrinth. David Bowie's face was currently scowling up at the blooder looming over me. Over me and between my thighs. Oh gods, he was going to rape me. I knew that bastard looked weird. Fucking blood-sucking sadist! If I lived through this, I was going to make him do horrible things to himself. Things involving enormous dildos.

"Shh." He pulled away, easing down to the end of the bed, and leaning over to grab the discarded blankets. He brought them up and over me, tucking me in like I was a child. "I'm not here to hurt you in any way, Elaria."

I tried to murder him with my stare.

"I had to restrain you," Banning said apologetically. "Cerberus told me you refused to talk to me, and I couldn't let you leave Kansas without at least trying to speak to you. I can't lose you again. Not after just finding you."

I felt my eyes widen. This blooder was bonkers. Or maybe he thought I was someone else. But no, he had used my name. He knew who I was. So he was just plain crazy.

"No, I'm not insane," Banning said as if he could read my thoughts.

I knew that wasn't true though. It wasn't a blooder talent. The old ones could sometimes control your mind, but they couldn't read it.

"I just want you to hear me out," he went on. "Just listen to what I have to say, and then I'll remove the restraints and the gag. You can do what you will then. Kill me if that's your wish. I only want you to hear me out first."

I went still. What the hell was this about?

"It has been over two hundred years since I've seen your beautiful face." Banning sat on the bed beside me. "But I recognized you instantly. The curve of your cheek, the bow of your mouth, even the color of your eyes–that strange mix of cerulean and amethyst. It's all the same. Your voice is still the same. Your scent. The only difference is your race . . . and your magic."

I was totally baffled.

"I know you don't understand." He sighed. "Do you not feel even the slightest bit of familiarity when you look at me? Do you remember nothing?"

Remember? What the fuck was this guy going on about? I shook my head. *No, Crazy Pants, I don't remember you.*

"Ah, I should have known that would be too much to hope for." Banning nodded. "Let me tell you my story then, Elaria, and perhaps that will trigger something."

Yep, he was batshit crazy, but at least he wasn't raping me. Maybe I could just calmly let this play out, and then kill the lunatic after he released me.

"I was blooded in 1641 when I was twenty-four years old," he began. "But we didn't meet until 1657. Your name was Fortune Selwyn, and you were the daughter of a ship's captain. Your family lived in London. Your father imported goods for the merchants there."

Oh, I wasn't liking where this was heading, not at all.

"I even remember the name of the street we met on." Banning smiled wistfully. "Beech. The tree not the shoreline. You were on your way home, with only a maid for your escort. I had never seen anyone as beautiful as you. You wore this pale blue dress, and it made your eyes appear violet. I stopped you and asked your name." He chuckled. "You sniffed indignantly, offended that I would approach you without a proper introduction, and stomped away. When I pursued, you told me, and this is a direct quote, 'Get thee from me this instant, you bull's pizzle!'"

40

I narrowed my eyes on him as he took a moment to laugh.

"I think I loved you instantly," Banning confessed. "I followed you home, secretly of course, and watched you daily for months. You were amazing. This vibrant, willful woman with the mouth of a sailor. I labored over how to introduce myself properly, how to get into your sphere. Finally, the choice was made for me." He swallowed hard.

I muttered against the gag that he had the wrong woman, but of course, he couldn't hear me.

"Your father had some very powerful enemies." Banning sighed. "They wanted to send him a message. I suppose it was a blessing that they didn't abduct and rape you, but what they did was still horrifying. They murdered you in the middle of the street. You'd just left your father's ship, after bringing him his dinner. He often stayed late in his office, and you enjoyed spending a few hours in his company, even if you had to walk through London during the evening hours to do it."

Something tingled inside me, some kind of creeping, seeping shiver. Dread.

"Being so newly blooded, I couldn't come out until full dark." His jaw clenched. "Your evening walks were just a little too early for me. I reached you just before you died. A few minutes later, and I probably wouldn't have been able to save you. As it was, the screams of your maid alerted me, and spurred me on. I found you bleeding out from a wound in your chest, lying on the dirty cobbles. They had simply stabbed you through the ribs, and fled."

Banning stopped, and gave me a hard look. His eyes flashed emerald.

"Know that they suffered, Elaria," he proclaimed. "I found them, all of them, and made them pay for what they did. Still, it was a blessing in the end. I don't think I would have had the heart

41

to blood you if you hadn't been on the verge of death. To turn you into a monster seemed like such blasphemy. But as I held you, I knew I couldn't let you die. I took you away from that filthy street, and I made you mine."

A flash of Banning in some kind of fancy, Elizabethan outfit danced in my head. Despite all the frills, he still looked good in it, manly even. Lace and gold bordered his throat, a silk ribbon bound his hair, yet his face was fierce when it lowered to my neck. No. No fucking way. I was letting this guy's story get to me. My imagination had filled in the images. There was no way I could remember that. I hadn't even been born yet.

"We fell in love, deeply in love, and we made the mistake of showing it." His eyes flashed again. "I was just starting to gain my power, just an infant blooder really, and I had joined the London Gura for their guidance and protection. As my blooded, you were brought in as well. The gheara was a woman. Cosmina. We gave her our loyalty and lived beneath her rule for nearly a hundred years before our love began to annoy her. Most immortals, as I'm sure you know, don't remain in relationships for more than a few decades. We grow bored so easily."

I must have made some kind of expression indicating agreement because he nodded and went on.

"Cosmina wanted me." Banning didn't say it with ego, just stated a fact. "She thought she could wait out my love for Fortune. After a century though, it became apparent that Fortune and I were special. We had a love strong enough to last forever. No one could turn my affection away from you. I have always, since the moment I first saw you, thought you were the most exquisite woman who has ever existed. But that wasn't why I loved you. Your face drew me in, but your heart held me prisoner."

His expression changed from romantic to ferocious.

"Cosmina hated our love," he growled. "The more she

watched us, the more bitter she grew. Until finally, she acted upon her jealousy. She murdered you. She took my beloved away, and I was too weak to stop her. That was the year 1760."

Banning stopped, hung his head briefly, and swallowed hard. When he looked back up at me, there were tears in his eyes.

Another flash of images came. A cruelly smiling woman with blazing auburn hair. She was standing over me, her greedy mouth bloody. Banning was behind her, being held back by a group of men. He was shouting, straining against them, his face streaked with tears and blood. What the fuck? Seventeen sixty was when this woman had died, Banning's Fortune. That was the same year I had been born. Was it a coincidence? I didn't believe in reincarnation. Did I?

"I fled London." His jaw clenched. "I am ashamed for fleeing, even to this day, but there was nothing I could do. I had to either submit to the woman who had killed my sweet Fortune or escape. I couldn't set sail from London. She would have known. So I made my way through Europe until finally, I reached another shore, and booked passage to America. My power had grown enough to establish my own gura, and I became a gheara." He stopped and pulled off his shirt, showing me his muscled chest.

There were tattoos down his right arm. I recognized one immediately. It was the mark of a gheara, a circle with a curving shape angled inside it, near the top. The form of a sharp fang But below and around this prominent tattoo were other, more-detailed pieces. Some tribal and some more realistic, but all in black ink. Stark against his pale skin.

"My gheara mark"–Banning waved to the one I'd recognized–"and marks for my gura," indicating swaths of designs below it. "But this one is for you." He pointed to a tattoo of a woman, near the bottom of his upper arm.

My eyes lost focus for a second, and then the image

became glaringly clear. It was me. The blooder had a portrait of me tattooed on his gods-damned arm! All black and gray wash, with my eyes done in their odd, bluish-purple color. The face was remarkably similar, but it was the eyes that sealed it. I'd never met anyone with eyes like mine.

"I had it made from an old painting of you. I wanted you with me forever," Banning went on. "After I left, I promised myself that I would never be weak again, and I would never live with regrets. So before I solidified my gura, I went back to London, and I killed Cosmina."

Why did hearing that make my blood race with satisfaction?

"It was why that army came for me." He shook his head. "I avenged you, and it brought you back to me. I cannot believe this to be anything but fate. You are Fortune returned, and I have brought you proof."

He reached to the bedside table, and picked something up. It was laid down flat, a little leather book, so I hadn't noticed it before. He opened it, and revealed a miniature painting. Maybe eight inches tall. It was of a couple in Elizabethan dress. They looked supremely happy. The man was obviously Banning, and the woman was me. It was identical to the tattoo.

"I knew the tattoo would be too modern to prove anything to you," Banning said softly. "But this painting is something you can verify. You can have an expert examine it, and they'll tell you the same thing I will, that the date inscribed here"–he tapped the bottom of the painting, where the artist had signed the piece with the year 1753–"is accurate. This is Fortune, and it's also you, Elaria. Look closely at it." He angled the painting beneath the light.

Every feature of the woman's face matched mine, down to the freckle I had on my right cheek. Banning propped open the painting on the bedside table. I stared at it in shock as he got up from the bed.

Banning went to my feet first, undoing the straps that held me. Then he removed my gag. I flexed my jaw and wet my lip as he leaned across me to undo the wrist restraints. He was freeing me, just as he'd promised. It was brave and kind of stupid. But then, he hadn't really offered me any harm. I didn't have a good reason to kill him, not really. I sat up, and stared from him to the painting as I rubbed my wrists.

"Did I make them too tight?" Banning gestured to my wrists. "I'm sorry I resorted to such treatment of you. I understand if you feel the need to strike out at me. I will not defend myself."

"Are you seriously trying to pull a Dracula on me?" I finally asked.

I was scared. He had truly frightened me with this tale of doomed love and reincarnation . . . and the images it brought forth in my head. When I'm scared, I react with bravado. I make jokes or offer insults. But Banning didn't seem to understand this one.

"What are you talking about?"

"Dracula and Mina?" I huffed. "Mina is his wife, and she commits suicide because she thinks Drac is dead. But he really isn't, and he comes home, and lashes out against god, who turns him into a vampire. Then Dracula finds Mina again, in fucking London, no less. His reincarnated bride."

"That's not the story of Dracula." Banning frowned.

"Of course it is." I grimaced. "I've watched all of the movies, even the new one with that hot guy from *Lord of the Rings*."

"The movies are inaccurate." Banning started arguing with me like we'd known each other for years. "The original story has no previous relationship between Dracula and Mina. In fact, Mina is the one who helps Van Helsing find Dracula, and Dracula pursues her to punish her for it."

"Well, I'm not talking about the book," I crossed my arms.

"The movie is a coincidence." His forehead creased in thought. "Perhaps someone got wind of my story and told it to the producers."

"Now you're saying you *are* Dracula," I laughed.

"No, I" He stopped and started to laugh. "This is just as we were before. The only thing that's changed is the language."

"Don't do that." I pointed at him. "I don't believe in reincarnation."

"How can you not?" Banning looked shocked. "You've been to the other worlds, haven't you? You've seen the souls in their heavens. And their hells."

"It just proves that there are souls," I shrugged.

"Aren't you descended from Greek sirens?" Banning tried again. "The Greek gods send souls back to be reborn, don't they?"

"Yes to the first." I frowned. "I'm not sure on the second."

"You're not sure?" Banning laughed. "I thought sirens were the companions of Persephone? Your people would know better than most."

"Mom never really talked about souls," I said. "And Persephone is kind of, well, annoying. I don't hang with her anymore."

"The Greek Goddess of Spring is *annoying*?" Banning burst into laughter.

"Yeah." I broke my stern resolve, and chuckled a little. "She's like a diva florist."

"Elaria"–his expression softened–"I know Fortune. She was the love of my life. Not a moment goes by that I don't see her face in my mind."

"Or on your arm." I nodded pointedly to the tattoo.

"You are her." He ignored my attempt at levity. I started to protest, but he held up his hand to stop me. "I know this is a lot to process. Take your time. I've said everything I wanted you to hear, and I will be content knowing that you understand what you mean to me." He took my hand and kissed it, as he had when we'd first met. But this time, it felt even more intimate. "If nothing else happens between us, I will still be eternally grateful to know that you live again. To see you, be here with you, is miraculous."

"Banning"–I shook my head–"I'm not your girl."

"Yes, you are."

"Even if I did believe in reincarnation," I huffed, "and I'm not saying I do. But if I did, this still makes no sense. Why would a soul return to life inside a body that looks exactly like her old one, except it's an entirely new race? Do you know how rare my kind is? Do you know how many spellsingers have ever been born?"

"I believe . . . six."

"Six." I frowned when I realized he'd gotten it right. "Yeah, I'm number six. Ever. Just enough of us to have a name for our kind, though not enough to procreate and really make it a race."

"I don't know why you were born in the same form." He shrugged. "Perhaps so that I would know you. I dare say, even had you been born in a different body, I would have recognized your soul eventually, had I been given the opportunity to speak with you. But you weren't going to allow that."

47

"So what?" I scoffed. "You think that destiny or fate or whatever put me in this body just for you?"

"Yes." He smiled.

"Rather arrogant," I observed.

"Not arrogance in the way you mean," he said confidently. "It's arrogance in our love. That's how strong it is, Elaria. If fate ever made an exception, it would be for us."

"You're mistaken," I said gently. "I'm sorry, but you are. I'm not Fortune."

"You are my love, Elaria." Banning stood. "I know you. I can feel you here." He laid his hand to his chest. "And I have faith that someday you will remember who you are. Who you were. When that day comes, I shall be waiting."

He pulled on his shirt and headed to the door.

"Wait," I called after him. "Your painting."

I held the leather-bound portrait out to him.

"That one belonged to Fortune," Banning said. "Therefore, it's yours. As is everything else that once belonged to her."

He closed the door on my stunned face.

Chapter Six

I knew I was dreaming. Still, it felt so real. More like a memory than a dream. The air was scented with expensive perfume: jasmine, rose, and musk. Beneath it was the sharp tinge of unwashed bodies, and farther beneath that was the aroma of old blood. Strange. I couldn't remember the last time I'd noticed scents in a dream.

"There you are." The male voice was low and familiar, both to me and in its tone with me. There was the knowing sound of intimacy within it, and a purr that heralded more to come. I turned toward the man expectantly.

He was blooder-blond, the color a lot of vampire hair turned when their original shade had been a blander, human version. The magic infusing blooders with immortality also liked to enhance what Mother Nature had given them. Blond turned into something more golden, more gleaming, and more glossy. Something too beautiful to be natural. Yet no one questioned it. To question would lead to receiving answers, and most people in Elizabethan London didn't really want to know the truth.

"Banning," I purred back as I leaned into him and drew my hand over his body.

His clothes merely hinted at the amazing physique beneath, and I couldn't resist a little reminder of what I'd be holding later that evening. Wait. My mind balked a moment. This was only a . . .

"Dream." Banning kissed the sensitive spot just beneath my ear.

"What was that?" I asked.

"I said, you look like a walking dream." He frowned at me, then looked me over carefully. "Have you partaken today?"

"Yes... I think so."

"Come, my love, let's get you another drink." He slipped my arm around his, my long fingers curling into the silk velvet of his jacket as if they'd done so a million times before.

I rubbed the fabric absently. They didn't make velvet like that anymore. Anymore? What was I thinking?

"Fortune?"

Banning was suddenly standing beside a young woman, holding her hand, and I found myself taking her pale palm from him. I turned her hand over, but instead of biting her wrist, I yanked her up against me, and latched onto her neck. Banning loved watching me feed on women. Softness against softness, he called it. I loved Banning watching me, so I tended to make a performance of it. I focused on his gaze as I drank, enjoying the way his eyes went from emerald to a deeper, forest green. Lust was practically pouring off him.

And the blood. I groaned, and sucked harder, closing my eyes to the sensations. Salty sweetness that tasted like magic, heaven, and sex all in one. It filled my mouth as the power of it filled my body. Heat surged through me, making me feel alive again, not just a cold corpse. I opened my eyes to find Banning breathing hard, his jaw clenched, and a bead of sweat dripping down his temple. I released the woman, and licked the last drop of blood from her throat. She fainted, and I casually helped her sit on a nearby bench.

"Shall we?" Banning held his hand out to me, and I took it silently.

We moved through the shadowed halls like phantoms, until the golden lights of thousands of candles lured us into the grand ballroom. Music poured out even farther than the grasping light, its bright notes touching our ears long before the candlelight hit our feet. As soon as we stepped within the room, the music boiled up around us. The scent of hot wax, flesh, and heady perfume circled on the lazy eddies of air. Bodies pressed close, laughter even closer, but Banning navigated us expertly out into the flow of dancers.

One arm went tight around my waist, almost imprisoning me with its vehemence. Another lifted to hang suspended at our sides, and I clasped it with my own. Even with the layers of clothes separating us, Banning managed to pull me in tight enough to feel his excitement. I sighed, my hips angling farther into him as he led us around the floor. The musicians played vibrantly, yet I could still hear the tinkling of crystal from the chandeliers above us. Everything called out to me, clamoring for attention. It was always like this after a long drink.

And Banning knew it.

"Your lips looked so lovely on her neck," he whispered into my ear. "Stretched tight. Sucking."

I chuckled, knowing exactly where he was leading me.

"I am enjoying the dance, Banning," I chided him. "Stop trying to lure me away from it."

"A little longer then." He swung me around. "But I hope you shall take pity on me soon. We can find an empty room."

"I'd prefer an empty corner." I smiled wickedly. "I saw one in the hall we passed through."

"Now you seek to make me spill before we even leave the ballroom," he growled.

"As if you are some young country lad." I cast my eyes upward. "You know more about drawing out pleasure than most

men in this room."

"You give me far too much credit," he admonished, but smiled as he did so.

"Do I?" I shocked him by taking the lead and steering us off the dance floor. "Maybe I'll put that to the test. Shall we see how long you can last with my lips locked upon your staff?"

Banning's eyes flared vivid green. "An inspired idea, my love."

We hurried out of the room, running through the hallways like a couple of young lovers off for a secret rendezvous. Finally, I found the spot I was seeking, and pushed Banning up against the stone wall. My hands went to his breeches, expertly undoing the laces as I fell to my knees. Just before I took him in my mouth, I looked up to see his eyes glowing in the shadows.

"I shall last as long as you want me to," he promised, "my sweet Fortune."

I came gasping awake. My skin slicked with sweat, my breath rasping out of my chest furiously, and I was as turned on as Banning had been in that dream. At least I hoped it was just a dream.

"A fucking Blooder ball," I muttered. "Parasitic bastards. There's no way I was one of them. No fucking way."

I didn't get much more sleep that night. I kept looking over at the antique painting. The resemblance was uncanny, but was it really me? Was I Banning's blooder girlfriend brought back to life? No. Even if I was, I wasn't interested in him anymore.

A sharp pain flared in my chest. I sat up and gasped.

"What the fuck is wrong with me?" I asked the early dawn.

I looked down at my shaking hands, and then at the happy

52

painting. With one smack, I closed it and knocked it over. That made me feel a little better. But the sun was rising in Kansas, and as it crested over the treetops, I thought of the Blooder king who was just now going to sleep beneath that ridiculous country club of his. All those people would be scurrying about, chasing tiny balls into holes in the ground, while beneath them, an entire gura of blooders bunked down for the day.

Suddenly, I wanted to get as far away from Kansas as I could. I reached for my phone, and hit Cerberus's number. He answered on the fifth ring.

"It's eight fucking thirty!" Cerberus snarled. "In the gods damned, motherfucking morning!"

"Yeah. Now you know how it feels, dog breath," I laughed.

"I let you sleep till three before I showed up," he groaned.

Someone murmured in the background.

"Go back to sleep; it's just work," he said to them.

"Who are you talking to?" I asked with glee.

Cerberus groaned, and the sounds of a lumbering, giant, dog shifter came through the phone. I heard a door open and close before he spoke again.

"Some hottie I found on the way out of your hotel last night." I could hear the smirk in his voice.

"You dog," I chuckled.

"Guilty as charged," he agreed. "Now, why are you really calling me, El? You wanna come over? I'll kick the bitch out for you."

"She's not a bitch, or you wouldn't dare kick her out. You'd try to have little puppies with her," I teased. "Oh, hey, Banning

53

showed up here last night."

"What?" Cer growled.

"Did you tell him where I was?"

"Fuck no."

"Then you were followed, my friend," I gave him the bad news with a huge amount of delight. It wasn't often that someone got the drop on Cer. Like never.

"No, I wasn't."

"Yeah, you were."

"Nope, hell no. Not possible."

"Either you were followed, or you told him where I was, Cerberus," I snapped. "Because I woke up tied to the bed, gagged, with Banning between my legs."

"What the fuck?" Cerberus roared.

"Yeah, but–"

"What happened?" I heard a female voice ask.

"Get the fuck out!" Cer yelled at her.

The woman must have been smart, because she didn't argue. I heard a few running footsteps, and then a door slammed.

"What the fuck did you just say to me, Elaria?"

"He didn't hurt me." I thought I'd better get that out before Cerberus had a meltdown. "Banning knew I'd shut him down with a song before he had a chance to speak. So he gagged me and tied me up, then he spoke to me."

"And then?" Cerberus's voice had mellowed, but only

slightly.

"And then he released me."

"And you didn't kill him?" Cer sounded shocked.

"No," I whispered. "It surprised me as well."

"Holy fucking shit!" Cerberus swore. "Fuck! Fucking Hades! Fuck!"

"Would you please stop dropping f-bombs?" I asked dryly.

"It's true, isn't it?" Cer finally got some non curse words out. "You're his ex. You're a reincarnated blooder! Persephone's pink panties! This is un-fucking-believable."

"I don't know." I took a deep breath and finally admitted what I'd been thinking. "It's possible."

"Holy fucking–"

"All right, enough already," I ground out.

"What are you going to do?"

"I'm leaving, of course," I huffed. "I don't do blooders, remember?"

"Yeah, I wonder why that is." Cerberus was sounding cocky again.

"What? You think I subconsciously wrote them off because I was waiting for Banning?"

"You said it, kid," he chuckled. "You and Banning, eh? Interesting. I pictured you with someone bigger. Someone more like–"

"You?" I asked with a laugh. "You would probably crush me."

"As if Banning couldn't," Cer snickered.

"I want you to contact that fairy," I was done joking around.

"What?" Cerberus went serious. "Really?"

"I'll go to Tír na nÓg."

"What the fuck, El? Hawaii isn't far enough away from Kansas? You need to go to fucking Tír na nÓg to escape Banning?" Cerberus's voice dropped to a dangerous level again. "Did he threaten you? Is he harassing you?"

"No, it's not like that." I sighed. "Just make the call, Cer."

"Are you sure, kid?"

"I thought you wanted me to take this job?"

"I do, but–"

"Just make the call," I growled. "I won't commit to the job before talking to the guy, okay?"

"All right, Elaria, I'll call him."

Chapter Seven

The Shining Ones loved gemstones. Anything that could make them even shinier. No, I'm kidding; that wasn't why they liked jewels. Crystals, including precious and semiprecious stones, were a natural source of magic. They had a base power of their own, but could also store, release, magnify, and even create energy. Different types of stones had different properties. Rose quartz, for example, was a great stone for romance. If a fairy already had a love-oriented magic, rose quartz might call to him or her, offering its assistance. It might even align with them or, in rare cases, bond with them entirely.

A lot of human myths talked about fairies and their courts. About how there were kings of summer or queens of winter. Actually, there are no seasonal courts in Tír na nÓg. The Shining Ones can't control the weather; they're at the mercy of the whims of the worlds right along with the rest of us. So there were no seasonal references, but there were gemstone courts. The Jewel Kingdoms. Fairies could live in any kingdom they chose, but those with the most power gravitated to a region that magnified their magic. The land within these kingdoms was usually full of the gems aligned with its ruler, and therefore provided the Shining Ones with more stones to call upon.

Now when I say "ruler," I'm talking fairy monarchs. Those rare fairies I mentioned before, who bond with gems? They become kings or queens. They rule. Outside of Tír na nÓg, their power would be impressive. Inside the Fairy Realm, with lots of pretty rocks to call on, their magic would be terrifying. They'd be able to use any gem in the vicinity to amplify their abilities, and depending on what that magic was, they could do some serious damage with it. Even love magic can kill. In fact, love was one of the most murderous magics there were. You'd die believing it was exactly what you wanted, and you'd probably do the deed yourself. But that's not all. A Shining One monarch could access all of the properties of the stone they're bound to. So not only did they have a jacked-up primary magic; they had all of the stone's magic too.

The courts of these powerful rulers were full of fairies who were nearly as magical as their monarchs. Men and women who could align with the stones. They couldn't access all of the stone's properties like the monarch could, but they could use the gems to magnify their own magic immensely. Generally, the closer a stone was to a fairy, the easier it became for them to connect with it. Because of this, the Shining Ones tended to wear a lot of jewelry, and you could usually tell a fairy's kingdom affiliation from said jewelry.

This guy was from Sapphire.

He wasn't dripping in jewels. All he wore was a masculine ring–a gold band with a cabochon sapphire set in it. That in itself was very telling. The fewer jewels a fairy wore, the more powerful he was. Shining One monarchs could walk around without any jewelry on at all, and still be able to connect with their bonded gem. Most adorned themselves anyway because . . . royalty. But some of the monarchy flaunted their power by wearing only their crown. This guy was basically doing the same thing. If he'd been a king, he'd be sitting here in a crown–nothing more. He was in the human world, where his magic was diminished, and yet he still only wore a ring.

Fuck me. Why did I agree to this? And why did such a powerful fairy need my help?

"Mistress Tanager." The fairy bowed over my hand. Oh yeah, they're usually very old school in their manners, even though most are surprisingly modern in their speech. Except for maybe this guy. "I'm honored to meet you."

58

"I'd say the same, if I knew who you were," I lifted a brow.

"Forgive me." He blinked his pale, husky-blue eyes in surprise. "I thought Cerberus had already provided you with my lineage."

"I told you, man." Cerberus shook his head and crossed his arms. "She don't care about your pedigree."

Cer was barely sitting in a chair in the corner of my hotel room. I say "barely" because his bulk was oozing over the creaking arms. We'd decided to do the meeting in my hotel room because if I didn't take this job, I'd be heading home anyway. And if I did, I'd be heading to Tír na nÓg. Keeping my hotel room a secret wasn't really an issue anymore.

"I am Duke Finbar of the Sapphire Kingdom," he introduced himself. "Son of the Diamond Queen, Isandra, nephew of–"

"Okay, that's good," I interrupted him.

"Told you," Cer chuckled.

"Hold on," I frowned at Finbar. "You're a *sapphire* duke born of the *diamond* queen?"

"Yes." Finbar looked confused.

"Had to leave home, huh?" I considered him. "That sucks."

"It's more comfortable for me in Sapphire," he shrugged.

"All right, fine." I waved him to the bed. There weren't any other chairs in the room, so I sat a little ways down from him. "Who do you want me to kill, Finbar?"

"It is not I who–"

"Just tell me who," I interrupted again.

"But you need to know that I speak on behalf of my king, who is also my brother, King Galen of Sapphire" Finbar insisted. "He bid me to come here and enlist your aid."

"My services, you mean," I corrected. "I won't be helping you out of the goodness of my heart."

"No, of course not." He seemed a little offended. "I've already given our offer to your consort."

"My *consort*?" I lifted a brow as Cerberus burst into laughter. "Try the word 'boyfriend' next time you visit Earth. Consort is a bit dated."

"Unless you're royalty," Cerberus snickered.

"Even then." I shook my head at Cer before looking back to Finbar. "He's not my consort. That's something we tell clients so I don't have to deal with unwanted attention. We're just friends."

"Regrettably," Cer sighed.

"Ah." Finbar's eyes suddenly glittered. "Of course. I'm sure you would be overwhelmed by suitors if he didn't offer you his protection."

"Nice." I grimaced. "You can drop the fey flattery bit. That won't work with me."

"Told you she's a tough cookie." Cerberus was just chortling it up over there.

"But delicious by the looks of her," Finbar surprised me by saying. "The extra chewing would be worth it."

"Knock it off," I growled at Finbar.

"My apologies." Finbar was instantly contrite. "I meant no offense. I thought it was the way men and women interacted here."

60

"Um, no," I said dryly as Cerberus chortled louder.

"Again, I apologize." Finbar angled his head respectfully.

"Who does your brother, the Sapphire King, want me to kill?" I got us back on track. "And why can't he do it himself?"

"The Onyx King," Finbar said. "King Torin. Do you know the properties of onyx, Mistress Tanager?"

"Call me Elaria," I said absently as I tried to remember. "Balance, protection"–I frowned–"grounding, I think."

"Grounding of spiritual energy into the physical plane," Finbar expounded. "It's a coveted power among our kind. The protection properties of onyx magnify King Torin's innate magic, but the grounding abilities of the stone allow him to dissipate any psychic attack against himself. He simply sends it into the earth."

"But you think my type of magic would not be dissipated?" I narrowed my eyes on him.

"Oh it probably would." He nodded. "But King Torin must call upon his magic, and then access onyx, before he can reach the grounding energy, as that is not his innate ability. It's also doubtful he would think to protect himself against a song. We already have a plan to sneak you into his court as a singer traveling with a band of minstrels."

"Did he just say 'minstrels'?" I asked Cerberus, who started laughing all over again.

"Musicians," Finbar corrected with irritation. "It doesn't matter what you call yourselves. You can walk right up to King Torin and sing for him without raising his suspicions. He'd be under your spell before he knew what was happening."

"And then?" I asked.

"And then?" Finbar asked back.

"And then what do I do?" I asked him. "I assume this would be in front of the entire Onyx Court. You think I can murder their king and then just walk out? They might have a problem with that."

"Yes, but I witnessed your power against the blooder army," Finbar shrugged. "You could simply keep singing."

"And slaughter the entire court?" I lifted a brow. "You're contracting me for one man. Yet now you're saying you want me to kill an entire court of Shining Ones."

"Well," he frowned. "I believe the compensation is generous."

"For one fairy king it is," I agreed. "For an entire jewel court, full of who knows how many top-level magic users? It's a pittance. Tell your brother to shove it where the fairy sun don't shine."

Cerberus sighed, all of his humor gone. I was throwing away the job, and therefore his commission.

"One hundred million," Finbar said immediately.

Cerberus's eyes went circular.

"No," I said firmly.

"El, come on," Cerberus cajoled.

"One hundred fifty million," Finbar upped it.

"Fuck me hard," Cerberus snarled. "Elaria, for the sake of Hades."

"No," I ground out. "This doesn't feel right."

"Two hundred million American dollars," Finbar nearly shouted. "Wired into your account tonight."

"I think I just came," Cerberus groaned.

"Why?" I asked Finbar as I leaned into his face. "Tell me why your brother wants this man dead so badly."

"He killed our sister," Finbar whispered.

"He killed your sister?" I lifted a brow. "Why?"

"They were romantically involved." Finbar closed his eyes briefly before continuing. "She tried to leave him."

"And the fucker killed her for it?" Cerberus asked.

"Yes," Finbar's lips quivered as he said the single word. "He killed my sister."

"Gods damn it," I swore.

Chapter Eight

I would step into Tír na nÓg $200 million richer. If I lived through this, I could take a very long vacation.

I packed up, and checked out of the hotel, then went to see Cerberus at Crouching Lion. Banning had provided Cerberus with a room at the country club, and Cer said it shouldn't be a problem for him to hang around until I got back. I was a little anxious visiting Crouching Lion, but it was the middle of the day, so there wasn't any chance of running into Banning.

I left my bag and wallet with Cer, not wanting to risk taking them with me into the land of the Shining Ones. If I needed a change of clothes, I was sure they could supply me with one, but I didn't intend on being there that long. So I stepped through the Veil with nothing but the clothes on my back and a song in my heart. Sorry, just some spellsinger humor. Actually, the songs were on my iPod, and that was tucked into a little evening bag, along with some earbuds, and a tube of Fresh's Sugar lipstick. What can I say? I hate having dry lips.

Tír na nÓg. Damn. I'd heard it was beautiful, but "beautiful" seemed like the cheap, ghetto cousin of the word needed to describe this place. We came out of the Veil into a little clearing at the edge of a packed dirt road. Just a sweet meadow surrounded by forest. No big deal.

Except the meadow was covered with velvety flowers in deep crimson, canary yellow, and peacock purple. The scent wafting up from them was intoxicating, practically painting the air. Then there were the trees–as slender as Finbar and nearly as pale. Their trunks shimmered silver in the buttery sunlight, and their delicate branches wove together, creating a spiderweb over the sky. They swayed gently, making soft creaking sounds that were closer to music than noise.

Vibrantly colored birds flew through the air, trailing insanely long tail feathers behind them like ribbon dancers. Beasts roared in the distance, and smaller creatures poked their heads out of the thick underbrush, giving me glimpses of things with large, liquid eyes and long fur. Even the damn air seemed to sparkle, it was so pure.

"Dear gods," I whispered.

"Lovely, isn't it?" Finbar seemed pleased by my reaction. "Come along, Spellsinger; our carriage is waiting."

Sure enough, there was a carriage pulled up beside the meadow. I hadn't even noticed it among so much natural beauty, but it was impressive as well. It was as if it had rolled out of Louis XIV's courtyard. Covered in gilded carvings with a base of black enamel, the door boasted a crest with a golden scale, like the one Lady Justice holds. Chunks of sapphires were set into the design, looking as if they were being weighed on the scale's plates. At the front of the carriage, a team of white horses was tethered, and several fairies were standing at attention nearby. They bowed as we approached, and one of them opened the door for us.

I had changed into a dress for my foray into the fairy world–a sleek, black, silk number with long sleeves, and a slit at one side. It was form fitting, but the slit allowed for movement. So climbing into the coach wasn't difficult. Especially since the fairy attendant helped me up the little steps that hung beneath the door. The only jewelry I had on was Finbar's sapphire ring. It turned out to be the diplomatic charm Cerberus had promised me. Finbar swore it would protect me from all manner of fey attacks, including abduction. I rubbed a finger absently over the cool stone as I settled into the velvet seats. Hopefully I'd be returning it to Finbar by the end of the day.

The carriage set into rumbling motion. Outside my window, the scenery began to change. The spindly silver trees gave way to thicker oaks, with deep blue flowers growing wild beneath them. Then those oaks became groves of blossoming orange trees. I leaned my head toward the window, and inhaled the scent of orange blossoms. I loved that smell. But we eventually passed through the grove too. Open grasslands spread out to either side of us, spotted with lakes, and then came a line of massive objects that glinted blue in the sunlight.

"What are those?" I narrowed my gaze, and realized they were statues.

Some soared into the air hundreds of feet–some were only around my height. There were all sorts of animals, plants, people, and strange shapes represented. Some were carved intricately, while others were polished smooth. But all of them were made of the same, deep blue stone.

"The Sapphire Gardens," Finbar said as if it were obvious.

"Those are all made of sapphires?" I asked in shock.

"Every kingdom has a guardian garden surrounding their stronghold." Finbar shrugged elegantly. "The stones protect us."

"Wait." I looked over the army of art. "Are you saying that they're like some sort of sentry?"

"They are charged with the intent of the king." Finbar seemed to finally realize that I'd never heard of these jewel gardens. "If we are under attack, these stones will become our first line of defense. King Galen can use them to conduct his magic. When empowered, they become a border nearly impossible to cross."

"Whoa." I blinked at the sapphire statues, which stretched out from both sides of the road. "You guys don't get a lot of wars here, do you?"

"No," he chuckled, "not many. But when we do fight, the battles are epic."

Then I caught my first glimpse of the Sapphire Castle. It had been directly before us, which meant I wasn't able to see it as we approached. As we drew closer, it stretched into my line of sight. Finally, the carriage angled along a curve, which wound around a miniature version of the Sapphire Gardens, and brought us to the front steps.

The castle was made from sapphires. Not really that big of a surprise after I'd seen the gardens. But to think that the castle would probably be made of sapphires, and then to actually see the reality of it, were two very different things. Frankly, I didn't know you could mine sapphires that large.

In their rough state, sapphires look similar to any other stone, except for their blue color. It was when you polished and cut them that they turned into something spectacular. The Sapphire Castle was constructed of rough, polished, and faceted sapphires. All three types, and several versions of each. Rough sapphires formed the foundation, cut into blocks, and placed together like stones in any human castle. From this foundation, several more rough pieces rose in a matte framework. Within the frame, walls consisted mostly of polished sapphire plates, shining like glass. But set in dizzying designs among the polished stones were faceted sapphires which sparkled randomly. Not too much, just enough to make me sigh in appreciation.

Maybe I'd buy myself a gemstone castle with my recent windfall. Or an island. Or a gemstone castle on an island.

Our carriage came to a gentle stop. Even the steps leading up to the main doors of the castle were made of sapphire. These were of the rough variety, and I was grateful for that when I made my way up them. I would have hated to try to navigate polished stone stairs in my human heels. Walking through the meadow had been bad enough.

Fairies stood at attention to either side of the white, wood doors. They pulled them open in an orchestrated movement as Finbar and I approached. Finbar barely batted an eye at them; he just led me into the depths of the castle. Inside, the walls were a simpler stone, creamy white, and covered with fairy masterpieces–paintings of elegant lords and ladies, fey creatures, and magical landscapes. Blue carpet stretched out before us, and curving beams of white wood arched above us. But there was little reason to the way the halls were laid out. Finbar led me in a winding manner, making so many turns, I felt hopelessly lost.

The castle was full of Shining Ones, and they all paused to watch our passage. They paused and bowed. Finbar was evidently a big deal. Not so surprising, since he was related to the king. Still, it was kind of weird walking beside him. I was getting even more attention than he was. The Shining Ones of the Sapphire Court looked at me like I was a celebrity. They probably thought I was human–gods know I looked it–which would cause them to wonder what their duke was doing with me. Or maybe they were speculating over the price I'd fetch. I'd heard rumors of slave markets in Tír na nÓg, sex slave markets full of humans stolen from Earth.

I thought I'd be taken to some elaborate throne room, but Finbar led me up a spiral staircase, and into a wing of the castle that had significantly fewer people in it. Those who were there looked to be servants, and rushed away after bowing to Finbar.

"Here we are." Finbar pushed a door open, and ushered me into an opulent sitting room.

I saw the dog first. At least, I think it was a dog. It was the size of a cat, with lavender fur, and so fluffy it would make a little girl squeal. It had sharply pointed ears, a sharply pointed muzzle, and a sharply pointed stare. That was one pointy pup, and it was looking at me like it wanted to gnaw my nose off.

It sat on the lap of a woman whose massive dress seemed to

mimic the fluff of her pet. The gown was also lavender, and so puffy, she was nearly lost in it. If she let go of that animal, it would probably disappear into the froth too. The woman was thin and willowy, as most fairy women are, with caramel skin and orange hair. Yep, orange. Orange like a pumpkin. And yet somehow, she pulled it off. It looked wonderful with her chartreuse eyes.

"I've brought Lady Elaria Tanager to you, Brother," Finbar declared grandly. "Lady Elaria, this is King Galen of Sapphire."

I followed Finbar's stare to another corner, tearing my eyes away from the softly smiling woman in her frothy frock. There sat a man who looked very similar to Finbar. Except this man's white hair ended in cerulean tips, and his features were a touch more masculine. Then there was the magic. It practically boiled off him. I could feel it like a vibration in the air. Or maybe I could hear it like the buzz of electricity. Or was that the taste of earth and salt in my mouth? Like licking a river stone. My senses were so confused for a moment, that I started nervously humming. Music calms me.

All three of the fairies in the room tensed, until I calmed myself and stopped humming. The tune had seemed to correct my perception, and turned Galen into a normal guy. Well, not normal exactly, but not the magical vortex he seemed to be mere seconds before.

"Sorry, Your Majesty." I gave him an elegant curtsy. My mother made sure I was trained properly, able to walk into any gathering, in any of the worlds, and feel comfortable. I didn't have a problem with addressing kings. "Your magic confused me for a moment. I had to get my bearings."

"How intriguing." The king stood, and cocked his head at me. "You could feel it?"

"You can't?" I asked in surprise.

Galen, King of Sapphire, burst into laughter, earning surprised looks from Finbar and the fluffy woman.

"Of course I can." King Galen held his hand out to me, and I placed mine in it. He lifted my fingertips to his lips and pressed a kiss to them before continuing. "I am its master, so I know the magic intimately, but usually it takes a great sapphire Shining One, one such as my brother or my bride"–he nodded to the woman, who smiled wider–"to be able to sense the flow of the sapphire power around me."

"Huh," I took back my hand. "Weird."

"Yes, quite." The woman laughed, and it was a high, tinkling sound.

"This is Queen Ava." Finbar nodded to the woman.

"Your Majesty." I curtsied to her.

"Spellsinger," she nodded, "it's lovely to meet you. I never thought I'd have the honor of speaking with one of your kind."

"You are the first spellsinger to enter Tír na nÓg," King Galen added.

"I am?" I lifted my brows.

"Oh yes." His smile turned wicked. "Most are too afraid we'd keep them. You know how much we treasure magic, art, and beauty. Spellsingers are full of magic, musically talented, and I'm told all of them are rare beauties. If you are a fair representation of your race, I'm inclined to believe the rumors."

"Thank you, Your Majesty." I bowed my head to him. Galen was much better at flattery than his brother. "And thank you for the charm." I held up my hand to show off Finbar's ring. "Without it, I would not have risked a trip here. And now that I've seen Tír na nÓg, I can safely say that would have been a tragedy."

"Ah, yes, there is no world like ours," King Galen agreed. "And you are most welcome here. At least, in my court."

70

"Yes, Finbar has told me what this job entails." I got to business, feeling more at ease talking shop than exchanging pleasantries with a Shining One. "I'm ready to head out whenever your group of musicians is."

"Oh, no, no, no." Galen waved his hand. "First, we must celebrate your arrival. In the morning, you can set out with our faux troubadours."

"As you like," I said stiffly.

"Take her to a guest room, so that she may freshen up," Galen said to his brother.

Finbar nodded, and we began to leave.

"And Lady Elaria," King Galen called out.

I turned back.

"You have my deepest gratitude for bringing my family the justice that I could not supply."

"Don't thank me yet," I said grimly. "I may not survive this."

Galen didn't bother to deny it.

"Then thank you for trying," he amended with sincerity.

Chapter Nine

Yep, fairies were perverts.

Sweet gods, I thought they'd at least tone it down during dinner. But I guess a *Welcome to Tír na nÓg* feast was a time to bring out the serious kinks. And the sex slaves. I got a bird's-eye view of it all from my seat at the high table–literally high. Like we were on a pedestal practically. I had to climb a set of stairs to get to the platform that the high table was on. Then I had to sit beside Finbar. Yay. And endure his endless attempts at seduction. Yay.

The rest of the dining room spread out before us in a surreal collection of mismatched tables, chairs, and china. There were round tables covered in fancy linen, with the finest silverware on them. There were also long, rectangular tables without tablecloths at all, to showcase the detailed carvings in the wood. There were chairs that appeared to be Victorian, and heavy wooden ones that looked like a lumberjack had made them. There were flying fairy globes emitting soft glows from above, as well as crystal chandeliers and modern art lamps. A plethora of carpets covered the stone floor at odd angles, like they'd been haphazardly thrown there. Persian, geometric, even–gasp–shag. It was utterly bizarre and yet felt fantastical.

Finbar explained that several fairy families lived at court, and in an effort to make them feel truly at home, King Galen had given them each carte blanche to decorate a small section of the dining room to their individual tastes. I nodded distractedly, contemplating this, as food was set before us, and the fun began.

Thank goodness there were no children there. Oh, that's another misconception I should probably clear up. Humans seem to believe that fairies have an issue with fertility. That's complete BS. Fey females can get knocked up just as easily as any other woman. Hell, they could probably use their magic to get pregnant whenever they wanted. But they don't because they aren't stupid. They're immortals. If they had children willy-nilly, whenever they wanted, they'd overpopulate their world within a few generations. Shining Ones are very in tune with nature. They know the stress an immortal species can cause, and they try to mitigate it with fertility restrictions.

For the most part, the Shining Ones used spells to prevent pregnancies. But every kingdom had a special season which came once every few hundred years, during which fairies could procreate. The only exception was royalty. Monarchs, with their strong magic bloodlines, were encouraged to have babies whenever they damn well felt like it. But what happened at that dinner had nothing to do with procreation, it was pure pleasure. A carnal display that would have made even the most jaded of porn stars blush.

First, like an amuse bouche, the kissing began. I noticed a few couples here and there start some light make-out sessions. I shrugged–no big deal. I'd seen people make out in public before. Just a little kissy-face. I could ignore that. Then the first course arrived. Almost as if they'd timed it with the food, the couples started getting a little more serious. Naked humans were led into the room, made to kneel next to tables, and sometimes beneath them. Beside me, Galen started feeding his queen little pieces of food. She giggled, sucking on his fingers, and I began to squirm.

Please, no. Please, if any gods can hear me in Tír na nÓg, make these paranormal perverts stop.

Third course. Couples turned into thruples, quadruples, quintuples, and whatever comes after that. They added partners and subtracted clothing. Hands disappeared up skirts and down bodices, popping back out with scraps of silk or mounds of flesh. Humans were draped across laps and tables. Legs spread and mouths descended. The silverware began to shiver. I gulped wine as Finbar leaned closer, and tried to look down my top. Moans began to filter up to us, and servants had to step over a few prone bodies, writhing away on the weird carpets.

"Are you all right, Lady Elaria?" King Galen asked me casually, as he played with his wife's you-know-what. Right there! He was rubbing away at her frantically, her fluffy skirts flopping about so violently they nearly hit her in the face, all while he had a conversation with me.

"Fine. It's fine. I'm fine," I gulped, and tried to find a safe place to look. My plate–that was the only safe zone. Even the chandeliers were showing signs of debauchery; lacy underthings draped the glittering crystals.

"My brother is an accomplished lover," Galen offered. "And I believe he would be more than happy to see to your pleasure tonight."

"Thanks"–I cleared my throat–"but I'm good. Ah, I think I see a free female over there, Finbar." I waved to a corner. "Maybe you could–no, never mind, they got her. Sorry, you might be alone tonight."

"You don't like sex?" Finbar was aghast.

"Oh, I do." I nodded. "I even like it with men. Just not men I barely know."

"How *human* of you." Finbar frowned, and started scoping the crowd for a couple to join.

"Actually, this is pretty much just a fairy thing." I waved my hand at the undulating crowd. "I don't know a lot of other supernatural races who feel so . . . free about their sexuality. At least not in such numbers."

"We are celebrating." Galen lifted his face from his wife's

74

nipple, his mouth coming free with a popping sound. "Don't you celebrate with pleasurable pursuits?"

"Sure," I nodded. "A glass of wine, a good meal, maybe some chocolate cake for dessert. Dancing maybe. An orgy? Not so much. But don't let me stop you."

I stood, and they all gaped at me like I was the worst party pooper around.

"Please, go back to what, er–*who* you were doing." I waved toward the queen. "I'm going to retire for the night."

"I can walk you to your room," Finbar offered with a gleam in his eyes, like maybe I was shy, and this was code for him to follow me.

"Oh no." I shook my head. "I wouldn't want to ruin your fun. You stay and enjoy."

"But this celebration is in your honor," Finbar whined. "I was going to lick your little flower right here, beside the king."

"Very noble of you, Brother," Galen muttered with his mouth full. You'd think a royal would have better table manners.

"My little" I choked. "Back off, fey boy. I don't do this kinky shit, and you ain't getting anywhere near my little flower."

"You say that now"–Finbar slid up to me–"but when I'm lapping at your pleasure bud, you will scream my name."

"Oh my fucking fairy gods!" I nearly shouted. "I didn't know I needed a rape whistle in Tír na nÓg."

"My apologies." Finbar immediately stiffened, and not in that way. *That* was already stiff. "I have offended you."

"Yeah you have." I waved a finger in his face. "Go lap at someone else's bud. I'm going to bed. Alone!"

I stomped from the hall, hoping I could remember how to get to my room and that I wouldn't have to murder a bunch of horny fairies along the way. Seeing them ravishing those enslaved humans didn't sit too well with me either. Part of me wanted to go back into that room, pull those fairies off those poor humans, and leave Tír na nÓg with them tonight. I could probably sing our way out of there. But that would mean murdering the entire court, because I definitely couldn't sway all of their minds at once. And then there would be the knights on guard duty to deal with. Not to mention the fact that I wasn't even sure if I could navigate my way out of the castle. I could just see me singing as I wandered lost through the Sapphire Castle with a line of naked humans behind me.

Ironically, I may be facing that exact same situation when I kill the Onyx King. Just without the naked humans. Then again . . .

That sobered me. I might have to kill lots of innocent fairies. Taking out a murderer was one thing, but his entire court? Why had I agreed to this? I dearly hoped that I'd be able to make a clean getaway without resorting to mass slaughter. Hadn't I killed my quota for the month? Damn it all, I shouldn't have taken this job. I shouldn't have let Banning get under my skin enough to send me running, and I definitely shouldn't have let that freaky Finbar sway me with his sad story.

I was feeling like a chump. Big-time.

Chapter Ten

The morning brought a repentant Finbar to my door.

I had made it safely back to my room the night before, then had locked and barricaded my door. You can never be too safe. I'd slept relatively well after that. I didn't hold it against Finbar. As I may have mentioned before, fairies are freaks. It was just his culture. His freaky, debauched, sex-slave-owning culture. After sleeping undisturbed for eight hours, I was able to see everything clearer, and get over the previous night.

But I wasn't looking forward to singing in another fairy court. Hopefully they wouldn't be celebrating anything. Well, I suppose when I was done, the only party they'd be having would involve burying their dead.

"I deeply regret any offense I offered you last night," Finbar said.

"It's okay, Finbar," I gave his shoulder a pat. "I get it. It's your thing. I'm just not into that."

"Good." He sighed in relief. "I was worried you might refuse to do the job."

"I'm a professional," I chided him. "I wouldn't walk away like that. Especially not after getting paid up front."

"Excellent." Finbar recovered. "I mean, yes, of course. Uh, the musicians are waiting in the courtyard. As soon as you break your fast, you may leave . . . if you're ready."

"*So* ready." I nodded, and we headed down to the dining

hall. "And thanks for the dress and shoes." I waved a hand down the blue cotton dress I was wearing. It was plain, but I figured that was the point. I couldn't blend in with a group of traveling musicians if I was wearing silk. And it also had some convenient pockets in its full skirts. My iPod, earbuds, and lipstick were stuffed into them. The shoes were more like boots and would make running far easier than my heels.

"My pleasure." Finbar nodded.

There were a lot fewer people roaming Sapphire Castle so early, and that was a blessing in my opinion. I ate quickly, then Finbar led me out through the labyrinthine passages. The musicians were an assorted group of stone users instead of being solely sapphire, so they wouldn't raise any alarms when we rolled into Onyx. They were sprawled among their instruments in the back of a horse-drawn cart (I'm not even kidding), and there was a spot next to the driver saved for me. I shrugged and climbed aboard. I've traveled in worse conditions.

As we pulled around the turnabout, Finbar waved goodbye, and I waved back, happy to see this thing started. After getting a taste of King Galen's magic the day before, I knew for certain that I couldn't face that kind of power in a fair fight. On an even playing field, the Sapphire King would probably wipe my blood up with my own face. I doubted that the Onyx King would be any less powerful. Which also made me doubt whether I could kill him, even with the element of surprise. People in my line of work didn't last long unless they were very good at what they did and very smart in how they did it. A mistake could mean the end of your career and your life. There was a significant chance that I had made that fatal mistake.

But there was nothing to be done about it now. I was committed. So I pushed away thoughts of my potential, gory death, and concentrated on the plan. If I followed the plan, the king wouldn't be able to make even a single strike against me.

I had a song chosen, and Finbar had given the sheet music to the musicians the previous night, before dinner thankfully. They had practiced, and were confident they could play the song perfectly. We were selling ourselves as a band of fey musicians with a human singer they'd magically enslaved. There was the allure of humanity as well as the appeal of otherworldly music. I'd prepared something sexy, but deadly. A climatic kill. Meg Myers's "Desire."

What I hadn't known was that it would take three days to reach the Onyx Kingdom. It was obvious once I thought about it. It would be a hell of a coincidence if the Sapphire Kingdom was set directly beside Onyx, and even then, we'd still have to cross an entire kingdom to reach it. Kingdoms are generally large. And Tír na nÓg had tons of kingdoms. Luckily, there were shortcuts for us to take that would lessen our traveling time a bit. Still, we had a fair amount of a journey ahead of us.

The Jewel Kingdoms of Tír na nÓg were oddly shaped, and depending on which road you took, you could cross varying quantities of them while covering the same distance. This was explained to me while we passed through a thin strip of the Garnet Kingdom. The borders between the kingdoms were abrupt and obvious, due to the extreme differences in their landscapes. So it wasn't difficult to see the odd layouts that the guitarist, Alex, told me about.

We'd already traversed Jasper, and I was told we'd have to ride through Opal, Citrine, and Amethyst before we reached the Onyx Kingdom. Then we'd have to go through several Onyx villages before we came to the castle. And all this traveling was being done in a wagon, which took significantly longer than if we'd simply rode out on horseback. But we needed the wagon to haul the instruments and to look like true traveling musicians. People on the road for long periods would have supplies, too many supplies to carry on the back of a horse.

I was nervous about making camp in the woods, and

sleeping out in the open. I was not into bugs or stretching out beneath the stars. I preferred to have some solid walls and a roof over my head. But the men assured me that we would stop at inns to rest each night; there wouldn't be any kind of camping involved. Also, as musicians, we were sure to receive warm receptions at these inns. So at least that fear was put to rest. It was a shame there was no assurance to be had over killing King Torin.

We were indeed welcomed warmly in both Opal and Citrine, where we stopped for the two nights we were on the road. It gave us all a chance to practice together, though it was a delicate procedure. I obviously couldn't use the same intent I would employ when singing for King Torin, but I couldn't sing without spellcasting. It was one of my biggest gripes about my magic. If I tried to simply sing a song for pleasure, the magic would scramble inside me, demanding release. If I didn't mentally direct it into a spell, the magic would choke me, literally lodging in my throat, and blocking my ability to speak, until I gave it purpose.

So I had to come up with another focus for the song. That actually wasn't the hard part. The problem was that once I sang a song in a particular manner, my magic grew accustomed to it. The more I sang it in that way, the more accustomed my magic got, until it simply added it to my arsenal of lyrics I could whip out at any moment. This was usually a good thing. It allowed me to sing something quick without too much focus. However, in this case it meant that I'd have to concentrate harder when I performed in Onyx. And that wasn't the only issue. "Desire" is a sexy song. There was little else to use it for, beyond seduction or slaughter. Since I didn't want to kill anyone before I reached Onyx, my only option was seduction.

Singing a randy song in a Shining One tavern was bad enough. Adding magic to the words amped up the bawdy blend of loose women, horny men, and general fairy freakishness into a stew of simmering sexuality ready to boil over. Making it unmolested to my room each night had been a feat of diplomacy and physics that I wasn't prepared for. At least the musicians had enjoyed themselves.

When we finally arrived in Onyx, the musicians were sexually sated and musically confident, ready to play our assassination song. We had even discussed our escape. The instruments would have to be left behind, possibly used as weapons to clear our way out of the room. Then we would split up and run for it. It's harder to chase six people, running in six different directions, than a group going one way. I didn't work with others often, and never in such a capacity, but I was confident in the musicians. We were as ready as we could get.

We rode through several villages, stopping only once for some lunch before we continued on to the castle. The sky was darkening to deep indigo by the time we rumbled past the Onyx Gardens. Statues of sea creatures, snarling beasts, winged monsters, and imposing Shining Ones ranged out in a wide swath around the dark castle, looking far more foreboding than the sapphire statues had. Perhaps it was the sin-black stone, which gleamed silver in the light of the glowing moon. Or maybe it was the shadows cast by the looming guardians, which seemed even darker than the gemstone. I don't know what gave me the willies, but a shiver coasted over my arms. I had a fleeting urge to jump down from the cart and go running home.

"We're not in Kansas anymore," I whispered to myself. "What did you get me into, Toto?"

"What was that, my lady?" Rupert, our drummer, asked me.

"Uh, nothing," I muttered.

"We're here; it'll be over soon." He smiled at me, but in the shifting moonlight, it looked more like a leer.

"All right; good," I nodded, ignoring my misgivings, then swallowed hard as the Onyx Castle loomed before us.

81

Sapphire had been beautiful, but Onyx radiated power. There were no faceted stones in its edifice. No sparkling light or patterns of alternating textures. It simply seemed to flow up out of the ground, going from rough rocks at its base to polished onyx at its crest, as if its king had summoned it forth like that. Several wings spread out from the main tower, making the castle seem more like a city than a single building. A fortification instead of a palace. Out of its far-reaching base, several sturdy keeps rose. Then, around and on top of the keeps, stood numerous minor towers. They shot up toward the sky aggressively, a battalion of soldiers with their spears at the ready. Their placement led the eye inward, toward the main body of the castle, where the central tower dominated.

There was light filtering out from the castle, but the glow didn't reach us. It was confined by the massive walls that surrounded the edifice. Funny, Sapphire didn't have walls around their castle, but Onyx, with its menacing looks, added even more of a "keep away" vibe with their defenses. The courtyard gates were guarded by a full retinue of fairy knights, and my stomach started to clench when I spotted them. If I had to make a run for it after killing Torin, I'd need to sing my way past these guards too. That was a lot of singing. No wonder Finbar had wanted to see me in action against the blooder army. But a blooder was practically human when compared to the magic of a Shining One knight. The odds against my survival were climbing steadily.

I rubbed my arms as a chill breeze blew by, and the wagon came to a lurching stop. Rough, male voices demanded to know who we were and what our business was at the Onyx Castle. The fairy musicians explained cheerfully that we were traveling about, singing at all the Jewel Courts, and wanted to offer our services to His Majesty, the Onyx King. If he wasn't interested, we'd be on our way. Oh yes, very casual, no big deal. It doesn't matter if you let us in or not.

The guards conferred with each other, and I looked over to

see them exchanging secret smiles. Those smiles set warning bells to ringing in my head. But I calmed myself when I realized that it was probably just the prospect of some entertainment that had them excited. Sure enough, the guards asked how soon we could be ready, and as they waved us in, they started conversing animatedly among themselves over what time they'd be done with guard duty. So perhaps I was being paranoid.

We found a place to park the cart, and then quietly unhitched the horses. Riding horseback would make for a much faster getaway. The cart would have to be left behind. We loosely tethered the horses so they wouldn't wander. Then we gathered our stuff, and headed to the main doors. I helped to haul some of the drums since I had no instrument of my own.

It had been so easy to get in. We didn't even need to provide much of a story. Those gate guards had heard that we were musicians, and that was all they needed. Based on that, I thought we were just going to waltz right into the dining hall, and this would all be over relatively fast.

But as soon as we stepped into the castle, a steward herded us into a small room off the antechambers. He directed us with the air of a man who'd done so numerous times before. Then he launched into a speech on what was expected from us and what we could expect when we were brought into the dining hall. He went over how he wanted us to walk in, where exactly we would place ourselves, and asked us how many songs we had prepared. The usual schtick wherever musicians went. Then we had to cool our heels for a bit.

When the time finally came and we were led into the dining hall, I was actually nervous. I hadn't been nervous about singing in decades. But the whole atmosphere of the place seemed to be geared toward intimidation. It was an entirely different feeling from that in the Sapphire Court, and I wasn't at all surprised to find that no one, and I mean *no one*, was making out in the dining hall, despite it being mid-meal when we walked in.

There weren't random tables or weird decorations either. This was a clean, well-organized room, with tables placed in neat rows down each side, and a high table set horizontally at the end. No elevation required; it was obvious who was in charge there. The Onyx King didn't need height or glitz to proclaim his power. His throne was elegant and understated, carved from ebony and stained even darker. His clothing was dignified, unadorned by jewels or frills, and predominantly black. He sat behind a sleek, ebony table, and wore a thick band of onyx, with a low point in the center, for his crown. The man had a thing for black.

And damn if he didn't look good in it.

I felt my jaw unhinge as I laid my eyes on the Onyx King for the first time. The musicians were busy around me, setting up their instruments in the space before the high table. It wasn't a long process, but it seemed to take forever as I stared at King Torin. And he stared back.

Blue eyes. That sounds so plain. So common. But these eyes were the shade of the deepest, clearest, glacier-fed lake. They seemed to shine from within, as if his magic could barely contain itself and needed a way out. Those eyes matched the gleaming highlights in King Torin's blue-black hair, which fell haphazardly around his face and over his shoulders in silken disarray. Wide and muscular shoulders that belonged on a linebacker or a lumberjack, not a fairy king.

In fact, Torin's entire body was impressive, built bigger than any fairy physique I'd ever seen. I wouldn't be surprised if he had some human blood in his ancestry. Or maybe some loup. Werewolf genes would explain the swarthy tint to his fair skin, but his features were too striking for wolfkin. A slender nose was bracketed by high cheekbones, and he had a sensual mouth that slowly smiled at me.

Oh fuck, he was a fairy sex god.

I nearly forgot to sing as the music rose around me. But then it called to me. The low thuds, like a heartbeat. The scraping squeal of guitars. The unformed magic undulating up inside my chest. Waiting for me to transform it into something powerful with my voice. Music was my life, as important as the blood in my veins, and I knew that if there ever came a day when I could no longer sing, I would be as good as dead. That was the weakness I had to accept. The flaw that kept me cautious, if not humble. Kill my voice, and you kill me.

I started to sing, my hips rolling to the erotic grind and whine. The sensual words suddenly seemed appropriate. Achingly appropriate. I didn't want to kill this man. I know, it was really unprofessional of me to let a handsome face sway me, but damn, what a waste. I wanted to do all the naughty things I was promising him. Images of bare skin and blue eyes formed in my mind, and went to war with my prepared intent. I pushed them away. I'd already accepted payment, and the magic was filling me. The entire room would sense the spell in seconds. Either I killed the Onyx King, or he would surely kill me.

Yet I found myself confessing to King Torin with the help of the lurid lyrics, explaining that I had to do this, I was sent there to destroy him. I wanted him, but I must murder him. I had no choice.

I wove the words around him, setting my trap, holding him hostage. I couldn't risk King Torin calling on onyx. Then the song started to delve into darker regions. Darker and dirtier. A drowning serenade of seduction and hostility. I found myself connecting with the music in a carnal way, nearly purring to the Onyx King about the wicked things I wanted to do to him. It was so wrong, feeling aroused during a kill, but I realized it was the only way I'd get through it. I had to trick myself into believing this was about sex, not death, or I'd never be able to deliver the fatal blow.

By this point, he should have been paralyzed. But instead of his being frozen in fear, King Torin's eyes were filling with lust.

His chest was starting to rise sharply with his rapid breaths. His hands clenched on the arms of his throne. He was listening to my song, but wasn't falling under my control. The Onyx King was *enjoying* my performance. I tried to push away the unease and regret I felt, and sang out the line that was meant to kill a fairy king.

My voice echoed around me, vibrating through the air like a swung sword. There it was, the moment he should have been torn apart from the inside out. Killed in an instant. A merciful death, if a bit messy. But King Torin was unharmed. Alive and . . . smiling. Oh gods, he was smiling.

Then I felt it—the pull, the drain. Something was absorbing my magic. As soon as it left my mouth, the spell was grounded. Nullified. Just another pretty melody without any physical power to it. I faltered, stumbling over the words, and the Onyx King stood. He made a swift gesture, his eyes never leaving mine. Knights rushed out of the crowd and seized the musicians. The music died a squeaking death, and my spell died with it. I gasped as my hands were grabbed and roughly yanked behind me. Then I was gagged for the second time that week. I screamed futilely against the leather, fought against my restraints, and got nowhere but more firmly bound.

Torin, the Onyx King, strode over to me, and I finally saw how huge he really was. Way over six feet tall, but that wasn't uncommon for Shining Ones. It was the breadth of him that was so surprising. Muscles for days. All over. Amid the sleek Shining Ones, he seemed massive. A monster of a man. Damn. This guy had killed Galen's sister? It must have been a quick death. As I hoped mine would be.

"What an erotic song you chose for me." King Torin looked me over slowly. "And you were going to kill me with it? That seems more like something a succubus would do than a spellsinger. But not nearly as much fun. As enticing as your words were, I think I'd rather have the succubus. At least she would have made

86

good on her promises."

The Shining Ones around me laughed, and I blanched. Oh fuck, I'd been set up. But why? How? Was it Galen? Why would the Sapphire King hand me over to the Onyx King? Why go through all this subterfuge? If King Galen had wanted me dead, he could have killed me himself. He was definitely strong enough.

"I don't believe you truly desired to kill me, did you, Spellsinger?" Torin gently brushed a lock of my hair back from my face.

My blood chilled, my body shivered, and my throat constricted. He wasn't going to make it fast. My death would be slow and very painful.

"No, you didn't. I saw that in your eyes. Regret. And you didn't know what you were getting into either. Poor little bird. Let's put it behind us, shall we? Welcome to my court, Elaria Tanager. Welcome to your new home." King Torin turned to his knights. "Take Ms. Tanager to her chambers"–he barely spared a glance for the musicians–"and kill them."

The musicians started to scream, begging for their lives.

"Fine." Torin held up a hand and they quieted. "Kill all but that one." He pointed to Rupert. "You will return to the Sapphire King and tell him to stop fucking with me. I ceased being amused by his incompetence after his fifth assassin. Tell Galen that I have her, the Spellsinger, and that he just let the most precious woman in all the worlds slip through his fingers. To waste her on an assassination attempt was foolish. Tell the Sapphire King that if he would stop sucking on his wife's tit for more than five minutes, he might have figured out how important Elaria Tanager was. But now it's too late; he's delivered her right into my hands, and I will use her to destroy him."

Torin's gaze went back to me as the musicians were dragged from the hall, most in one direction, Rupert in another.

87

The Onyx King looked me over with supreme satisfaction. He nodded to the men holding me, and I was dragged away too. Precious indeed. The only reason this guy thought I was precious was because he believed he could make me into a supernatural assault rifle.

I was so fucked, but at least I wasn't dead.

Chapter Eleven

I was strapped into a chair, a rather comfortable chair actually, and then my guards and I waited patiently for the Onyx King to join us. Some of us may have been more patient than others.

I searched the room while we waited, my eyes frantically looking for a weapon or a way out. I found neither of those. No windows, no sharp implements, no doors beyond the one we'd entered through. My chair was facing that door, placed perfectly in line with it. These guys were good at building tension. But then, they'd probably been perfecting the art for centuries. Or maybe they watched a few imported spy movies. This could be a strategy stolen from James Bond. Thanks a lot, Ian Fleming.

The image of a bunch of Shining Ones sitting around a human-made television, watching OO7 while they took notes, did make me smile. Combined with the fact that I wasn't facing imminent death, it also made me relax a bit. Where there's life, there's hope, and all that other suicide hotline crap. But seriously, as long as I was breathing, there was a chance for escape. In fact, with my skill set, it was pretty much guaranteed. I started to smile wider against the gag.

When the Onyx King finally entered the room, I lost that smile. I was struck again by how gorgeous he was. He was the kind of handsome that hit you in the face and left you gasping for more. That unreal kind of attractiveness. But more than that, the man had a presence. Charisma. The room felt smaller with him in it. He just walked in, and bam! It was hard to breathe. Damn, it was always so much worse when the villains were beautiful.

King Torin nodded to the guards, and they left, giving him sharp bows as they passed. A knight closed the door behind him, and locked us inside the bedroom. It was a luxurious bedroom too. Even more beautiful than the one the Sapphire King had provided me with. The walls were hung with cream silk, as was the four-poster bed. The carpets were plush and crimson, the furniture delicate and gilded. It was the room of a fairy princess. It even smelled pretty. And Torin, with all his aggressive masculinity, still looked perfectly at ease within it.

"Elaria Tanager." The Onyx King sat in a slightly more masculine chair than mine. His voice was deep, but not as deep as Cerberus's gravely rumble. Torin's was more tiger than freight train, with a sexy purr to it. "You're a long-awaited blessing."

I was a what now?

"This won't help you." He slipped Finbar's ring off my finger, and tossed it into a corner. It clanked on the stone floor like rattled chains. "As soon as you tried to harm me, the magic of the diplomatic charm was negated."

I swallowed past the nervous lump in my throat.

"Now, I'm going to do something that may seem stupid, but I assure you, you can't kill me before I restrain you." Torin smiled, and it was, *of course*, breathtaking. "I think I've proved that already. Should you attack me, I will simply deflect your magic into the onyx, just as I did earlier. You can't sing the stones into your control, Elaria. Do you understand?"

I nodded. Was this dumb motherfucker about to remove my gag? Couldn't sing the stones into my control, my ass. I was going to teach this Shining One a lesson about spellsingers.

"All right then." He reached forward and undid the leather straps.

I worked my jaw, and moistened my lips as he leaned into

me farther, as if he were embracing me. But he was only untying the leather around my wrists. Still, my heartbeat sped up. Torin's cheek brushed against mine, and I felt a zing of desire shoot through me. Wow, I needed therapy. This guy had just murdered nearly all of the men I'd traveled to Onyx with, had taken me prisoner, and was intending to use me to destroy King Galen somehow. And I still wanted to jump him.

Then again, we did crash his party with the sole purpose of assassinating him, so I suppose all's fair. And from the sound of it, this wasn't the first time Galen had tried to kill Torin. But Torin had killed Galen's sister. Of course Galen would try to get some revenge. The Onyx King was a murderer, and I needed to remember that. Not like I had any right to point fingers. I'd done my fair share of murdering, and I did it for money. But I chose my clients carefully, and I never killed innocents.

Something wiggled in the back of my mind with that last thought. Normally I'd have Cerberus check out the claims of my potential clients, or I would investigate them myself. Especially in an assassination contract. I liked to be certain of exactly what I was walking into. And exactly what kind of an asshole I was about to kill. But Cerberus had been blinded by the money, and I had been distracted by Banning. Neither of us had verified Finbar's story.

Sloppy, Spellsinger, very sloppy.

Torin leaned back slowly, as if giving me the opportunity to attack him. I wasn't stupid enough to take it. Oh no, I would wait, lure him into believing that I was complacent, and then I would pounce. I would kill this son of a bitch, despite his unearthly hotness level, and then I would get the fuck out of Tír na nÓg. At this point, his guilt didn't matter. He'd taken me hostage and now it was personal.

"Torin." He held his hand out to me, like we were two humans meeting at a cocktail party.

"Elaria." I shook his hand.

"Nice to meet you." He smiled brilliantly, as if he were tickled pink to use such a common human mode of greeting.

Something quivered inside me. Down, girl, down.

"Likewise, I'm sure," I said snidely.

"Why did you try to kill me?" King Torin asked casually. "Was it just about the money?"

"*Just?*" I laughed. "They paid me two hundred million dollars to kill you. That's a massive fortune in the human world, in case you're not aware. But actually, it had more to do with you murdering King Galen's sister."

"Nila?" Torin's brows rose. "Galen told you I *killed* her?"

"Yes" I narrowed my eyes on him. I had just realized that Galen had never told me his sister's name. How odd. "Do you deny it?"

"Of course I deny it." He laughed, "Nila isn't dead."

"What?" I blinked as all of my bravado fled. My shoulders fell, and I gaped at him momentarily. "What do you mean she isn't dead?"

"Nila attacked me." Torin grimaced. "We had a bit of a squabble when I ended our relationship. It got vicious, and I'm afraid I pulled too much of her magic away from her. I was merely trying to calm her, ground her, but in all the violence of it, I couldn't judge how much she had left. I took too much. All of it, in fact. I completely grounded her."

"You *grounded* her?" I asked flatly.

"Not like a human adolescent." He chuckled. "In a—"

92

"I know what you meant," I snarled. "But you *didn't* kill her?"

"No. I care about Nila; I would never hurt her purposefully. But I suppose I can understand why Galen would say that I did." He shrugged. "Magic is everything here. Without it, Nila's status dropped down to that of a commoner. She tried to go home to Sapphire, but they turned her away. It was the same in the Diamond Kingdom with her parents. She had become an embarrassment to them, and was forced to return to me. I would have given her a place in my court, but she didn't want to stay in Tír na nÓg. She was humiliated, and wanted a fresh start in the human world. So I set her up in Santa Monica. She's modeling now, doing pretty well actually."

"She's a model?" I blinked at him.

"Yeah, she's a . . .," he frowned as if he were trying to remember the word. "Supermodel? Is that the right term?"

"That fucking bastard!" I was livid.

That idiot Galen had sent me out to kill a guy over a lover's spat. I couldn't help it; I normally don't agree with breaking things, but I needed to hurt something. And at that point, Torin was out of the question. So I stood, picked up a nearby vase, and chucked it against a wall.

Torin laughed, "My, you are feisty."

"I'm feisty?" I snarled at him. "Are you fucking insane? Do you know what I could do to you?"

"I know precisely what you're capable of." He smiled sensually. "And as I told you, I can handle your magic."

"Yeah, about that." I dropped back into my seat, leaned forward on my knees, and regarded him intently. "Who betrayed me?"

"What?"

"Who warned you that I was coming tonight? I was told it would take you time to reach for onyx. That you wouldn't be able to ground my spell so quickly."

"That's true." His lids lowered.

"Then who warned you?"

"The stones did," he said in complete seriousness.

"The stones?" I frowned. "Somehow I don't think you mean Mick Jagger and the rest of the boys."

"No, but good music reference. Though I suppose that's your area of expertise." Torin grinned. "I meant the stones I'm bonded with. Onyx has the power of prophecy."

"Shut up, it does not," I huffed.

"It does, I assure you." He chuckled, his cobalt eyes sparkling. "The stones whisper to me sometimes, and they told me about you. In fact, I was given a full prophecy. Would you like to hear it?"

"Oh, I would love to," I said sarcastically.

"Excellent." He launched right into it. "Child of the sky and sea. Daughter of earth and fire. Rare bird of sunlight and darkness. Sent to sing death to Onyx, she brings life instead. Hope for all the realms."

"Poetic." I gave him a scathing look, though part of me shivered.

His words resounded within me. Sky and sea, earth and fire, bird of light and dark. They all referred to pieces of my ancestry. My siren mother flying through the sky as she drowned men in the sea with her song. My father's people thought of

94

themselves as keepers of the Earth, but his magic leaned toward fire, and I had inherited a little of it. Calling fire through my songs was easier than trying to work with other elements. The bird thing was obvious–all sirens took the names of birds for their surnames–and I was definitely rare. And, of course, there was the singing.

"There's more." Torin held up his hand, not at all irritated that I had interrupted him. "A king will fall to her song, but she will raise him up, stronger than before. The Jewels will sing under her sway, and Tír na nÓg will tremble in joy and fear."

"Uh-huh." I cracked my neck. "And you got what from that?"

"I shall be that king, and together we shall make Tír na nÓg tremble," he said confidently.

"Tremble. Great. And where's the part where you knew I was coming tonight?"

"Oh, that was something else." He waved his hand. "Something far less romantic."

"Oh?"

"Onyx said, 'The sixth spellsinger comes to slay you this night.'" He shrugged.

"Are you messing with me right now?" I narrowed my eyes on him.

"No, I swear to you." He held his hand up like a boy scout taking an oath. "Onyx told me those exact words."

"And you knew to look for me in a bunch of traveling musicians?" I scoffed.

"I assumed you would sneak yourself in by some devious means." He shrugged. "I warned the guards at the gate to look for you, and they spotted you easily enough. We readied the entire

95

court while you and the minstrels waited."

"Are you kidding me?" I gaped at him. "Why didn't you just kill us?"

"Did you not hear the prophecy?" Torin frowned. "You will raise me up."

"Yeah"–I frowned–"and how exactly am I supposed to do that? You got like a hundred pounds on me. I swear, you're the biggest fucking fairy I've ever seen."

Torin laughed, and it was even deeper than his voice. Hot. Oh so hot.

"Not literally raise me up." He sat back in his chair and studied me. "I think we shall be lovers."

"Oh, is *that* what you think?" It was my turn to laugh. Though a part of me did kind of sit up, and pant like a dog for a . . . bone . . . yeah, that was a bad choice of analogy.

"Yes, I do." He leaned forward and licked his lips. "And you're thinking it too."

"You're really arrogant, you know that?"

"And you're not?" Torin lifted a brow.

"Well, you have me there." I chuckled. "But I'm arrogant about my magic, you're arrogant about"–I waved a hand at him–"everything."

"Nothing wrong with knowing your own worth." He smirked.

"Except I don't like cocky guys," I smirked back. "And I don't feel like sticking around your Disney Villain's Castle. I'm going back to Kansas, and possibly looking up a blooder who I may or may not have shared a past life with. He's got some hot tattoos, and isn't nearly as arrogant as you are."

I stood, and Torin followed suit. It brought us within inches of each other. I was left staring at the solid muscle revealed in the gaping V of his tunic. And he smelled good too, damn him. Something woodsy, spicy, and pure fairy male. I didn't know if I wanted to inhale him or lick him. Possibly both. At the same time. The man was like a pot brownie–delicious, with the potential of delivering a high that made you hungry.

"You're not leaving, Elaria." His hands slipped around my biceps. "I don't like the thought of holding you prisoner, but I will. You're too precious to let walk away."

"*Precious* again." I tried to pull back, but he held me firm. "I won't be your weapon or your prisoner. You can't cage a spellsinger."

"I'm sorry, Elaria, but I can." Torin released me, his hands sliding down my arms and leaving a trail of sensitized skin in their wake. He came to the end of my forearms, and slipped his hands around mine. "I hope that you'll come to understand my actions, and that the cage becomes unnecessary, but you *are* precious. Far too important for me to allow you to leave. And not just to me, but to all life, in all worlds. We need you." He lifted my hands, and kissed the back of first one, then the other. "Sleep well, Spellsinger. We'll talk again in the morning."

Chapter Twelve

I waited till late in the night to make my escape. No, I wasn't going to stick around. I don't care what kind of cryptic shit Torin spouted about all life in all worlds needing me. That was ridiculous. Please. All of the worlds depended upon me? Yeah okay, me and Obi Wan Kenobi. I'll just go grab my lightsaber. And by the way, I was speaking the absolute truth when I told Torin he couldn't cage a spellsinger. You could kill us, yes. Gag us and make us powerless, absolutely. But when we could literally sing things into being, it was rather hard to trap us.

I bent near the keyhole in the door, and began to sing one of my favorite Madonna songs. An old stand by that had opened many a lock for me. The words were perfect, even though Madonna was obviously referring to love when she sang them. I mean, it was in the title, wasn't it? "Open Your Heart," not open the door. Still, I sang the upbeat tune into the keyhole. Then I tried the handle. The door remained locked. I scowled and tried again, to lyrically sway it into setting me free.

Nothing. I stood up with dawning horror. No. No way. I went to the wall like a man on the way to the gallows, and pushed back the hanging silk with a trembling hand. Solid onyx. Torin had put me in an onyx cell. I rushed back to the door, which, to all appearances, was wood, and looked closer. There was a black border running around the edges. I peered at the lock. It was gilded. A few scratches at the gold revealed the polished surface of onyx below. Charged onyx, if I was guessing correctly. *Grounding* onyx.

Dear gods, the man had thought of everything.

No problem. I took a deep breath, and tried to calm myself. I would simply change the stone into something else with a song. Nothing was impossible for me. Altering an onyx lock into a traditional metal one should be a breeze. But getting past all of the grounding within the walls might require the use of some backup. I fished my iPod out of my pocket, and stuck the earbuds in my ears with determined shoves. I found my selection quickly, smiling down at the image of a blonde woman with her hand held to her forehead in lament. Lacey Sturm. Her song, "Impossible," was perfect for fighting the onyx drain. I just had to get ahead of the magic, fight the grounding until I pushed past it, and change that little piece of stone to metal.

The jolting music began and I let it take me, let the magic rise inside me. The energy was immediately yanked away, but I kept pushing. The happy melody screeched up into a pounding punishment. It became a lamentation. A cry of emptiness. Of giving until I had nothing left, and then giving more. I could do this, go beyond my limits. I would shove magic at this prison until the enchantment broke. Until that lock turned to metal and busted open. Nothing was impossible for me.

I shrieked out the words, bringing more and more of my magic to the surface. Nothing happened except for a shaking exhaustion that crept over me. My legs trembled, my hands shivered, and my lips quivered. The song slammed out its anger between bouts of coercive, rolling arias. It soon felt as if it were punching into my gut. Still, I pushed onward. I had to get out. I wouldn't let a few rocks stand in my way.

The lyrics began to shift into hope, urging me to keep going. Failing is only an opportunity to try harder. I reached for the stone with my words, trying to force a sliver of my magic into it. A crack would give me an in, enough to wedge into, and then break, the rock. I tried to feel the strength of the victorious music, tried to make its power mine. But it all just seeped through my grasp like wine poured into my palm. All that was left was the stain.

On and on I fought, until the song wound down to its screaming end. I fell to my knees, choking out the last of the lyrics. My fists pounded against the lock, and my words took on a new meaning. Hope changed to despair. The inspiring declaration of surmounting odds became a statement of oppression. This was . . . impossible. I bent over and laid my forehead to the floor.

I really was caged. My heart started to race. I should never have come to Tír na nÓg. I should have taken the thirty mil I'd earned and gone home. I whimpered, thinking about the sweet ocean breeze that I could be feeling on my cheek even now, had I not been swayed by greed and misplaced righteousness. By lies. Oh, and had I not wanted to put an entire realm between me and Banning Dalca.

Banning. I curled up into a ball on the floor. Was there really history between us? Could there be a future? Did I want one? He was gorgeous, but also a bloodsucker. His leech-like nature kind of grossed me out. The possibility that I had once been a blooder too was really ironic. I had seen strange things when he spoke to me, and there had been some kind of feeling that rose inside me. Emotions for him. About us. But I also thought it would be stupid to repeat my mistakes, especially those made in a past life. If there was such a thing as reincarnation, I would think its whole purpose would be for a soul to experience new things. For it to move on, and not go right back to someone it had loved before.

New life. New love.

And what of Torin? Could his prophecy be true? Would I make Tír na nÓg tremble? How could I? I couldn't even handle a fairy lock. The thought of me making the Fairy Realm tremble in fear was absurd. And raise him up? Make him stronger than before? What could I possibly do for a king of the Shining Ones? Torin was obviously powerful enough as he was. And then there was that pesky premonition bit. He didn't need my help. The Onyx King would be warned of danger before it stepped one foot in his direction. Hell, I was surprised Tír na nÓg wasn't already

100

trembling for him. I know I was.

In so many ways. Damn the man and his Shining One hotness.

I was scared, and it was becoming a habit. Banning had given me the courtesy of removing my fear quickly, but it looked as if Torin wouldn't be so obliging. The Onyx King wouldn't kill me, but remaining in Tír na nÓg against my will sounded nearly as bad. At least death might bring me another go at this.

No, that was stupid; I didn't want to die. And I wasn't sure I believed in reincarnation, despite those weird visions I'd had of Banning. But I didn't want to stay locked in an onyx cell either. So that meant I had to escape. There would be a way. Torin would slip up. Maybe I could use this attraction between us, make him think he had won me over, and then he'd drop his guard. As soon as that happened, I was outta there.

I looked around at all the luxury, and a chill went over me. The room suddenly seemed much smaller, and I had the strangest desire to curl up beneath the bed-covers and have myself a good cry. I didn't approve of crying. It was pointless. But at the moment, it seemed like it might feel really good. I compromised with my inclinations and just got back into bed. Under the covers, I felt warmer and stronger. The urge to bawl abandoned me, and the determination to escape burned brighter.

I would get out of Tír na nÓg, even if I had to sing my throat raw to do it. Nothing would stop me, not the onyx or its king.

Chapter Thirteen

"His Majesty requests that you join him for breakfast." A woman stood beside my bed, looking mulish.

She was as elegant looking as every other Shining One, but she was dressed simply, in layers of sturdy cotton, similar to what I was wearing. Her platinum-blonde hair was nearly white, but still had a hint of gold to it. Her eyes were a darker version of her hair, golden brown and long-lashed. She was pale, but not overly so, and had a pouty mouth, which I was pretty sure was putting extra effort into turning down, especially for me.

"What?" I rubbed at my eyes and sat up. "Who the hell are you?"

"I am Sara, my lady." She gave me a grudging curtsy to go along with my grudging title. "King Torin has appointed me as your maid."

"Yeah?" I huffed as I heaved myself out of bed. "Well you can tell your king he can shove his maid" I frowned. "No, scratch that. Tell him . . . oh, forget it. I'll tell him myself." I stretched my cramped muscles. "You guys got showers here?"

"We're not barbarians," she grumbled. "Of course we have showers. Water pressure was discovered by the Romans. Did you really think we couldn't figure it out?"

"Wow, he stuck me with the snarkiest maid ever." I looked her over and smiled. "You know what? I like you. I think we're going to get along just fine. Now show me where the damn bathroom is, Snarky Sara."

Sara gaped at me for about five seconds before she rushed to the wall and pushed aside the silk hangings to reveal a narrow door. She opened the door, and gave me another curtsy. I slid past her, into a sumptuous room of rose quartz walls, gold furnishings, and a porcelain tub shaped like a blossoming lotus. A golden stem wrapped around the tub, with thick leaves jutting out from it, to hold assorted bath products. Then it continued up, arching overhead, to dangle a showerhead into the center. There were no shower curtains, but the bathtub looked wide enough to catch any spray.

Fluffy towels were set on the lotus-carved lid of the toilet, candles were placed on the layers of petals spreading out from the sides of the tub, and a full-length mirror, which might or might not have once belonged to Snow White's wicked stepmother, dominated one wall. I walked over the cool, onyx floor, and sighed in disappointment. I guess it had been too much to hope that Torin would have forgotten to add onyx to the bathroom.

"He could have told me about the hidden door last night," I muttered to Sara. "What if I'd had to pee?"

"I imagine you would have used a vase." She grimaced.

I burst out laughing, startling her again.

"Actually I couldn't," I smirked. "On account of throwing the vase at the wall last night. Now, did you happen to bring me anything to wear?"

"Yes, of course." She rolled her eyes. "As if His Majesty would allow you to attend him in that." Sara looked disdainfully at my simple dress.

"How shocking that would be." I gave a fake gasp and clutched at my invisible pearls. Aka, the gasp and clasp.

Sara snickered.

"I shall be outside when you're ready to get dressed." She shut the door on me.

"Thank the gods," I called out to her. "I thought for a second you were going to stay and watch. Damn perverted fairies."

I heard her surprised laugh through the door.

Then I took a nice, hot shower, and worked some of the tension out of my shoulders. I went out into the bedroom naked, carrying only the contents of my pockets. Sara hadn't brought the change of clothes in to me, and I'm not really shy in front of other women. What's the point? They have the same goods, and they're usually not interested in mine. Plus, this woman was there to help me dress; she was gonna see me naked eventually.

Sara lifted her brows, her gaze stuck somewhere it shouldn't be unless she was into ladies. Possible, totally possible, but it was more likely that something else had caught her attention. Or a lack of something else.

"It's waxed," I told her. "Warm wax is applied, then a cloth, and after it cools a bit, the whole thing is yanked off, pulling out all the hair."

She gaped at me in horror.

"It's not as bad as it sounds." I chuckled. "Plus, I like it smooth–feels cleaner to me."

"This is a human practice?" Sara waved her hands at my lady bits.

"Yep." I made a motion for her to hand me the dress she was holding hostage. "You got any underwear, or just the dress?"

"Undergarments are right there." Sara waved distractedly to an elaborate chair, set in front of an even more elaborate vanity. There was a stack of silky things on the seat.

"Thanks." I went over, deposited my items on the vanity, and pulled on the underwear. I wasn't sure how well the little scraps of silk would hold up my full breasts, but I gave it a go, and it seemed to work fine. Sexy in a barely there, scandalous sort of way.

"My lady." Sara held up the much more formidable heft of the fairy dress. It looked like yards of silk and velvet had been sacrificed to construct it.

"Okay," I sighed, and ducked beneath the skirts.

I came up through the neck hole, my arms slipping through the silk chiffon sleeves like a swimmer surfacing for air. Sara settled the massive amounts of material around me, laced up the back with sharp pulls, and pushed me down onto the vanity seat. I was pretty sure that fairy princesses weren't manhandled like this, but I didn't really mind.

I tucked my iPod into my bodice, swept on some lipstick, then sat back to watch her work on my thick hair. Sara was a pink tourmaline Shining One. It looked as if she had some kind of beauty magic that the tourmaline magnified. Kind of perfect for a lady's maid. Sara twirled her fingers above my head, while her jewelry glowed with power. My hair seemed to curl and braid itself, settling into elaborate configurations under Sara's supervision. So elaborate that I began to have concerns over ever getting my hair loose again. But the end result was very pretty. And dry. Somehow she had managed to dry my hair as she worked.

"Nice," I said when she was done.

"Nice?" Sara huffed. "That's a coiffure worthy of a countess."

"Yeah? Well, a countess coiffure gets 'nice.' If it had been worthy of a queen, I would have come up with a better word."

She stood glowering at me for two seconds before she gave

in, and twisted her pouty lips up into a smile.

"Okay, Sara, enough primping. Where's your king?" I stood.

"I shall take you to him, my lady." She walked to the bedroom door and rapped briskly on it.

A knight in full livery opened the door, nodded to Sara, then looked at me warily. "I have to put these on you, m'lady." He held up a pair of steel bracelets. Just slim bands of polished metal . . . with thick bands of onyx set inside them.

"What do they do?" I asked, though I already knew the answer.

"Ground your magic," he said grimly as he stepped into the room, and shut the door behind him with an ominous click.

Oh, why couldn't Torin's men be as stupid as MacLaine's had been?

"Fine." I held out my hands.

The knight handed the bracelets to Sara and stood watching me carefully as she put them on. Another smart move, damn him. Sara flipped them open, there was a discreet hinge at one side, and some kind of keyhole at the other. Once open, I could see the onyx clearly, nicely polished bands of it. The stone was surprisingly warm when placed against my wrists. They clicked into place, and I was left with a shiny new set of bracelets. Just like Wonder Woman's Bracelets of Submission. Except I was more like Weakened Woman, and these bracelets worked their submission powers against me instead of my enemies. Their name was appropriate though.

"Happy?" Sara snapped at the knight after she finished locking my magic up.

"I'm only doing my duty, Sara." The knight huffed and walked out.

"Oh damn," I whispered to her. "Got 'em all under your thumb, eh?"

She gave me a saucy wink. Yep, I liked this girl.

Sara led me downstairs and through several twisting hallways until we came out into an overturned punch bowl. Yep, the ceiling was a big, glass dome. Beneath it was a garden of luscious blooms, fruit trees, other assorted foliage, and onyx statuary. Onyx stepping-stones led to an onyx fountain, bubbling happily beneath the stretching arms of a maple tree. The air was misty cool, fragrant with the scent of fruit and flowers. Sunlight filtered through the lazy tree branches, scattering shifting patterns across the grass. If I hadn't already noticed the glass dome above, I could have easily believed we were outdoors.

Torin sat at a full-size dining table, set beside the gurgling fountain. He stood as I approached, and came around the table to pull out a seat for me. I lifted a brow at the silver settings, porcelain dishes, and crystal glasses. There was a vase of massive flowers and ivy in the center of the table, trailing the sharp leafed vines around steaming platters of food. Above all this, hanging from a sturdy branch, a crystal chandelier sparkled with fairy lights. A chandelier. Of course there was a chandelier hanging from a tree in Tír na nÓg. Why wouldn't there be one?

Sara bobbed a curtsy, and hastily retreated to the entrance of the dome. I guess it was a garden room. Or an atrium, solarium, arena . . . whatever. I sat, Torin sat, and then he poured me tea from a silver teapot that looked as if it belonged in seventeenth century Russia. I watched Torin with utter bewilderment as he placed the cup before me, nudged the sugar bowl in my direction, and then started filling my plate with an assortment of strange food. The scent of vanilla and fresh bread wafted up to my twitching nose, pushing away the scents of the garden.

"Thanks, Hatter." I shook my head as he daintily took a sip of his tea.

"Yes, I suppose that's fair." Torin looked around the room, then down the table filled with food. "I would have invited the Dormouse and the March Hare, but they were busy this morning."

I smiled at his quick response. I knew the Shining Ones were as well versed in human culture as I was, but it was a little startling to come face-to-face with a fairy who spoke like a modern man right in the middle of a Tír na nÓg Wonderland.

"And thanks for my Bracelets of Submission." I lifted my wrists. "Do they deflect bullets too?"

"Not quite," he smirked. "Though I can assure you, you won't be shot at in Tír na nÓg."

"What a relief. So"–I looked around–"there's something that's been bugging me."

"Yes?"

"Where are all the lesser fey?" I peered suspiciously at him. "The pixies, goblins, and all those other critters you have here. I've only seen Shining Ones. Do you have the lesser fey locked up in your sex dungeons with your other slaves?"

Torin choked on his tea.

"My what?"

"Your sex dungeon. You know"–I sipped my tea–"the place where you keep all your human sex slaves. S&M Central, Fifty Shades of Fairy, Fuc"

"Yes, I get it." He held up a hand and cut me off. "I have no dungeon or sex slaves."

"No?"

108

"No." Torin cocked his head at me. "I admit that my people are prone to pursuing pleasure, but there are varying degrees of hedonism here. Not all of us are like King Galen. I, for example, am more reserved in my tastes."

"So where are the lesser fey, if not in your dungeon?" I teased.

Who knew a conversation with my captor could be so fun?

"The lesser fey live in Primeval," Torin explained. "They're too wild for the Jewel Kingdoms."

"Primeval?"

"The ancient forests that lie on the outskirts of our kingdoms. They are happiest there. We don't force them into banishment or anything horrid like that, so you can remove that nasty expression of disapproval, Elaria," he chided. "They choose the freedom of Primeval over the restrictions of kingdom life."

"Oh," I thought about it. "I suppose they would be happier in the wild. I can't see a kelpie enjoying this," I waved a hand at the room.

"Just so," Torin nodded. "There's an ocean in Primeval, as well as several lakes. The aquatic fey rarely leave, for obvious reasons." Then Torin looked pointedly at my dress. "You look lovely in blue."

"I just realized that the color matches your eyes," I noted. "Did you choose this dress?"

"No," he smiled, "and the color matches your eyes also. Well . . . sometimes. They're currently turning a deep shade of amethyst."

I went still, my smile falling away abruptly. I've had lovers tell me how my eyes went deep purple when I was feeling

109

amorous.

"What did I say?" Torin frowned.

"Nothing." I cleared my throat, and took stock of my emotions.

Yeah, okay, so Torin looked really amazing this morning. He had on a deep gold tunic and brown, leather pants. The earthy colors actually turned his eyes a darker shade of blue. The velvet tunic stretched across the expanse of his wide shoulders, pulling tight in places and giving me glimpses of smooth, muscled flesh in its gaping neckline. Damn it all; I needed to kick this guy's ass before I did something naughty with it. Too bad I was a little restricted by my jewelry at the moment.

"I have something to show you." Torin handed me a fashion magazine.

"What's this?" I took it, looking over the smiling woman on the cover.

"*This* is Nila." He pointed at the blonde model. "I thought it might be a good idea to offer you proof of life." He tapped the corner. "See the date?"

"I believed you." I tossed the magazine into an empty chair beside me. "You didn't have to shove her in my face."

There was a strange twinge of something in my chest. I didn't like looking at the woman. The supremely gorgeous woman. It made me feel . . . oh, fuck me, it made me jealous. I was feeling jealous! Oh, I was going to kiss this guy's . . . er, I mean kick, I was going to *kick* this guy's ass so hard. I hadn't been jealous in like . . . like . . . ever. It was her blonde hair, and her perfect face, and her big eyes, and her . . . ugh! This was his last girlfriend? And *he* broke up with *her*? Now he wanted me? Yeah, right.

"You have no reason to believe me, so thank you for your

trust," he said sincerely. "Elaria, uh, I . . ." He sighed. "May I call you Elaria?"

"Sure," I smirked as I popped a berry in my mouth. "If I can call you Torin."

It was a ridiculous request, and I knew it. The man was a fairy king; to drop his title suggested a familiarity that was

"You may absolutely call me Torin." He smiled, and my mouth went dry. "Until you come up with something more intimate."

"Wow," I snickered as I reached for my cup. "That big head of yours must get heavy. How do you manage to hold it up?"

"The stones said we'd be together." He shrugged as if it were a foregone conclusion.

I don't think any woman enjoys being a foregone conclusion. I liked it even less than seeing his last lover plastered over the cover of a magazine.

"The stones said you would fall." I lifted my chin. "But they didn't say I would."

Torin's smile faded.

"And how do you even know that's what they meant?" I went on. "They could have been warning you that I was going to kick your ass. Or trip you."

"Elaria." His voice was so damn sexy, especially when he was serious, which he suddenly was. "There's so much more that I need to tell you."

Why did he have to speak like that? Dear gods, why? I was susceptible to sounds. It's a spellsinger thing. It was like my hearing was an erogenous zone.

"Yes?" I prompted him when he hesitated.

"You have been thrust into a war," he said gently. "Galen sent you to kill me, not because of any familial loyalty, but because he needed me dead so he could further his own agenda. He couldn't kill me himself, so he's been sending assassins."

"Yeah, well, I failed at killing you too." I frowned. "Among the humans I'm powerful, even in the Beneath. But here, in Tír na nÓg, I'm nothing special. All you needed was a little warning from your rocks, and you were able to subdue me. Hell, a pair of bracelets are subduing me right now."

"You're stronger than you think." His eyes shifted into a brighter blue. "And Galen is a fool. He sent me the only person necessary to winning this war."

"I couldn't even break out of my bedroom last night," I huffed without thinking.

"I knew you'd try." Torin laughed.

Internally, I groaned. I probably shouldn't have told him that. What was with me and this guy?

"My point is"–I rolled my eyes–"if you could trap me so easily, how could I be imperative to winning a Shining Ones war?"

"Witchcraft," he said succinctly.

"Witchcraft?" I blinked at him.

"The craft of the witches." He nodded. "Spells, magic, enchantments, etcetera."

"Yes, I know who the witches are."

"I would hope so," he chuckled. "But did you know they nearly wiped us out once?"

"What? No, I didn't."

"Yes." Torin frowned. A flicker of something more than irritation, possibly something truly painful, crossed his face. "It was before I was born, but it has been well recorded in our histories. The Shining Ones decided that Earth was wasted on the humans, and that we should control it. The witches got wind of the plot and acted first. They tore open the Veil and marched through Tír na nÓg, leveling kingdoms and obliterating any who opposed them."

A chill coasted over my skin. My father had said something to me once, which I'd thought to be bravado, but now realized it had been simple truth. "If not for us witches, those fucking fairies would have taken over the Earth long ago." He had to have meant this war Torin was talking about.

"How did it end?" I asked.

"Thankfully with a truce," Torin made a gruff sound. "The witches pulled back their armies, and agreed to leave Tír na nÓg on two conditions."

"Which were?"

"First, that we never try to take over the human world again." He waved his hand as if that were obvious. "And second, that we allow them to leave a relic within Tír na nÓg. A magical object that would awaken should the truce ever be threatened."

"Like a warning bell?" I frowned. "Does it alert the witches if the Shining Ones begin scheming to invade Earth again?"

"No, actually, the warning is for us." Torin looked deathly serious. "The witches had been right to attack us. If the Shining Ones had taken Earth, it would have upset the balance of magic. The Veil between Earth and Tír na nÓg would have faded and possibly disappeared entirely. If that piece of the Veil was ever to fall, what do you think would happen to the other boundaries? The rest of the border?"

"It would fall as well," I whispered. "Like a disease, the fade would spread until there was nothing left to separate the different planes of existence.

"Yes, precisely," he agreed. "So this relic was left here to warn us against our own hubris, our own destructive natures. Because if one portion of the Veil fell, all of the worlds would fall with it. The damage would spread until the Veil disintegrated, and the planes would merge. Then the strain of several layers of matter, all trying to occupy the same space, would result in a cataclysmic explosion. Nothing would survive. Less than nothing. I've theorized that the result would be a black hole."

"Scary," I nodded, "Horrifying even, but what has this relic to do with me?"

"The witches swore that if the relic ever awakened, a champion from their world would come to claim it." Torin stared at me intently. "This warrior would be someone rare, someone special, and someone who was only *part* witch. The witches knew their own limitations, and the relic they created was too powerful for any of them to wield. The warrior would need to be a halfling, a witch whose blood was strengthened by another race. There have been endless debates over what the other half of this witch warrior would be. Perhaps part fey, part shifter . . . or part god."

"And you think that's me?" I laughed. "The half-witch warrior come to claim the relic?"

"Elaria."–Torin shook his head–"I've read the scrolls myself. They say that one such warrior will be born every five hundred years. Each new birth frees the previous soul from its responsibility to the relic. If the relic awakens, the current warrior is drawn to Tír na nÓg, pulled to the relic itself, and then they shall forge a bond. Together, the relic and warrior will quell the uprising and reinstate the truce."

"Five hundred years?" I asked, and he nodded.

I recalled something my mother used to say about the strangeness of spellsinger births. They seemed to occur once every five hundred years. Like clockwork. To the exact day, and even occasionally, to the exact hour. All spellsingers had the same birthday. May first. Beltane, the witch festival of growth and protection. The perfect birthday for a warrior. A guardian. A shiver coasted over my skin.

"No." I stood abruptly, sending my chair crashing back onto the onyx tiles. "No fucking way. I'm not a warrior witch. The magic is in my song–that's all."

"Elaria." Torin got up and approached me carefully. He reached out slowly, as if to a startled horse, and took my hand. "Maybe you aren't the warrior. Maybe I've read the signs wrong. But there's one more thing you should know before you turn your back on this."

"What?" I whispered, not really wanting to hear it.

"The relic has awakened."

Chapter Fourteen

"The relic has awakened?" I blinked. "What is this? *Dune?*"

Torin had been so serious, so intent, it took him a few seconds to respond to my joke. He blinked back at me, then let out a surprised laugh.

"No, this isn't a person; it's an object." He tugged on my hand. "Come with me and I'll show you."

"You've got it here?" I smirked. "Has it been keeping you up at night, claiming that it's the Kwisatz Haderach?"

"No." He wrapped my arm around his as he led me through the garden. "Do you always use humor to deflect uncomfortable conversations?"

"Yes."

"At least you're honest." He chuckled. Then we reached a soaring, glass wall, and he pointed out through it. "Look there."

I looked in the direction he indicated. It led my gaze off into the distance. A mountain so sheer, and so perfectly formed, it was practically a pyramid, rose above the varied landscape. At the mountain's apex, a light shone. It sparkled with a multitude of colors, making it seem opalescent. As soon as I saw it, my whole body lurched forward into the glass. My face made a resounding thump when it hit.

"Ow." I cringed, and pushed myself away, not registering what had really happened. "What the hell? Did you push me?"

I glared at Torin in accusation, but he was staring at me in wide-eyed wonder.

"You didn't push me, did you?"

"No," he whispered. "Sweet stones, it's true. You're the awaited warrior."

"Now, hold on." I rubbed at my nose. "I probably just slipped."

"You were standing still." Torin shook his head. "It was the relic calling you."

I risked another glimpse back at the light, and again, I felt a physical pull. But this time, I was prepared for it. I stood my ground. Just barely. My body shifted forward, making me feel like a piece of metal being drawn to a magnet, and a tremor coursed through me. I took a deep, horrified breath, and laid my hand to the glass. I could feel it, that witch relic, and the longer I stared at the light, the stronger that feeling became. Until suddenly, I saw it.

The image was HD clear. I saw the relic waiting atop all that stone. An ancient guardian anxious to get to work. It spoke to me. Not with an actual voice, but with intent and emotions. Claim. Defend. Kill. I inhaled sharply. Oh, it was angry, very angry. The magic of thousands of witches had been poured into it. All that power, just sleeping on a mountaintop like a hibernating dragon. Now someone had poked the beast, and it was grouchy. Aren't we all, when we get woken up too early?

It also knew why it was awake. Yes, it was sentient. It sensed that someone had disobeyed the truce, and now it wanted that someone to pay. It *needed* them to pay. As far as it was concerned, the fate of all the worlds depended upon making that person pay.

And it wanted my help. No . . . it demanded my partnership.

117

"Nope." I shook my head. "Not for me. Don't want it."

"What?" Torin gaped at me.

"I can't help you."

"You're the warrior."

"Nope, you've got the wrong girl."

"Elaria." He sighed. "I know this is a lot to take in. The responsibility is"

"Not mine," I growled. "I don't have time for this shit. Look, I'll go home and call my dad. Maybe he can recommend someone to come out and help you."

"Recommend . . ." Torin made a huffing sound of disbelief. "That's not how this works. You feel it, Elaria. You know you must wield that relic."

The pull rushed through me again, even though I turned away from the light. It had taken root already, and I knew I wouldn't be able to leave Tír na nÓg. Not because Torin would try to stop me–he wouldn't have to. My own body would betray me. I wouldn't be able to make it fifty feet in the wrong direction. Torin was right. This wasn't something I could just say no to. I had a feeling that if I tried to head away from that relic, I'd simply turn around and run faster toward it.

"This isn't me." I swallowed hard. "I don't actually fight. I *sing*. The songs do the fighting for me. I'm not a warrior–I'm an occasional killer. There's a big difference. You can hand a child a gun and turn him into a killer, but one weapon doesn't make a warrior. I don't care how strong that thing is; I simply don't have the necessary skills."

"Yes, you do. You don't have to fight physically," Torin said gently. "You will stand at the back of the army and sing, that's all."

"That's *all*?" I scoffed.

"That and whatever else the relic requires of you," he shrugged. "But I don't believe it will be physical."

"This isn't even my fight."

"Did you miss the *cataclysmic explosion* portion of our conversation?" Torin asked snidely. "Of course it's your fight. It's everyone's fight."

"Why doesn't someone just explain this to whomever is trying to take over Earth?" I huffed. "Just tell them what you told me. I can't imagine anyone would risk destroying all the worlds in order to conquer one. That's just plain stupid."

"The promise of power can make even the smartest of men ignore the truth," Torin sighed. "Galen believes he can keep the Veil intact. He has a team of sorcerers who have promised him that they can create a magical counter balance that will pull back the energy, should the Veil ever start to fade."

"Wait . . . Galen?" I blinked in shock. "You're telling me that the Sapphire King is the one who's plotting to invade Earth?"

"Why do you think he sent you to assassinate me?" Torin gave me an impatient look. "He could never beat Onyx in a war, so he's been sending assassins to kill me before it comes to that. I'm his strongest opposition. I've been petitioning the other monarchs to band together and stop Galen before the warrior was called to claim the witch relic and a war became unavoidable."

"But then Galen brought me here." I made a sound of disbelief.

"Yes, the irony was not lost on me." Torin smiled. "In trying to clear the way for himself, he only placed a bigger obstacle in his path."

119

"You really believe I'm this relic-wielding warrior?"

"The onyx spoke to me." He shrugged. "Yes, I believe it, and judging from the look on your face, Elaria, I think you believe it too."

Chapter Fifteen

I went back to the table and sat down. Torin followed me a little hesitantly, and reclaimed his chair while continuing to watch me. I pulled my iPod out of my bodice, tucked the earbuds in, and hit play. I didn't care what came on, as long as it was music. I needed something to relax me. Something to take my mind off this situation long enough for me to work it through. I know that sounds crazy, but studies have shown that the brain works better when you don't force it to think. I always find solutions in the songs, but that might just be a spellsinger thing.

Then I realized that I could sing.

I mean, duh, yes, of course I can sing. But with my new bracelets, I could sing without casting a spell. I could simply enjoy the music. I started to smile.

"What?" Torin asked. I didn't actually hear him–my ears were full of Halsey–but I saw his mouth form the word.

Instead of answering, I sang the lyrics to "Castle." A fairy tale of old kings and new queens. Misogyny given a furious, yet elegant, middle finger. The melody made its tick-tock climb to an ethereal apex, and then slowly slid down to a rocky bottom. An insistent, bring-it-on type of song that was perfect for my mood. I stood and spun happily, allowing the rhythm to shift into my soul.

Torin stared at me.

I went on, singing the fantasy, loving the lyrics for just being words, sounds to sway to without any magic to direct. I let them shift me closer to the Onyx King, and then I started to dance. I went on singing, and Torin went on staring, but he also began to smile. The fairy tale unfolded between us with a magic that had nothing to do with me being a spellsinger . Torin stood and shifted forward, sliding his hands around my waist. I followed the lead of the lyrics, and trailed my fingertips across Torin's lips playfully.

Torin took an earbud out of my ear, and put it in his. "You need to learn how to share."

He pulled me closer, and we began to dance.

The song became a protest, then a cry of conquering. I let it carry me along. No direction, no intent, only the music. I placed my palm on Torin's chest and began to enjoy the simple satisfaction of singing to a man. Just singing, and maybe tempting a little. The words took on a personal meaning suddenly. They were both warning and seduction. I wouldn't be an easy conquest, but I would definitely be worth the battle.

Torin's hands slid up my back, sexy but not too grabby. I liked that, and I liked being close to him. In the middle of the music, that freedom of singing without focus, I allowed myself to like all of it. Everything had become complicated so fast. I needed this moment of pure pleasure, simple happiness. So when he picked me up and spun me, I found myself leaning back into it, and laughing through the next line. And when Torin lowered me back to the ground, I wrapped my arms around his neck and held tight.

Torin didn't ruin the moment by trying to kiss me. He just swayed with me like we were teenagers at our first dance. Nothing too crazy, just a slow bit of motion to go with the melody. It wasn't till after the song ended and I was left staring up into those darkening eyes that I felt a growing presence around us. I frowned, and as soon as I did, Torin looked away from me. And then he smiled.

The man had a smile that could make sirens weep.

"You have an audience." He nodded to our left.

I turned, and found the lurking presence I'd sensed. A crowd of Shining Ones was staring at us, waiting for me to look in their direction before they launched into applause.

"What the hell?" I scowled. "Why are they doing that?"

"Why?" Torin grinned and gaped at me simultaneously. "Because you have an amazing voice. Because they enjoyed listening to you sing."

"*Enjoyed* listening," I blinked as the next song started to play in our ears. "I can't remember the last time someone applauded my singing just because they enjoyed the sound of it. Maybe my mother, when I was little."

"That's ridiculous." He frowned, then saw that I was serious, and frowned deeper. "How is that possible?"

"I can't sing without casting a spell." I shrugged like it didn't bother me. "For me, a killer song is quite literal, and if there's applause when it's over, it's not in response to my voice."

"Well you have an eager audience now." He held his arm out to me.

"What do you want?" I scowled at him.

"Come now, Elaria." Torin smiled wickedly. "Don't tell me you're shy."

"No, of course not." I huffed. "But . . . you want me to sing? For them?"

"Why not?" Torin took the buds out of our ears. "I have a sound system you can plug this into."

The crowd continued to watch us, listening avidly to our conversation with hopeful expressions. They were mostly members of the court, but there were a few servants huddled at the edges, including my maid, Sara. She gave me a taunting look, the little minx. She probably knew that would compel me more than any amount of cheering.

"Wait." I hesitated. Torin's words finally registered with me. "You have a sound system? As in a human-made stereo?"

"The whole dining hall is wired." He squished up his face in offense. "We are not heathens."

"Then why don't you have cars?" I shot back.

"Ghastly things." Torin shook his head. "They spew pollution into the air. The only thing a sound system spews is music, and we Shining Ones love music."

"Huh." I considered it. "How do you power it? You don't have electricity here, do you?"

"No, we have something much better," he smirked.

"Magic? You figured out how to use magic to power human technology?"

"Not I, personally, but yes," Torin said. "I'm told it wasn't that difficult. Energy is energy. Magic can create lightning, and lightning is a form of electricity."

"I didn't notice any power outlets," I said.

"Outlets? No, we aren't restricted by such things. Magic functions more like a Tesla Coil, transmitting energy wirelessly."

"So my iPod?"

"Charging as we speak," Torin smirked. "Would you care to connect it to the stereo now?"

"Okay, but I get to pick the play list."

"Of course, my lady." Torin winked at me as I took his arm.

Then he looked at the others. "The Lady Elaria has consented to sing for us."

They cheered. These people, whose king I'd come to kill, actually cheered for me. So weird. But then maybe they knew the prophecy too. Maybe they, like Torin, thought that my arrival was a blessing, and that I was a savior instead of an assassin. I looked into Torin's impossibly blue eyes and wondered if he was right. I had felt the pull of that relic. I knew I wouldn't be able to leave Tír na nÓg without at least holding it in my hands. Did that mean I was destined to defend Earth from an army of Shining Ones? I couldn't fathom it. Frankly, it was ridiculous to think that I could go from mercenary to messiah. But a little, teensy-weensy part of me wanted to.

And I discovered that I liked the sound of applause.

Chapter Sixteen

I woke up on a throne.

I'm not kidding, and I don't mean a porcelain throne either. I woke up the next morning, draped across an ebony throne, with Torin leaning against the foot of it, his cheek pillowed on my thigh. At first, I had no idea how I'd wound up there. Then it all started to come back to me.

"Oh gods," I groaned and sat up, dislodging Torin.

Torin yawned, and stretched languorously, coming awake easily and with the grace of . . . well, a king. Hell, the man looked royal even when he was stretched out on the floor before his throne, instead of in it. Speaking of which . . .

"How did I end up in your throne?" I peered around the room to get my bearings.

We weren't the only people passed out in the dining hall. Or was it a throne room? There was a throne in it, but I think it was just Torin's dining throne. He probably had another one someplace else, where he did kingly things. This one was for eating in, and apparently for passing out across. Anyway, there were lots of Shining Ones strewn about the hall, passed out in heaps and rows with other Shining Ones. Thankfully, all of them were clothed, and I didn't recall it being different at any point in the evening. Which was probably why I had stayed long enough to pass out in a throne, instead of running to my room to hide from an orgy. Perhaps not all fairies were freaks after all.

"It was when you finished your last song, and then fell over from exhaustion." Torin stood, then shouted, "Breakfast!"

And a massive scurrying began. The sleeping fairies began to awaken as well, rubbing at bleary eyes and helping each other up. Some stumbled off, but most just crawled to a table and sprawled across it, waiting for the food to arrive.

We had evidently partied a bit hard the night before.

"Right." I recalled drinking an excessive amount of fairy wine, then singing.

I sang and sang and sang until everything went dark. Evidently that was what passing out felt like. I frowned and tried to get up, but the world wobbled.

"Easy now." Torin helped me back into the throne. "Just relax. We'll have breakfast here shortly."

Had I really spent a whole day singing? Wait . . . Nope. I also drank and ate a little bit. Then I sang. Then I drank and danced. Then I sang some more. It had gone on that way till late in the night. Or possibly early in the morning. I'm a little fuzzy on the time. I think I may have even sung some Gaga. Oh dear gods.

"But this is your throne," I protested. "I shouldn't be sitting in it."

"It's just a piece of furniture," Torin shrugged, and took the smaller seat beside mine. With him in it, it suddenly seemed to be a more intimidating chair. "That hunk of wood doesn't make me king. Nor does a crown for that matter." He gestured pointedly at his bare head. "If I relied upon such things to rule, I'd never have been able to build this castle in the first place."

"You built this place?"

"Many years ago"–Torin shrugged–"with a lot of help. But yes, it was my design. Everything in my castle is here because I wish it to be. And every*one*." He reached over, and took my hand, then surprised me by laying a kiss on it.

"Sweet baby Jesus." I jerked my hand away from him. "It's way too fucking early in the morning for you to be kissing my hand."

"I think it's perfectly appropriate after the night we shared." He smirked. "In fact, I think your hand is the least of what I should be kissing."

"Half of yesterday is a blur to me," I narrowed my eyes on him. "What did you put in that wine?"

"Magic," he said, again with that *duh* tone. "Give yourself a few minutes to clear your head, and then it should come back to you."

"Right, of course." I rolled my eyes. "That's why Cerberus says to never drink with a fairy."

"We prefer the term 'Shining Ones.'" Torin teased, but then he frowned. "Who is Cerberus?"

"You haven't heard of the three-headed dog who guards Hades?" I was a little shocked. I mean, the guy had a sweet sound system, but he didn't know Greek mythology?

"I know the myth, yes," Torin said. "I've even heard of the man. Works in security, correct?"

"Owns a security company, yeah." I smirked. "He's damn good at it too."

"How could he not be?" Torin's face went aloof. "He is a guard dog after all."

"Hey!" I pointed in his face. "Watch how you talk about my friend."

"Friend or lover?" Torin narrowed his eyes on me.

I froze with my finger right beneath Torin's nose, and then I

128

laughed. Torin scowled even more fiercely. Which made me laugh harder.

"Seriously?" I leaned back in the throne and regarded him. "You've known me a whole day, and you're already jealous? That's adorable."

I wasn't going to contemplate my own jealousy over Nila.

"More than a day," Torin muttered, "and we've had a few moments. I thought . . ." He shrugged and looked away.

"We had a few moments?" I laughed again, and he started to get up in a huff. I grabbed his hand and pulled him back into his seat. "Relax, Onyx." I shook my head at him. "I'm not dating Cerberus. We've been friends for most of my life. I wouldn't risk it with him."

"Oh." He sniffed.

"Adorable," I said again.

"Do you deny that we connected last night?" Torin turned to me with an intense stare.

"Yeah, it was fun." I smiled at a servant who placed a mug of coffee before me. "Oh, you wonderful woman," I said to her. "How did you know exactly what I needed?"

"A lot of visitors from the human world like this brew." She giggled, laid out a silver pitcher of cream, and a bowl of sugar, then ran away.

I mixed some cream and sugar into the coffee, sipped it, then sighed in delight.

"Fun?" Torin huffed. "What about the gardens?"

"The gardens?" I frowned into my coffee.

Then it all came rushing back. The *gardens*. My eyes widened. I'd done something naughty with Torin in the gardens, hadn't I? Oh damn, I'd gone and made out with a Shining One. A king! A shiny king! Damn. And it was good too. Double damn. He'd tasted like red wine and cinnamon. Damn, damn, damn. I swallowed hard, remembering when I'd brushed a certain part of Torin's anatomy with my hand. It was as impressive as the rest of him. Damn his fairy wine and damn me! At least our clothes had stayed on–no harm done really. But honestly, I was a little disappointed that our first kiss had occurred while we'd both been under the influence of magic alcohol.

And now Torin would really be certain that we were going to get together. But then hadn't that been my plan? I was going to lure him into a false sense of security, possibly by seducing him, and then bail. Except now there was this relic thing that I may, or may not, believe I was connected to. Perhaps leaning toward the *may*.

"Yes, uh . . ." I cleared my throat. "That was a bit more than fun. Sloppy on my part, and potentially embarrassing, but definitely more than just fun."

"I don't recall anything sloppy or embarrassing." He scowled. "We talked for hours before our more intimate interlude. Or did the wine wipe that away too?"

"Uh . . ." I blinked as I thought back.

Oh yeah. I had told him things. *Personal* things. Why did I do that? The memory rose in full clarity.

"Through here," Torin's voice echoed to life inside my head.

He was smiling softly, secretly, as he led me up the stairs to his private, roof-top garden. We'd gone through his bedroom to get there, offering me a good look at his enormous bed along the way. My stomach clenched as the memory rolled onward.

130

A midnight sky scattered with more stars than I'd ever seen. Wind sighing through the intricate designs of onyx partitions. Moonlight stroking sleeping flowers, shimmering over the night-blooming blossoms. There were spots of brilliant white, soft lavender, and pale blue in the velvet shadows. Fragrance more delicate, and more complex, than any expensive perfume, wafted through the air. A seductress calling to her lovers. The stone of the roof had ended at the edge of the garden, where a ledge was surmounted by stairs. I climbed them with Torin, and realized that the whole garden sat in a massive planter.

Trees shivered in the slight breeze, grass cushioned our steps, and a night bird cooed softly to its mate. A gazing pool was set in the exact center of the garden, with a small circle of bare grass surrounding it, and three onyx benches placed at precise distances apart, in the grass ring. This was where Torin led me, to sit on one of the cool, polished seats beneath the open sky, before the mirrored surface of the pool. It was filled to the exact level of the grass around it, so that it seemed to be an extension of the earth. If you weren't careful, you could easily slip into the water.

"This is my sanctuary," Torin had whispered to me as he stared contentedly around the garden.

"And you brought me here?"

"I had the urge to share it with you." He shrugged.

"It's beautiful," I offered. "It reminds me a little of where I grew up. Though there's no ocean nearby to salt the air."

"You lived by the sea?"

"I lived on an island." I smiled. "I still do, though it's far different from the one I was raised on."

"What was your first island like?" Torin's eyes had gone as liquid as the pool before us, and I felt a sudden urge to tell him. To speak of things I normally didn't like to talk about.

"The island was beautiful," I whispered, caught by his intense gaze. *"It was full of magic, as my entire childhood was. I have no right to complain."*

"But you were unhappy?"

"No." I found myself staring into the mirrored water, seeing my childhood play across the surface. *"Not exactly. I didn't understand why we were so isolated. Why there were no other children on our island. No other people at all. Just my parents and me, and the occasional siren visitor."*

"It was your magic," he guessed.

"Yes," I said. *"As soon as my mother conceived, she knew she would bear a spellsinger. It's simple genetics. When witches breed with sirens, this is what you get."* I waved a hand toward myself. *"I was the first spellsinger to be born in five hundred years, and each one before me had shown erratic growth with their magic. My parents isolated us to protect me, and everyone else, until I could learn to control my power. But at the time, I'd thought there was something wrong with me. Like I had been born bad and had to be hidden."*

"I understand." Torin swallowed hard. *"Our parents do their best for us, but they don't have as much control over our lives as they would like. Several things can turn paradise into hell, all beyond a parent's control."*

"That sounds like personal experience." I slipped my hand into his, and his gaze jerked back to mine.

Torin searched my eyes for awhile before answering, *"I was isolated as well, but mine was more of an ostracization than a physical remoteness."*

"You were ostracized?" I blinked in surprise. *"You?"*

"Me." He gave a mirthless laugh. *"I'm not entirely fey."*

132

His arm lifted, as if to display the obviousness of that statement. "Mixed blood usually doesn't bother the Shining Ones. As long as you have some fey blood in you, that's enough. There are more important things than purity. Things like magic and beauty."

"Well, you have both of those in spades," I grimaced.

"Thank you." His lips twisted in a sweet smile. "But my beauty wasn't the right variety."

"It's okay for you to be different, as long as you don't look it?" I asked with a little anger on his behalf.

"Precisely." He turned my hand over in his palm, laying it upright before cradling it between both of his. "I was so much bigger than the other children. And my face was too... feral. That's the word they used most often."

"Fucking kids." I shook my head. "They can be so cruel. Maybe I was better off on my island."

"Maybe," he shrugged, "but I don't regret my childhood. I had love from my parents to support me through any viciousness those children offered me. And those trials, those rejections, made me stronger. I'm grateful for them now. They gave me a valuable perspective on my own kind, and those friends I did make, I knew were true."

"That's a pretty Zen attitude to take," I noted. "I suppose all those children changed their tune when you grew up and became a king?"

"Oh yes." He chuckled, a low, satisfied sound. "I remember vividly the first time one of my childhood tormentors approached me. She had matured into a beautiful fey woman, and she thought her beauty would be enough to sway me into forgetting our past. She tried to seduce me."

"You told her to shove it where the fairy sun don't shine?"

133

I asked with a wide smile.

"In a manner of speaking." He laughed loudly, and the sound echoed around us. It was a little startling in the quiet night, but I loved it. It was the sound of triumph.

"Good for you," I curled my fingers over his, and shared the victory with him. That small, harmless vengeance that nonetheless tasted so sweet.

I let go of the memory on that happy note.

Torin had vowed that he was grateful for his harsh childhood, but I knew immediately that this was the reason he was so arrogant. He had bonded with onyx because he'd been born with protection magic, and that's exactly what his cocky attitude was about–protection. His flippant way of flirting ensured that he could laugh off a woman's rejection. Torin could simply pretend that he wasn't really interested, and then scorn her arrogantly.

But Torin had been truly interested in me. He had dropped his arrogance last night, and let me see the man behind the onyx mask. A man with vulnerabilities just like mine, despite the power he held. And it was unbelievably sexy. That was what had compelled me to kiss him. Yes, *I* had kissed *him*. I recalled it now vividly–the way his lips had parted slightly as I moved closer, the way his hand hesitantly lifted to my cheek. There had been stars reflected briefly in his eyes before I had eclipsed their light, and I couldn't decide which I preferred; the star-filled eyes or those full of my shadows. I remembered the feel of Torin's breath on my lips just before I pressed my mouth to his. His tongue was velvet against mine, and his fingers like dictators in my hair–demanding, pulling, and directing me. Our chests were pressed tight together, hearts pounding through our clothing to synchronize their beats, and it seemed as if nothing would quench the heat between us.

It was a hell of a first kiss.

"I remember it now," I cleared my throat. "That was . . .

special."

"Humph." Torin settled back. "All right then. I thought we could leave in a few hours. That will give us enough time to eat, bathe, and prepare for the journey."

"Journey? What journey?" I scowled at him, a little hazy after experiencing the rush of memory. Did he want me to go somewhere? I didn't have enough caffeine in me yet to even think about standing, much less taking a trip. No coffee, no walkee.

"To the relic of course." Torin scowled back.

"Who said I was going to claim that thing?" I growled at him as the urge to get up, and start running toward the relic, nearly consumed me. Crap, simply talking about it was too much for me to handle.

"You did, last night." Torin was slowly beginning to understand that I had been a bit more affected by all that fairy wine than he'd been.

"Yeah, well, I don't do favors for my jailer." I held up my onyx-bound wrists. The steel coating glinted in accusation.

Torin stared at the bracelets long enough for me to drop them, and then he continued to stare. I sipped my coffee, and he followed the movement up to my face. Then he stared into my eyes. Like he could see the future in them. I was beginning to get really uncomfortable, when he pulled a silver key out of his pocket.

"Give me your wrists," Torin said softly.

"What? Really?"

"Yes, Elaria," he sighed. "I'm choosing to trust you, to trust in the woman I got to know last night. I already told you, I don't want you to be my prisoner. How do you think it feels for me to kiss a woman whom I've bound?"

"I don't know," I whispered. "Kinky?"

"It feels reprehensible." Torin ignored my horrible attempt at humor, and took my left wrist. He inserted the little key into the tiny lock, and opened the bracelet. "It feels wrong. I don't want to force you in any way. Not to remain here, or to be with me, or to claim the relic. But please remember that we're not only fighting to save Tír na nÓg; we're in a battle for the safety of all the worlds. And we truly need you, Elaria."

The other bracelet came off, and he slipped them into his pocket. Then he just stared at me, waiting for me to do something. Anything.

"That key has been in your pocket this entire time?" I snapped. "I could have taken it off you when you were passed out at my feet."

Torin laughed, relaxing a bit. "Except that you passed out first, and I awaken very easily."

"Awaken easily while looking like a Calvin Klein model," I muttered.

"What was that?" Torin's smile turned into a smirk.

"Nothing." I rubbed at my free wrists. "I may want to borrow those sometime."

Torin lifted his brows.

"So I can sing again," I explained. "I told you I had fun."

"They're yours." He pulled them out of his pocket, along with the key, and handed me the lot.

"Thanks." I stuffed them into one of my skirt pockets.

"My pleasure." Torin gave me a sexy smile, then thanked the servants, who placed platters of steaming food on the table before us. He filled a plate, set it before me, then casually asked me, "So, the relic?"

"Yeah, give me a few hours," I muttered with my mouth full.

Torin smiled wider, cutting into his meal with gusto.

Chapter Seventeen

The journey to Relic Mountain (as I was calling it in my head) had to be done furtively. We'd be passing through some kingdoms that were known Sapphire sympathizers, and Torin didn't want to attract any attention. So we all donned some rugged clothing (leather pants, cotton tunics, and leather vests) and tried to look as plain as possible. By "we," I mean Torin, myself, and four of his knights. I found it interesting that he had other gem users in his Guard, not just onyx. There were knights wearing bloodstones, Fluorites, labradorites, and even diamonds, in addition to a large onyx pin that proclaimed their allegiance. I found that strange. I knew the Shining Ones lived in whatever kingdom they wished, but I'd thought that generally those with more power gravitated to the kingdoms whose stones they aligned with.

When I asked Torin about this assortment, he'd said that he believed it was wise to have a diverse selection of abilities in his personal Guard. Onyx was great for protection, but it wasn't a stone for any kind of offensive attack. The men in his Guard had more aggressive magics, and therefore bonded with more aggressive stones. There were a few exceptions of course, one of them being the Fluorite knight, who used his stone's energy to enhance his mental abilities, and for a bit of good luck. Torin said a little good luck never hurt.

He had also advised me to bring my music. So my iPod was tucked into an inner pocket of my leather jerkin. I had some thick boots on my feet, Sara had braided back my long hair, and I even had a little dagger hanging off my belt. I felt like Robin Hood. And Torin kind of looked like a hot Little John. I shook my head at that. Torin could wear the plainest clothes around, but nothing could disguise his thick build. Maybe he could hunch in on himself when he was in the saddle.

The six of us set off around mid-afternoon on horseback. At first, it was kind of fun. I enjoyed the ride. Horseback riding was something I rarely did, and the scenery kept shifting, keeping things interesting. But after awhile, my backside started to go numb, and my thighs started to ache. And the mountain still seemed so far away.

I would not whine. I would not whine. I "Do you have an ETA?"

"An estimated arrival time?" Torin looked as if he could ride for hours more without a problem.

"Yep." I eyed the mountain in the distance. "An estimate, a guesstimate, whatever. How much more of this torment will I have to endure?"

The knights chuckled.

"Uh . . ."–Torin chuckled too–"we'll probably get there sometime tomorrow afternoon."

"Tomorrow?" I nearly screeched. My horse shied away from the others, and I had to sing to her a little to calm her down.

It had been an automatic response, the singing thing. So I was surprised to find Torin smiling at me softly.

"What?" I scowled at him. "Taking joy in my pain?"

"No." He smiled wider. "Taking joy in your kindness. What you just did for the animal, that was nice. I didn't know you could use your magic so casually. Or that you *would* for such trifling things."

"An upset horse isn't trifling." I tried to act as if his praise wasn't a big deal, even though I was kind of feeling warm and tingly inside. Or maybe that was just my numb limbs coming back to life. "My butt hurts enough already without me landing on it."

More laughter from the men.

"Laugh it up, you Legolas impersonators," I called back to them. "I'll remember this when I hold that relic."

That shut them up.

"And the assassin returns," Torin observed, but he also smiled.

"I'm not just an assassin." I rolled my eyes. "I kill only if all other options have been closed to me. I'd much rather sway someone than murder them."

"How charitable," Torin smirked.

"Don't be a dick," I huffed.

The knights started to sound as if they were choking.

"I am never a dick," Torin said as he straightened in his saddle, and gave me a disdainful look. "When you're a king, it's called being firm or assertive. Being a dick is for lesser men."

I burst out laughing, as did the knights behind us.

"Must be nice to be a king," I noted.

"It has its perks," Torin agreed. "Not ever being a dick is the least of them."

"All right, get over the dick thing," I said, and then made a incredulous expression. "Wow, those are words that should have never come out of my mouth."

"Indeed." Torin laughed, and then glanced at the darkening sky. "Perhaps we should stop for the night."

"We are still in Malachite, Your Highness. Just a little

farther, and we'll reach Turquoise." The Fluorite knight nodded to a swath of tall grass up ahead. We were currently riding through a lush jungle.

"Sound advice, Sir Arnet." Torin nodded. "We'll ride a little into Turquoise, and then make camp."

"What's wrong with the Malachite Kingdom?" I searched the surrounding jungle warily.

"They are Sapphire supporters," Torin followed my gaze. "Don't worry. If they attack, I'm prepared."

"We all are, Your Majesty," the diamond knight assured us.

"We all are," Torin repeated the words to me with a smug smile.

"Yeah, you're damn straight." I tapped my jerkin where my iPod rested. "I can even sing a cappella if necessary."

"Excellent"–Torin smirked–"but look, we are out of the jungle already."

Sure enough, we were. As I'd been talking to him, our mounts had sped up, as if sensing that rest was near. Sweet-smelling grass rose to almost hip high on my horse, and grew right up to the edge of the dirt road we traveled. Grasslands stretched out flat for a few miles before us, then ended abruptly in a thickly wooded area.

"There." Torin pointed to what appeared to be a random spot in the middle of the grass.

I didn't question him. He was a fairy king, so I trusted that he knew where he was going in Tír na nÓg. His knights followed just as blindly, even Arnet, so I suppose Torin had made an acceptable decision. Soon, I saw why it was wise. The grass parted for our horses, and after a few dozen feet, it fell away entirely, revealing a little lake and a small clearing clinging to its shore. Torin's height must have allowed him to spot it.

Torin dismounted gracefully, then helped me out of my saddle. I nearly fell, and he had to grab me by my waist to prevent my face-plant.

"Sorry," I whispered as he held me tight. "I'm not used to riding for so long."

He gave me a wicked grin.

"Get those dirty thoughts out of your head, Onyx," I huffed and tried to push him away.

"I merely smiled." Torin shrugged and held firm, helping me over to a sandy spot near the water. "Here, sit down. I'll get your sleeping mat out for you."

"Thanks." I sighed, and watched him head back to our horses. It was a nice view, watching him walk away.

Soon, he had a thick sleeping mat unrolled for me. I scooted over onto it, and then just plopped onto my stomach, to give my ass a rest. Torin laughed, and got up to help his men with the horses. I watched the easy way he interacted with his knights, noting how comfortable they were around him. He treated our horses with the same casual care, doing a thorough inspection of their legs and hooves before he led them to the water's edge. I liked a man who was kind to animals. In my opinion, it said a lot.

Once the horses were taken care of, settled near the lake, the men set about making a small fire and settling on their own mats. Dry rations were passed out, as well as flasks of water. I munched thoughtfully on a piece of jerky as I looked over the placid surface of the lake. Night had fallen while the men worked, and the moon had brightened. It turned the surface of the lake into a silver mirror, reminding me of Torin's gazing pool.

142

A light breeze blew through the grass, setting it to rustling softly, and the sound became whispers in my head. I felt my mind drift away as my gaze went unfocused, caught by the glittering reflections on the water. The whispers intensified and keened, like a thousand voices singing. I shook my head, but they only became stronger. Wait, they weren't singing; they were chanting. It was a spell.

Flames shot up before me suddenly, but I was lost to the vision, and I didn't flinch. Through the fire I saw the relic. It was being forged without the use of hands or tools, just tumbling in the forge, pulling itself together. The chanting continued as the fire died, and then water rained down, setting the relic to sizzling.

Wind blasted at it, blowing the rain away, and the thing dropped, diving deep into the wet earth below. The chanting escalated, and the surface of the soil bubbled, little things moving through it, toward the relic. Stones. The gems rushed to the cooled metal, setting themselves into place. The metal curved in on the jewels, embracing them. Then, with a crescendo of sound, the spell set, and the relic burst free of the earth. It hovered before the gathered witches in a ball of light, absolutely pristine, and then it fell slowly into the palm of one man.

"Elaria," the man whispered, "do not fail us."

His eyes were blacker than the shadows surrounding him, but they were also noble, full of righteous purpose. They expanded till they filled my vision completely, and I felt like a snake, hypnotized by his charm.

"Submit and conquer." The man's voice rumbled though my mind, setting me to shivering.

"Elaria?" A new voice echoed over the witch's. It was deep, and familiar, but I couldn't see who it belonged to. My sight was still trapped by those demanding eyes. "Elaria, are you all right?"

"They're coming!" the witch in my vision hissed. He pulled

143

back and slapped me across the face.

I jerked out of the vision and inhaled sharply, my eyes shooting around the campsite, as my hands went automatically to my iPod. I stopped myself from pulling it out though. I needed to be able to hear, interact with the others in my company. I wasn't alone this time, and the thought was briefly comforting. Until I remembered the witch's words.

"They're coming!" I repeated the warning, and all of the men tensed.

"Who?" Torin asked as he scanned the grass.

"I don't know." I got into a crouch, and lifted my head just above the choppy crest of grass. "But they aren't friendly."

"Prepare yourselves," Torin said to his men, though it was unnecessary.

The knights were already urging the horses closer to the water. Then they spread out in front of us, forming a line of protection between their king and whatever was threatening him. I heard a low cooing, like a night bird, and then the muffled sounds of feet approaching. I lifted my head a little farther, getting a good look at the advancing group of soldiers. A group much larger than our own.

"Perhaps fifteen," I reported to the others. "Get back by the horses."

Torin shook his head and said, "I can protect us."

"Get behind me, Torin," I said again, with a firmer tone. "I can end this a lot faster than you. And without bloodshed."

I saw the battle wage inside him. The one of his pride against his reasoning. Reason won out, and he nodded, waving his men behind us. The knights went to crouch beside the horses, hands on heaving flanks, soothing the already nervous beasts. But Torin placed himself directly behind me.

"I am here with you, Elaria." Torin settled his hands on my shoulders. "You sing, and I shall protect you."

Something shaky rose inside my chest, and for a second I couldn't breathe. Someone to protect *me*? Someone to watch over me as I sang. It was the sexiest thing a man had ever said to me. And it gave me an immense amount of confidence.

"Thank you," I whispered to him as I felt his magic settle around us.

Then I began to sing.

Soft and sorrowful at first, "True Colors" by Cyndi Lauper was actually a love song. It was uplifting, encouraging, a gentle urging to turn toward joy instead of drowning in sorrow. But I sang it to bring about an opposite reaction. I twisted the words into a heavy pall and directed it at the oncoming force. They stumbled to a halt as my magic seeped into them. The lyrics became accusations, hope turned to shame, and love to disgust.

Our attackers began to scream, weapons falling as their hands went to their ears, trying to block out the darkness that was worming its way inside them. The doubt. The insecurity. It wouldn't kill them. That wasn't necessary. In fact, it would be wiser to let them live, and carry the warning of what a spellsinger could do.

My voice burst out, echoing across the undulating grass, extending far into the open arms of the night. The words went back to being an encouragement, offering the men a chance to redeem themselves. The opportunity to change into something honorable. There was still hope.

So sweet. So romantic, those simple lyrics. But they were devious when woven with my magic. They showed the men before us their inner selves, as well as the truth of what they fought against. Those poor men saw exactly what their actions would achieve if they followed through with their plans to hurt us. Tír na nÓg would fall, *all* of the worlds would fall, and the destruction would start with this very moment. The weight of it would be on their shoulders.

They wailed, utterly converted, and then dropped to their knees whimpering. I stopped singing, though my magic still vibrated through the smoky-sweet air. Torin's hands slipped down my arms, his fingers wove into mine, and he squeezed gently as he eased his body against me. I felt his magic sink into the earth, grounding itself now that it was no longer needed.

"What have you done, Spellsinger?" Torin whispered as he wrapped our joined arms around me. I wasn't sure if he was offering comfort or asking for it.

The men, who moments earlier had intended to kill us, crept forward and bowed to Torin. To me. They began to beg for forgiveness. For us to allow them to live and make amends for their wrongs. They would tell all of Tír na nÓg about the true threat, that of the Sapphire King and his evil intentions. They would warn everyone who would listen.

"I've opened their eyes," I said to Torin. "That's all."

"The Jewels will sing, and Tír na nÓg will tremble," one of our knights said reverently.

"In joy and fear," Torin added as he swung me around and kissed me.

Chapter Eighteen

I woke up nestled against Torin, my body aching from the previous day's ride, but not so much from sleeping on the ground. The mat had been surprisingly comfortable, and Torin had kept me warm. I guess sleeping outside wasn't so bad, when you had a fairy king and his magic to keep away the insects and the cold.

After I'd subdued the men who attacked us the night before, we had interrogated them. Well, I guess it wasn't much of an interrogation since they freely offered to answer our questions. They had been sent by the Malachite Queen, Riona. It appeared that Rupert had made it home to Sapphire and spilled his guts. King Galen had then warned his supporters that Torin had me and intended to use me as some kind of weapon. It was the Malachite Queen who came to the conclusion that I might be the foretold witch warrior and that perhaps they should watch the roads leading to the relic.

Queen Riona had sent her knights out to patrol her stretch of road, giving them orders to kill anyone they deemed to be suspicious. She had warned them to be wary, that King Torin himself might be among the travelers, and all knew of the Onyx King's magical, as well as physical, prowess. Evidently, Queen Riona was a shrewd one. Just not smart enough to realize that conquering Earth would kill us all. Anyway, the men had heeded their queen's warning and had waited till after we'd settled in before they came to kill us.

After we got as much information as we could out of them, we released them back into the wild. They didn't pose a threat to us anymore. We advised them to get out of Malachite entirely. Queen Riona wouldn't take well to their change of heart. Speaking of changed hearts, I couldn't believe the direction mine was taking.

"Good morning," Torin whispered as I tried to extricate myself from his embrace.

"Good morning," I whispered back, looking over my shoulder to see that the other men were already up, and getting the horses saddled.

"Just give me a few more minutes." Torin pulled me back against his chest and nuzzled his cheek against mine. "I haven't been so comfortable with a woman in a long time."

"Yeah, me either, but that's probably because I'm straight," I said in a deadpan tone.

He laughed, but it was a soft, intimate laugh. We were fully clothed, and nothing more than some light petting had happened the night before, but somehow it felt like we'd crossed a bridge. We were a "we" now. There was something between us, something we were both acknowledging. And Torin was right; it was exceedingly comfortable to lie there together. I fit against him perfectly, and his thick muscles bracketed my body like they were made to curve around me. We fit, and that's very important to me. I liked to feel like I had a me-shaped nook that I could lean into on a man's body. Perhaps that was one of the reasons Cerberus and I had never got together. I just knew we wouldn't fit. Torin was large, but not as massive as Cer, and his body worked well with mine. It hinted that it would work exceptionally well in so many ways.

"All right." Torin sighed. "I suppose we must get on with the day."

He eased me up with him, and squeezed me one last time before unwrapping the blankets that had bound us together. We pulled apart slowly into the chilly morning, and started gathering up the mats and blankets. One of the knights came over and took our things from us, exchanging them for dry rations. Torin and I ate as the knights readied our horses.

148

Then we were off again. Riding hard toward the mountain which seemed to loom much closer that morning. The night before, it had been a bright beacon in the darkness, and I had often found myself half-awake, turning toward it. Now, in the haze of early morning, it still shone, but not quite as brilliantly. Yet no matter the illumination, the pull was the same. I could have headed toward it blindfolded. When I closed my eyes, I could still feel it, and if I concentrated hard enough, I could see it. It was growing impatient.

We passed through the sage-scented grasslands of Turquoise and into the vast forests of Quartz. Torin said we were safe there. Even though the Quartz Queen wasn't exactly a firm supporter of his, she had a well-known animosity toward King Galen. She would not be sending men to intercept us. So I relaxed a little and took in the scenery.

All the landscapes of Tír na nÓg were similar to those in the human world, just a bit more beautiful. A bit more magical. It was as if some god had turned everything up a notch. The world was more vivid, more fragrant, more clear. Just more. The trees in Quartz were particularly pretty. Their bark glimmered, each rough edge sparkling when sunlight hit it.

A little critter scurried up a trunk. I watched in amazement as its claws loosened a piece of bark and pushed it free . . . to shatter on a boulder below.

"Did you see that?" I pointed back to the boulder. "That piece of wood just shattered."

"It's quartzwood," Torin smiled at me. "The trees are nearly as strong as stone, but their outer husk is brittle. It allows the bark to shed as the tree grows."

"Quartzwood?" I blinked.

"They only grow in the Quartz Kingdom," Torin said. "You can find unique flora in every kingdom. We believe it's a way for the magic to continue to evolve. All life evolves in one way or

149

another."

"Fascinating." I looked closer at the trees.

They weren't the only unusual things in Quartz either. There were luscious blooms spreading out beneath the jagged branches, some of them venturing upward on waxy vines. Berries ripened on bushes in all sorts of strange shapes and colors, and the animals feasting on them were unlike any I'd ever seen before. Fur in all the colors of the rainbow, some accented with scales, and eyes ranging from beady to bulbous. I was so intrigued, I barely registered how far we'd gone, until the forest faded into a barren desert.

The desert had no life at all within it. No cacti or hunched trees. No lizards or burrowing creatures. It was desolate. Not even a tumbleweed to roll by and enhance the desolation. But the wasteland spanned only a few hundred feet before it met the base of Relic Mountain. I took a shaky breath, my whole body suddenly vibrating, as I craned my neck up. This was no ordinary mountain.

We reined our horses in at the base of the monolith. And it *was* a monolith. This was a stone construction, not a natural formation. It was obvious now that I stood before it. Smooth, cinnabar stone soared up thousands of feet, without any crevice or ledge to break its sleek progress. Entirely unscalable. Its color was like old blood in the sunlight, and it seemed to be a warning. Approach at your own peril.

The warning didn't matter. I couldn't stay away. But then, I don't think it had been meant for me. No, this mountain knew me. It beckoned me forward eagerly. I dismounted without waiting for Torin, and strode toward the expansive base with a determination that didn't feel fully like my own. The men remained where they were, dismounting only to stand before their horses and watch me. I could feel their intense stares on my back as I laid my hand to the glassy surface of the mountain. A low vibration, like that of a large bell being struck, rippled through the rock. The men behind me

150

inhaled sharply.

Nothing else happened.

"Sing to it, Elaria," Torin urged.

Yes, of course. I needed to sing. But what? What would open this mountain's secrets to me? What would bring me the relic? Do I sing about opening? Or perhaps about crumbling? Do I sing about falling? Maybe if I sang about flying, the relic would simply float down. Then my whole body jerked forward like I'd been pulled. I had to brace myself at the last second, palms flat against the stone. It was just as it had been in Torin's glass room. I nearly brained myself on the mountainside, my nose just a hair breadth away. Which left me staring at my own dark reflection. My breath fogged over the stone, and that's when I had an epiphany.

"I need to sing to the *relic*, not the mountain," I whispered as I looked up the sleek expanse.

The relic was anxious. I was so close, and yet I was down there dithering while it sat waiting on its pedestal, awake but impotent. It was angry at being disturbed, but even more angry that I was wasting time. It needed me as I needed it. We were meant to be together . . . meant to be. *Surrender and conquer.*

"It needs a love song." I smiled, and pulled out my iPod.

"What's that? You said it wants something?" Torin stepped up beside me, but he did so cautiously.

I realized then that even though I'd sensed the warning emanating from the mountain, I didn't really feel it. Torin and his knights did. The witches must have laid some sort of *keep away* spell around the magic mountain. Just another layer of insurance that the Shining Ones would leave the relic alone. That Torin had braved his way past an ancient spell meant to keep him at a distance, was impressive.

"It needs to be seduced." I gave Torin a saucy grin before returning to searching my song database. "Ah, perfect." I gave his shoulder a pat. "Step back, baby; I got this."

Torin gave me an amused grin, and took a few steps to the side. He was still within my line of sight, but had given me some breathing room. It seemed like he had no intentions of leaving me there alone, and I have to admit I liked him more for that. I tried not to let it show though.

I went about the process of preparing myself. Instead of putting the earbuds in, I draped them over my shoulders. So I could hear the music as well as everything else around me. Then I pressed Play, and tucked the iPod back in my pocket. The first strains of Sarah McLachlan's "Possession" started to filter out of the little speakers on my sternum, rising around me in an eerie echo.

My voice lifted with the mysterious lyrics, flowing up the stone to the mountain's apex, where the relic waited for me. It was plaintive, yearning, an undulation of promises, seduction, and betrayal. I made my lyrical confession to the relic; I was lost without it. All this time, I'd been searching for it subconsciously, never knowing what I needed. Shivers coasted over me as I joined the poignant words to the haunting melody, and I felt the men drawing in closer to my back. The pull of my song was negating the push of the mountain.

Torin's eyes were wide, his lips parted as I continued. The music was sad, but also hopeful, a sweet urging to the weapon that had lured me there. The words seemed to be written for us, me and the relic. But as I went on, I knew I sang to Torin as well, and I could feel the magic seeping out toward him as my voice echoed around us. I made vows to him with the music, sensual promises steeped in romance.

The mountain shook, and I trembled with it. Everything that was me shivered–my blood, my bones, my flesh. I had this strange certainty that even my soul vibrated along with Tír na nÓg. The shivers turned into a low rumbling as the stone before me started to slide down into the earth.

The entire mountain was sinking smoothly, dry earth crumbling in to fill the gap as the mountain descended. And far above, I could feel the relic responding to me, its anger softening. It was listening, and it liked what it heard. I sang on as threads of power reached out for me, strengthening the bond I already felt between us. My song connected us, weaving those threads into a cord with my spell, tying me and the relic together.

The lyrics turned into a portrayal of my life, and I felt an ache inside me as the truth was revealed. The heartache of seeking something real, and only finding loss. The desire for more, for something to fill that emptiness in my chest. The sense that I wasn't complete, that I had been born broken. My arms lifted to the relic like a beseeching lover, but there was still a part of me that called to Torin.

The song was scraping me raw, baring the secret of how I truly felt. My work had exposed me to the worst sort of people. So evil, they often needed killing. And killing them had long ago become easy for me. I didn't have nightmares anymore. I didn't have regrets. I don't know when I'd lost my softness, my innocence. The infallible feeling that people were basically good. That evil was an anomaly. Something that rears up rarely, only to give the good guys a target to aim at. An objective to prove how damn good they really were.

That feeling was gone, and in its place was tough skin and cynicism. Yet I had still searched. I still *wanted*. I hungered for someone to prove me wrong, to be loyal and true and honest. To be a friend and a lover, without sacrificing anything for it. And I suddenly wanted Torin to know me. To see the cold reality of what I was, but also the tenderness I kept hidden. That small part of me that I'd saved. Tucked away like a nest egg for the future.

153

I could see Torin's face in the corner of my eye, enraptured with my song. He was hearing me, but more importantly, he was listening. Responding. And the relic didn't like that.

A sharp pain made me flinch, and I knew I had to let go of Torin for now. This wasn't about the love between a man and a woman. This was about the love between a spellsinger and her magic. The relic was magic given form, and it wanted to be mine. I just had to give myself to it in return, fully, in this moment. I had to want it as much as it wanted me.

So I focused on the vision of it inside my mind, and sang only to it. The erotic words became so much more between us, a gateway to life and victory. Together, we could conquer this world. The song became a sexy slide into obsession, consuming everything that kept us apart, until two became one.

The mountain kept descending, until the top of it stood level with the ground. A crystal temple took up the entire apex of the mountain, and its steps smoothly came to rest on the barren earth. The mountain was gone; all that remained was the temple. Four pillars of crystal supporting an arched roof. The walls were glass, and so were the doors before me, set on golden hinges. I sang on as I walked up the crystal steps, and those doors swung out toward me like a welcoming embrace. I felt Torin move up behind me, but as soon as I stepped foot in the temple, the doors slammed shut between us.

I didn't bother to glance back. This was between me and the relic. Our relationship. Our love. I walked to the pedestal in the center of the temple, singing the last refrains of our song. I reassured it that we would be together, that no one could keep us apart. As I sang the last chorus, I reached for it. But it lifted all on its own, the clasp opening, and spreading wide as it moved toward me. I opened my arms, baring my neck to it in submission, and the thick collar wrapped around my throat. With my last words, it closed its clasp, and the multiple jewels set into it, one for every kingdom in Tír na nÓg, came to life. I felt our bond solidify, my

154

song and the will of the relic melding together in magic. The light of the gems burst out in blinding radiance, and I closed my eyes against the glare, letting go of the music, along with all of my doubts. Everything would be all right now that we were together.

Then the light faded, and I fell to my knees. The doors behind me opened, and Torin came rushing in. I saw his boots before me, and then his strong hand came into view. I took it, and he helped me to my feet. My eyes shifted up his leather-clad thighs, his trim waist, thickening into a muscled chest, then those wide shoulders. I took in the pulse beating in his throat, the hard angle of his chiseled jaw, the trembling of his sensuous lips, and finally, his amazing eyes. They had darkened to indigo, and were full of emotion.

"Elaria." Torin whispered, and then his gaze dropped to my throat. "A necklace." He shook his head. "I didn't expect that."

"Not a necklace." My hand reached up to spread over the smooth curves of the polished stones. "A collar. We are enslaved to each other."

"No." He frowned, his hand reaching out till his fingertips fluttered over the jewels. "Elaria, I'm so sorry. I didn't"

"It's not that kind of enslavement." I smiled peacefully at him, then caught his hand, and placed it firmly on the downward slope of the collar.

It swooped into a gentle V over my sternum. As wide as it was, it should have been uncomfortable, but the relic felt soft against my skin, and the links of metal encasing the jewels were flexible, giving me an ease of movement. I felt the stones respond to Torin's touch, warming with my attraction to him. Now that we were one, Torin wasn't a rival. It could want him *with* me.

Torin gasped, and flattened his hand so that his fingers wrapped around my throat. The stones pulsed between us, magic rising to tickle our flesh. His free hand went to my waist, and he

155

pulled me closer with both hands. Remnants of magic were still on my lips, and it tingled through our kiss. Power and pleasure became one. Torin groaned, and lifted me, pressing me tight to his chest with one hand as his other continued to caress the collar. He was romancing us both, and the relic loved it.

"Your song," Torin whispered when we finally pulled away from each other, "it brought me to my knees. I have never heard anything so beautiful."

"Let's hope it will do the same to the rest of Tír na nÓg," I said, and the relic flashed in agreement.

Chapter Nineteen

Later that evening, we were camped in the tropical Jade Kingdom. This is going to sound racist, but I expected Jade to be more, well, Asian. So dumb. Jade is a popular stone in a lot of Asian cultures on Earth, but that had nothing to do with Tír na nÓg. Here, Jade meant harmony, wealth, beauty, and healing, among other things. It was a vibrant kingdom, alive with color and heat. It reminded me a lot of my home in Hawaii. The way the climate changed, along with the landscapes of each kingdom, was a bit disorienting, but in this particular instance, I appreciated it. The night we spent in Jade was nearly as humid as the day. We didn't need a fire; we just stretched out beneath the stars, and enjoyed the balmy evening.

Torin was on his side, angled toward me. The knights were spread out around us, but Torin's mat was laid directly alongside mine, and he was only a heartbeat away. His hand lay on mine, over my stomach, as I stared up into the star-riddled sky. Just another sparkling facet of Tír na nÓg. I could feel Torin's stare on me, but it didn't make me anxious. In fact, I felt calm, calmer than I had been in ages. Though honestly, that had nothing to do with Torin.

My free hand trailed up to the collar. It vibrated beneath my fingertips, and I hummed to it in response. We were quickly becoming in tune with each other, literally. I smiled at that thought.

"Sing for us, Elaria," Torin's purring voice urged.

"What?" I looked over at him.

"I think it wants you to"–he nodded to the collar–"and we'd enjoy it as well."

"Yes, my lady," Arnet agreed as he shifted over on his mat to face us.

"Your song has haunted me all day," Jameson, the Fluorite knight, added.

"But I'll need to weave a spell," I protested.

"That's even better." Torin nodded. "You need to practice with the relic, see what you can do together."

"But I don't want to hurt any of you."

"So sing a song of beauty." Torin shrugged. "Or peace. Your spells don't have to change a person's will or hurt them. You can do anything, right?"

"Right." I smiled, and sat up. "And I shouldn't need a fairy king to remind me of that."

I had a brief flash of my childhood: standing before my mother, singing about summer as we watched flowers spring up from the earth. She had cried, and I'd stopped singing, instantly afraid that I'd hurt her. But then she held me, and whispered how beautiful my gift was. How she wished she could sing like I did, and create life instead of death.

And what had I done with all that life? I had turned it into an echo of my mother. I had been given the choice of miracle or monstrosity, and I had picked the monster.

"A king of the Shining Ones." Torin corrected me with a kiss, pulling me out of my musings. "And this king wants nothing more than to hear you sing him a lullaby."

"As long as it's not your last." I frowned, thinking of Cerberus.

"What is it?" Torin asked.

"I need to send word to Cerberus," I said. "I want him to know I'm all right, and that Finbar was playing us. Cer's waiting for me to return to Kansas."

"I can have a message sent to him." Torin assured me. "It will be done when we return to Onyx."

"Thank you," I said.

He looked at me, then pointedly around us, at the knights waiting patiently for me to sing. I laughed in delight. I'd never had fans before.

"All right, all right." I held up my hands. "Let me think . . . okay, I have one."

I began to sing a cappella to Ruth B's "Lost Boy." The words were simple at first, innocent. Sad, and sweet, and a little haunting. A lonely child staring at the moon.

The men sighed, and lay back on their mats, staring at me like children listening to a bedtime story. Torin laid his chin on his bent knee and watched as the gemstones in my collar began to softly glow. I felt the magic lift, but instead of rushing out of my mouth, as it always did, it was pulled through my throat and into the collar. The stones collected the magic, intensified it, and directed it with the barest of thoughts from me. Our spell seeped into the air along with the light of the collar's glowing stones. The soft feeling of longing was slowly replaced by hope, and then pure joy, as my voice lifted.

An immortal friendship, an end to all unhappiness. The impossible promise that only a child could believe in. Yet it became real for all of us. Chills rose on my arms as the night seemed to embrace me. It was the magic, thickening the air into a physical entity. The lyrics became lighthearted, soaring up with my voice.

I felt like a little girl again, playing make-believe, safe

159

under that false sense of security all children are born with. The world was wonderful, and no one wanted to hurt me. Everyone loved one another. War was a foreign word. Along with hate and death. I looked around, and saw my emotions mirrored in the expressions of the men. My voice surged higher, and we all became children of that make-believe world, wild and young forever. I crooned out the final words, cementing the feeling of joy and freedom.

The stones in my collar pulsed happily, and the peace of innocence spread out around us. Fairy animals, scurrying through the night, stilled. The chirping insects hummed happily into sleep Even the breeze seemed to blow softer. Then the glow faded, and I found myself looking up into Torin's night-blackened eyes.

"I was wrong," he whispered, and a flash of fear skittered across his face. "A single song from you is not enough for me. I don't think a thousand songs would be."

"Why do you say that like it's a bad thing?" I asked.

"It's not." Torin shook his head and gathered me in against him. "It's not," he whispered before kissing me.

But I caught that flash of fear again, and I wondered at it. Had I acquired more power than the Onyx King had imagined? Was I becoming a threat to him too? Most men didn't like being with a woman stronger than they were, be it physically or magically. Was Torin that kind of man?

Whatever he was, he was a damn good kisser, and I soon forgot his strange look. I forgot about everything but the feel of him pressed to me and the taste of him on my tongue. Heartbeats through leather and wine lingering on lips. Later, I would remember his fear, but for now, I let the peace of my spell lull me away to Neverland. I fell asleep listening to Torin's strong, steady heartbeat. That was my lullaby.

Chapter Twenty

I was surprised when we made it back to the Onyx Kingdom without any interference. That mountain rumbling down must have attracted a lot of attention, and yet no one came to investigate. I mentioned my thoughts to Torin as we rode through the shiny, black, castle gates.

"They know you have the relic now." Torin dismounted and handed his reins to a servant. He came around to my horse, and helped me down casually, as if he'd done so all of our lives. "They'll be more careful with us." He paused with his hands still around my waist. "With you."

"It seems to magnify my abilities." I lifted a finger to brush the collar.

"I think it does far more than that." Torin held his arm out to me, and escorted me into the castle. "Come, Lady Spellsinger, let's get you up to your chambers so you may refresh yourself, then we can speak further on the relic."

"My onyx cage, you mean?" I grimaced.

"It's a cage no longer." He slid me a disappointed look. "I thought you knew me better by now." He made a huffing sound. "I thought you knew yourself better."

"What's that supposed to mean?" I frowned up at him as we passed hordes of people, all of them bowing to us as we swept by.

Whispers were spreading down the line of them, and by the time we reached the staircase, the Onyx Court was cheering. I gaped at the Shining Ones. What was this now? Oh . . . right. The hope for all worlds, yada yada.

"See?" Torin smirked at me. "Even they know better."

"Better than what?"

"Better than you."

"*About* what?" I growled. This was getting idiotic.

"That room can't hold you prisoner now, Elaria." He shook his head at me. "Nothing can. Don't you see? You aren't just a spellsinger anymore. You hold the power of all the stones of the Jewel Kingdoms."

"What?" I stopped halfway up the stairs.

"I'm not sure how it will work." Torin held up a conciliatory hand. "But I felt a pull when you sang last night. One of onyx's properties is relaxation, and you were accessing it. You wove your spell of peace, and the collar translated it to the stones." He angled his head to the side. "At least that's my theory. And if you can call on onyx, it's safe to assume you can call on all of the jewels in the collar."

I grabbed Torin's hand, and pulled him up the stairs with me. His eyes widened, but he didn't try to stop me. We reached the landing, and I gave him a pointed look. He blinked, then gestured down the hall.

"We can speak privately in my chambers." He waved his hand toward a large, ebony door. I vaguely recalled it from the drunken night when he'd taken me to see his garden.

Torin pushed open the door, and pulled me inside. I shut the door behind us with a firm click. The room barely registered with me. I got a flash of a lot of black, including the mammoth bed which I recalled vividly from my last visit, but that was all. I was too intent on Torin.

162

"Is that why you looked frightened last night?" I asked him.

I hadn't wanted to say it in front of witnesses. Calling a king a scaredy-cat was just bad form. To do it in front of his court was suicide. But I had to know. That look in Torin's eyes kept flashing through my mind.

"Why I what?" Torin looked horrified.

"Don't get all butt hurt." I shook my head at him. "I get it; I just came into a lot of power. If it scared you, it's nothing to be ashamed of. But I need to know, Torin. Is that why? That *look*. Was it because you realized I have power over the stones of Tír na nÓg?"

His face went blank, his jaw dropping, and his gaze skittered away from me. "No."

"No?" I cocked my head into his line of sight. "Then what was it?"

"I wasn't scared of you," Torin growled, and turned away from me entirely.

"Oh, that's great. Okay." I sighed in frustration. "Make me think there's something between us, and then shy away because I get a little magic."

"I'm not shying away." He swung back around, his eyes a furious, blazing blue. "I wasn't scared of your magic!"

"Then what the fuck are you scared of?" I got in his face. "I know I saw it. Stop trying to deny it. You looked at me like I was going to hurt you!"

"Because I'm falling in love with you!"

We both froze, our chests heaving, and stared at each other with wide eyes. I think my mouth fell open, but I'm not sure. I was too fixated on him. On his perfect, Shining One beauty, tempered

163

with that other ancestry. How it gave him that rough edge I found so sexy. I was enraptured by the sunlight streaking over him from the nearby window. It turned his eyes into luminous pools. I was obsessed with the way the muscles of his chest curved down into the V of his tunic, and the way his scent rolled off him. Earth, metal, spice, and the musk of man. Torin smelled unique and amazing.

And he had said he was . . .

"That's what spooked you?" I whispered.

"When I first heard the prophecy"–Torin cleared his throat before he continued–"I thought to myself that this war might bring me some pleasure. When I saw you that night in my hall . . . when you sang those words to me . . ." He shook his head and sighed. "I knew for certain we would become lovers. I knew we'd have a passionate affair. I *knew* it would be wild, and beautiful and unforgettable. But I also knew that was all it would be. I never once suspected that you would become more to me. Especially not so quickly. And even when I began to feel it, I still didn't understand."

"Understand what?"

"What love is." He threw up his hands. "I thought I knew. I'd even believed I'd felt it before, several times. It was something warm, a clenching in my chest. It was a wanting, a hunger, and sometimes an obsession. It was base, but beautiful, an attraction that could make a man place one woman above all others in his esteem." He gave a self-deprecating laugh. "Sweet stones, that isn't it at all. I'm merely touching the surface of what I could feel for you, and I already know that everything I've ever known in the past is dust compared to it."

I wobbled, and he rushed forward to catch me. My breath was coming rapidly, and my skin felt hot and cold all at once. There were little zings going down my arms. What the hell was this? *Love,* a voice whispered in my head. Was I feeling it too? Was I touching that surface with him? Gazing into the mirrored pool of my heart and seeing his face reflected there? It had only been a few days, but I did feel something for him already. What would it be like to dive into this with him? To plunge past the surface, and plumb the depths?

"I understand," I whispered to him. "I think I'm scared too."

"Elaria," he groaned, and pulled me against him. "We shall conquer this fear together."

Then his mouth was on mine, and his hands were everywhere else. I started yanking off his clothes; his belt and sword fell to the floor with a thud. I pushed my hands up under his shirt, and groaned as I slid my fingers over the smooth, muscled planes of his chest. Air kissed my skin as Torin divested me of my outer clothes. When my underwear slipped away, he inhaled sharply.

"What's this?" Torin's hand went to the bare skin between my legs.

"I have the hair removed." I watched his eyes flash as he trailed his fingers over me. "Do you like it?"

"Oh yes." Torin smiled. "And I plan on showing you just how much. With fingers"–he slipped one into me, and I gasped–"and tongue." He went back to kissing me.

We were getting lost in each other once more, in the feel of skin on skin, when Torin reached for the clasp on the collar.

"Ah!" Torin yanked away, holding his hand out in shock.

"What was that?"

"The collar." He rubbed his fingers, and then looked at my

neck. "I thought you'd be more comfortable without it on. I only tried to remove it for you, and it attacked me."

I lifted a hand around to the back of the relic, and felt a sizzling energy rush through the clasp. I wasn't actually surprised. I'd had a suspicion it was there to stay. At least until I vanquished the threat.

"I told you we were enslaved to each other," I whispered to him. "Are you all right?"

"I'm fine." He reached for me again with a little smile. "I guess I did have something to be afraid of."

"Well, hopefully the worst is over." I slid against him, grinding my hips into his until he rose proud between us.

"On to better things," he agreed and picked me up.

I wrapped my arms around Torin's neck, and he carried me to his silk-draped bed. Again, the luxuries around us faded away as I concentrated on him. He laid me down, covered me with his body, and filled my whole world. And that world became pleasure. The slide of skin, the heat radiating between us, the taste of his lips, the clenching of his hands on my flesh. Then completion, the ultimate physical apex a man and woman could achieve together. The little death. We moved together perfectly, like a symphony, like a song, and by the time the sun rose on the next day, all the fear between us had faded.

Chapter Twenty-One

Torin couldn't spare a messenger for a few days, not with the war preparations starting, but he had finally kept his word, and done so at the first opportunity. I didn't think Cerberus was in any danger or I would have insisted on a message being sent sooner. Nor did I think there would be any kind of response back from Cer. Especially not the one I received.

It had been four days since we'd returned with the relic. Torin and I were in the dining hall, finishing dinner. Our days had been spent with his advisers and representatives from other kingdoms, planning for the inevitable war. You'd think that King Galen would have been smart enough to know that this wasn't a fight he could win, that he'd just call the whole thing off after hearing of our success with the relic. But yet again, Galen believed that fairy magic was stronger than witch. Not only was he not backing down Galen was actively petitioning other kingdoms to stand with him. And some of them were buying his bullshit.

So information needed to be collected and analyzed. We had to plot out where they might attack us, or if we should stop worrying about all that and simply take the fight to Sapphire. Every day brought us more allies as word of the claimed relic spread. But according to our intel, King Galen wasn't exactly lacking in supporters either.

The highlight of my days was Torin. Stolen kisses between meetings and scandalous make-out sessions in dark corners, were what kept me going until night fell. Then we'd dine, casting hungry looks at each other, feeding one appetite while the other starved. After dinner, we'd stroll as casually as possible to his bedroom, where we would fall savagely upon each other. I'd slept in Torin's bed since the first night we'd returned.

It was official; we were a couple.

In fact, I was in the process of doing some precoupling, slipping my hand up Torin's thigh under the cover of the tablecloth, when Cerberus strode into the hall. He was closely followed by our nervous messenger, a pack of his security men, and a gura of blooders. A gura I happened to be familiar with.

My hand jerked back into my lap as I sat up. "Cerberus?"

"Hello, my darling!" Cerberus boomed as he walked through the hall. "Miss me?"

Behind Cer, one of the blooders separated himself from the pack, and came forward. Banning. Sweet gods, Banning Dalca had come to Tír na nÓg. The onyx messenger hastened away, eager to have his part in the debacle over with.

"This is your friend?" Torin lifted a sardonic eyebrow at me. "The one from hell?"

"Hades. But yeah, that's him"–I sighed–"and he's brought a bunch of his friends with him."

"You wound me, Elaria." Banning smirked, but I could see true hurt lingering in his eyes. "I thought we were friends too."

"I barely know you, Banning," I said gently. "Why are you here?"

"And who is he?" Torin had yet to address any of our visitors.

"Banning Dalca, Gheara of the Kansas Gura," I told Torin. "This is the guy who I slaughtered that band of blooder mercenaries for. The fight Finbar witnessed."

"And is there more between you that I should know

168

about?" Torin's voice lowered so only I could hear him.

The men were still down the hall, but they were closing in fast.

"No, but he thinks there is." I shook my head. "I'll explain it later; just know that there's nothing between us."

"All right." Torin nodded to me, then looked up just as Cerberus and Banning reached the edge of the high table.

"Not in this lifetime at least," I muttered.

Torin shot me a questioning look, but Cerberus started talking.

"Your Majesty." Cerberus bowed to Torin, then winked at me. "Looks like you've been having fun, El."

"Shut up, Cer," I groaned.

"Hey, I brought your stuff." He shook my bag at me, the one I'd left with him. "A little gratitude might be warranted."

"You were supposed to keep that safe in the human world." I rolled my eyes. "That was the whole point of me leaving it with you.

"I figured that if you were staying in Tír na nÓg awhile, you might appreciate having your own things." Cerberus gave me a look. "You saying I was wrong?"

"No." I gestured for him to give me the bag, and took it from him. "How the hell did you even get here so fast? We just sent that messenger yesterday."

"I would have been here sooner if I didn't have to wait on Banning." Cerberus shrugged. "It's just a hop, skip, and a jump."

"What do you mean?" I scowled. "When I arrived, I had to

go through Sapphire, and then it took me three days to get to Onyx."

"You didn't have a traveling stone," Torin explained.

"A what now?" I looked at him.

There were several ways to cross the Veil, but most involved parting it magically and stepping through into the corresponding location. The reason they called all the different worlds "Planes of Existence" was because they were laid over each other like pages in a book. Going from one page to another was like piercing the pages with a pin; it took you to the spot laid directly over or beneath you. Evidently, traveling stones did things differently, but I'd never heard of them.

"A traveling stone," Torin said again. "Any Shining One strong enough to pull back the Veil is also strong enough to create a traveling stone." Torin took something out of the pouch hanging from his belt and placed it on the table before me. It was a clear stone about an inch in diameter, with light swirling inside it. "The messenger I sent employed one. He obviously used it to bring your friend here."

"And what does it do?" I picked up the stone and felt the zing of magic against my fingertips.

"Focuses your journey to a specific destination." Torin closed my fingers over the stone. "Keep that one; I have more."

"Really?" I looked at him in surprise. "Thank you."

"You may need it." He shrugged. "I want you to be able to move freely from your world to mine."

"How specific can I get?" I smirked at him. "Can I focus on a particular room? Say a certain royal bedchamber?"

"Absolutely." Torin smiled sensuously.

Cerberus cleared his throat. "Still standing here."

"Sorry." I laughed. "Torin, this is Cerberus Skylos, Hound of Hades, and Banning Dalca, Gheara of the Kansas Gura. Gentlemen, this is King Torin of Onyx."

"Nice to meet you, King Torin." Cerberus grinned.

"Your Majesty." Banning's reply was more clipped, and he kept looking at me like I was cheating on him. Awkward.

"When I got your message, I was with Banning," Cerberus said to me. "I immediately decided that if you were going to war, then so was I. I told Banning, and he chose to tag along."

"Tag along? To a war?" Torin narrowed his stare on Banning.

"I'm a blooder." Banning shrugged. "We like war. It's an all-you-can-eat buffet."

"And yet you needed Elaria to save you from your last buffet," Torin said snidely.

I gaped at Torin as Banning inhaled sharply, and started forward with violence burning in his eyes. Cerberus grabbed Banning by the back of his shirt, and hauled him away, just as the floor began to vibrate with Torin's power. His knights hadn't even bothered to move forward; they knew their king could handle one measly blooder.

"Easy now, lad," Cerberus growled, his expression going serious.

"Torin," I hissed, "that wasn't cool."

Torin shrugged, completely unrepentant. "I find his face irksome. He irks me."

"Fair enough." I snickered.

171

"I enlisted Elaria's aid against overwhelming odds," Banning ground out. "But I was more than prepared to fight." He turned his hurt glare on me. "What did you tell him, Elaria?"

"Just the basics." I sighed. "Can you three please stop the pissing contest? Cerberus, for fuck's sake, seriously? You come to Tír na nÓg with a bunch of shape-shifters and a blooder gura? This isn't your war."

"I think it is." Cerberus shook his head. "You said in your message that if Galen succeeds, the Veil will fall and threaten all existence. I happen to be a part of existence, El. I'm here to fight for it."

"Well said." Torin stood abruptly and held his hand out to Cerberus. "Welcome to the Onyx Kingdom, Cerberus Skylos. We are glad to have your assistance."

Cerberus gave a start, then grinned broadly and shook Torin's hand. "Happy to be here, King Torin. You got a nice place."

"Forgive my rudeness," Torin said to Banning. "My relationship with Elaria is fairly new, and new knots always creak when tested. You appeared to be pulling my rope, and I was simply creaking." Torin held his hand out to Banning.

"That was a nice way of saying I made you jealous." Banning smirked, but shook Torin's hand. "In all fairness, I should warn you that I intend to pull that rope again, and often. Elaria is meant to be with me. She simply hasn't remembered it yet."

"Oh, sweet baby Cupid," I groaned. "If you're going to be like this, Banning, go home. We don't want your help."

"It's fine, sweetheart." Torin smiled wickedly at me as he resumed his seat, and pointedly placed his hand on my thigh. "Let him pull all he wants. Our knot is strong. The creaking will stop with time, I promise."

172

"Even the Gordian knot was severed." Banning smiled back. "All it took was one strike."

"Interesting." Torin looked Banning over. "Your sword doesn't seem sharp enough to make such a strike."

"There are a lot of metaphors flying around, gentlemen." Cerberus frowned. "Are you talking about your cocks in reference to my girl here? Because I'm starting to get mad."

"You're not the only one." I gave Torin and Banning hard looks. "Banning, we discussed this; I'm not interested. If you're here to help, fine, but if you're just going to put stress on a relationship I actually want to be in, you can leave right now."

Banning's strong jaw clenched, his regal nose lifted, and his stunning green eyes flashed. He looked back at his gura and considered things, then finally nodded.

"The blooders I brought with me came of their own free will," Banning said. "We are here because this is a battle that needs to be fought, and won, here in Tír na nÓg. None of us want it to spill into the human world. The European Falca has been notified, and they will send more troops if we require it. They have also offered me a clean slate, as it were, for being here."

"So you didn't just come for me?" I smirked.

"There were multiple reasons for my joining Cerberus," Banning offered. "But you are among them."

"Two songbirds with one stone, eh?" I shook my head. "How very like a blooder."

"You should know," Banning said smugly. "You were one."

Torin shot me a look, but wouldn't show his hand by asking in front of Banning.

"Decide now, Banning." I narrowed my eyes on him. "Me

173

or the Falca? Why are you here?"

"So I must reject you, if I'm to be allowed to stay near you?" Banning lifted a brow.

"Yep," I said as I grabbed Torin's hand. It had begun to slide up my thigh inappropriately.

"As you like." Banning nodded to me. "I choose the Falca then."

"A wise decision." Torin nodded. "One that ensures my hospitality and your continued existence." He waved some servants forward. "Show our guests to their seats, and prepare some rooms for them, it seems as if they'll be staying awhile."

"May all the gods help us," I muttered.

Chapter Twenty-Two

Banning hadn't meant it when he said he chose the Falca, of course he hadn't. He had made the best tactical maneuver, the one that kept him closest to his goal. And then he'd waited, biding his time. His opportunity came the very next evening, when I'd gone to Torin's library for some private time. I needed to search through my iPod, and find songs for the battle. I had my earbuds in, so I didn't even hear Banning come in.

I gave a startled yelp when he sat beside me on the leather couch.

"Sorry." He gave me an apologetic grin. "I didn't mean to startle you."

"Banning," I sighed, and scooted down the couch, away from him.

Torin's private library was just three doors down from his bedroom. Between them was a study (a sort of Shining One version of an office) and his private dining room. The entire floor was reserved for the Onyx King. There were guest rooms, but only a few, and I was the only guest occupying one . . . technically. I kept some stuff in the room across the hall from Torin's, the one he'd originally imprisoned me in, but I never slept in it anymore. I mainly used it for getting dressed in the mornings.

Torin had removed the enchantment from the walls of my guest room. But as he'd pointed out, now that I had the relic, it didn't really matter. I could have removed the enchantment myself. Anyway, I didn't expect Banning to be up there, much less to come striding in like he owned the place.

"Why, Elaria?" Banning didn't try to touch me, just stared at me as if I'd betrayed him. "Are you still angry with me for letting you die?"

"Banning, I'm not angry with you. You didn't do anything to me; that was Fortune." I held up a hand when he started to ease forward. "I'm just not interested. Even if it is true, and we were once lovers, it has no bearing on this life. I'm sorry; I don't feel anything for you."

"Yet . . ." His jaw clenched, and I got a flash of the gheara he was–relentless, determined, ferocious. "I'm certain that if you'll just give it some time, the memories will surface, and you'll feel as you once did."

"I'm certain that I won't." I knew I needed to just rip this Band-Aid off as fast as possible, and get the pain over with. "I admit that I saw some images of the past which may or may not have been created by the power of suggestion."

"You think your mind is making it up?" Banning scowled. "Elaria, you must feel the truth in them. What did you see?"

"I'm not getting into this." I started to stand, but he grabbed my wrist.

"Just tell me what you saw. Please."

"Fine." I sighed and sat back down. "But I'm not telling you what I saw until you confirm something first."

"What? Anything." He leaned forward eagerly.

"What color was Cosmina's hair?"

"The woman who killed you?" Banning's eyes went wide. "Did you see her?"

"What color?"

"Red," Banning said, and my stomach flopped. "A vibrant auburn. It didn't look natural. Like my own hair, it was enhanced by immortality. Was that what you saw?"

"Yes," I whispered. "She was above me, laughing."

"As you died." His eyes shut, and his features twisted with pain. "She laughed as you died. The endless years can make some of us very cruel."

"Indeed"–I huffed–"and not just blooders."

"What else did you see?"

"You, dressed in lace." I gave him a little smile and flicked his blond hair. "Your hair pulled back with a ribbon."

"That was the fashion of the time." He smiled back.

I felt a twinge of attraction, which I immediately stamped out. Nope, not going there with a blooder, no matter how hot he was. I didn't want this, even if there had been no Torin in my life. But there was a Torin, and our relationship made me want Banning even less. What was some dusty memory compared to the vivid ones I forged with Torin every day?

"I still don't want to be with you, Banning," I said softly.

"You just haven't remembered fully yet," Banning offered. "Give us a chance, Fortune."

"Elaria!" I hissed as I stood. "My name is Elaria. Now please leave."

"I'm sorry." He shook his head. "I just... your face... I got a little confused. Forgive me."

"You're forgiven if you leave." I pointed at the door.

"As you like." He sighed heavily as he stood. Banning

177

started for the door, but paused when he came abreast of me. "You will remember more, *Elaria*, and then you will understand. This is not a love that can be ignored."

And then he left.

I crumpled back onto the couch with a relieved huff, but there was a nagging tickle in my chest–this horrible feeling that he might be right.

Chapter Twenty-Three

"I can't believe you brought Banning here when I expressly told you I was going to Tír na nÓg to get away from him," I hissed at Cerberus.

We were behind the castle, in the training fields, working out maneuvers that would keep our side safe from my spellsinging. This was more complicated than you might think. We were preparing for a huge war, and I wasn't sure how many soldiers I could enchant at a time. So we had to do practice runs using non-lethal spells, such as singing them to sleep. Once I knew roughly how many men I could manipulate at once, as far as mind control went, we then needed to work out how I could attack certain areas on the battlefield without hurting our troops.

First we'd tried a series of horns. But we'd had to make a different type of horn call for each of our twelve units. Cerberus, his shifters, and Banning's gura made up their own fighting force, while Onyx had another. Then there was Jade, Peridot, Topaz, Chrysocolla, Citrine, Jet, Howlite, Garnet, Fluorite, and Alexandrite. So far. Other kingdoms were still deciding which side to be on. We had some intel on Sapphire that had told us they had support from Diamond, Malachite, Jasper, Opal, and Tiger's Eye. However, we didn't know for sure if there would be more joining Galen's cause.

Our allies hadn't given us their whole fighting forces to train with, but they had sent some of their commanders, with small units of men, to work out the details. Then they would return to their kingdoms to train the rest of their soldiers. I'd had no idea that the tactical aspects of war took so much time. On top of all that, there was the traveling to consider, the location of possible battle sites, and the spying.

The Shining Ones loved subterfuge, and they were fantastic spies. This was great because it meant we received a lot of information on potential threats. But it also meant that we were probably being spied upon as well. It was hard to keep battle plans under wraps when you had so many allies. The more people involved, the more lips to let things slip, and the more ears to overhear the slippage.

But that was all for later. At the moment, we were working out the movements of units. As I mentioned, we'd tried horn calls, but there were so many different groups, we'd had to make a type of horn Morse code, and assign a series of bursts to each one. It had been a disaster.

Men had fumbled about, going in all sorts of directions, bumping into their compatriots, and generally causing a big mess equivalent to a twelve-car crash on a highway. It was simply too hard to count horn blows while trying to battle an opponent. Everyone was confused. It looked like a comedy act, except with armor and a lot of clanging. The Shining Ones meets the Marx Brothers. It would have been funny if the fate of all the worlds didn't rest upon our shoulders.

Finally, we'd decided to simply use some human technology. The European Falca had sent reinforcements at Banning's request, and Cerberus sent some of his men back into the human world to meet the new recruits and ferry them over with traveling stones. While there, Cer had his men gather supplies, including communication devices. Each commanding officer would have a set. Sir Hugh, the onyx knight assigned to guard me while I sang, would have a set as well, and would relay my orders to each commander on when to pull their men back out of my magic's reach.

So now that we had that worked out, the teams were trying to figure out how to fight together. The commanders had all given their input as far as tactics went, Cerberus contributing a fair amount, and now those plans were being put to the test in a mock battle. Cerberus had handed control of his men over to Banning, deciding to take a back seat so their unit could function more smoothly under a single leader. There were more blooders in their group than security men anyway. So Cerberus was able to sit out the maneuvers. Torin, however, was with his soldiers, working them through the movements efficiently. He looked amazing in his jewel-studded leather armor, riding horseback among his knights.

I hated to admit it to myself, but Banning looked pretty impressive too, even though he was on foot. There was an air of confidence and control around the blooder, and he led his group expertly. If he hadn't been so outnumbered at Crouching Lion, I doubt he would have needed my help. His soldiers looked strong and capable, and they obeyed his commands as if they'd done so for centuries, even the reinforcements from the Falca. He just had that aura about him that made people want to follow him.

I had very little to offer the proceedings, so I was standing upon a little rise with Cerberus and Hugh. We had a nice view of the proceedings. Hugh was intently watching everything play out, writing notes down for the report he intended to present Torin with later. So Hugh wasn't listening to our conversation. Or if he was, he wasn't letting on.

"I had no choice." Cerberus defended himself. "Banning was there when I got your message. He announced that he would be joining me, and then went to gather his blooders. I didn't even have the chance to refuse. Besides, I figured you'd need all the help you could get."

"All right, fine," I huffed.

"And he's a good guy." Cerberus smirked. "I mean, if you're not going to be with me, he's an acceptable alternative."

"I'm already with Torin"–I smirked right back–"in case you

hadn't noticed."

"Yeah, I noticed," Cerberus huffed. *"Everyone* has noticed."

"You got a problem with Torin?"

"No, actually." He chuckled ruefully. "He seems like a good guy too. It's just loyalty to my friends, you know?"

"Well, how about being loyal to *this* friend, and support my choice of boyfriend?" I nudged his shoulder with mine.

"Yeah, I guess." Cerberus gave in. "But what happens after this is over, El?"

"What do you mean?"

"This is convenient now." Cerberus shrugged. "You guys are working together to save all the worlds. But when this is over, what then? You gonna move out here for good? Give up the human world? All that money you just made?"

Of course Cer would focus on the money.

"Why would I have to choose?" I frowned. "It's a little soon for that, and I have a traveling stone now."

"So you're just going to jump back and forth through the Veil?" Cerberus lifted his brows.

"Why not?" I huffed. "Maybe he can come visit me too."

Cerberus gave me a look that clearly said what he thought the chances of that were.

"You never know; he may want to." I rolled my eyes. "It doesn't even matter right now. We'll talk about it when it does."

"All right." Cerberus said it like it was no big deal, but the damage had been done. He'd planted the seed of doubt.

I looked over at Torin, where he stood, directing his troops, and I felt myself scowl. Torin looked up at me as if he could sense my stare. He frowned, seeing my expression, and started toward me. I waved him off and forced myself to smile nonchalantly. Torin narrowed his eyes, and my smile brightened. Nothing to see here, move it along, sir. He stared a little longer, gave me an intimate look, and then went back to work.

"He's kind of big for a fairy," Cerberus noted.

"Yeah," I said appreciatively.

"You like big guys?" Cerberus transferred his speculative stare to me. "How did I not know this?"

"Down, boy," I teased him. "You know we would be bad together."

"Yeah, we'd go down in flames." He smiled brightly. "But what a way to burn."

"It would be." I winked at him.

Then an echoing boom filtered back to us from the front of the castle. An explosion. A big one. Everyone started running toward the sound, Cerberus and I included. It was a bit of a sprint to get around the massive edifice of onyx, and it took us a few minutes more to reach the main courtyard. There were already numerous knights rushing about, some returning from the site of the disturbance.

"What happened?" Torin asked one of them.

"The Onyx Gardens, Your Majesty," the knight reported as he pointed back from where he'd come. "Some of the statuary has been destroyed."

"That sly bastard," Torin growled. "Bring me a horse!"

183

There was a lot of movement around the stables, but one of the knights dismounted before a horse could be saddled for Torin.

"Take my mount, Your Majesty." The knight offered Torin his reins.

"My thanks." Torin mounted, then held a hand out to me. "Elaria."

"Oh." I rushed forward and let him help me into the saddle before him. "Okay, I guess I'm going too."

Torin smiled briefly, and slid an arm around my waist. He maneuvered the horse back toward the Onyx Gardens expertly with just one hand. The guardian statues actually formed a circle around the castle grounds, and I had a vague thought that it was strange to choose the front as a point of attack. Wouldn't the back be better? We'd been training back there and might have caught them if they had gone that route. But they shouldn't have known that. Maybe they'd heard the commotion; training for war isn't exactly quiet. Still, the thought nagged at me.

The other knights went into formation around us, and the sound of hoof beats vibrated through the shivering air. It seemed like my heart was beating along with the pounding hooves. We rode through the gates, and down the packed dirt road in tense silence. Torin had warned me that there would probably be skirmishes before the big battle, but this sneaky attack had shocked me. We reached the edge of the gardens quickly–it was right outside the courtyard–but we had to travel a ways in, before we arrived at the site of the explosion.

There was a huge, black smudge marring the vibrantly green grass. Roughly circular, with long streaks shooting out from its center like a star. Across this smear were the remnants of several onyx statues, just a mass of debris now. Torin stopped our horse at the edge of the soot circle, and dismounted before helping me down. He headed over to the spot, and stared down at it, fists on hips, frowning.

My feet took me past Torin, straight into the eye of the explosion. The men started muttering behind me. My gown, one of the many Torin had provided me with, swept through the cinders, snagging on bits of stone. I didn't care. I could feel the pain radiating from the broken gem, and it was calling to me.

Crystals can hold energy; that was the purpose of these gardens, to store enough magic to form a protective shield around Onyx. A shield that could also be turned into a sword by the king. But gemstones could absorb things other than magic, trauma being one of them. The stone may not have actually felt pain, like you or I would, but it carried the weight of it. I don't know if I'm describing it right. The stone held the memory of the hurt. A record of the explosion, which included a jarring break of its enchantment. In my mind, I registered the feeling as pain.

"Elaria, what are you doing?" Torin stepped carefully over the bits of stone, as a squeamish man might do at a gory crime scene. "Come away from there. We'll have to . . ." He swallowed hard, and I turned to see the strain on his face.

"You feel it too," I said gently, and held my hand out to him.

"They've injured my onyx." Torin's eyes looked wounded, as if he'd taken the damage himself. He latched onto my hand, and stared into my eyes, "Of course I feel it. I created these guardians. Their spells have been broken, the stone shattered. It cries out to me. But *you* shouldn't be able to sense it. What exactly are you feeling, Elaria?"

"Pain," I whispered, and looked back at the broken bits of onyx.

"What the fuck?" Cerberus growled behind us. He was seated on a massive stallion, and Banning came riding up behind him on another. "This is your first line of defense, isn't it? They're

185

weakening your boundaries, testing your strength." Cer considered it, then nodded like it was a good thing.

"And they've done their job well," Torin growled back. "It will take me months to replace these statues. In the meantime, our defenses are down. We are vulnerable."

"But they've also given us some insight into their capabilities," Cerberus noted.

"Not now, Cer." I waved him off distractedly. There was something tingling around me, something teasing my skin, and compelling me. "Torin." I pulled him closer. "Hold onto me."

Torin gave me a confused look, but didn't question me. His arms slid around me from behind, and I felt his body settle against my back. I gave his hand a quick, reassuring stroke, and then let the collar lead me. I knew it was the relic's magic pulsing over me, the relic that was truly responding to the hurt in the onyx. We were merging more and more each day, and I trusted in the collar now as much as I trusted in myself. It knew what needed to be done; all I had to do was give it a voice.

"Help me guide the magic," I said over my shoulder to Torin, just before I began to sing Cher's "You Haven't Seen the Last of Me."

The echoing, beating notes of fury burst out of me, a little startling in the sorrowful quiet surrounding us. The strength of the words surged through the stones in my collar, to combine all of the necessary properties from several different crystals into exactly what I needed. This unified magic took the pain around me and transformed it into power. Hurt became determination, and the song turned into a declaration of survival. Not just survival, but triumph.

I felt like I was singing for them, on their behalf. Those broken guardians who had fallen in the line of duty. I was giving them a voice.

186

Torin's hands moved over my body, as if he were feeling the flow of the magic within me. Then he lifted his right arm, laying it directly below mine, pushing up to support me. I placed my palm over the back of his hand, aligning our fingers. Together, we reached toward the shattered remains of the statues, and we began to manipulate the magic. I could have done it alone, but this was his kingdom, and I wanted his magic to be a part of this healing. Healing was another property of onyx, but it was difficult to heal yourself. So the relic and I would help Torin.

My voice resounded out of me, words of suppression becoming a battle cry, and the collar flared bright. The depths of heartache had been delved, and the music was pulling us back to the surface. We came gasping into the air, belting out defiantly that we could not be drowned. We could not be destroyed so easily. We would shake our fists at the sky and fight on.

The pieces of stone lifted around us, trembling as they came together. Every chunk, every shard, rose and found its way to its proper place. I guided them, urged the pieces home, while Torin filled them with his intent. His cheek slid down to press against mine, his heartbeat radiating through me. I'd never felt so close to another person. It was more intimate than sex. I could feel *him*, Torin, all that was him on a spiritual level. The magic tingled between us, mine pushing through him, blending with his before pulling back into me. Our intent was unified. Protect the Kingdom, protect the people. *Defend*. The stones started to vibrate proudly, ferociously, fitting perfectly together until the statues stood whole once more. But they stood by our will alone, the cracks of their injury still visible across their slick surfaces. I knew that as soon as we let go, they would fall.

The power of the song rose with a tide of emotion in my throat–anger that this had been done, determination that it wouldn't happen again, conviction that these guardians would come together stronger than before. We would prevail despite the most harrowing damage done to us. I drew out a powerful note and felt Torin pull

187

me tight against him, his magic soaking through my skin to blend with mine even more intimately. For a brief moment, I couldn't tell where he ended and I began. Then I pushed our united magic out through the collar with the last lines of the song, shouting out its challenge defiantly. The statues burst with dark light, a glow rising from base to tip as the stones joined seamlessly back together–healed completely.

My voice echoed out across the Onyx Gardens, and with it a brilliant flash that flared through all of the statues, until my song faded grudgingly into silence. I sighed, and leaned back into Torin's embrace. He set his face into the nook of my neck and breathed softly against my skin. We let the vibrations of the magic drain out of us, and then Torin kissed my cheek tenderly.

"I've never been a part of anything so wondrous," he whispered into my ear. "Thank you."

"My pleasure." I smiled and turned to face him.

"What the fuck just happened?" Banning ruined the mood.

"We fixed the statues," I said simply, stepping an arm's length away from Torin, but keeping his hand in mine.

"Yeah, we see that," Cerberus chuckled. "Damn, girl. That was mighty impressive."

"I believe the phrase is 'You haven't seen anything yet.'" Torin smirked at Cerberus. "Elaria is just beginning to delve into the powers of the relic."

"Great. Fucking fantastic," Banning nodded. "There's just one more question I have for you two lovebirds." He sneered the last bit.

"What's that?" Torin lifted a brow, not at all bothered by Banning's tone.

"How did someone manage to blow up your special, magic statues, whose whole purpose is to guard your damn castle?"

Torin's face fell, and he looked around the still-scorched earth for some sort of clue.

"Don't strain yourself, Your Majesty." Cerberus chuckled as he held his palm out to us. There was something lying across it. "I've already figured it out."

"What is that?" Torin walked over to Cerberus, taking me with him.

"Something I'm betting your stones weren't prepared for," Cerberus said.

I stared at the bits of metal and melted wires, my blood going cold. I knew exactly what Cerberus held.

"It's the remnants of a bomb," I said as I met Cerberus's grim stare. "Galen got his hands on some human weapons."

Chapter Twenty-Four

"How can human weapons harm magic statues?" Banning folded his arms across his chest. "I think perhaps your magic was flawed."

"It wasn't flawed," Torin's eyes narrowed on Banning.

"No, it wasn't," Cerberus agreed. "Here; feel this." He placed the bomb remnants in Torin's hand, and the Onyx King inhaled sharply.

"There's magic in them," Torin looked at me in surprise.

"Someone was able to infuse a human bomb with magic? How? Magic can only empower pure, natural objects." I scowled and touched a fingertip to one of the pieces of metal in Torin's palm. Sure enough, it vibrated against me. Most of the magic had been dispelled, but there were traces left. "Copper," I whispered. "They must have covered the explosives in it. That's kind of brilliant actually."

"And deadly," Banning added.

"The Copper King and I share a long-standing animosity," Torin growled.

"Why?" I asked him. "What did you do?"

"The Copper Queen." Torin gave me a look that said it all.

"Ah," I chuckled.

"Your guardians weren't made to withstand that combination of physical and magical attack." Cerberus looked over the new statues, and then down the thick swath of the gardens. "Though I think they are now."

"What? All of them?" Banning scoffed. "Elaria only fixed the three." He waved his hand toward the statues we'd reassembled: a gryphon, a dragon, and a winged horse.

"She fixed only three," Cerberus agreed, "but can't you feel that thrumming in the air? I think her magic spread out to include the others. What exactly were your intentions, Elaria?" Cerberus looked back at me.

"What do you mean?" I narrowed my eyes on him.

"When you sang," Cerberus explained, "what was the intent for your spell? I mean, beyond repairing the stone."

"I focused on them coming together even stronger than before." I thought about it. "And that this would never happen to them again."

"Ha!" Cerberus slapped his thick thigh. "You've empowered them all to withstand any kind of attack. This is fantastic. They've just tested your defenses and run home, thinking they know your weaknesses. But when they return, they'll find that the attack has only made you stronger."

"She will raise him up, stronger than before," Torin mused as he looked over the statues.

I absently touched the collar, and felt a zing of magic. It seemed happy to me, satisfied with itself. I had the distinct feeling that the relic liked working with Torin. Or perhaps it liked fulfilling the prophecy. Whatever it was, the relic was relishing this moment.

"Let's go home," I said to Torin.

"As my lady commands," Torin smiled brilliantly. "*Home* it

is." He swung himself onto his horse, and then held a hand down at me. After I settled into the saddle before him, he looked at his knights. "Back to the castle. Our gardens will stand firm now."

The knights cheered, and we all rode triumphantly back to Onyx Castle. It was a rather unexpected result from such a horrible event, and I think that made it feel even more successful. Everyone was smiling, except for Banning, who kept sending me brooding looks. I ignored him on principle.

Chapter Twenty-Five

"I think we should leave," Banning said to me.

I laughed at him.

"We're perfectly safe here." I shook my head at the young man who offered me his right wrist. I'd already drunk my fill from his left one, and his blood was still sweet upon my lips. With a shooing motion, I sent the feeder away. "Cosmina wouldn't dare hurt me. She knows you love me too much. If she harmed me, she'd never have you. Her only hope lies in keeping me safe until you tire of me."

"Which will never happen," Banning had already discarded his jacket and vest, they were thrown over the back of a dainty, gilded chair.

His crisp, white undershirt was open at the neck, showing off his pale, muscled chest, and his tan breeches were unbuttoned at the top, threatening to slide down his slim hips. I was hoping they'd make good on their threat. Banning padded across the thick carpet to me on bare feet, then knelt in front of the chair I lounged on. I watched his hands as they reached for mine.

I loved Banning's hands. He could tone down his blatant masculinity beneath lace and satin and curl his long hair into the latest style, but he couldn't hide those barbarian hands. Inherited from his Romanian father, those hands were wide and rough looking, with thick fingers that worked magic on my skin.

"I will never give you up, Fortune"–those strong hands wrapped around mine tightly–"and Cosmina will see that eventually. Then you will be in danger. We must flee now, before

she has time to learn how enduring our love is."

"Where will we go?" I frowned at him. Banning had been singing this tune for years, and I was growing tired of it. "You want to give up our position in one of the most prestigious guras, to go into hiding on the chance that our gheara decides to kill me? It's ridiculous, Ban." I leaned forward and kissed him. "Stop talking nonsense. The only place I want to escape to is our bed and your embrace. Take me there now."

Banning groaned and shook his head, but did as I asked. He lifted me, and my layers of skirts, as if I weighed nothing. As soon as I was in his arms, his anxiety disappeared, and he was caught up in our passion. It was always like this for us, from the instant I had awoken to my new existence. As a human, I'd wanted him. I cherished our first meeting, even though I'd spoken harshly to him for daring to approach me. It was the way things were done. You couldn't let a man know that you found him attractive. So I had been cruel, and hoped that he found me intriguing enough to pursue me regardless.

I'd seen him watching me often, but he'd never approached me again. Not until the day I was stabbed in the streets and left to die. Banning had saved me, and taken me away from my mortal world. He'd given me a new life, an eternal one, and all the gifts that came with it. Including the gift of freedom. The boundaries of society held sway over me no longer. I could give into the desire I felt for Banning, without worry over ruining my reputation. What did human restraint have to do with me anymore? Nothing. I wasn't just a woman now; I was a blooder.

What was so surprising was that the passion between us had never lessened, not in nine decades. If anything, we'd grown more attracted to each other through the years. It was hard for us to touch each other in any kind of manner without growing excited by it. And, as I mentioned, restraint was no longer an issue. So we gave into our needs as often as we wished.

194

Including this very moment.

Banning undid my petticoats and skirts, pulling them off, and tossing them to the side of the elaborately draped, Baroque bed. I had silk stockings on, held up by lace garters, and high heels on my feet. He yanked the heavy, wood heels away, and then slid the stockings down my calves. I scooted up onto the high mattress, teasing him by moving out of his reach, and then lay back seductively across the fluffy, silk pillows. My bodice was still tightly laced, displaying my breasts while simultaneously denying him access to them.

Banning smiled and stepped out of his breeches with sensual intent. I sighed appreciatively as his manhood came free, lifting proud before him. I knew every inch of this man, and yet seeing him nude never got old for me. Banning yanked off his shirt, and then climbed up on the bed, stalking me like a predator. I shimmied farther back into the pillows, and he pounced. Those barbaric hands went beneath my knees, parting and lifting. He pushed me deeper into the mound of pillows, laughing a little as my curls fell into my face. I pushed the curls away, and pouted at him, making him laugh harder.

Then he revealed the silk stockings in his hand. My eyes widened as he tied my forearms to my thighs, keeping my legs up where he wanted them. I lifted a brow, giving him a saucy look. He responded by tearing the front of my bodice open. I inhaled sharply as my breasts spilled free, the cool air tightening my nipples. He tweaked them playfully before settling in against me.

"I love you, my sweet Fortune," Banning said softly.

He lowered his lips to mine as he slid inside me. I reached for him, but my arms were bound tight. So I settled for lifting my hips to meet his thrusts. I moaned into his mouth. The angle set him in me to the hilt. Nothing was better than being with Banning, than having him deep inside and pressed up against me. Life would never be sweeter than in these intimate moments, and I knew we would have thousands of them together. More moments than I had numbers to count with. That's how long our passion would burn. Our love would outlast the gods.

I keened as we came together faster, my pleasure lifting inside me. At its apex, I cried out, finally answering him.

"I love you too, Banning. Forever!"

I sat up straight in bed, coming violently awake with the words shivering on my lips. My entire body was shaking, going from hot to cold, and I ached with need. I could still feel Banning inside me, still taste him in my mouth. Oh gods. I took deep breaths, trying to calm my racing heart, and looked over at the man beside me. Torin, not Banning. It had just been a dream. Hadn't it? Was I truly remembering? And what was this pain in my chest? It was even stronger than the ache between my thighs, and yet felt similar. I was empty inside.

I lay back in bed carefully, trying not to wake Torin. He didn't stir, and I ended up staring at his striking profile. Moonlight streamed in through the balcony, outlining his face in silver. Just seeing him there, beside me, settled my mind. It didn't matter whether I'd just dreamed up Banning or if it had been an actual memory. Fortune had been wrong about so many things. She and Banning hadn't been destined for eternity, and their love hadn't outlasted the gods. That mistaken woman was long gone, dust in the ground, and Banning was all that was left of their love.

Tragic yes, but that's the risk you take when you love so intensely. Fortune had been murdered, just as she'd been in her mortal life. Perhaps that's what was meant to happen. Fortune had to die so that I could be born. And maybe Banning was right about our meeting. Maybe we had been drawn together. Not to return to our love, but to give him the closure he needed to get over it. Because even after that erotic dream, I had no desire to seek out Banning. My hand reached for Torin automatically and gently smoothed back a lock of his hair.

196

"I'm exactly where I want to be," I whispered, and the stones in the relic glowed softly in agreement. "Where I'm *meant* to be."

Chapter Twenty-Six

I woke early in the morning, the mist of a new day still hanging over the land. I slid from the warmth of Torin's bed and body, then padded across the silk carpets to the balcony. I was still half-asleep, mind fuzzy from dreams, eyes drifting open and shut. The metal handles were frigid under my fingertips as I pushed the balcony doors open, and the stone beneath my feet was nearly as cold. A wall rose up seamlessly from the balcony's ledge, enclosing the wide space like the rim of a bowl. Absently, I noted my wavering reflection in the smooth onyx. My sheer nightgown turned me into a ghost.

The thought comforted me in an odd way, as if being a specter would be preferable to being solid in this moment. A spirit could walk the worlds without hindrance. It could stand there, on that onyx precipice, and not be seen. I didn't want to be seen as I reached out to the border between the worlds.

Oh. Was that what I was doing?

My vision hazy, I let it go, and mentally focused farther across the sleeping land. Over the steep hills, covered in pointed trees. Across glimmering lakes, turning gold with the sun's awakening. Abruptly, I veered up, feeling for that invisible energy that separated the Planes of Existence. The Veil. That nebulous membrane that held us all together while keeping us apart. There it was, a condensed sheet of energy, vibrating like a struck drum. I could almost touch it with my hands. I *knew* I could touch it with my voice.

I faced the East, and began the chanting lyrics of Wendy Rule's "Circle Song."

It was a witch's chant, used to cast a circle of protection in preparation for spellwork. An odd choice to sing to the Veil, but I hadn't really chosen it. The words had risen inside me all on their own.

My mother used to sing this song; she loved it, but it was my father who had taught it to her. He told me once that I was a natural progression in the evolution of witches. Words had power, so it made sense that singing them could cast a spell. Dad had sung this particular song to me only once, to show me how regular witches were already headed toward the evolution I represented. But they had a long ways to go. For now, they needed tools and ingredients to cast spells, not just the magic they were born with. It was much simpler for me, especially when I sang a song that already had magical intent within its lyrics. I didn't even have to focus much. I faced the direction in which I wanted the magic to go and sang. The words vibrated into the air and hung there.

East was complete.

I turned to the North, and chanted more of the powerful warding. Calling the corners as my father used to do. Between each line, I moaned out the sounds that connected the corners, dragging the magic with me to the next direction. I shifted toward the West, and my voice lifted higher, the lilting sounds seeming to gather their power in preparation for the finale. I turned to look to the South, and felt the air sizzling around me as the last of the chant surged through the relic.

My spell intensified within the jewels, like sunlight through a magnifying glass, and I was briefly pulled along with it, out to the Veil. I saw the border as a shimmering thing, a collection of limitless energy around each realm. My spell pulsed out to touch it, hardening that energy into an impenetrable shell. A circle of protection closed around Tír na nÓg.

My awareness pulled back into my body, and I came fully awake, staring across the Onyx Kingdom from Torin's lofty balcony, as the sun blazed over the horizon, warming my skin, and lifting my spirit. I inhaled deeply. The bright scent of evergreens helped to clear my head further. As much as my siren's blood loved the ocean, my witch's heart gloried in the alpine feel of the Onyx Kingdom. Such a contradiction. Half of me longed for salt on the breeze while the other half craved the scent of snow. Had I been born to never be satisfied?

"Elaria." Torin's low whisper wrapped over me from behind. A warm cloak against my chilled thoughts.

Then his hands replaced his words, sliding over my shoulders, skimming down my chest to finally rest at my waist. His heat surged around me as he leaned into my back, his hips set firmly to mine. Torin's hands closed in tighter until he had his forearms crossed over my belly and I was fixed perfectly into his angles. I sighed, and leaned back into him.

"What have you done now, little bird?" Torin's cheek slid down beside mine.

"Can't you feel it?" I looked over at him. "I think the relic was guiding me."

"You've closed the Veil." His eyes lifted, caught the rising sun, and turned into fire. "How is it possible?"

"I don't know." I followed his gaze to the fading crimson that had streaked the sky with the last echoes of my song. "The collar must possess more magic than we'd thought."

"Indeed," Torin whispered. "It knows what to do before we do. Healing the guardians. Closing the borders of our world." He shook his head in disbelief. "We have the threat contained now. No matter what happens here, Earth is safe."

"Yes." I trailed a fingertip over the relic. "Earth is safe. Now we must make sure it stays that way."

200

"When Galen realizes what you've done, he'll come for you," Torin said with a smile. "He'll have no choice."

"Or we could go to him," I suggested. "Take him unaware. After this, he won't be expecting us to march on Sapphire."

"True." Torin frowned in thought. "But here, we'd have the advantage."

"And here, they would be free to ravage the rest of your kingdom." I turned in his arms to face him. "I don't like that possibility."

"Neither do I." Torin sighed, and brushed his lips across mine. "But I like the thought of you riding through several enemy kingdoms even less."

"I don't think I've ever been so powerful." I slid my hands up his back. "It's kind of ironic that I've found someone who wants to protect me after I no longer need protecting."

"You can still be hurt, Elaria," Torin's gaze went grim. "Don't make the mistake of thinking yourself indestructible."

"I know I can be hurt," I assured him. "I just don't think I need your protection."

"And I think you're wrong." He pulled me in closer, so I could feel his words upon my lips. "You need someone to watch over you, and I intend to be that man."

"If you insist." I smiled into his kiss.

Torin eased me backward until I was pressed against the stone railing. As I lifted my hands to his face, smoothing the tension I found there, he lifted my sheer, silk sheath, and wedged himself between my thighs. I sucked in a breath, feeling him hard through the fabric of his cotton breeches. One of my hands went to his shoulder, to help pull myself up, and the other slid into the front of his pants, pulling him out. In seconds, we were together, moaning our desire into the morning.

As the sun finally settled into its full glory, lighting the Onyx Kingdom in brilliant clarity, Torin and I found our own brilliance together.

Chapter Twenty-Seven

"Well, that will stop the importing of explosives," was what Cerberus said to the news of my closing off the Veil.

"You trapped them, just as you did Lincoln's army," Banning nodded. "Well done."

"She's kind of trapped us all." Cerberus frowned a little.

"I'm sure her spell will be broken once this is all over," Banning defended me.

"It wasn't really me." I shrugged. "The relic guided me into doing it. I was only half-awake."

"More susceptible to magic's influence," Cerberus said. "Your will was weakened."

"The relic has its own agenda," Sir Hugh observed. "Interesting."

"It was created with a purpose," Torin said, "and it's extremely powerful. It makes sense that it would work toward its goal with or without Elaria's help."

"It had my help." I shrugged. "I would have done it anyway. I just didn't *think* to do it."

"Whatever the case," Sir Arnet said, "we'll have to patrol the kingdom more diligently now. Lady Elaria has crippled their impetus. They'll need to get free of her restriction before they can do anything else. And they know exactly where to find her."

"You're right," Torin agreed. "Add more patrols. We want

to make sure our people are safe as well. Galen is just the sort to take out his frustration on innocents."

"Yes, sire." Arnet stood. "I'll dispatch more patrol units immediately." He strode from the room.

We were in Torin's study, meeting with the generals and Torin's advisers. When Torin and I had come downstairs that morning, we'd found the generals impatiently awaiting us, pacing the hall. They'd felt the difference in the Veil as soon as the spell had been cast, all of them being strong magic users, and they wanted an explanation. The one we'd supplied had shocked them into silence. And necessitated this meeting.

"I need to inform my queen," the Howlite commander said. "She'll be worried, I'm sure."

A murmur of agreement went around the table. He wasn't the only one who had important Shining Ones to reassure.

"Of course." Torin waved regally. "Why don't all of you return to your kingdoms, and put your monarchs's minds at ease? We will continue to prepare for battle while you're gone. But tell the royals that we will need their troops soon, as this new development has sped up our anticipated schedule."

"Yes, Your Majesty," the Chrysocolla Commander stood, followed by the others. "I'll return with our troops as soon as I'm able. I dearly hope that this is a sign that the war shall both start and end swiftly." Then he surprised me by turning to me, and bowing, "By your leave, Queen of Song."

The room went quiet, but only for a moment. The other commanders in the room bowed as well, echoing the new title Chrysocolla had offered me. I managed to give them all a shaky nod, as Torin started to smile. By the time all the commanders had exited, Torin was beaming.

"Queen of Song," he repeated smugly.

"I'm not a queen." I frowned at him. "I'm not even a Shining One. Why did they call me that?"

"You know why," Torin chided gently. "How do Shining Ones become royalty?"

"They show a powerful affinity to a particular stone." I shrugged.

"You currently control *all* the stones," Torin smirked. "And you do it through song. Your new title is both fitting and diplomatic."

"Diplomatic?" Cerberus cocked his head at Torin.

"The other monarchs would have felt threatened if Elaria had been named Queen of Jewels or something encompassing like that. It would essentially put them under her rule."

"So he called me 'Queen of Song' to acknowledge my talent without acknowledging my authority." I chuckled. "Smooth."

"But he also asked for your permission to leave, instead of Torin's," Cerberus noted. "He did acknowledge your superiority; he just did it subtly."

"Cunning," Torin nodded. "And he did it before I could claim a title for Elaria. The words have been spoken, and they've been accepted by you." He gestured to me. "You are now the Queen of Song. There's nothing anyone can do to change it."

"Tricky," I said. "He played on my ignorance."

"I would have stopped you from accepting if I'd thought it was a hindrance to you," Torin assured me. "As it is, I believe Sir Barret has done you a great service. I shall remember to thank him, and to be wary of him. It's best to keep a man like that within your sights."

"I like the way you think, King Torin," Cerberus laughed.

205

"Thank you."

"So do I get a kingdom now?" I smirked.

"In Tír na nÓg, you can have anything within your power to claim," Torin said seriously. "If you want a kingdom, Elaria, we will get one for you."

"Are you fucking serious?" I gaped at him.

"Told you," Cerberus muttered to me.

"Shut up, Cer." I kept my eyes on Torin.

"I'm very serious," Torin said. "May I recommend Sapphire? It matches your eyes."

Chapter Twenty-Eight

"Don't trust him," someone whispered.

I swung about, fists at the ready, searching my guest room.

"Are you all right, Your Majesty?" Sara asked.

"Didn't you hear that?" I scowled. "And also . . . are you fucking kidding me? How did you know to call me 'Your Majesty'?"

"I heard nothing but your heavy, human-like tread across the carpet." Sara grimaced. "And gossip spreads fastest among the servants. I knew you were a queen, practically the moment you were declared one."

"Betrayal . . ." The word drew out in a creepy hiss.

"There!" I pointed to the air in accusation. "You had to have heard that."

"Are you losing your mind, Your Majesty?" Sara cocked her head at me consideringly. "It's been known to happen to great magic users."

"Shit"–I blinked–"maybe I am. I swear I just heard someone talking."

"Yes, Your Majesty." Sara sighed. "That was me."

"Not you, you ass," I growled. "It sounded like a man's voice. Deep. Rumbly. Powerful."

"Powerful?" Sara seemed to consider. "What did this deep,

rumbly, powerful voice say to you?"

"It said"

"Don't trust him." The voice came again, right on cue.

"Damn it, there it is again," I snapped. "Don't trust who? *Which* him? You wanna be a little more specific, Mr. Creepy?"

"Perhaps your power over the stones has provided you with a precognition talent?" Sara suggested.

"Perhaps." I scowled at the room in general. "I highly doubt that I'm the Heir of Slytherin."

"Elaria." Torin strode into the room. "Would you come with me please?"

"Don't trust him." The rumble came again, and a shiver went down my spine.

Torin? Was that who I wasn't supposed to trust? Oh dear gods.

"Elaria?" Torin frowned, and came farther into the room. "Are you all right? You look a little pale."

"Yes." I swallowed hard, and sent a quick, silencing look to Sara.

She nodded once, crisply.

"I'm fine." I went to Torin. "Where are we going?"

"Just to my study." He gave me one last, piercing look, then offered me his arm.

I took it and let him lead me down the hallway to his private office. The door opened to reveal a spacious room with a curving bank of windows directly across from the door. A padded bench was set into the curve, its cushion wrapped in forest green velvet. The walls were covered in expensive, tapestry wallpaper in a slightly lighter green, but most of the wall space was taken up by ebony bookshelves, filled with leather-bound books.

The ebony shelves matched the grand desk, crouching before the windows. It was hand-carved and looked heavy enough to require a troll to move it. Or possibly the animal whose skull hung over the desk. The bleached skull leered at me, eye sockets and gaping mouth full of fey lights, which came on as soon as Torin waved his hand in the room. Magically powered, motion-sensing fairy lights. At least he didn't have to clap them on.

Torin walked over to a table, set off to the left of the desk. He waved me into a seat before it, then pulled a velvet-lined tray over to me. There were chunks of crystals on the tray. Too many to count. My hand went to my collar subconsciously, and Torin smiled.

"All the kingdoms of Tír na nÓg are represented here," Torin took the seat beside mine.

"Okay." I cocked my head at him.

"I thought you might like to have some loose stones to focus on," Torin explained. "Maybe it will be easier for you to discover the properties of each jewel if you have them separate, and can concentrate on them individually."

"You want me to hone my skills," I said thoughtfully.

"We are all preparing for war." He nodded. "I thought you might like to have a way to train as well. These are the jewels of our known enemies, you may want to start there." He pointed to a grouping that was separated from the rest.

"Thank you." I picked up a jagged-looking, lavender-blue chunk.

"You're welcome." Torin set a quick kiss on my lips before standing. "I'll leave you to it. No one will bother you in here."

"Okay." I rolled the rock in my palm, and immediately felt the magic flare within it.

"If you don't make an appearance at the mid-day meal, I'll return for you." Torin winked at me, and closed the door behind him.

"Sure," I said absently as the power of kyanite revealed itself to me.

One after another, the properties of the jewel rolled through my mind. Images of what was possible flashed like movie trailers, each one describing what kyanite could create. But most of its properties were too general or were useless in a war. I needed something to help me in battle, to fight back against those who already held power over this gemstone.

As soon as the thought formed, more images flashed into my head. I gasped as the creativity of kyanite showed itself capable of forming unusual battle tactics. The property of commitment revealed that it could band our assorted armies together. Loyalty would make sure that no one betrayed us. Meditation would calm us, and open paths we had not considered. Communication would keep our orders precise, and our troops focused. Cleansing offered me purity to face the fight without the past hindering me. Dreams whispered about finding truth in my subconscious. And finally, honesty promised to discover the truth in others.

I dropped the stone and fell forward, catching myself on my palms. Instantly, I saw more images, and I jerked back. My palms had fallen over other gemstones. I pushed my chair away from the table to get some space. Jagged breaths sawed in and out of my lungs, and I slowly realized that the relic was glowing. The light spread over my chest, seeping into my skin, and my hands went to the collar in fright.

But it wasn't trying to hurt me. The relic only sought to comfort me and show me how to handle the influx of information. The collar was the key. I shouldn't have tried to delve into the jewel energy without its help. I sighed as the heat of its compassion eased my tension, and I found myself sliding back to the table, and picking up another stone.

The process began again, but this time, I was prepared for it.

Malachite, Selenite, Tiger's Eye–I went through each gem carefully, analyzing its properties with cool calculation. I could weave these talents into my music, and use them to hobble our enemy before they employed them against us. It was devious, but the fate of all existence was on the line, and I was down with devious if it meant winning.

By the time I'd worked my way through half of the known Sapphire supporters, my head was spinning and my stomach rumbling. I'd forgotten all about the creepy voice in my guest room. I was lost to the jewels and their multitude of powers. I got to my feet in a daze, and headed for the door. Surely it must be time for lunch.

A few steps was all it took to clear my head completely. I took a deep breath, feeling strong and confident at last. Torin had been right; I needed this. Every other warrior was out honing their combat skills daily. I'd practiced with the relic, but it felt as if I were fumbling through the spells. I was grasping in the dark, trying to guess my way into mastery. When all along, this was what I'd needed. What better way to understand a thing than to learn about its components?

After focusing on each stone separately, I could better focus on the relic as a whole. And the collar was helping me along, so I knew I was on the right path. Learning the properties of each jewel would open up a world of possibilities. This knowledge, combined with my own innate talents, would make me the perfect partner for the relic.

"Don't trust him." The whisper startled me, and I stumbled.

"What the hell?" I hissed at the empty hallway. "Who are you? And who shouldn't I trust?"

"Trust misplaced," the voice hissed.

"Damn it; I got that part," I growled. I was so hungry, and combined with my sudden frustration, I became hangry. "If you aren't going to tell me anything useful, then shut the fuck up!"

"Do not . . ." The whisper faded away.

"Good." I nodded smugly, and headed down to the dining hall. "So many stairs," I muttered as I held my skirts high so I could take the steps faster. "Fucking Shining Ones. They have magical hand-waving lights, but they can't manage an elevator?"

I jerked back right before I slammed into someone.

"Your Majesty." The man flinched, his dark eyes widening. Then he bowed. "Forgive me."

"No, that was totally me," I sighed. "Sorry about that."

"Don't trust him." The rumble came back with a vengeance.

"Son of a bitch," I growled, swinging around like a crazy person.

"Your Majesty?" The poor guy was trembling.

"Sorry." I shook my head at him. "I'm just really hungry. Don't mind me."

I rushed off before the guy questioned me further. Maybe my hunger was making the voice stronger. Cerberus had said that weakness made me more susceptible. Food was what I needed.

Food and maybe some Torin. Not necessarily in that order. No, wait . . . yes, in that order. I wouldn't be able to handle Torin without some sustenance first.

I headed into the dining hall with a hungry smile.

Chapter Twenty-Nine

"Did you study onyx yet?" Torin purred as he slid my dress off.

"Not yet," I was determinedly divesting him of his clothing too.

His hands coasted over my skin carefully, then tenderly, stopping for a more thorough inspection in prime locations. I inhaled sharply as Torin's fingers tightened around my nipples. Then I paid him back by biting his earlobe. He only chuckled, and lifted me off my feet, carrying me to his bed.

The silk was cool beneath me, emphasizing the heat of Torin's skin when he laid his body over mine. I sighed and wrapped my legs around his waist, drawing him in closer. His mouth was at my neck, and then his teeth closed around the sensitive skin there. I dug my fingers into the thick muscles of his back, but he suddenly pulled away.

Torin flipped me over onto my stomach, then pressed down over me, angling his mouth to my ear, "Relaxation is a property of onyx."

"Oh?" I looked back at him. "What if I don't want to relax?"

"I know what's best for you." He smiled, and shifted away from me, his hands sliding over my back as he did so.

Energy pulsed beneath his fingertips as he drew them over my skin. I gave a gasp as the tingles went deeper, invading knotted muscles and unwinding them. Sharp pain slackened into relief quickly, and soon, my whole back was putty in his hands. I couldn't move; he had massaged me into paralysis.

"That's better." Torin sighed as if he could feel my relief. "Now your legs."

His strong hands kneaded my thighs, then up over my ass, performing the same magical massage he'd performed on my back. Torin swept down, all the way to my feet, then back up again, working on my arms. I was slipping away into a drug-like haze when his fingertips brushed against the sensitive flesh between my thighs.

I inhaled sharply, a little shocked at the sexual sensation after so many innocent strokes. Torin chuckled low, and turned me over. His eyes were nearly black in the shadowy room, his thick hair falling forward to cast even more darkness over his face. He looked like a demon, a fallen angel sent to torment me. Except I wanted this torment. Wanted it bad.

"Elaria." He drew his hands over my chest. "You're so beautiful."

"It's dark in here," I teased him.

"Then I'd best judge by feel." He pushed my thighs apart, and settled himself between them.

The magic continued to tingle through his fingertips as he stroked them over my breasts. My head rolled as he replaced his hands with his mouth, sucking hard, as his fingers continued to quest downward. Relaxing then exciting, it was a head-spinning ride. I sighed into the pleasure, and then jerked as a magic-filled finger slipped inside me.

Working steadily, Torin brought me over the edge of ecstasy, then once more, set his mouth to the task. I came with a screaming, but oddly relaxing, orgasm, clutching at his shoulders as he lifted above me. Torin licked his lips, then set them to my

215

own, and slid himself inside me. I cried out, but it was lost to his gasp. I inhaled into his chest, my pleasure sustaining his.

As he led us both back to that apex of desire, I clung to him, my flushed face pressed to his shoulder as my moans grew louder. Torin's hips were slamming my own apart, ensuring that his full length was sheathed, and the muscles of his biceps bunched with strain as he lifted himself to stare down at me.

A strip of late afternoon sunlight streaked across his face like a mask, illuminating his eyes till they seemed to glow from within. Then they flashed, a spark of magic igniting in their ocean-like depths, and they held my own eyes hostage.

"I love you, Elaria."

Those words meant so much to me, and I was delighted that he'd said them first. The sweet declaration that would take our relationship even further. I was about to declare my feelings back, when that rumbly whisper interrupted me. Shivers coasted over my arms and then through my heart.

"Don't trust him."

Chapter Thirty

"Fuck you, Mr. Rumbles," I shouted.

"And who is Mr. Rumbles?" Sara walked into my guest room, holding yet another gorgeous gown to add to my fairy princess fashion collection.

"That voice." I heaved a sigh. "It's talking to me again. If I'm not already crazy, it will soon make me so."

"You're still hearing it?" Sara frowned as she set the dress on my bed. "Tell me about it again."

"Whispers." I shrugged. "Sometimes louder. It's deep and rumbly. Strong. Definitely male."

"And what's it saying?"

"The same thing, over and over, 'Don't trust him.'" I rolled my eyes. "Who? Who am I not supposed to trust?"

Sara put her hands on her hips and stared thoughtfully around the room. Then she walked over to a wall and pulled aside the silk. "Your Majesty, please come here a moment." She motioned me over.

"What?" I went over to her.

"Place your palm to the wall, and ask that question again," Sara nodded to the slab of onyx.

"Okay." I frowned and placed my hand to the stone.

Before I could say anything, the voice roared inside my

217

head, "Don't trust him!"

"Holy wailing walls, Batman!" I jerked back. "What the flying fuck was that?"

"Your language is lyrical, Your Majesty." Sara rolled her eyes.

"Yes, thank you," I huffed. "Now tell me what just happened."

"Are you really so daft?" Sara gaped at me. "You heard a voice, I told you to put your hand on the onyx, and you heard it again, correct?"

"Yes."

"So who do you think is talking to you?"

"Oh," I looked at the onyx. "No way."

"Onyx speaks to King Torin, and now you hold power over all of the stones." She waved a hand toward my collar. "So onyx tells you things as well."

"Cryptic things." I glared at the wall, then slowly placed my palm back on it. "Who can't I trust? Is it Torin?"

My heart plummeted at the thought. I was falling hard for the guy, and it would be just my luck if he turned out to be a two-timing bastard. When I thought about it, I wondered how he could not be. A man that hot was bound to have women throwing themselves at him, and Torin was a king to boot. He must be up to his eyeballs in you-know-what. I wasn't up to the task of holding that kind of man's interest for long. I knew I was beautiful, but in my world, beauty was everywhere. I was technically part goddess, and I've known quite a few divine ladies. They're all gorgeous, jaw-droppingly gorgeous. And a guy like Torin could have his pick. His last girlfriend became a super model. Enough said. So what did he want with me?

I had nothing special to offer him. Except for power. My stomach turned as I realized that I was most likely being played. Yeah, the passion felt real, and it was a little more difficult for a man to fake desire than a woman, but just because I was pretty enough to get it up for him, didn't make me special enough to keep him faithful. Torin was probably with me because the prophecy told him I'd make him stronger. I could only do that because of the collar, and I had no illusions over keeping said collar. I'd already sensed that it was with me for one reason only, to stop an attack on Earth. Then it would most likely return to its slumber, going into hibernation until the next idiot decided it was a good idea to rule the Human Realm. As soon as this whole thing played out, and I went back to being me, Torin would lose interest.

"Stupid girl." The voice rang out in my head again. I'd completely forgotten that I was standing there, leaning against the wall, as I mulled it all over.

"Are you talking to me?" I asked the wall. "Like actually having a conversation with me? I thought you just spouted cryptic shit!"

"The more power the listener possesses, the more strongly we can speak," the voice said. Correction: the *onyx* said.

"Damn," I whispered. "All right, Onyx, then tell me why you think I'm stupid."

"Oh, where will it start?" Sara flounced off and sat on a lavender loveseat.

"You are as lost as he," the voice proclaimed. "So lost, for so long, that being found becomes suspicious."

"You like those riddles, huh?" I grimaced at it. "You're saying I can trust Torin?"

219

"He is my king," the stone huffed.

"So you're saying that even if I couldn't, you wouldn't tell me?" I shook my head at it.

"Stupid girl!" Onyx growled like the slide of mountain rocks. "I'm not as fickle as other jewels. When I choose a king, I make certain that he is worthy of my magic."

"Do you mean that the stones choose their monarchs?" I gaped at the shiny surface, and it reflected a shadowy, shocked image of myself back at me.

"Of course we do!" Onyx vibrated against my palm. "The Shining Ones possess power that calls to us, but we decide whose call we answer. Like attracts like. I am a steady jewel. A stone of stability and balance. I am faith and protection, grounding spiritual energies into the Earth. I am prophecy, and I am relaxation. I am not flighty like Sapphire with its fertility properties. Or moody like Rose Quartz with its casual love. I don't have a greedy nature like Ruby or a nervous one like Peridot. I am the steadfast Onyx, and King Torin is my chosen representative."

"All right, I got it." I rolled my eyes, but my heart was calming into a happy tempo. "Torin's a good guy. So who can't I trust?"

"There is a spy in your midst."

"We kind of figured that," I shrugged. "There are spies in all the courts."

"This particular spy is dangerous." Onyx went deadly serious, I could feel its intensity. "He has human weapons with him. Weapons that recently destroyed my guardians."

"The explosives?" I gaped at the wall again. "There's a guy here, in the castle, who has *more* explosives?"

220

"Yes."

"Well, why the fuck didn't you just say so?!" I shouted, and then I turned to Sara, "Go get the king!"

She gaped at me a second, then jumped up and ran from the room.

"Who is he, Onyx?" I gave my attention back to the wall.

"A tiger among men," the stone growled.

"A tiger among men? Seriously? That's what you're giving me? Have I just been magically transported to Oz?"

Torin swept into the room, stopping short when he saw me standing with my hand pressed to the wall. I was half-dressed, still waiting on that gown Sara had brought me. So I probably looked as if I were leaning there in a saucy pose, hoping for Torin to come ravish me. I saw that the thought had struck him too, but Torin was too smart for that. He looked again at my hand, then closed the door behind him, and strode over to me.

"What is the stone saying to you?"

"See?" Onyx growled. "He is wise. I chose well."

"Yeah, yeah, good on you." I rolled my eyes. "You are stability, yada yada."

"Are you speaking to Onyx?" Torin's eyes widened. "In that manner?"

"Yeah, we have a rapport." I waved off his concern.

"And he is respectful," Onyx added approvingly.

"I'll respect you a whole lot more if you'd tell me who *exactly* has the explosives?" I snapped at the wall.

"Someone has explosives?" Torin laid his palm to the onyx beside mine.

"The tiger," Onyx said, and Torin flinched.

"Dear stones," Torin whispered. "The voice is so strong."

"It's the collar." I said. "Its power allows Onyx to speak more clearly. At least it did"–I growled at the wall again–"until Onyx decided it liked annoying me with riddles. What the hell does 'the tiger' mean? Give me a name, damn it."

"I know only the names of those I've connected with," Onyx huffed.

"Tiger." Torin frowned. "Do you mean he bonds with Tiger's Eye?"

"Yes, of course." Onyx sighed. "Is that not what I said?"

"See?" I said to Torin. "This is what I'm dealing with."

"Thank you, Onyx," Torin said as he rubbed the wall affectionately. "I will take care of this."

He headed to the door, and swung it open with a determined air.

"Hey, hold on," I stumbled after Torin, and grabbed his arm. "What are you doing?"

"There are very few Shining Ones within these walls who work with tiger's eye." Torin's eyes dropped to my open chemise. His fingers trailed over the tops of my breasts and he sighed. "I hate myself for saying this, but get dressed, Elaria. We have a traitor to catch."

Then he left.

"I chose well." The voice was much softer without me

touching the wall, but I could still hear the smugness in it.

"Fucking, self-righteous rock." I made a face at it.

Chapter Thirty-One

The tiger's eye fairies were all investigated, their rooms searched, and the traitor was found quickly. He was a knight named Emmet. The same guy I had nearly plowed into on the stairs. Emmet's betrayal shocked and dismayed Torin, who had thought he'd chosen his knights carefully. But power can sway allegiances, and King Galen had offered Emmet his own little kingdom on Earth. All he had to do was blow up the spellsinger. Yep, the assassination attempts had transferred from Torin to me.

Emmet had ten bombs in his room, all of them charged magically with the help of copper casings. It was pretty damning evidence, and he didn't bother to deny his guilt. He did beg for Torin's forgiveness though, and freely offered up all the information he had on Sapphire. That didn't stop Torin from magically interrogating him, using a combination of several of his knights, who employed their jewels to pull the truth from Emmet. Just in case he was holding something back. Fool me once and all that.

It was a good thing Torin did go the extra mile, or put in the extra magic rather, because Emmet had even more to offer us. Like the locations of several bands of secret agents hiding in Onyx. King Galen and his supporters had been quietly infiltrating the Onyx Kingdom. They were coordinating an attack which was set to take place in four days.

"Kill him," Torin said tiredly to Arnet.

"Please, sire," Emmet began to beg for his life again.

"Son of a bitch." Torin stopped, his jaw clenching, and turned back to Emmet. "You were going to kill the woman I love," he sneered in Emmet's face as I gaped at them. "Do you think I have any compassion for you? In fact, tradition be damned." Torin pulled his sword from its sheath in a dramatic swish of steel. "I claim this satisfaction for myself," and he rammed the sword into Emmet's chest. Torin's eyes blazed as he pushed the blade farther in, watching every twitch of pain on Emmet's face, and relishing every cry from his throat. "May your soul find no peace, you fucking traitor."

Torin pulled the sword free and took the cloth Arnet calmly offered him, nodding crisply to the knight. The Onyx King wiped his sword clean, slid it back into its sheath, then extended his hand to me. His eyes were shaky with emotion, but his arm was steady.

"Shall we hunt down the vipers in my kingdom, Song Queen?"

"Absolutely." I took his hand.

"Deliver those bombs to Quinlan, and ask him to carefully analyze them." Torin nodded from the stack of bombs to Arnet. "Stress the word 'carefully.'"

"Yes, Your Majesty." Arnet bowed.

Torin escorted me out of the room, and we started to make our way upstairs, to his bedroom.

"Are you all right?" I whispered to him, then nodded and smiled to the people we passed in the corridor. Sure, everything is fine here, your king just executed a traitor, no biggie.

"I'm . . ."–Torin's jaw clenched hard enough to flutter his cheek–"angry."

"Yeah, I can see that." I wrapped my arm around his, and leaned in. "I'm sorry your knight betrayed you. That's rough."

"You think my anger is about the betrayal?" Torin turned to

225

me sharply, stopping us in the middle of the hallway.

People gave us hesitant looks as they passed, but no one looked for long. It was better not to question a king. Especially one who looked upset.

"What else could it be about?" I eased him over to the side.

"What else?" Torin gaped at me a second before he jerked me against him, and kissed me till my head spun.

I floundered at his shoulders as his passionate assault overwhelmed me. Torin's hands were clawing into me like he was afraid I'd escape. His mouth was demanding and bruising, slashing like a weapon. His body crowded, then enveloped me, so that I felt entirely surrounded by him. Torin's scent, his skin, his touch–I was wrapped in it all. Finally, he eased back, and we stared at each other as we caught our breaths.

"I am angry that someone thought to take you from me," Torin whispered. "That they were able to get close enough to nearly be successful. I'm furious at Emmet and Galen, but especially at myself, for failing to protect you. You were given into my keeping, Elaria, and I nearly allowed my own knight to slaughter you. You, the hope of all the worlds."

"Is that what I am to you?" I asked softly. "The hope of all the worlds?"

"No." He closed his eyes briefly, and leaned his forehead to mine. "You know that you're more than that to me. But I must remind myself that you are precious to us all. Losing you would be the greatest tragedy my heart has ever suffered, but I wouldn't suffer it alone. Not for long."

"I love you too." I kissed him gently, and he groaned into it.

"Elaria," Torin sighed. "I've been waiting for those words."

"I know; I'm sorry." I swallowed hard. "I wanted to be sure before I said them."

"Then they mean even more to me." He smiled.

"But I wasn't given to you." I pushed at his chest. "And I can take care of myself."

"I know you're powerful," he sighed, "but I still feel protective of you. Is that really such a bad thing?"

"I suppose not." I took his hand again, and we resumed our walk. "Now, let's go get ready for our hunt. I'd better let Cerberus know. He'll be disappointed if we don't include him."

"I'm not sure if I'll be able to refrain from making hunting dog jokes," Torin warned me in mock seriousness.

"And I'm not sure if I'll be able to stop Cer from making you his prey if you do," I teased.

"Hmm." Torin seemed to consider it. "A fight against the Hound of Hades. It would be a match to remember."

"Wondering if you could win?"

"Wondering how mad you'd be at me if I were to cripple your friend." He smirked.

"Arrogant." I shook my head. "I have no idea what I find so attractive about you."

"I could make you a list," Torin offered smoothly. "There are a few things you say in bed that should be at the top somewhere."

"Oh please." I rolled my eyes.

"Yes, that would be one of them."

Chapter Thirty-Two

I was getting ready to leave, slipping my feet into a pair of boots while Sara fussed with my hair, when something exploded in my room.

Sara shrieked, and I stared in shock at a corner table that had become a pile of sooty splinters.

"Was that a bomb?" I frowned and headed over to the wreckage.

"No," Sara screamed and pulled me back. "Don't go near it!"

"Sara, it's fine." I tried to calm her, rubbing her arms gently. "It's already detonated."

"What if there's another one?"

"Doubtful." I eased her back toward the bed as Torin and several knights came rushing in.

"What happened?" Torin scanned the room, and his eyes came to rest on the mess. "Something *exploded*?"

Torin started toward it.

"No, Your Majesty!" Sara screamed again. "Don't! It's not safe."

"Sara, calm down." I said gently to her, and then approached the corner with Torin. "It was a little bomb." I bent down to inspect the pile of wood and ash.

"Damn that fucking bastard!" Torin pulled something out of the pile.

"What? Who?" I peered at the blackened thing. It was a ring. "Is that the ring Finbar gave me?"

"Yes"–Torin's jaw clenched–"and it's a good thing I pulled it off your finger that first night. He had a killing charm placed beneath the diplomatic one. Emmet must have been wearing some sort of charm as well, something that warned Finbar that his plan had failed and his rat was dead."

"So he decided to just blast me to smithereens?" I glared at the ring.

"It was a slim chance, depending on your wearing the ring. He must have been desperate when his first attempt failed." Torin smoothed the soot from the sapphire and showed me the cracks within the stone. "The spell is so fatal, it destroys the jewel upon activation. They're rare, due to the casting difficulty. It's basically suicide for the stone, so most gems reject the magic. I never would have thought to look for it."

"That fucking bastard." I echoed Torin's words.

"I'm going to kill him slowly," Torin promised me.

"If I don't get to him first," I stood and looked back at Sara. "It's okay, Sara. It was the ring Finbar gave me."

"What?" Sara screeched as she shot up. "That slimy son of a sea-goat!"

"Yes, indeed." Torin chuckled, then looked me over. "Are you ready to leave? I'm now extremely anxious to find these infiltrators."

"Yeah, I'm ready," I held my hand out him. "Let's go get-'em."

We paused at the door so Torin could give the shattered ring to one of his knights. "Destroy this thoroughly."

"Yes, sire."

Then we made our way down to the courtyard, where we found a large group of men waiting for us. Cerberus and Banning had both wanted to come along to help find the groups of Sapphire supporters hiding in the Onyx Kingdom. Since there were four groups we needed to locate, Torin formed four units of knights to go out to the different locations all at once. He sent Banning with one, Cerberus with another, and he took charge of a third group. Torin wanted me to go with him, but I didn't like feeling as if I needed babysitting. He argued that I'd just nearly been blown up, which prompted explanations to Cerberus and Banning, who then agreed that I should accompany one of them. This brought out my special spellsinger death stare, which I used on all of them until Torin agreed to let me lead the fourth team.

So I rode out with fifteen knights, feeling confident and capable. I'm not a woman who normally relies on men for protection, and these assassination attempts had brought out a need in me to take action, and prove to myself that I was competent. I would handle this threat myself.

My unit found our designated group quite easily, thanks to Emmet's information. It turned out that Emmet had been using his influence to find them places to stay in Onyx. The group I went after had been hiding in a town called Evervale. The infiltrators were pretty surprised when we showed up on their doorstep and took them into custody. So surprised that they barely put up a fight. The spies were shackled and loaded into a wagon within thirty minutes.

Torin wanted them all brought back to the castle so they could be questioned. Then he would decide their fates. So the round up didn't involve any killing, just a bit of manhandling. I hung back after the initial foray had been finished, and let the

230

knights gather the criminals. A few of my knights were inside the hideout, searching for weapons and information. I lounged against the wall outside, my eyes flitting around the area cautiously.

Evervale was around thirty miles across, sizable for a fairy town. There were several buildings in the center of it, businesses mostly, and then homes spread out around the hub. Most of the homes were actually farms. Which made sense; the food had to come from somewhere. I just hadn't thought to see Shining Ones out tending fields. Especially not with magic. They cut wheat with waves of their hands, pulled vegetables with barely a finger curl, and then directed their haul into waiting barrels with little more than a few gestures. I suppose hard labor was unnecessary when you had magical talent. It was fascinating to watch, and the sight distracted me enough that I wasn't as cautious as I should have been. When I heard a strange sound coming from behind the cottage, I simply went to investigate.

And I was grabbed by three men.

I was gagged first, then lifted off my feet and drug away. I fought viciously, but there were multiple men restraining me, and they were able to subdue me quickly. Ropes wrapped viciously around my wrists and legs, and then I was thrown over the back of a horse. A rough hand held me down onto the bruising saddle as we galloped away. Branches slapped my face, and I sought shelter against the horse's hide. The smell of horse sweat and unwashed man stung my nose. Combined with the bumpy ride, I almost lost my lunch. Which would have resulted in me dying á la Janis Joplin, choked to death on my own vomit. Not a way I wanted to go. So I did my best to suppress the urge, hardening my abs against the torment.

As the world sped by beneath me, all I could think was that I had failed. When had I become so weak? When had I lost the ability to defend myself? Or perhaps I hadn't become weak, but stupid. Careless. I had taken risks I wouldn't have normally taken, all because I felt threatened by a man who wanted to protect me.

Torin's words came back to haunt me; was it really so bad?

Yes, damn it! I didn't want to rely on anyone, especially not a lover. In a relationship, I needed to be on equal ground. Torin's romantic declaration had been sweet, but it had undermined my ability to reason. I'd been thrown by it, and had focused on my pride instead of my safety. I had to go and prove to myself that I was a big, strong spellsinger. Well, I'd forgotten one small fact. I was in Tír na nÓg, and in the Shining Ones's Realm, I wasn't a big, strong spellsinger. I was just another magic user, except I needed my voice to access that magic. And that made me vulnerable.

After what seemed like hours, we finally came to a halt, and I was yanked off the horse. I tumbled across the grass to awkwardly roll my way into a sitting position, difficult to do with my hands bound. I shook my hair out of my face, and finally got a good look at my assailants. Three Shining One males. I was pretty sure they were all from Sapphire since they were covered in the blue jewels. Perhaps I'd even met them while I was there, but I hadn't really been paying attention during that perverted party.

They didn't start a fire or unpack their supplies–normal things done when camp was set. Instead, they instantly began arguing. Over my life.

"You should have just killed her when you had the chance," the blond one said to one of the dark haired men.

"She may be worth more to us alive." The guy who I had rode with defended himself.

"Finbar already promised us fifty gold pieces each," the final man said.

"And you think King Torin wouldn't give more?" My abductor scoffed. "They say he's in love with her."

"In love with her powerful voice," the blond sneered.

232

"She's beautiful." The second brunette eyed me speculatively. "Unusual. Those eyes"–he shook his head–"they shift colors. I've only seen that once before, and it was on a man."

"So what?" the blond huffed. "Beauty has nothing to do with her worth, and Torin is known to be shrewd. If he cares about her, it has nothing to do with her eyes." He glanced down at the V of my tunic, which had fallen open a bit. "Or her tits, though those are nice too."

I grimaced at him through my gag. Men.

"Whatever we decide"–the speculative brunette started to ease closer to me–"we shouldn't waste such an opportunity. It's not every day that you get handed a king's mistress to do with as you please."

The blond started to smile.

Panic flooded my limbs, but more than that, I felt a rush of anger. I had this relic around my neck, this witch tool of such power that it was fated to save all the worlds. Yet I was still hindered by the same spellsinger weakness. Gag me, and I was vulnerable. It was so frustrating, and in that moment, it was horrifying. I had never been sexually assaulted, but the possibilities of it were enough to send tremors through my limbs. Panic turned to fear, and anger turned to rage. I screamed against the gag, all of my fury at my own limitations rising up to combine with my dread of what was about to happen. I felt so helpless, and for me, that was the worst part.

My magic lifted with my extreme emotions, crawling up my chest to burst out of the collar. The stones didn't glow softly, they flared to blinding brilliance, making me shut my eyes against the glare. I winced and fell back as the magic shot out of the relic. There was a brief wave of heat, the smell of cooking meat, and then strangling smoke. When I opened my eyes again, the men were gone. All that remained were three startled horses and three

233

piles of ash. I stared at those piles, utterly transfixed, as the wind caught them, lifting them gently into the air. It was almost beautiful, the spiraling designs of delicate gray flakes twirling through the eddies of the cleansing breeze. My would-be rapists were nothing but dust in the wind.

The lyrics of that old song rose in my mind, and I laughed insanely against my gag. Kansas probably hadn't envisioned such a quick transition to dust when they wrote that song. Then my laughter failed me, and I began to cry. Sure, I'd been saved from unwanted attentions, but now I was bound and gagged in the middle of some Tír na nÓg forest, with no way of getting free. Just my fucking luck.

The relic!

I sat up straight, sniffled, and focused on it. If it had killed those men with only my rage to focus it, then surely it could undo my ropes. Right? Right! Wrong. I tried for hours, humming sounds against the tight fabric filling my mouth, as I visualized my ropes breaking. Please! I begged the relic, I bargained with it, reasoned with it. I did everything I could think of to get it to help me, but my magic stubbornly refused to rise. The relic remained dormant on my chest.

I fell back in exhaustion.

The horses had long since calmed and taken to grazing on the thick grass, but I began to panic more and more. I couldn't even get to my feet; those bastards had bound me around the knees as well as my ankles. Maybe I could crawl, squirm along the ground like an inchworm. But my hands were tied behind my back, and that meant I either had to butt shimmy or squirm on my face. I knew I'd end up caught hopelessly on something or perhaps drown in a puddle. Wouldn't that be a glorious end? Oh hell, I needed to calm myself and think.

Think, Elaria!

It had to be the emotions behind my intent that had powered the relic, but what emotion should I use to free myself? Rage had killed those men. But I didn't want to accidentally kill the horses while I was trying to destroy my bonds. So what then? Fear? I tried to fuel the relic with my panic, but nothing happened. I tried the feeling of being trapped. No go. Nothing worked. Finally I gave into my exhaustion, and just laid my cheek to the cool grass and wept more. At least there was some release in that.

I don't know how long I lay there, but my hands began to go numb, my shoulders screamed with pain, and my jaw started to ache from the strain of the makeshift gag. The fabric was wet and disgusting from my spit and tears. My hair was ragged around me, full of leaves and dirt, which was doubtless streaked across my face along with my tears. I must have looked a horrible mess when Banning found me.

I heard Banning's horse approaching before I saw him, and I tensed. Company could have gone either way. It could be more Sapphire supporters, roaming the woods for their friends, or it could be someone on my side. In the brief moments before his horse broke through the foliage, I tried to prepare myself for some kind of defense. But then I saw Banning, and I gave a wrenching sob of relief. He spotted me, and gaped at me for a second, taking in the empty clearing, my bound state, and the happily munching horses, before he jumped down, and rushed over to me.

"Elaria!" Banning's hands went to my gag first, trying to untie it. He finally cursed with frustration, pulled his dagger, and simply cut the thing loose. "Are you all right?"

I worked my jaw loose, and wet my lips before answering, "Now I am," and then I fell forward into his arms, wailing in the most embarrassing way.

I'm not a crier. Really. But it had been hours of waiting like that, wondering if I had managed to save myself from rape only to die of exposure. Hours of lying there helpless and in pain while

235

those damn horses had their dinner. The aches in my limbs didn't even bother me anymore, now that Banning was there. I just needed to vent, let all that anxiety out.

"Shh now, you're safe," Banning cooed to me as he worked at the ropes with his dagger. "Elaria, shh, it's all right now. Let me untie you. Please, darling, stop crying. I've got you now. You're okay."

"Yeah, okay." I leaned over his lap so he could get at my wrists, and I felt him sawing at the rope. My hands came free, but my numb arms ended up just swinging limply forward. "Oh sweet gods, thank you, Banning," I moaned into his thighs, and ended up pressing my cheek to them. I couldn't move yet; the tingles of life were spreading through my arms with painful jolts. "Thank you."

"You're welcome, sweetheart." He brushed my hair back from my face, and then went to work on the ropes around my legs. "Here; I need to unwind this. Can you roll over, or do you want me to help you?"

"Just push me," I moaned. "I can't move yet."

"All right." He ended up pulling me farther across his lap.

"Thank you," I said again, and looked up, realizing I was lying in his arms like a child.

"You're welcome." Banning's lips pressed together, his eyes filling with some kind of strong emotion. "Your team searched Evervale, and then sent word to the rest of us of your disappearance. I don't know what the others are doing, but I'm sure they're all out looking for you. We're supposed to meet back at Evervale in an hour." He stopped and took a deep breath. "I don't think I've been so scared since the moment Cosmina first grabbed Fortune around her throat. Elaria"–Banning shook his head–"I thought I'd lost you again."

He pressed a gentle, chaste kiss to my lips. It was too much

236

tenderness for my vulnerable state. I kissed him back. Nothing sexual really, just a stronger pressure between us. I held his face in my hands and leaned my forehead to his, trying to silently convey the depth of my gratitude to him. I suppose I was still in shock, but a shivering took hold of me, and I couldn't stop it. Banning pulled me into his chest and rocked me, murmuring sweet things to me as he rubbed warmth back into my arms. At one point, he scooped up my legs so that he was holding all of me, pressed tight to his chest, and we just sat there, clinging to each other.

That was how Torin found us.

I would have felt awkward about it if I hadn't been so distraught. There I was, trembling in the arms of a man who had declared his intentions to take me from Torin. It must have looked pretty damning. But Torin wasn't an idiot. He came crashing into the clearing on horseback, took one look around, and then focused on me.

Banning had lifted his knife, but hurriedly lowered it when he saw who it was. I witnessed it all through the corner of my eye, still too upset to remove my head from the security of Banning's chest. I felt Banning tense beneath me and stand, taking me with him.

"Give her to me," Torin said with cool command, and his voice was enough to gain my attention.

"Torin," I whispered.

Torin's eyes widened when he saw the state of me, and he seemed to forget Banning altogether. He leapt from the saddle and rushed over to me. One of his warm hands went to my cheek, and the other smoothed the hair back from my face. His throat convulsed harshly before he spoke.

"Are you hurt?" Torin whispered. "Did they hurt you, Elaria? Tell me."

237

"No, I'm okay," I said shakily. "I've just been here alone, tied up for hours. I wasn't sure anyone would find me."

"They just left you here?" Banning asked.

"No." I looked at the horses. More horses than people in the clearing. "They . . . they tried to . . ."

"But they didn't?" Torin asked before I had to finish saying it.

"No." I took a deep breath. "I was afraid and angry that I could be so easily restrained. The rage just boiled up, and I screamed. Something happened. There was a light. I closed my eyes against it. When I opened them, the men were piles of ash."

"You burned them with your rage?" Banning whispered in awe.

"I think the relic did." I shook my head. "I can stand now, Banning. Thank you."

"All right." Banning reluctantly lowered my feet to the grass. "Are you sure?"

"Let go of her, Banning." Torin took my arm and carefully eased me over to him.

"I'll let her go when I'm good and ready," Banning growled, holding tight to my arm.

"You'll let her go now or I'll remove your hand with my sword," Torin snarled back.

I started to cry again, falling limply forward, and both men reached out to catch me.

"Damn it all," Torin cursed, and swept me into his arms, yanking me out of Banning's grasp. "See what you've done?"

"What I've done?" Banning scoffed. "You're the one acting like a barbarian."

"The horses," I moaned before they could start fighting again.

"What's that, sweetheart?" Torin asked me.

"The horses." I turned to Banning. "Can you bring them back with you? I don't want them left here alone."

"Of course," Banning said immediately.

"Thank you." I gave him a look that expressed both my gratitude, and my hope that he would back off. I couldn't handle a fight between Torin and him. Not right then.

"You're welcome, Elaria," Banning sighed, and then nodded. "I'll take the horses with me to Evervale, and let the others know that she's been found," he said to Torin.

"My thanks." Torin set me into the saddle of his horse, a massive black beast, and then swung up behind me. "I'll take Elaria home."

Torin swung us about and set off at a gallop, racing through the forest like we were being chased by demons. I didn't care. I felt safe again, and that was all that mattered. I snuggled in against Torin, burrowing my face into his tunic, and inhaled his scent. It settled me further, and I kept my face pressed there, my cheek to his heart, so I could keep breathing him in.

I must have fallen asleep because the next thing I recall is being carried up the stairs to Torin's bedroom. He went straight to the bathroom, and set me on a padded stool as he ran some water in the bathtub. The tub was porcelain, stark against the rest of the dark room, and set down into a pedestal that filled the entire far end of the room. Behind it was a short ledge, and then a wall of windows, but the drapes were pulled shut.

I blinked more awake, pulling my eyes from the silver curtains, and caught Torin staring at me. He was crouched beside the tub, one hand trailing in the water to test the temperature, but he was focused on me.

"What?"

"I've never known such fear," he confessed in a whisper. "Panic. The threats against your life made me angry, but I wasn't truly afraid until today, when they took you from me. They *took* you." He slammed his fist into the water, sending it splashing up in a torrent and making me flinch. "Just snatched you away, and there was nothing I could do about it. I wasn't even there! And I wasn't even the one who found you."

"Torin," I whispered, "I'm okay."

"I let you sway me." His chest was rising and falling rapidly. "I let you go out into a dangerous situation alone. Never again, Elaria."

He began removing my clothing efficiently. The shoes went first, then my dirty tunic. Torin helped me stand so he could get my breeches off, and then he pulled off my underwear. All with a grim expression. It was the most awkward strip ever. When I was completely naked, he picked me up, and laid me gently in the water, being careful to hang my long hair over the edge of the tub.

"Torin." I finally spoke when it became evident that he wasn't going to. "I was just a little shaken. I'm all right now."

"They could have raped you." He set a hard stare on me. "Is that not what you were trying to tell me? They were going to rape you, but the relic helped you defend yourself?"

"Yes," I whispered.

"Never again will you be put in such peril." He stood and fetched a comb from the counter behind him.

Torin's bathroom left the castle's onyx walls bare, no tapestries or silk to cover them. Just polished onyx everywhere– walls, ceiling, and floor. What wasn't onyx was silver, and what wasn't silver was mirrored. It seemed like Torin's savage expression was reflected everywhere. Magnified in the stone.

The ferocity in his face made me shiver, but when he crouched behind me, his touch was tender. Torin began to run the comb through my hair, carefully untangling it. I sighed and reached for the soap. We both worked silently, me washing my body while he combed my hair. Then he washed my hair, using a silver bowl to pour clean water over it when he was through. His hands were stroking, soothing, but every time I looked at his face, I found him scowling.

Finally, I was clean and mostly dry. Torin swept me up, and carried me back into the bedroom, where he laid me gently on the bed. That's where his gentleness ended. He stepped back and flung his clothes away, then climbed onto the mattress with me, staring at me like I was prey.

"Torin?" I frowned.

"I was in a panic, Elaria," Torin told me again. "I searched everywhere, until I finally found your trail. Then I come upon you and him together. He held you as if he'd done so a thousand times before."

"Torin . . ."

"And you looked like you belonged there." He loomed over me, slid his knee between my legs, and shoved my thighs apart.

"I was upset," I pushed at Torin's shoulders, but he kept angling closer to me. "He was comforting me."

"You're mine. I am the man who gives you comfort, not Banning," Torin whispered harshly, right before he covered my mouth with a passionate kiss.

I melted into his desire, but his words were triggering a stubborn response. "No, I'm not."

"What?" Torin pulled back to stare at me.

"I don't belong to you."

"Of course you do." He scowled. "You love me, you said so."

"Love isn't about ownership." I tried to ease away, but he slid inside me, and I groaned.

"Is it not?" Torin began a steady rhythm, driving harder and deeper with each thrust.

"I told you before." I clung to his shoulders even as I tried to rebuke him. "You can't cage a spellsinger."

"I've done it once already." He bit at the tender skin of my neck, making me arch into him.

"I would have freed myself eventually." I clawed my hands into his thick hair.

"No, my darling." Torin smiled against my neck. "You wouldn't have, and you won't now. You're mine."

"No," I said simply.

Torin snarled and pounded the mattress with a fist. He pulled out of me, sitting back on his heels to glare down at me.

"I will have all of you or none of you, Elaria." His massive chest rose and fell with deep, forceful exhalations. "Just admit that you're mine."

"Why?" I eased up on my elbows. "Why this need to possess?"

"You told me you're enslaved to the relic." He waved an angry hand at the collar. "Yet you will not submit to the same bond with me?"

"Oh gods." I shook my head. "Why do you have to use words like 'submit' and 'enslaved'? The relic is different; it's not a man. It's a tool that I must use to keep us all safe."

"It's *not* different." Torin leaned over me again. "You have given yourself to it. Now I want you to give yourself to me. You already have." He laid his palm to my sternum. "I can feel it. Why won't you admit it?"

"It's too much, too soon," I looked away from him. "We barely know each other."

"Oh, is that it?" Torin grabbed my hips and slid inside me again. "That's the excuse you're going to use? You know, as well as I, that time has nothing to do with knowing someone, especially not with people like us." He moaned as he ground his way deeper. "You know me, as I know you. You couldn't love me if you didn't."

"I won't be a possession, Torin." I grabbed his jaw to get him to stop his sensual attack, and see how serious I was. "You still don't know what love is."

He laughed. I scowled harder.

"A possession?" Torin's hand slipped up over mine. "You could never be that to me. When I say that you're mine, Elaria, I mean that I own your heart, as you own mine." His hand clenched, pushing my fingers more firmly into his face. "That you will not allow another man to touch you because of the love you bear for me. Just as I will not be intimate with another woman because of the love I have for you. We belong to each other, an equal enslavement." He released my hand, and when I eased my grip, he kissed my palm. "There is no master here."

"Equal enslavement?" I whispered as he began to move

243

inside me again.

"Words have power; you know that." Torin trailed kisses over my face. "I crave the magic of your voice. I need to hear you claim me, as much as I need to claim you. So I will say it first, if it makes it easier on you. I am yours, Elaria."

"You are?" I looked over his striking features, outlined in silver moonlight, and felt the cage settle around my heart.

"I am," he vowed. "Now say it to me, little bird. Bind us together."

"I'm yours." I put a musical lilt to the words without thinking about it, just something I did when I was happy, and my magic responded, lifting up and pushing through the relic.

The collar glowed softly between me and Torin, and we both stared down at it in surprise. An enchantment rose, a warm glimmer that coasted over our skin as our bodies strained toward completion. It sank into our flesh, and as it did, I saw an image of Banning. My hand was reaching out to him, but I knew it wasn't the same hand I held Torin with. It was Fortune's hand. As the vows between me and Torin settled into place, Fortune's hand faded, and so did the image of Banning. The relic was completing the spell I'd begun with Torin the day I'd first claimed the collar.

"We belong to each other." Torin's voice rumbled between us, shivering with magic and setting the spell.

We cried out in ecstasy, both of us clinging to each other through the pleasure of physical and magical completion. When it was over, I knew the memories of that other me were gone. Banished by the relic's blessing on this relationship. One tie broken while another was made stronger. Something inside me mourned, but that was soon banished too.

Chapter Thirty-Three

Five days later, my bond to Torin was tested, and surprisingly, it wasn't by Banning. Banning had actually backed off a bit since my abduction. He continued to give me brooding looks in typical blooder fashion, but he never said anything to me about our past. I was beginning to wonder if he had felt the separation of the relic's spell as well.

On my end, Banning looked the same, as gorgeous as ever, but there was no ache in the depths of my chest. No nagging feeling that I was forgetting something important. I had already forgotten, and released it. There was peace in that.

There wasn't any peace in *her* arrival though.

Royals had started to show up in Onyx with their armies. Our allies. The monarchs were given rooms in the castle, but their armies had to make do with camps in the courtyard and the surrounding area. There simply wasn't enough space in Onyx Castle.

I was standing around the war table, in a meeting with Torin, his advisers, Cerberus, Banning, the royals who had already arrived, and their generals, when the Snowflake Obsidian Queen swept into the room. She was blonde to the point of being colorless, and her skin matched her hair. Delicate, almost frail looking, she was one of those women who made men want to take care of her. But her eyes were black, and they stared out at the world with a severity that revealed her true nature. She was a queen of the Shining Ones, after all; she had to be powerful. This woman didn't need a man for anything except pleasure.

"Queen Oonagh"–King Declan of Alexandrite was the first

to spot her–"greetings. You look lovely as ever."

"Thank you, King Declan," Oonagh nodded regally, her riot of curls, piled high on her head, swishing forward with girlish charm.

Then she turned to Torin and I saw him tense.

"King Torin," Oonagh purred.

"Welcome, Queen Oonagh," Torin nodded, "We're happy to have you with us."

"Of course." She sidled up close to him, wedging between me and Torin, even though I'd been only inches away from Torin. "We've always supported each other. I wasn't going to abandon you now."

I hadn't moved back for her, which meant that she was pressed against me. Tight. Ridiculous really. I lifted a brow at Cerberus, across the table from me. He was barely containing his mirth. Cer knew I wasn't a woman to back down when someone tried to intimidate me. In fact, I was quite the opposite. I wasn't about to let anyone push me around, not literally or figuratively.

I leaned forward and whispered in Oonagh's ear, "You're standing on my dress."

"Oh!" Oonagh exclaimed.

She was so startled that she lurched sideways and nearly fell. The Alexandrite king was behind her, and he steadied her, giving me a gleeful look in the process. Instead of being pleased by King Declan's help, Oonagh appeared perturbed that Torin hadn't been the one to assist her. In fact, both Torin and I stared at her calmly, as if waiting for her to do her next trick.

"I do apologize," Oonagh finally said, the words sounding brittle. "I didn't see you standing there."

It was one of those snide remarks that you're just supposed to let slide in polite society. You didn't actually call a queen a liar to her face, not even when it was obvious. But I was a queen too, wasn't I? And I liked calling things as I saw them.

"You didn't see me?" I lifted a brow. "You didn't see me right *here*, standing two inches away from my man? You must have at least *felt* me since your back was squishing my breasts flat . . . and that's quite a lot of squishing, in case you haven't noticed."

"Your what?" Oonagh made a disgusted face at me, ignoring my comments about her being pressed intimately into my chest. "What did you call King Torin?"

"My man," I smiled brightly at her. "My lover, my boyfriend, my sweetheart. The keyword here is 'mine', so back your scrawny ass off my man before I break it in two."

"Oh damn!" Cerberus laughed. "You go, El!"

The rest of the room went silent, watching us face off with a mixture of horror and delight.

"Who is this cretin?" Oonagh looked to Torin with shocked revulsion. "Are you going to allow her to talk to me like that?"

"Queen Oonagh"–Torin's lips were twitching as he slid his arm around my waist–"this is my . . ." He at me and smiled brilliantly as he said, "My *woman*, Queen Elaria."

"Feels good, doesn't it?" I smiled up at him. "Feeds into those barbaric inclinations of yours."

"That it does," he agreed as Oonagh gaped at us.

"Queen of what?" Oonagh finally asked. "I don't know this *woman*, but I'm fairly certain she isn't one of us. Is she queen of some tiny island in the human world?"

"She is the Queen of Song." Torin cocked his head at

247

Oonagh. "I would have thought you'd heard of her, and of my relationship with her, by now."

An irritated look crossed Oonagh's face. "I hadn't believed such base rumors." She looked me over. "I suppose she's pretty enough, but I had expected the witch warrior to be more . . ."–she frowned–"*more.*"

"Pretty *enough*?" Banning growled. "Elaria is the most beautiful woman in all the worlds."

The room went silent again, and I turned to gape at Banning. He didn't falter, but met my gaze steadily before looking back at Oonagh. Banning's stare was hard, daring her to dispute his claim. The Snowflake Obsidian Queen was sputtering, and I was still gaping at Banning.

So I guess he hadn't felt that separation spell after all.

"And who are you?" Oonagh hissed at Banning. "Another lout with bad manners?"

"Banning Dalca, Gheara of the Kansas Gura," Banning continued to stare at her.

"A blooder?" Oonagh looked at Torin. "You've let a blooder into our alliance?"

"This war will determine the fates of every living being on every plane of existence." Torin frowned a little, and looked over his shoulder at Banning consideringly. "I suppose he's a type of living being. Whatever he is,"–Torin looked back at Oonagh,–he is welcome here. In *my* court and *my* alliance. I will not have anyone questioning my decisions or mistreating my allies."

Queen Oonagh paled, if that was even possible, "Of course not." She bowed her head demurely. "I was just surprised."

"Queen Oonagh, would you care for a glass of wine?" King

Declan had been standing off to the side of our group throughout the entire exchange, his blue eyes shifting to violet, just like his allied gem.

He was a handsome man, with the elegant features most fey men possessed, and his lustrous auburn hair was pulled back in a tight braid to emphasize his good looks. But what struck me the most about Declan was the color of his eyes, which were nearly identical to mine.

Oonagh perused Declan's beautiful features thoughtfully, then took the Alexandrite king's hand, and let him lead her away from us, to the far end of the table. I caught Declan's eye, and nodded my thanks to him. He sent me a saucy wink. The rascal.

"Now that my relationship status has been settled, let's move on." Torin smirked at the others gathered around the war table, which was covered in maps, notes, and stone figures.

The group laughed nervously. Yeah, I guess that exchange could have gone badly. Even fatally. It wasn't surprising that it had made them nervous. I wondered what they would have done if Oonagh and I had started rolling on the floor, clawing at each other like a couple of teenage girls. The imagery brought my behavior to light inside my head, and I realized that I'd just defended my boyfriend with all the grace of a ghetto chola. Dear gods, all I needed was some long nails, red lipstick, and a flannel shirt. The words "cut a bitch" also came to mind. Maybe I should buy a switchblade.

I was mortified. Then Torin's hand slid into mine, and I looked up to find him smiling at me. There was a smugness to his smile that made me laugh. He had enjoyed it. Of course he had. What man doesn't enjoy two women fighting over him? Even if one of them happened to do it in a slightly less sophisticated manner. But I also knew that the whole interaction had been a test. If I hadn't stood up to Oonagh, she would have continued to behave as if Torin were hers. And then I would have had to kick her ass. As one does.

"As I was saying . . ." Queen Teagan of Jet spoke, and we all gave her our full attention with a fair amount of relief. "I believe it would be best if we simply marched on Sapphire and put a swift end to this." She smacked a pile of papers with the flat of her hand.

I liked Queen Teagan. She was very clear in her manner and speech, lacking a lot of the guile most of the Shining Ones possessed. It probably didn't make her the best diplomat, but her husband, King Edmond, seemed adept at the art. He eased around his wife, and laid an elegant, tanned hand over her dainty, pale-gold one. She looked up at him with a little smile, her ice-blue eyes warming a bit.

"Or"–King Edmond swept back his queen's indigo hair, kissed her cheek, and then suggested–"we could come at them from multiple sides, perhaps in a more secretive fashion? So they would have less time to prepare."

"I like the way you think, King Ed." Cerberus grinned.

King Edmond winced at the slaughtering of his name.

"I do as well, King *Edmond*," Torin stressed the name, and shot a chastising look at Cerberus.

Cerberus shrugged, as unrepentant as usual.

"*Can* we do that?" I asked, pointing down to the map. "Jasper, Opal, and Diamond are all supporters of Sapphire, and two of those border the Sapphire Kingdom, while the last, Opal, lies between us."

"And I've had word this morning that Carnelian joined Sapphire as well." Sir Kean of Howlite pointed to Carnelian's location on the map. Right above Jasper and bordering Sapphire.

250

Sir Kean was the first gray-haired Shining One I'd met. I guess technically his hair was silver–it shone like metal in the light and was actually pretty–but it registered as gray in my mind. It didn't help that he had gray eyes to match. However, Kean also possessed a confident manner, and a solid, soldier's build. He in no way looked old.

"Any other news to report?" Torin scanned the rest of the room.

"We've heard that King Jarlath and Queen Isandra have already joined their sons in Sapphire," Queen Teagan added.

"Those are the Diamond royals?" I asked.

"Yes, and they're formidable," Torin said. "Jarlath is especially good with war tactics."

"Galen is no idiot either," Queen Oonagh added, then sipped her wine. "He plays the part of the hedonist, but he inherited his father's talent for strategy."

I looked at Oonagh, surprised that she had anything useful to say. And there I'd thought she'd only come to try and steal my boyfriend. How small minded of me.

"The Malachite Queen is with them as well," King Declan reminded us. "She's quite brilliant. I can attest to that personally." His eyes met mine again, and his lips twisted into a sensual smile.

"Nice." I grimaced at him. "What happened to gentlemen who don't kiss and tell?"

"I believe you'll find them in the human world," Declan smirked. "Here in Tír na nÓg, we love kissing and telling, sometimes at the same time."

"Indeed, King Declan," Oonagh twittered, winding her arm through his. "Human reservations are so boring."

"Fucking fairy perverts." I muttered, and Torin chuckled.

"You seemed to enjoy my perversions last night," Torin whispered.

"Yeah, but that was in private, and you're not announcing it to everyone this morning," I countered.

"That doesn't mean I don't want to," he leaned in and purred into my ear. "Or that I wouldn't love to take you right here, on this table, in front of everyone."

I must have blushed because Cerberus burst out laughing.

"What are you two whispering about that has El looking like she's sixteen again?" Cerberus asked Torin. "Scratch that. I don't even remember her blushing at sixteen."

"Tactics," Torin said smoothly. "I was asking the Song Queen her opinion on mine."

"Oh, uh-huh." Cerberus chuckled. "And what was your response, El?"

"That we should just chuck you at them in a catapult," I smirked. "They'd be dead in ten minutes."

"That they would!" Cerberus chortled. "Show me to the closest catapult!"

That lifted the tension in the room, and everyone laughed, but I caught some uncomfortable attention coming from the end of the table. Oonagh was staring at me like she wanted to know how my blood would look soaking my dress, and Declan like he wanted to know how I'd look without the dress entirely. What a match those two were. It appeared that I might have more than one front to fight on.

Chapter Thirty-Four

"There's one more person we need to speak to today." Torin guided me away from the meeting room.

"Who's that?" I glanced over my shoulder and saw Oonagh scowling at me. I may have smirked a little.

"Quinlan," Torin whispered.

"Quinlan?"

"My alchemist." Torin hurried us away.

"Oh, right." I slipped my hand down to his. "You sent him the bombs to investigate."

That whole escorting bit, with my arm around his, always made me feel awkward. It was too close, too difficult to walk, especially when doing so with a man Torin's size. His fingers laced with mine and squeezed. Much better. Just like in a love affair, a little space went a long way.

"Yes, and he's discovered something." Torin took me through the twisting halls of the Onyx Castle, down into the lower levels.

We entered a room that did nothing to meet my expectations of an alchemist's chamber. There were no bubbling beakers filled with vivid liquids or jars of pickled creatures. Though there were lots of jars set into shelves along one wall, and a heavy, wood desk pushed up to a small window. Light glared down from a magical chandelier above, illuminating the scene far too well for my tastes. Aren't alchemists supposed to work in the dark? Preferably in some damp cellar? This guy had a setup closer to a CSI crime lab than a medieval wizard's lair. I half expected Grissom to walk in and start explaining how the bomb would lead us to the killer.

Quinlan himself didn't fit my image of what an alchemist was supposed to be either. I expected someone with bushy brows and a long beard. Someone dressed in robes, wearing a wizened expression. Quinlan looked more like Lancelot than Merlin. He had golden-blond hair, cropped short, intense brown eyes, and biceps that looked like they lifted more swords than beakers. If he hadn't smiled so sweetly at me when I walked in, I would have turned around and left in baffled disappointment.

"Your Majesties." Quinlan bowed to me and Torin, then focused back on me. "It's an honor to meet you, Queen Elaria."

"Nice to meet you too." I nodded to him. "So, alchemy, eh? I wouldn't think the Shining Ones needed alchemy."

"It's just science." Quinlan shrugged. "What the Shining Ones need are pretty names for common things."

"Well said." I chuckled. "So you're a scientist then?"

"I'd like to think so." He looked over at a collection of gears and parts strewn across his desk. "Though I'm not usually a bomb expert. I had to consult a few books."

"There are men in the human world who are specially trained to defuse bombs. I'm impressed that you were able to manage it with just a book." I sidled closer to the desk and looked over the carefully laid out pieces.

Most were from one of Emmet's bombs, but a few were from the detonated bomb that had been used to destroy the onyx guardians. It looked as if Torin had the area searched, and a few more pieces had been found for the alchemist to analyze.

"Books are powerful tools," Quinlan smiled warmly at me.

"Yes, it's where they hide the information," I gave him a wink, and he burst out laughing.

"Just to be clear"–Torin rumbled, and put a hand on my shoulder–"Queen Elaria and I are exclusively intimate."

"What the fuck, Torin?" I looked at him in shock.

"My apologies, Your Majesty." Quinlan bowed his head respectfully.

"He was flirting with you," Torin said. "I stopped it before it went too far. Just as you did with Oonagh."

"He didn't press up against me, bat his eyes, and swear he'd always be there for me." I grimaced.

"Men flirt differently than women," Torin folded his arms across his chest. "And you winked at him."

"It was a casual, friendly wink."

"Uh-huh."

"Begging your pardon." Quinlan held up a cautious hand. "I *was* flirting with you, Queen Elaria. King Torin was right to inform me that you were exclusive. I knew of your relationship, but not of the exclusivity. I'm sure you've realized that we Shining Ones tend to be a little more . . . free in our sexuality."

"This is not the conversation I came down here for." I cleared my throat. "Maybe we could just get back to the bomb?"

Torin chuckled.

"Of course." Quinlan gestured to the unused bomb components, all shiny and neatly laid out beside the twisted rubble of the detonated bomb. "This is not the time to discuss pleasure.

Though I would like to . . ."

"Quinlan," Torin shook his head.

"Right." Quinlan nervously straightened his tunic. "Queen Elaria, allow me to explain what I do. I am a rhodonite fey, and my base magic is understanding, especially that of new concepts or teachings. I've found an outlet for that magic in the study of science."

"Kind of ironic actually," I said.

"Yes, if you believe that science and magic are separate things," Quinlan said.

"And you don't?" I lifted a brow.

"No." Quinlan grinned wider. "I think they are closely related. Both work with the world and the energies in it. Both create amazing shifts in reality through study and application. I've spent my life combining the two and learning from their interactions."

"Interesting." I nodded. "So what has your magical science revealed to you about the copper bombs?"

Quinlan instantly looked grim. He set his stare on Torin.

"Quinlan." Torin stepped closer. "What did you find?"

"It's not what I found that bothers me." Quinlan swallowed hard. "It's what I didn't find."

Quinlan picked up a crumpled ball of copper. It looked similar to the sort of thing you get when you smash a piece of paper into a wad. Then he picked up a shiny, flat sheet of copper. He held them out for our inspection.

"These are the same components," Quinlan said. "One is predetonation, and one is post. Hold your hand over each, and tell me what you sense."

Torin immediately did as Quinlan asked, frowning when he came to the sheet. I didn't have to reach for the pieces of copper; I knew just by looking at them.

"The flat piece is charged with magic," I said, earning a surprised stare from both men. "The crumpled copper has nothing."

"Precisely right." Quinlan's brows lifted as he looked at Torin.

"Yes, Queen Elaria is as sensitive to the stones as the rumors say." Torin nodded.

"Why is this important?" I asked.

"You are, of course, familiar with the Atom Bomb?" Quinlan asked.

"The A-bomb is a world destroyer." I narrowed my eyes on Quinlan. "This bomb took out a few statues, that's all."

"Yes," Quinlan agreed. "But this bomb wasn't built to destroy physical things."

"It did a fine job of demolishing our guardians," Torin growled.

"Yes, Your Majesty," Quinlan agreed, "but only because they were full of magic."

"No." I felt my stomach drop as I reached the conclusion Quinlan was leading us to. "Not possible."

"What isn't possible?" Torin snarled. "What does this bomb destroy?"

"Magic," Quinlan whispered.

257

"Explain that." Torin's jaw clenched. "Thoroughly."

"The Atom Bomb explodes because an atom is split." Quinlan carefully placed the copper pieces back on the table. "This bomb exploded because a piece of magic was split, and the resulting wave of energy wiped out all other magic in the vicinity."

"Not thorough enough." Torin's jaw was now ticking.

"This piece of copper is infused with magic." Quinlan held up the copper sheet. "A very tiny amount, and nothing truly harmful on its own. It was placed within a metal casing"–he pointed to a shiny box–"along with another piece of charged copper. This second piece"–he pointed to a green square set aside from the other pieces–"is separated from the first by a steel strip." Quinlan pointed to a length of metal. "Then it is all encased in more protective steel, lined in even more magically charged copper. The bomb is primed by removing the separating strip, which allows the two charged pieces of copper to come together."

"One magically charged piece touches another," Torin shrugged. "I fail to see how this becomes explosive."

"The first piece is charged with common magic." Quinlan tapped the copper. "But the second is a nasty spell. It's this spell that changes everything. I don't know who contrived it, but he has created a means with which to kill any supernatural being, no matter how powerful they are. This spell unmakes magic."

"Then why bother with a bomb?" Torin asked. "Anyone could rule Tír na nÓg with such a spell."

"Ah, but it's still magic." Quinlan smiled. "Magic has its limitations, and its rules, just like science."

"The unmaking spell can't be wielded," Torin whispered.

"Correct, Your Majesty." Quinlan smiled wider. "The spell is too nasty to cast at a level to do any major harm. It would kill its caster. A small amount of it can be used to charge an item with. But even then, it dissipates quickly, as soon as it comes in contact with air. Magic is like any living thing; it does not wish to die . . . or to kill its kin."

"Air." I frowned at the corroded piece of copper. "The spell caused this piece to oxidize?"

"Yes, Your Majesty." Quinlan looked like he wanted to give me a gold star for getting the correct answer. "It discharges rapidly, especially in copper, which has a releasing property. As soon as I opened a side panel of the constraining box, the copper corroded."

"Then why choose copper?" Torin asked.

"*Because* of its quick release." Quinlan started speaking faster in his excitement. "Whoever helped this spell caster create this bomb, he was brilliant. The spell couldn't be wielded by a magic user because it would turn on them. But it also couldn't be kept in a charm because it released too quickly. So a second spell was needed to contain the first." Quinlan tapped the metal box. "And then, once that was created, they had to come up with a way to deploy the unmaking spell. A contained spell. The only way would be to destroy something in containment with it. Something to trigger the response and blow apart the bomb, freeing the unmaking spell to do its damage."

"The first piece of copper." Torin nodded.

"One little, insignificant piece of magic." Quinlan sighed. "Just barely a zap of power. But once that power was unmade, it resounded like a split atom. Luckily, it doesn't have nearly the amount of range of an Atom Bomb, but it spreads wide enough to kill a few Shining Ones or explode a few magically charged statues."

"Diabolical," Torin growled.

"I have a suggestion, sire," Quinlan said softly.

259

"Yes?" Torin's eyes flashed indigo.

"Find this Shining One and anyone associated with him," Quinlan said steadily. "Kill them all and destroy any evidence of their work."

"I intend to," Torin vowed.

Chapter Thirty-Five

Hosting a war assembly of numerous Shining One monarchs meant that Torin also had to provide royal entertainment each evening. We had feasts every night, celebrations that lasted late into the evening. It frustrated me to no end. We were preparing for war, and, in my opinion, this was not the time to be partying it up. Bad enough that we had to wait for all of our allies to gather, but to have to entertain the ones that were already there? Ridiculous.

And unsettling. Torin may be more reserved than other Shining Ones, but there were several royals visiting his court now, and they did not all share in his modesty. Every night there came a point in the revelry when the fun became more of the bedroom variety. Except without the bedroom.

The first night had been stressful for me. I'd left the feast as soon as it became evident that Torin was not going to put an end to the erotic behavior. I had looked at him in surprise, but he had merely shrugged and smiled. He said I could enjoy the show without participating in it. I shook my head at him and left. Torin hadn't followed. That was what really pissed me off. But then he'd climbed into our bed later, and made love to me for hours. So I guess I had reaped the benefits of his voyeurism. What did I care where he'd worked up his appetite? As long as he ate at home.

The second night, I stayed longer, and each night thereafter made the events a little easier to watch. It's funny how quickly you can become numb to such things. Still, I wouldn't last very long. It was hard to have a conversation while people were moaning in the background. And it was very difficult to ignore certain, shall we say, positions that the Shining Ones achieved. So there always came a time when I bailed. Torin would stay a bit longer, and then he'd release his pent-up aggression with me in private.

But I had no intentions of leaving early on this particular night. Not with Oonagh prowling the hall, her tiny breasts shoved up to show them off to their best advantage. Her hair was free and flowing down her back, way past her hips, in impossible curls. An obvious invitation to be touched. And her pale cheeks were blushed like a young girl's. She looked stunning.

I had no doubt that her clothes would be coming off in that dining hall, and she'd be removing them as close to Torin as she could get. But Oonagh wasn't the only thing keeping me there. I wanted to talk to Torin about the bombs. I'd had some time to think things over, and I wanted to discuss my thoughts with him, but we hadn't had a private moment together since we'd met with Quinlan. Ironically, the sexual activities going on around us, and our lack of participation in them, pretty much guaranteed that no one was eavesdropping on our conversation.

"I think we should sneak into the Copper Castle and find that bomb maker," I whispered to Torin. "We need to eradicate this threat before we go to war."

Torin tore his eyes away from a particularly flexible couple and looked at me. "I agree."

"Good." I let out a sigh of relief. "I was afraid you'd say something silly like, 'You're too precious to risk,' or some nonsense like that."

"Oh, *you're* not going." Torin lost interest in the entertainment immediately, and intensified his stare on me. "I will send in some of my best knights."

"To find a bomb maker who can destroy magic?" I asked him. "And to look for research? They could be up against any number of different jewel fairies, and they won't know how to spot the research. I need to go and so does Quinlan."

262

"Quinlan?" Torin growled. "You want me to send you off to Copper with Quinlan?"

"I'd be leaving you behind with Oonagh," I snapped. "This isn't about our relationship; this is about Copper having the ability to kill magic."

Torin stared at me hard, his jaw clenched and his breath coming fast. Finally he inhaled deep and let it out slowly. "You're right, this is nearly as important as preventing Galen from conquering Earth."

"Thank you," I sighed.

"But I don't like the thought of sending you out to Copper without me," Torin scowled. "And I can't go, not now."

"I know," I said gently. "You need to be here. It's okay. We'll be able to blend in easier without you."

Torin scowled deeper.

"Sorry, honey, but you're a fucking huge fairy."

Torin let out a low chuckle.

"And speaking of fucking . . . you've slept together, haven't you?" I eyed Oonagh as she fluttered about the room. All of the royals dined with us at the high table, but Oonagh had only pecked at her food and then floated off to display herself before us like she was dessert.

"Yes, of course," Torin said casually.

I shot him an annoyed look.

"I wasn't a virgin when we met, Elaria," he teased me.

"I know that," I huffed, "and neither was I. I just hoped you had better taste."

"She was available and eager, as well as beautiful." Torin shrugged. "I'm a man."

"Yeah," I huffed, "all right. But are all of your ex-girlfriends blonde?"

"Are all of your ex-boyfriends blond?" Torin shot back, and flung an annoyed glance at Banning.

"He's not my ex-boyfriend," I pointed out.

"Technically, he is," Torin argued. "You told me you believed it to be true."

I had explained my possible past with Banning, to Torin, and Torin had questioned me extensively on it. I'd been as honest as possible, telling him about the memories, and all the strange feelings I had for Banning. But I'd also told him about the relic's spell, and how I wasn't receiving any new memories of my past with Banning anymore. Torin knew better than to bring it up. Which meant something was bothering him.

"The relic broke all of my ties to Banning." I narrowed my eyes on Torin. "Why are my questions about Oonagh bothering you?"

"They're not." He looked away. I saw his glance skitter over the Snowflake Obsidian Queen.

"Uh-huh," I sighed and sat back in my seat. "Whenever you'd like to tell me the truth, I'd be happy to hear it."

"I don't lie to you," Torin said sharply. "Your questions never bother me. I love talking to you, and I love how honest we can be with each other. It's just Oonagh . . ." He scowled, and I followed his gaze to her.

She was in a passionate embrace with Sir Kean.

Wow, I didn't see that coming. I assumed she'd go for

Declan. I looked around the room, and saw why Oonagh wasn't with the Alexandrite king. He was nowhere to be found. Strange. Dinner was over, but I'd thought if anyone would stay for the evening's more intimate entertainments, it would be King Declan. He'd made it abundantly clear that he enjoyed them.

"Does that bother you?" I nodded to Oonagh and Kean.

The Howlite knight had his face buried in Oonagh's cleavage. What there was of it. Yeah, I know that was catty. Meow.

"No," Torin laughed. "If it were you down there, I'd tear Sir Kean apart. But Oonagh"–he shrugged–"I find that I don't even feel the urge to watch."

"That's it," I said in surprise. "You're upset because you don't feel anything. Do you think the relic did that? It took my past from me; maybe it took yours too."

"Possibly," Torin admitted, "but I don't think that's entirely the case. When we spoke those words to each other"–he leaned in and rubbed his cheek to mine–"and the relic bound us with our own desires, I believe that it sought to remove obstacles to our love."

"Obstacles?" I asked as my eyes sought out Banning.

He was seated beside Cerberus, who had a beautiful woman sprawled across his lap. Another stunning fey woman sat next to Banning, but he seemed to be resisting her advances. Banning caught me looking and lifted his glass to me. I lifted mine back and nodded. But then Banning downed the contents of his goblet, stood, and left the room.

"Yes, obstacles," Torin said pointedly. "Whether you wish to admit it or not, Elaria, Banning had some kind of hold on you."

"Not anymore."

265

"Precisely."

"And Oonagh had a hold on you?" I asked. "I thought you said she was convenient."

"She was"–he sighed–"at first. Then things progressed. I thought I loved her once, but then she left me."

"*She* left *you?*" I made a shocked sound.

"I know," he chuckled. "Hard to believe."

"Shut up." I rolled my eyes.

"I wanted more and she didn't." Torin shrugged. "There were issues. It's rare for monarchs of different jewels to marry. It can be difficult, but I had thought she loved me enough to make the effort. And she may have, but there was always my lineage to consider. Having an affair with the Mongrel King is one thing, but to marry him would be a different matter entirely."

"What did you just call yourself?" I growled.

"It's what *they* call me." His jaw clenched. "Because of my witch blood."

"Hold on . . . witch? You're part *witch*? That's the mix in your ancestry?" My anger faded into shock.

"Not just that." Torin closed his eyes briefly. "I didn't want to tell you this. I was afraid of what you might think."

"Tell me what?" I leaned closer, blocking out the rest of the room.

"My grandmother was raped by a witch during the war." He met my eyes steadily, but there was a tick in his cheek. "There was so much magic running rampant, she wasn't able to protect herself from pregnancy."

266

"Raped?" I breathed in horror. "And she still had the baby?"

"A shining woman would never kill a child because of its parentage," Torin scowled. "Of course she had the babe. That was my mother. Mother found happiness despite the stigma of her birth. But then, my mother is very beautiful, and it's hard to hold such things against a beautiful woman."

"Witch blood," I whispered as something tingled at the base of my mind. "That's why we work so well together."

"What?"

"Like when we rebuilt your guardians," I explained. "I could feel our magic blending. It was so smooth. I had wondered at the ease of it, and attributed it to the relic. But then we cast that spell together, on each other. I've never done that before."

"Perhaps we just meld well, all on our own." Torin began to smile.

"In so many ways." I smiled back.

"So that night"–he took my hands earnestly–"when we spoke those powerful words to each other . . ."

"Our magic blended with that of the relic." I nodded. "I think it was responding to both of our needs. My need to let go of Banning."

"And my need to let go of past wounds, to not allow them to infect what we could have together," Torin added. "I've found it difficult to trust again after Oonagh. I've cared deeply for women since then, but it always turns sour. I get jealous, and start to . . ." He shook his head.

"Start to behave barbarically?" I teased him. "Like you did that night I was taken?"

267

"Exactly." Torin made a self-deprecating sound. "I can't guarantee that I won't behave like that again, but I think the spell removed my tendency toward insane jealousy, the piece of me that had been broken by Oonagh."

"So we start fresh then, Onyx King." I slid my palm along his cheek.

"Just you and I, no past to haunt us," he agreed.

I wrapped myself around him and kissed him. I didn't care about what was happening around us or even who was watching us. In that moment, there was only Torin, our kiss, and our vow to each other.

Chapter Thirty-Six

I didn't have to wait for Torin that night. After our public display of affection, he'd taken my hand, and we'd left the hall together. Much to Oonagh's chagrin. I'd secretly snickered when I saw her push Sir Kean away petulantly, and go flouncing off. All just a show, as I'd suspected. Torin didn't even notice; he was too intent on getting me to his chambers.

Honestly, I didn't understand that kind of behavior. It was one thing to make your ex jealous by dating someone else, maybe flaunting the relationship by holding hands, something like that. But to actually make out with another man in front of the man you truly wanted, even go as far as having sex in front of your ex? I just didn't see how that would get him back.

It definitely hadn't worked on Torin, but then we'd had a little help from our friendly neighborhood relic. Maybe it would have worked on him if we hadn't woven the spell together. I guess I'll never know, so there was no use in dwelling on it. I had enough drama in my life without creating more. So I forgot all about Oonagh, and Torin's past with her, choosing instead to focus on my future with him. Especially the immediate future which involved a lot of kissing . . . and hopefully no telling.

The next morning, I woke up before Torin, relaxed and refreshed from our naughty activities of the night before. We'd been having breakfast together in his private dining room so we didn't have to be all polite and royal with the other monarchs first thing in the morning. It was kind of nice to sit there with Torin in our dressing robes and eat together. It felt nearly as intimate as sleeping together. But I needed to pop across the hall to my guest room first. I wanted to wear something of my own. I was getting tired of all the fairy gowns with their heavy fabric and sparkly adornments. Though I suppose they suited my new irremovable jewelry better than a pair of jeans and a hoodie.

I didn't care– that was exactly what I wanted to wear. I was beginning to lose myself to Tír na nÓg, Torin, and the relic. I needed to connect with something of my own, and remember who I was. So I slipped into my guest room, and then into some old jeans, a Hawaiian T-shirt, and a soft leather hoodie.

"Right, *this* is me." I breathed in the scent of Jo Malone's Red Roses, my favorite perfume, which had entrenched itself within the leather jacket. "So much better."

"Damn the diamonds!" Sara cursed as she came into the room. "You're supposed to call for me when you want to . . . What the hell are you wearing?"

"My clothes," I smiled at her.

"Are you serious right now?" Sara shook her head at me. "That frigid bitch is downstairs looking like the Goddess of Tír na nÓg, and you want to wear *that*? I had a whole outfit planned for you, an ensemble meant to take her down a few notches. You can't walk out among Shining One royals and face that pale-faced slut looking like a human."

"I appreciate your loyalty," I chuckled, "but this is something I've worn to work in. It feels like armor to me, and I need that kind of confidence if I have to deal with the Queen Bitch."

"Humph." Sara crossed her arms and considered me. Then she walked around me, taking her sweet-ass time. "You know what?" She tapped a finger to her nose. "When you look past the fact that this isn't worthy of royalty, your ensemble is quite flattering. Your posterior is shown off like no other woman's here will be. Jeans, right? That's what they're called?"

"Yes." I lifted my jacket higher to show them off. "Nothing helps an ass look finer than the right pair of jeans."

"No kidding," Sara said. "Okay, yes." She circled to the front. "But this"–she waved her hand at the loose T-shirt–"take off that atrocity immediately."

"I like it." I pouted at her. "It has local flavor."

"And *here* the local flavor is much more palatable." Sara grimaced. "Take it off, Your Majesty, or I shall tear it from you. I would sooner be whipped for insubordination than allow you to walk out that door looking like a backwoods bumpkin."

"Hawaii is not backwoods." I scowled.

"I'd never have guessed." She looked pointedly to the shirt. "What happened to coconut bras? Don't they wear those there?"

"You want me to wear a coconut bra?" I laughed. "Shall I see if I can find a grass skirt too?"

"It would be preferable to this sack of cotton."

"Show me a better option then," I challenged her.

Sara's eyes lit up, and she smirked before running out the door.

"Sara!" I called after her, but she didn't come back. "What am I supposed to do? Sit here and wait while she goes shopping?"

I flounced onto the bed, and wrapped the sweet-smelling leather tighter around me. Actually, I didn't have long to wait. Sara was back within minutes, brandishing a piece of crimson silk like a flag of war. I narrowed my eyes on it.

"What is that?" I stood.

"Your ticket to winning over the entire male population of

271

Tír na nÓg." She tossed it at me.

"Also known as a bustier." I grimaced at it. "You called Oonagh a slut, and yet you want me to wear a bustier? This is the core piece of slutty outfits."

"You have these on Earth?" Sara scowled. "I just tore the skirt off a gown for you. This is the bodice. I thought it was something new. Something exciting and creative."

"It probably is," I hastened to assure her, "in Tír na nÓg. On Earth, they have something similar which is either called a bustier or a corset, depending on how tight you lace it."

"Your tits will look fantastic in it," Sara said boldly. "And with your ass on display, the men will be salivating. Especially since you're *not* a slut, and they all know that's the most they're ever going to see of you. Unlike some women . . . I won't name any names." She made a coughing sound that turned into, "Oonagh," cough, cough, "who tosses her skirts up as soon as the cake is cleared."

"I have to say, I'm surprised at your attitude." I cocked my head at her. "I thought all of the Shining Ones viewed sex with an extremely open mind."

"You mean you thought we were all a bunch of debauched degenerates." She grimaced.

"Can you blame me?" I asked. "If this is how your celebrations go."

"Not everywhere"–she gave me a churlish look–"as you well know. Our king doesn't approve of such displays, and a lot of us came to his court simply because we feel similarly."

"Seriously?" I blinked at her in shock. "I had no idea."

"Sex is natural," she amended. "But it's also sacred. I don't

272

think it's something that should be flaunted about like a new pair of earrings. It's a private treasure."

"I agree," I said seriously. "I knew I liked you for a reason, Sara."

"Well"–she cleared her throat awkwardly–"do you like me enough to try on the bodice?"

"I suppose," I sighed, and shucked off my jacket and shirt.

I pulled on the bodice, and Sara quickly laced up the back for me. Then I turned to look in the mirror, expecting something sort of sexy. It would be under the hoodie, so it shouldn't be so . . . holy canaries!

"Is this a magical bodice?" I gaped at the mounds of flesh reflected in the mirror. "I look like I've grown two cup sizes!"

"It's all in the way you lace it," Sara smirked. "You gotta tighten it from the center out. What you have is not as important as how you display it."

"Evidently." I turned and admired the way it nipped in my waist to Elizabethan proportions, how the laces trailed over my butt, and how the relic poured jewels across my breasts in the most intriguing way. "Damn . . . just . . . damn." I pushed my fist out to Sara for a bump, "Well done."

"What are you doing?" Sara eyed my fist.

"You're supposed to make a fist and knock yours into mine," I explained, keeping my fist out there. "It's called a fist bump."

"Okay." Sara hesitantly followed my instructions. "And now what?"

"That's it," I said. "It's like an expression of victory between two people."

"Oh"–Sara thought about it–"so it's like a physical huzzah?"

"Yes, it's a physical huzzah," I chuckled.

"Then, thank you, Your Majesty." Sara held out her fist.

"Huzzah, Sara." I bumped it back. "Now"–I swung on the leather hoodie–"what do you think?"

"Most excellent, Your Majesty." Sara smirked. "In fact, I hope this becomes the new fashion. I'd like to wear one myself."

"I'll bring you back some jeans when I go home," I said casually, but her face fell, and she just stared at me blankly. "Oh shit, did I say something wrong? Am I not supposed to do that?"

"No, it's just . . ." Sara blinked. "You'd bring me a gift? Me? I'm just your maid."

"Oh please," I pushed her shoulder. "You aren't *just* anything, and you know it. You're kind of awesome and you're my friend."

"I'm your . . ." She blinked again. "I'm a huge bitch! Why would you want me to be your friend?"

"Cause you're the right kind of bitch, and I need to hang with my own kind." I hugged her. "Plus, you made me feel welcome here. Thank you, Sara."

"You're welcome, Your Majesty," she sniffled.

"Don't go all crybaby on me," I teased her.

"Oh please"–she mimicked me–"I was just trying to make you feel special."

"And she's back." I headed to the door. "Let's see how Torin likes my new look."

Chapter Thirty-Seven

Torin was already gone when I got back to his bedroom. He'd left me some breakfast in the dining room, and a note asking me to meet him at the training field. After eating, I went downstairs to find him.

He wasn't with the troops this time, but standing on the rise I had used to view the training before. The other royals were with Torin, as were the commanders of the armies, going over the maneuvers they had mapped out. If we went with King Edmond's more sneaky approach, we'd have to change our tactics. But it was good to have contingency plans.

By the time I crested the rise, I'd completely forgotten that I had dressed differently. I was just so comfortable in my old jeans, and the jacket covered most of the corset. With my hands stuck deep in the leather pockets, I felt ready for anything the day brought me.

Except for the utter amazement I was greeted with.

"What is it?" I looked around at the shocked faces.

"What are you wearing?" Oonagh sneered.

"And where can I get my own?" Queen Teagan swished her way over to me in her heavy skirts.

"Nice bustier, Lady Marmalade," Cerberus teased.

"I felt like being comfortable today." I shrugged. "These are my normal clothes. With exception of the bodice, which my maid, Sara, created for me this morning. She refused to let me out of the room in the T-shirt I'd been wearing."

"Who is this woman?" Torin slid his hand along the inner edge of my jacket, casually pushing it open and inhaling sharply in appreciation as he did so. "I must thank her personally. She deserves jewelry. Lots of jewelry."

"And please ask her to inspire more women to dress in this fashion." King Declan subtly angled his head to check out my ass.

"It's Sara." I pushed Torin's hand away with a grin, and ignored Declan's ogling. I'd become accustomed to it within hours of his arrival. The man was a typical fairy flirt. "You know Sara, the snarky one. She's wonderful."

"I need a Sara," Queen Teagan said to her husband.

"Yes, my love," King Edmond agreed as he stared at my ensemble, "you most certainly do."

"Or you could just buy clothing from her," I offered.

"Buy clothing from her?" Teagan perked up. "Yes, that sounds easier. Please introduce us later, Queen Elaria. I'd like to place an order." She looked over the delicate beads of faceted onyx sewn along the hemline of the bodice, and added, "A large order."

"It's obscene," Oonagh sniffed.

"Can she make these breeches as well?" Teagan ignored Oonagh completely.

"Um, I don't know." I looked down at my jeans. "But I'm sure you can get someone to purchase them for you in the human world."

"Ah, perfect." Teagan kissed my cheek. "Thank you."

"My pleasure."

276

"Not as much as it is mine." Torin slid his arm around my waist, inside the jacket. "Is this what you were doing this morning? I woke up lonely."

"Oh no, what a tragedy." I gave him a quick kiss.

"It is. Especially now that I see this." Torin lowered his face to the leather and breathed in. "Sweet stones, what is that smell?"

"My perfume," I said. "I hadn't thought to wear it lately, but I have a bottle in the bag Cerberus brought me. If you like it, I'll start using it again."

"I like it," Torin declared.

"If we are quite finished discussing women's clothing and perfumes, could we get back to the war?" A man I hadn't met spoke with irritation.

He had ebony hair pulled back into a severe club, an indolent stare of soft green, and skin that shone like creamy porcelain. A little taller than Torin, with the build of most fey men, he seemed even thinner because of his height. He nearly dwarfed the woman beside him, but he didn't diminish her in any other way. She was brightly beautiful, with glaring amber hair, pale skin, and warm, caramel eyes.

"Yes, of course," Torin said smoothly, steering me over to the couple. "Queen Elaria of Song, may I introduce you to King Parthalon of Jade, and the Duchess Branna. They've just arrived this morning."

"Pleased to meet you." I nodded to them.

"And you as well," Branna said warmly, while her husband just nodded.

"The others are due to arrive later today, and a few more

277

this week," Torin informed me. "Then our army will be complete."

"So we can set out soon?" I asked in surprise.

"I'm hoping to be ready within a week, maybe two," Torin agreed.

"Wonderful." I eased toward the map-strewn table. "So we're going with the divided, and hopefully unseen, approach?"

"Yes, we've all agreed that King Edmond's idea was best," King Odran of Howlite tapped the map. "We are just now resolving who shall march in from what direction."

"This is wrong." Oonagh pushed in beside Torin, and tapped a spot on the map. "Tiger's Eye moved over here, beside Turquoise, when Queen Moirin married King Sean."

"When did that happen?" Torin asked her.

"Two months ago." Oonagh shrugged. "Your map is out of date."

"All right." Torin picked up a discarded pencil and crossed things out, then scribbled others in. There was a bit of discussion between him and Oonagh over which kingdom had moved where. "All right, does anyone else know of any discrepancies on this map?"

No one did.

"Your kingdoms move?" Banning asked the question before I had a chance to.

"Sometimes," King Declan answered. "If monarchs unite in marriage, and they happen to be rulers of two types of gems, their kingdoms will shift into place beside each other. The other kingdoms will move to accommodate them."

"How the hell does that happen?" Banning scowled at the

278

map.

"Magic," Oonagh said as if it were obvious.

"Of course." I rolled my eyes at Banning, and he chuckled.

"Does that mean most royal marriages occur between rulers of the same stones?" I asked Declan.

"Yes," Declan said. "Most often, when two people ascend to a royal status under the same gem, they are drawn together. We believe it's a way for the jewels to let us know that we'd be compatible. They're usually right."

I remembered what Onyx had told me, about how the stones chose their rulers. So they chose couples as well. Fascinating. Little jewel matchmakers.

"And what happens when they're wrong?" I wondered. I could believe in magic predicting compatibility, but love was a tricky thing. Tricky, and sometimes fickle.

"War usually," Queen Teagan answered. "There can be only one kingdom per gemstone. If there are two rulers who refuse to unite, they must determine who the stronger is. The winner rules."

"And what then?" I asked. "Does the other have to die?"

"Absolutely," Oonagh scowled at me. "To leave a royal alive after they've been defeated would be both cruel and stupid."

"How savage." I looked at Torin. "Good thing there isn't an onyx queen."

"Yes." Torin's hot gaze flowed over me. "But I'd kill anyone to keep you beside me."

My breath caught. I stared at Torin for a second, fire infusing my limbs, before I answered, "And I for you."

Then he kissed me. Passionately. And I didn't give a hot damn that all those royals were watching and waiting on us. We had just declared that we'd kill for each other. I think some passion was required.

"How romantic," Duchess Branna sighed.

"Oh stop." Cerberus rolled his eyes, "I'm going to fucking cry."

Chapter Thirty-Eight

"I don't like this," Torin growled, his eyes straying to Banning.

"I know, but it's the best we can do," I slid into his embrace.

It was late, and all the royals were asleep except for us. We stood inside the stables, the sound of shifting, sleeping horses soft in the background. My mount was already saddled; the poor beast wouldn't be getting any rest for a while. He was a ballach, a type of speckled, fairy horse, and he was waiting patiently for me beside his friends, who already had their riders in the saddle.

We were headed to Copper, and Torin was staying behind. However, I had invited Banning to join us. I needed some extra muscle, someone of the nonshining variety, and Cerberus was too damn big to be stealthy. So I was taking Banning, as well as a group of Torin's knights, and the alchemist, Quinlan. Torin had agreed to the collection of companions for me, but he wasn't happy about it.

"If you have to kill the whole damn castle to get out of there alive, do it," Torin whispered to me. "Come back breathing and whole, Elaria."

"Just because you said so," I teased.

"Good." He smiled and set me away from him. "I love you."

"I love you too." I kissed him quickly, then went to mount my horse. One last wave to Torin, and our group headed out of the courtyard as quietly as possible.

The gate guards had been warned, so they carefully creaked the massive gates open for us, and my party snuck out into the night. We didn't want to tell the other monarchs about the copper bombs for several reasons, the biggest of which being the fact that rulers, especially those of the fey variety, tended to be power hungry. We were afraid that once the idea was planted in their minds, they might attempt to recreate the weapon for themselves. It was best to keep knowledge of the bombs to as limited a group as possible.

As the night closed in around us, the dim lights of the dreaming Onyx Castle fading behind us, I wondered if the humans would have banded together and sent a secret team to destroy all evidence of the A-bomb if they'd known what it would do to Hiroshima. Sadly, I didn't think so. Perhaps it was things like this that made Galen believe he'd be a better ruler of Earth than the humans were. I wasn't sure if I disagreed with that perspective. Unfortunately, the Earth belonged to them, for better or for worse, and the rest of us had to accept that.

Unless the Beneath rose up and claimed the world.

I gave a start as the thought struck me. Where had that come from? When had I become a revolutionary? The Beneath functioned well in the shadows. We supernaturals didn't want to be known, much less rule. Or, if we did rule, we'd prefer it to be under the guise of humanity. Even then, things could go bad. A race of supernaturals had been worshiped once. They had dominated the world, and demanded sacrifice in return. But humans are a plucky lot. They may not have as much power as the gods, but what they lacked in magic, they made up for in tenacity and numbers. The gods were overthrown.

Gods don't like to talk about it. Mostly, they say that humans slowly forgot about them. But the truth is, humanity rebelled. They chose a select few to worship, those who promised an utopian afterlife without demanding a lot in return. Then they cast the others aside. "Thou shalt have no other gods before me" was a commandment created by humans, not Jehovah. It was a way for humankind to remind themselves never to let the gods return to power. At least not in such great numbers.

So the magical masses slunk into the shadows. Not literally of course. We like sunshine just as much as anyone else. But we hid our magical natures, and we discovered that it's much better this way. The Beneath was formed, a secret society of supernaturals that spans the globe. We have our own government, our own rules, even our own territories. There are whole islands inhabited only by members of the Beneath. I should know; I was raised on one.

The point is, the Beneath likes things as they are, and unless humans try to destroy the world completely, I doubted that we would ever interfere with their rule.

"How about here?" Banning asked. "This is still Jade, right?"

"Yes, sir," one of our onyx knights answered him. "We've got at least ten miles before we leave the Jade Kingdom."

"Does this look like an acceptable camping site?" I asked the same knight, waving my hand toward a clearing just off the road.

"Let me scout it, Your Majesty." The knight angled his horse into the thick jungle, and took a look around the space that we'd indicated. He waved a hand back to us, urging us in.

"Looks like you can finally get some sleep, sweetheart." I gave my horse's neck a pat.

"I'm looking forward to it, honey," Banning teased as he rode past me.

Chapter Thirty-Nine

The Copper Kingdom was on the other side of Relic Mountain. Which meant that we had to go through the butt-numbing journey to the mountain, and then ride beyond it. It wasn't difficult terrain though, and we didn't encounter any aggression. We were able to blend in with the common inhabitants of the kingdoms easily. The fairy villages were bustling places, full of life and an assortment of Shining Ones. The few times we passed people on the road, people going about their business transporting wares or produce, they barely glanced at us.

I didn't feel a sense of unease until we reached Relic Mountain. Though really, that was an inaccurate name for it now. We rode out onto the barren stretch, hooves echoing over the dry ground, and my eyes shot to the temple which was all that remained of the witch-made mountain. It looked lifeless, empty, waiting for its heart to return. The glass doors were shut, and I knew they wouldn't open to anyone, not even me. It was an abandoned place, and would remain so until my work was done.

Even our horses sensed the emptiness and edged away from the temple, so we had to skirt the edges of the desolate circle until we made it out to Copper. If not for the road, I wouldn't have realized we'd left the relic's domain. The land shifted subtly into an open region of jagged slopes and even more jagged flora. It reminded me of an American desert, except sharper looking, and more vivid. The sheer slices of mountains were striped with crimson, mustard, and viridian. Even the earth was speckled with color, glints of metal within the soil. Massive blooms spread open like cabbages, their petals brighter than any sunset. They dug into the dry dirt with slick roots, and nestled in rock crevices. There weren't any cacti, but there were rubbery leafed plants ringed with thorns, and bushes hiding burrowing creatures. Enough similarities to be an alien echo of the Southwest.

Though this land was a bit more hospitable than the Painted Desert. There were vast lakes spotting the terrain in an impossible juxtaposition. As if Tír na nÓg was turning its nose up at the law of nature. Though the more I looked, the more I realized that Copper wasn't an arid kingdom. There was moisture in the air and more plant life than you'd expect to find in a desert. There were even farms, with rows of crops flourishing in the sandy soil. I finally gave up and asked Quinlan about it.

"The landscape is a mask." Quinlan shrugged. "If you dig but an inch past the topsoil, you'll find the rich earth of Tír na nÓg beneath. No matter how the monarchs wish to design their kingdoms, they cannot change the foundation upon which they lie. They can only work with it. So if you desire a stark vision such as this"–he waved his hand out–"then you must gather the water and force most of it underground."

"The monarchs design the land?" Banning asked.

"They work with the stones to come up with an environment beneficial to them both," Quinlan explained. "This landscape is most comfortable for copper."

"Bizarre." Banning shook his head.

"Not at all," Quinlan protested. "Jewels are affected by several conditions, including temperature, pressure, surrounding deposits, and the amount of space they have to grow in. Jewels formed in Tír na nÓg feel these conditions like you and I would feel a chill or the warmth of a fire. Certain landscapes can be ideal for one stone and yet detrimental to others."

"So the relationship between monarchs and jewels is a form of symbiosis," I noted. "The jewel provides power, and the ruler provides sanctuary."

"Precisely." Quinlan beamed. "You have the mind of a scientist, Your Majesty."

Banning gave Quinlan an odd look, but he remained silent throughout the rest of the journey through Copper. Our timing was a little off, and we neared the Copper Castle around midday. Night was the standard time for infiltrating a castle. So we decided to double back to a small town we'd passed through, and get some refreshment while we waited for dusk. Our horses were in need of some rest as well. Plus, if we could be subtle about it, we might even be able to gather some intel from the locals.

We chose a modest, but clean looking, establishment, more of a bar than a restaurant. I'd call it a tavern, but the Shining Ones weren't that medieval. They did dress more typically of that human time period, but they were just as advanced as the human realm was. In some ways, they were more advanced. I guess "pub" would be a good word for it. It looked like something you might walk into in the United Kingdom. Except for all the magic flying around of course.

I'd become used to it, pretty much immune to the sight of Shining Ones doing their daily chores with a little assistance from their stones. Banning seemed just as numb to it as I, adroitly maneuvering around a hovering drink as he took lead through the main room. Much more startling than the magic, were the human machines. A coffee maker sat behind the bar, gurgling away, and a jukebox squatted in one corner, belting out some very old songs. I blinked at the surrealism as we casually took over an empty table, and waited to be approached by a waitress.

When she came by, I gave Banning a look, and we both angled our faces downward, so the Shining One wouldn't notice our nonfey features. We needn't have worried. The beleaguered barmaid barely glanced at us, taking our orders with an air of bored indifference before heading back to the bar. And she didn't return either. Our food and drinks floated out to us, just as everyone else's did.

"Should I make some rounds, ask how things fare in the kingdom?" Sir Hugh asked me.

"No, hang back." I glanced to the side, where a group of men were avidly conversing. "I think if we're quiet, we may be able to simply listen in, without drawing attention to ourselves."

"I can hear the conversations at the back of the room, if you're interested," Banning said.

I looked up at him in surprise. "I didn't realize blooder hearing was so good."

Banning smirked. "*Old* blooder hearing is."

"All right." I agreed. "You listen to the conversations we can't hear, and we'll focus on the closer ones."

We all set to eating and drinking as quietly as possible, while focusing intently on the people around us. Mainly, it was just your average talk: harvests, women, cattle. But then I caught the trace of annoyance in someone's tone, and I honed in on his words.

"Why's it so damn important anyway?" the man grumbled. "Guarding an old farmhouse seems stupid."

"King Lorcan probably has a mistress out there," another man chuckled.

"Pft," the first man scoffed. "Ain't no women going in there, and ain't no royal mistress gonna accept that for a home. There's something devious going on there, you mark me!"

"It's probably that crazy loup the king hired to fiddle with human magic."

"No such thing as human magic."

"There is too. They call it science."

287

"Not magic," the man grumbled.

"Still, I seen lots of copper going into that farmhouse." The first guy was talking again. "Who knows what's going on out there? They could be fashioning poisons to kill the Onyx King. You know that King Lorcan still wants him dead."

"He ain't gonna mess with King Torin," another man scoffed. "Lorcan's got his queen. What does King Torin have? Nothing."

"I heard he's got a beautiful witch for a mistress," a man said wistfully.

"No, she's a siren," another corrected him.

"Whatever she may be, the Onyx King has his own cunny, and he don't want our queen anymore. King Lorcan's gotta know that."

"That probably just makes him madder," another said with a wise tone. "Poison. Must be. He'll send it in with a maid and have her sneak it in Torin's food."

"How can you make poison with copper?" another man scoffed.

"Can."

"Can't."

"What farmhouse are you talking about?" another guy asked, and I tensed expectantly.

"You know, the one that old Mavis abandoned when she went to live with her daughter in Opal. Just down the road to the castle, and off to the right. It's perfect for the king's poison-making experiments, as close as it is to Copper Castle, while still being outside the guardians. The queen will never suspect."

"The poor woman," another man said. "Rejected by one man, and coveted by another, to the point of being a prisoner."

"Hush," someone hissed. "What if the king has spies here?"

I felt their stares shift to us. We must have been the only strangers in the room. I lowered my face a little more and tried to be as unobtrusive as possible. Sir Carrick called to the waitress for another round, and the inspection from the table beside us ceased. I looked up at Banning, and we shared a victorious smile.

Chapter Forty

The farmhouse was fairly easy to find using those convenient directions we'd overheard. It wasn't in the best shape, tiles clinging desperately to the roof in places and windows dusty from neglect. The crops looked as abandoned as the house, overgrown to a state impossible to harvest. Each plant was entangled so thoroughly with its neighbors that their orderly rows had been completely obscured. Fruit rotted on the ground below, unseen but making its presence known through its death stench. A copper cistern stood to the side of this wilderness, corroded to deep umber with splotches of turquoise, like some kind of alien fungus.

We left the horses tethered to some gnarled trees and crept up to the shambling building in the deepening twilight. The lavender light cast everything into shades of purple and made the shadows seem more menacing. I ignored the sensation and scuttled around a boulder, peering at the guards posted around the perimeter.

"I think I can just sing them to sleep," I whispered.

"Wasn't the whole point to get rid of any who might know about the bombs?" Banning reminded me.

"But they're just guards." I didn't like the idea of killing men for nothing. "They probably don't know what's going on inside that building."

"*We* don't know what's going on inside that building," Sir Hugh muttered. "I think it might be wise to reconnoiter a bit, Your Majesty."

"Valid." I grimaced. "But your reconnoitering could catch

the guards' attention."

"Then you may sing your lullaby," Hugh said.

"All right, Sir Hugh," I agreed. "Have at it."

Hugh was more stealthy than I'd given him credit for. I didn't see him sneaking up on the building, and I knew to look for him. Not a single bush shook or rock slid to give away his location, and none of the guards even twitched. Hugh was back within ten minutes.

"There's a horde of copper inside, along with some suspicious pieces of metal, and some fully assembled bombs," Hugh reported. "And those men were right; there is also a loup present. We'll need to restrain him as soon as possible, or he might make use of one of his creations. But I saw no others in the building."

"A werewolf scientist." I shook my head. "I guess there are stranger things."

"Like a Shining One scientist?" Quinlan smirked.

"Maybe," I said with a grin. "All right, let me just send some relaxing vibes over to these soldiers. I'll put them to sleep, and then we can investigate. If it looks as if they're complicit, we'll kill them."

The men nodded their agreement.

I began to hum softly, visualizing the men across the field from us falling gently into slumber. Then I sang Brahms's "Lullaby," as sweetly as any mother tucking her children in at night. The relic glowed gently, gathering and intensifying my magic before sending it shooting out to the soldiers. They didn't even make it to the second line. I lifted my brows in surprise.

"Well done, Elaria," Banning noted. "All right, let's go.

Maybe we can get out of this kingdom before morning."

"You forget; we still need to kill the king," Carrick reminded us.

"Another king to murder," I whispered to myself.

"You had no problem killing those blooders." Banning slid a glance at me as we snuck quickly and quietly up to the farmhouse.

"They were running across a golf course ready to murder anything in their path." I shrugged. "It's a little easier to kill a man intent on killing you than to murder one who doesn't even know it's coming."

"Fair enough." Banning reached for the handle of the backdoor while the rest of us reached for our magic.

Then Banning held up his fingers: one, two, three. He jerked the door open, and we all piled inside like a black ops team. The loup was sitting at his desk, a lamp hanging directly above him, leaving the rest of the room in deep shadow. He was taken completely unaware, and we had him restrained within seconds. But he wasn't upset in the least. In fact, he started laughing. As I'd already learned from my experience with Torin, your target smiling was a bad sign. Laughing had to be ten times worse.

And it was.

"The Queen of Song." A man walked out of the shadows on my right, as if he'd been formed of them.

He was around the size of our knights, a muscled, but slim, Shining One. Dirty-blond hair, appearing a little more on the dirty side in the meager illumination of the farmhouse, hung about his shoulders. It was too dark to see his eyes, but I caught a metallic gleam when the lamp glow hit them. His skin was the nutty tan of a laborer, but I doubted that this man had seen a day's work in his life. He smirked at me, holding a copper bomb aloft like an apple at an archery contest. The fingers of his other hand gripped the steel strip that would activate it.

"King Lorcan?" I lifted a brow. "What a pleasant surprise."

"Is it?" Lorcan laughed. "And here I thought you'd be terrified to find yourself trapped by the Copper King. You enjoyed my little game then?"

"Those men were plants." I felt my teeth grind together. "Damn it, I should have known that was too easy."

"I had thought you'd be a little wiser." King Lorcan tsked me.

"Morons." The loup, who was the biggest man in the room, and had all the attractiveness of a worn-out, carny hawker, rolled his eyes and chuckled.

"You shouldn't have even known we were here." I defended us, as if a crazy fairy king wasn't casually holding a magical A-bomb.

"Oh, that's adorable." Lorcan smirked. "Little spellsinger, I knew the moment you stepped foot in my kingdom. I have spies everywhere. I knew when Emmet was discovered that it would be only a matter of time before you came to kill me. To *try* and kill me. I've had men posted at my borders ever since. They simply followed you to that tavern, and directed you straight to me."

"Fuck this." Banning, who had a knife to the loup's throat, growled. "Put the bomb down or I kill the wolf."

"Kill him." Lorcan shrugged. "I don't give a shit. He's already showed me how to make the bombs."

"What?" The loup stopped laughing. "God damn you, Lorcan. You need"

Banning called Lorcan's bluff, but instead of slicing his throat, he clutched the wolf tighter and bit him. The loup gurgled out the rest of his sentence, grasping at the air with hands shifting into claws and trying vainly to remove Banning from his neck. Banning stabbed the loup in the side as he continued to savage his throat. Our knights tensed as Banning drank his fill, then tossed the dead loup to the floor between me and Lorcan. The body landed with a heavy thud, its eyes managing to stare up at Lorcan in accusation.

"He was our only means for negotiation," Quinlan hissed at Banning.

"We had to kill him anyway," Banning wiped away the blood around his mouth, then licked his fingers. "And he's hardly our only leverage." He looked pointedly at me.

"Oh yes." Lorcan smiled sweetly, as if there weren't a dead man lying at his feet. "I've heard all about your talent. Go ahead, try and sing your spell before I pull this piece of steel. I don't think you'll be successful. And in case you haven't noticed, this is one of our newer, larger bombs. It has a radius of twenty feet. More than enough to kill all of you, while leaving me completely out of harm's way."

I noted the expanse of the room, and that the bastard was right.

"Now, back yourselves outside," Lorcan nodded to the door. "Slowly."

I looked at the others and gave them a slight nod. "Stay together," I whispered, "as close as possible."

"Nice job with my soldiers." Lorcan smirked. "So kind of you not to kill them. I never expected the Spellsinger to have a soft side. There." He nodded toward an open space in front of the farmhouse. "Go."

294

"I'm going to rush him," Banning whispered to me. "Grab the others and run."

"Banning"

"I can't let you die again, Ellie." Banning's eyes were wild. "Please just do it."

"Shut up and trust me, Banning," I hissed. "All of you, when the time comes, you gather around me tight."

Banning's eyes went wide, and he gave me a quick nod. Our knights also agreed, and started to look a little more hopeful.

"Stop," Lorcan called. "That's far enough. I almost hate to kill you so quickly. You've come so far, after all. I'll have to take comfort in the fact that Torin will suffer when he receives your head as a gift."

"Killing her will ensure your own death," Carrick said bravely. "If King Galen succeeds, it will"

"Yes, yes." Lorcan huffed, pulled the metal strip, and tossed the bomb at us. "She's the hope of all the worlds." He rolled his eyes.

I cast my hands out before me, already prepared with a visualization of a shield, and punched out with magic and music. I shouted the lyrics to Ashford & Simpson's "Solid." It wasn't the most pleasing rendition, but it did the job. The relic flared, magic rushed through the jewels at my throat, and the bomb bounced off an invisible barrier, heading straight back to its sender. Lorcan gaped in shock as it hit the ground a few inches away from his feet and burst open in a blinding pulse of murdered magic. I kept singing, yanking the men into a huddle as I envisioned an impenetrable shield around us.

We should have been far enough away from the blast, but I wasn't taking any chances. The relic flared even brighter, so bright,

I could still see its glow when I closed my eyes against the explosion. I heard Lorcan scream, then several others joined him, but the shouts were brief, cut short like someone pressed stop on a stereo.

I sang on, clutching the men tighter, focusing on that unbreakable shield until I felt like we were safe. I finally risked a glance, and saw the world calm around us. I stopped singing, the relic fading into rest. The men slowly fell away from me, a flower opening to a new day. We stumbled to our feet and then just stared about us in shock.

The ground before us was littered with bloody chunks of flesh and bone . . . and other things I don't even want to mention. The blast may have stopped short of us, but the carnage had spewed right up to my shield, forming a gory arc over the dry earth. The soil was already soaking up the blood, turning into garish mud. It had a lot of blood to drink several of Lorcan's soldiers had been caught in the blast along with him.

I walked through the carnage on unsteady feet, trying to breathe through my mouth, and then deciding that tasting the gore was worse than smelling it. I cringed at the way the earth sucked at each of my footsteps, and took a moment to tap off the mud when I reached dry soil. Bloody earth splattered, mixed with chunks of King Lorcan. I swallowed the bile rising in my throat and went steadily forward. Five sleeping soldiers remained, whole and peaceful. Completely undisturbed by the bomb or its repercussions. I sighed resignedly and looked at Banning.

"Is it dinner time, darling?" Banning smiled viciously at me.

"Bon appétit." I grimaced. The onyx knights gave me hard looks, and I stared them down. "Would you prefer I burn them alive? Or you could stab them in their hearts?" The knights looked away. "Yeah, Banning at least can benefit from their deaths. After that demonstration from their king, I just can't take the risk of

296

leaving them alive."

"We understand, Your Majesty." Carrick said softly as the sound of Banning's feeding filtered over to us. His eyes fluttered, but met my stare. "And I realize that you have the interests of all the realms in mind. The threat must be eliminated. That's the reason we're here."

"I'm glad you feel that way, Sir Carrick." I smiled ruefully. "Because I'm going to need your help gathering up the remaining bombs."

Chapter Forty-One

"What have you done?"

The men from the pub stood on the road before us, blocking our way into the copper city. We were just leaving the farmhouse, and it looked as if they'd come to check on their king. Finding him in thousands of pieces was probably unexpected.

"I've killed your king," I said succinctly.

Sir Carrick made a choking sound.

"Where is he?" One of the copper fairies looked around the bloody field with horror. "I see only a few soldiers. Where are the rest of them?"

"You'll find them in front of the farmhouse." My voice went cold and casual.

I didn't want to kill these men, but I needed to know if they had any knowledge of the bombs before I let them go.

"Don't play games with us." Another man strode forward, his palm starting to glow with the distinctive warning of magic to come. "Where is our king?"

"Everywhere." I spread my arms out to indicate the mess, and smiled viciously. "He has become one with his kingdom."

"Are you . . ." Another man stumbled back. "You mean that this . . . ? Impossible. No magic can do that."

The other men looked just as shocked.

"I think they're okay," I said to Banning. "What do you think?"

Banning stared at the terrified men hard, then looked at me. "I think they're ignorant. They can live."

Those cryptic words sent the men running, and when we started riding after them, they scattered, leaving the road entirely to scamper off toward shelter. We kept going, keeping our pace fast enough to discourage anyone from attempting to stop us. And we didn't slow our pace until we were well past the relic's temple.

We had destroyed every piece of evidence we'd found in that farmhouse. Every book, every note, everything. The only exception were the materials. We just couldn't carry all that metal back to Onyx. But they were just scraps of steel and copper; no one could figure out how to make a magic-killing bomb simply from looking at them. The copper was dormant, uncharged, and the steel was just metal. So we left them behind, and deployed all of the bombs within the farmhouse.

We figured that discharging the bombs in the building took care of two problems: the bombs, and any evidence that we might have overlooked. We must have found everything though, because after the bombs had detonated, we went back inside to collect the wreckage. The only casualties, beyond the bombs themselves, had been the fairy lights, which had exploded into dust. It was a relief to know for certain that no one else had been concealing themselves in the shadows like Lorcan.

So all that was left of King Lorcan's nasty weapon was debris, and even that we'd taken, to make sure no one analyzed it, as Quinlan had done. He was the one carrying the remnants, and he promised to have them melted down after we made it safely back to Onyx.

If we made it safely back to Onyx.

Two hours after we'd left the Copper Kingdom, we heard

rapid hoof-beats behind us. I looked to the others, and we veered off the road as one unit, taking cover behind a copse of quartzwood. I dismounted, and crept closer to the road with Sir Carrick and Banning. The others kept the horses quiet behind us. It wasn't long before we spotted them, a group of mounted knights, heading in our direction with deadly intent.

"Looks like Queen Eileen has been informed of her husband's death," Carrick whispered. "Shall we engage, Your Majesty?"

"No, leave this to me." I closed my eyes, and focused on the result I wanted.

The relic started to glow even before I began to sing. We were becoming so aligned that it knew when I needed it. I started to sing Bonnie Tyler's "Total Eclipse of the Heart." My voice filtered out of our cover to compel both men and beasts into changing their motivations. The horses reared, and the men floundered. I called out softly to them, coercing gently, using the words in their most basic definitions. The knights flailed as their mounts turned around in circles. The song turned sorrowful and plaintive, seeping in deeper. Into their conscious mind and then subconscious. The knights finally got control of their horses. They turned them about and headed back where they had come from.

"They're leaving," Carrick whispered. "Well done, Your Majesty."

"Thank you, Carrick." I looked at the others. "Now, let's get out of here. We need a place to camp for the night."

Chapter Forty-Two

"I'm sorry that I didn't have faith in you back there," Banning said.

We rode until we were within Turquoise, and made camp in the same site I'd used once with Torin. The horses were grazing near the lake, and we had our sleeping mats out, preparing for bed. I had somehow ended up between Banning and Quinlan.

"What do you mean?" I slipped beneath my blankets, my exhausted body flopping and twitching its way into relaxation.

"When we were faced with that Copper son of a bitch," Banning growled. "When I was going to rush him instead of following your lead."

"You didn't even know I had a lead," I said. "Banning, you were going to sacrifice yourself for us. Don't apologize for that. It was admirable."

"Even if it was unnecessary," Quinlan muttered.

"Quinlan." I gave him an annoyed look.

"Sorry"–Quinlan shrugged–"but you're the Song Queen. You're wearing the relic of the witches. I wasn't worried for a moment."

"Well, I was," Banning growled. "She's been abducted while wearing that necklace. It's not all powerful."

"Valid," I whispered before Quinlan could say anything. "You're right, Banning. Things could have gone badly, relic or no. We had to do some horrible things today, and you were a huge help. So, thank you for that."

"You're welcome," Banning lay back down. "I'm glad I was there with you."

"What we did was done for the greater good," Quinlan said. "We couldn't allow anyone to have such power."

"We should have kept the bombs," one of the knights muttered.

"Who said that?" I sat up and looked around the camp.

"It was I, Your Majesty," Sir Gerard admitted.

"And would you like to explain that comment?" I asked him.

"It's just that those bombs would have given us an advantage in the war," Gerard said.

The other men muttered angrily, but I was the one to answer Gerard.

"Those bombs were a threat to everyone who has magic within them," I said gently. "You saw how easily it was turned against Lorcan. Can you imagine throwing one out into a war? It's too unpredictable. Not to mention that as soon as we used one, everyone who was a witness to it would become a liability. They would see the possibilities in the bombs. If Quinlan could figure it out, there's bound to be another Shining One who could. Then every kingdom would have them, if for no other reason than to protect themselves against the other kingdoms that had bombs. Tír na nÓg would become dangerous for any supernatural."

I watched the gravity of it descend upon Gerard, his face going pale in the moonlight. Then he nodded; no other words were necessary.

"Uh, actually . . ." Quinlan cleared his throat, and we all

looked at him in shock. "I still have most of the bombs that were found in Emmet's possession."

"What?" I blinked at him in shock.

"King Torin wants to use them to destroy the sapphire guardians, so our armies can march into Sapphire unimpeded." Quinlan held up a hand when he saw me start to speak. "I believe he intends to send our scouts ahead with the bombs. No one else need know how we managed to destroy the guardians."

"Oh." I frowned, unsure how I felt about it.

"I was going to recommend these men here." Quinlan nodded to the knights. "That way, the secret stays with us."

"I suppose that would work," I conceded.

"You can talk to King Torin when we return," Quinlan offered. "I'm sure he'd be open to any suggestions you have."

"Would all of you be willing to carry those bombs into Sapphire, and detonate them around the guardians?" I asked the knights.

They looked a little shocked that I was asking, instead of ordering, but they all nodded their agreement.

"You can never divulge your part in the guardians destruction. Nor can we tell anyone else what happened today," I warned them. "We did a great service to Tír na nÓg, and the entire Beneath, but we cannot crow about it. To do so would make all of our efforts pointless."

"I don't require glory, Your Majesty," Sir Hugh said. "It's enough to know that those I love will never be subject to such a weapon."

"It's enough for me as well, Sir Hugh," I sighed.

"We have already been vowed to secrecy," Gerard added. "None of us shall speak of this. Nor shall we tell anyone how we'll destroy the sapphire guardians."

"Good." I slipped back under my blanket.

"I will not speak of this either," Banning assured me.

"Thank you, Ban." I said the nickname without thinking, and he smiled when he heard it.

"Anything for you, Ellie," Banning whispered, his voice like a caress on my cheek.

Chapter Forty-Three

We had to return to the castle under the cover of night. Torin had planned on giving the other monarchs the excuse that I was busy honing my talents, and Banning was helping me. We were supposed to be studying diligently within Torin's private apartments. So we couldn't exactly come traipsing in all la-di-da.

The same gate guards had to stand watch every night until we returned, making our re-entry as smooth as possible. They looked relieved when they spotted us. Probably because gate duty is boring as hell. I would have felt sorry for them if I hadn't just blown a king to pieces with his own magical A-bomb. Maybe we could call it an M-bomb. No, never mind, we weren't calling it anything because as soon as the last of them was detonated, it would become nonexistent.

We led our horses into the stables, made sure they were cared for, and then snuck carefully into the castle. The sounds of revelry drifted out from the main hall, and I found myself scowling.

"Doesn't seem right that they're enjoying themselves while we were out taking care of business," Banning gave voice to my thoughts.

"They didn't know what we were up to, remember?" I reminded him as I did myself. "And if Torin is in there, it's only to keep up appearances."

"Uh-huh." Banning grimaced. "Come on, let's go upstairs and change. Then we can go down, acting as if you've just finished your training."

"All right." I nodded to the others, and they hurried off to do the same.

All of us were more than ready to eat some real food. The last cooked meal we'd had was in Copper, at the pub, and saying it was a bland meal would be generous.

Banning and I made it upstairs without anyone the wiser. Everyone important enough to question me was already in the dining hall. I left Banning on the landing for his floor, promising to meet him downstairs, and then hurried up to my guest room. Sara wasn't there, but I hadn't expected her to be. It's not like the woman just sat around waiting in my room in case I needed help getting a dress on. But since she was unavailable, I had to find something I could get on without help.

I chose some of my human clothes, but went for something a little fancier than jeans. Actually, I rarely wore jeans, preferring the ease of a dress. Call me lazy, but it's faster to throw a dress on than wiggle into jeans and then pull on a top. The dress I chose was slinky, classy, and deep crimson. I felt strong in it, victorious. I needed to concentrate on our success so I could let go of the horror of its development. It wouldn't be too difficult for me, and I suppose that is a horror in itself. I'd seen a lot of gory things in my life, been the cause of most of them. So the mincemeat remains of King Lorcan and his men wouldn't give me nightmares. Not for long anyway.

I walked out of the guest room, intending to head downstairs, but a sound from Torin's bedroom caught my attention. It could have been one of the servants, tidying up, but I decided to take a look. When I opened the door, I was happy I had.

Torin lay across his bed, silky sheets bunched around his restless legs as he stared furiously up at the onyx ceiling. He was gloriously naked, his ebony hair spread around him in wild disarray, and the moonlight streaming in from the balcony turned him into a god of dreams. Sexy enough to protect me from any

306

nightmare.

I inhaled sharply, and his gaze shot to mine.

"Elaria!" Torin slipped out of bed, and strode over to me. He barely gave me any time to appreciate his magnificent nudity before he wrapped me in tight to his chest. "Great gems, I've been so worried." He pulled back to look me over. "Are you well? Did everything go as planned? The bombs?"

"I'm good," I assured him. "The plan kind of went sideways, but we improvised, and I'm pretty certain that we took care of all the evidence."

"Sideways?" Torin scowled.

"I may have led us into a trap," I eased him back to the bed. I wasn't about to go downstairs after seeing him au naturel, no matter how hungry I was. Other hungers sometimes took priority. "But it's okay; it worked out for the best."

"King Lorcan?"

"Dead," I grimaced. "Killed by his own bomb. He had a loup working with him. Banning killed the wolf."

"Banning did?" Torin's eyes narrowed.

"He didn't come along to twiddle his thumbs, Torin." I pushed him down, to sit on the mattress, and then turned my back to him. "Now help me with this."

He paused for all of five seconds.

Then my dress was on the floor, and my victory celebration was in full swing. Torin's kisses were better than wine, his touch far more satisfying than any fey food. We rejoiced together, and his body helped mine forget the savage things I'd done to keep us safe.

307

Chapter Forty-Four

"I can't believe we're finally doing this," I said to Torin as we rode out, away from the Onyx Castle.

There was a seriously long train of people setting out with us, but we were splitting up soon. We would be coming at Sapphire from seven different directions, two kingdoms's armies per direction. Except for us; we had a Shining One army and a unit of blooders and shape-shifters. Cerberus had insisted they fight beside us, of course. Torin and I had sent the bomb scouts ahead secretly. They would make the journey to Sapphire on their own, then split up and position themselves at predetermined locations in the Sapphire Gardens. Once there, they'd detonate the last magic bombs in existence and use them to clear our path into the Sapphire Kingdom. The other armies knew we were clearing the way, but had no idea how. Torin had told them we'd be using human technology, and they'd eventually accepted that answer.

As soon as we were in Sapphire, we'd attack King Galen's forces, and whoever else happened to be there supporting him. There were all kinds of plans in place about maneuvering the soldiers, but honestly, they blurred together for me. I had one job, and that was to sing. That's all I could focus on.

But first, we had to get there.

The journey took three days, nearly four because we had so many people to deal with. Camp had to be erected every night, and food had to be distributed. Then there was the mode of travel, horseback again. Hopefully I'd be able to stand when it was all over. I'll tell you what though, my thighs were getting a hell of a workout, and at least I wasn't one of the foot soldiers, doomed to walk the entire way.

Cerberus loved every step of the journey. He's one of those outdoorsy types, so he was completely in his element. He rode tall in the saddle, sometimes bellowing bawdy songs, sometimes bellowing bawdy jokes, and was a general source of entertainment for the troops. At night, the Cerberus Show continued. He'd hunt for fresh meat, then sit around the roasting carcass, drinking something potent while telling tales of the Greek Underworld and his adventures with the numerous gods inhabiting it. The one about Campe, the half-dragon, half-woman Goddess of Tartarus, was a crowd favorite.

The nights on the road weren't so bad actually. I did enjoy listening to Cerberus, and after dinner, Torin and I would retreat to the privacy of his royal tent. No one camped like Shining One royalty. Torin's tent was nicer than some five-star hotels I'd stayed in. It was a far different situation than when we'd been sneaking through the countryside, trying to get to the relic without anyone spotting us. The only sneaky part of this journey would be in our final approach. If someone spotted us along the way and somehow reported it to King Galen, it couldn't be helped. It simply wasn't possible to hide an army of this size.

"You have your songs prepared?" Torin asked as we snuggled together in his bed after a bout of particularly vigorous sex.

It was the last night of the journey. We'd reach Sapphire sometime the next afternoon.

"Yes," I assured him.

"Make sure to always keep Sir Hugh within your sight," Torin said. "He needs to be as close to you as possible, so that his protection spell is impenetrable."

"I know." I kissed his cheek. "I will."

"And if you see me fall, Elaria," he whispered, "don't falter. Keep singing."

"You won't fall," I said confidently, though my heart stuttered at his words.

"There will be a lot of powerful Shining Ones on that battlefield." Torin turned grim. "It's a possibility. Do not watch me; it will only distract you. Just as I shall endeavor not to look at you. We will perform our own tasks, and then hopefully reunite when it's all over."

"Hopefully?" I cocked my head at him. "You can't go into battle thinking like that. You *will* live through this war—we both will—and we will be triumphant."

"As you say." He swallowed hard.

"I want *you* to say it, Torin," I insisted.

"We will be triumphant," he sighed.

"And?"

"And we will both live through the battle." Torin smiled at me, then pushed me over onto my back. "But just in case, I think we should make love one more time."

"Just in case." I chuckled as he lowered his lips to mine.

Chapter Forty-Five

We made it to Sapphire without anyone attacking us. I had no idea if we'd been spotted or if we still had the element of surprise. But as we neared the Sapphire Gardens, an explosion rumbled out to us, and alarms sounded from the castle. The scouts had completed their missions, and they circled back to join us, looking very pleased with themselves. All of our armies would have clear passage to the Sapphire Castle. Not only that; Carrick had scouted the perfect place for me to make my stand and gave me full instructions on how to reach it.

The explosions should have given Sapphire fair warning, even if we hadn't been spotted. But as our forces closed in on the castle from all sides, their armies were scrambling to meet us. Torin and I exchanged one last, love-filled look, and then I broke off from our army, with Sir Hugh at my side. We headed for the vantage point of the low hill Carrick had advised me of. As we reached the crest, the clash of metal meeting metal began to ring up to us.

"I'm ready, Your Majesty," Sir Hugh said. "My magic is surrounding us."

"Thank you, Sir Hugh." I took in the scene, trying to determine where to strike first and whom Hugh should warn to fall back.

Torin had said not to look for him, but that was an impossible thing to ask of me. I had to search the battle anyway, and I couldn't do that without subconsciously searching for Torin. But there was a lot to distract me from the Onyx King.

Shining Ones rarely waged war on each other, and there

was a reason for that. How does one side win when both are so strong magically and physically? It was like watching a supernatural game of tennis. One opponent would sling something out, and the other side would block, then throw something else back. It was disorienting, with flashes of light and rapid maneuvers making it difficult to determine what was really happening.

Then suddenly, it all became clear. I could feel the relic warming on my chest, the stones starting to glow, imparting both their power and knowledge to me. My eyes widened as individual ribbons of magic became visible to me. I could easily determine which stone's energy was behind every attack. There, that blast was from the Diamond Queen. The power behind it couldn't be anything but royal, and the sparkling light was obviously diamond. Isandra was showering her troops with an extra coating of success.

That might have made a difference, if King Niall of Citrine hadn't negated Diamond's success spell with a flare of golden, citrine luck. Back and forth it went, streaks of multicolored magic turning the battlefield into a vibrant spiderweb, until one side managed to sneak something through. Like King Declan with Alexandrite's impressive manifestation magic. What a convenient power to possess in a war. Most of the gemstones had magic that needed to be twisted or coerced into causing harm, but Declan's was made to conquer.

King Declan's stallion, its coat the rich brown of fertile earth, reared up as he cast his magic against a unit of Opal knights. A giant scythe appeared mid-air before them, and slashed across the riders, beheading four of them in as many seconds. I inhaled sharply, the relic tingling in response to the violent display. Maybe I wouldn't be needed after all.

But it became apparent that Declan's strike was lucky. Most attacks, from either side, were parried with protection magic, or avoided with a stroke of luck. I would be needed to tip the scale. Without something stronger than all of this, the magical Newton's cradle would continue clicking back and forth indefinitely.

312

As if in confirmation of my thoughts, a group of Tiger's Eye soldiers rallied together, using the power of their connection to earth to throw boulders up into the path of some advancing Jade knights. Queen Oonagh caught the movement and flung out a hasty wave of Snowflake Obsidian magic to absorb the negativity. The boulders sank back into the soil as if they'd been pushed by giant hands. The Jade knights then countered with their growth magic, tripping the Opal foot soldiers with vines the width of anacondas.

Cerberus ran through it all with a happy howl. He had shifted into his other form, that of a giant, three-headed dog, and his security men had followed suit. The Hound of Hades led a pack of paranormal beasties into the fray, clearing a path for the blooders and Shining Ones behind them. Instead of looking like the second wave, Torin and his army seemed more like a British hunting party with particularly vicious hounds. They galloped after Cerberus as if they were allowing him to corner their prey, but they had no intentions of sharing the kill.

I determinedly turned away from Torin. I had to be sensible about this, unswayed by my affections. All of existence depended upon our success. I needed to choose my first target carefully. So I sorted through the chaos until I found the perfect place to start.

"There." I chose a group that hadn't yet engaged with the Howlite army, but was nearly within range. It was a central position, meaning that if there was magical spillage, it would seep into the enemy's ranks. "Tell Howlite to rein back."

"Yes, Your Majesty," Hugh began talking into his communication unit as I pushed my earbuds in and turned on my iPod.

I wanted to start with something impressive, a song that would grab the attention of our foes, and hopefully cause some of their men to become deserters. Seeing as this was Tír na nÓg, a land of magic, I decided that something more human, more scientific, would prove the most terrifying for its inhabitants. I'd chosen "Radioactive" by Imagine Dragons.

The beat was slow and insistent, the words harsh and full of devastation. My voice pummeled out the lyrics, and the magic flared immediately from the jewels in my collar. Power bypassed my mouth altogether and shot outward across the enormous expanse of battlefield, magnified by the relic. A wasteland was evoked by the devious ditty, full of festering contagion.

A putrid yellow fog encased the team I'd targeted. The soldiers within it began to cough, and then scream brokenly. Around them, other fighters froze, to stare in horror–even the soldiers of Howlite who had been warned to expect my assault. Without even realizing what I was doing, I called upon the power of Blue Lace Agate to calm the Howlite soldiers. I watched in fascination as the creamy, robin's-egg ribbon of Blue Lace Agate energy rushed from the stone embedded in my collar, and covered the Howlite soldiers in a blanket of calm. They instantly regrouped, and headed away from the bubbling, baneful clouds of toxic gas.

My song surged into a proclamation, a warning of the weapon I wielded. It seemed that everyone looked to me, quieting enough to actually hear my disastrous declaration. It echoed over the battlefield like a rung bell. Death was coming for them. He rode the wind with my words.

For a moment, it truly seemed as if I'd brought the utter devastation of an apocalypse to Tír na nÓg. The power of my magic was multiplied by the relic, but I also held authority over all the gemstones. For the first time in my life, I felt like a true goddess, not just a halfling wannabe. I could turn the magic of the Shining Ones against them. I saw it all so vividly in my mind, the whole process of rolling the tide of energy back toward the sea. But I knew that even this clarity was a product of the stones–the Wisdom of Chrysocolla, the Inspiration of Garnet, the Self-Confidence of Carnelian. Those particular gems were glowing just slightly brighter than the rest.

And beneath all of that, the spells of my ancestors fueled me. *Protect the Realms!* I could hear their voices, those powerful witches whose magic still echoed through the relic. I could feel their intensity. Their determination. We would win today because there was no other acceptable outcome. That clamoring compulsion was so strong, but somehow, it was also easily muted. It was intended to be a support, not a distraction. They were with me, and we would defend the worlds together.

The fighting had begun again, but it was frantic on one side and ferocious on the other. The kingdoms that had allied with Onyx were gaining in confidence, plowing into the other forces with sure strokes of magic and steel. Our enemy was floundering, unable to even concentrate enough to throw a flash of gemstone energy back at us. Then a group of sapphire archers ran toward me together, coming in as close as they could get, to launch a volley of arrows in my direction. The projectiles hit Hugh's shield, and fell harmlessly aside.

Their faces filled with fear.

My arms spread out as I sang a mocking message back to them. The end was unavoidable, my poison would find them yet, and together, we would choke the life from their throats. The noxious cloud spread with my motions, seeping toward my sapphire assailants like a sentient being. They screamed, fleeing the roiling tide of miasma, and I felt a savage satisfaction.

The more I sang, the more powerful the magic became, and the brighter the relic glowed. It became effortless; one casual thought would send gemstone magic shimmering out from me while I simultaneously continued to cast spells with my voice. I watched with cool detachment as the Malachite Queen rode purposefully toward me, surrounded by her knights. As soon as she was within range, she blasted pure power against me. Sir Hugh tensed. He knew his shield wouldn't hold against the direct assault of a fairy queen. But fortunately for us, so did I.

A casual flick of my finger sent an impenetrable wall up before me and Hugh. It churned with pale purple energy, fed by the pulsing amethyst in my collar, and seemed to solidify when Queen Riona's power hit it. The Malachite magic burst apart into a bunch of brilliant, green butterflies, flapping away in blissful ignorance. I paused a moment to appreciate the display. What a beautiful example of amethyst's ability to transform negative energy into positive.

Hugh fell to his knees in relief, and sent me a look that clearly expressed how equally grateful and impotent he felt. I'd reassure him later that he'd been needed, at least earlier in the war. But at the moment, I was a little too busy to assuage his male ego.

As my song wound down, the cloud of chemicals began to thin out, and the damage was revealed. Part of me flinched at the twisted faces of poisoned Shining Ones, and the burned skin of those who'd been irradiated. More men shouted in terror as the dead were exposed, but I pushed aside my squeamishness, and forged on. Billions upon billions of people would die if I didn't stop these armies.

I forged ahead to the next song.

"Pull back Onyx," I said to Hugh.

My heart lifted when I saw how brilliantly Torin fought. He slashed with his sword while simultaneously striking out with magic. The inky tendrils of onyx lashed out like a whip, striking every target it was aimed it. Torin's horse moved beneath him without the use of reins, directed only by the angle of his rider's knees. It was fatally beautiful, turning death into art.

"Yes, Your Majesty." Hugh's voice had taken on the awed tones of an acolyte.

But I barely paid Hugh any mind. My eyes were fastened on Torin. He looked amazing amid all that morbidity. The arcs of blood, the flash of metal in the sun, it was a barbaric background

316

that seemed perfect for Torin's harsh allure. His face was set in ferocious lines, his hair flying back like a pennant, and his teeth bared in a vicious grin. I've never seen such a hellishly handsome man.

Which made my next choice of song oddly appropriate.

I began to sing AC/DC's "Highway to Hell" as I watched Torin order his soldiers into a mock retreat. He glanced up at me, our gazes caught, and we shared a sweet smile. The rose quartz in my collar flashed, and I inhaled sharply as it momentarily intensified our love. Torin swayed in the saddle, and I yanked back the energy. The stone bowed to my will, and Torin nodded with a knowing grin, before focusing back on the war. I refocused as well, giving some imagery to my magic, directing it as clearly as I could.

That's when hell came to Tír na nÓg.

I hadn't been certain of what the song would accomplish, but I had visualized something terrible. Those visions had manifested accurately, the magic leaping to fulfill my wishes like a liberated genie. There was bravado in the lyrics, a dark reveling in their desperation. Fate was leading us straight into hell, but instead of allowing ourselves to be tormented, we were taking over. We would rule. I felt my body leaning forward into the intensity of the music. Evil infiltrated the words, and it coated my skin with a greasy film. I shouted out with the pounding blare of drums and screaming whine of guitars while the land directly before Torin's team opened up, spewing forth the denizens of the Underworld.

And not just one type of underworld. Demons from the Christian hell came crawling out of crevices, emerging gleefully from foul belches of toxic fog. Garm, the four-eyed, massive hound of the Norse Helheim, appeared in a circle of frost, icicles shooting from his spiked fur as he shook himself with canine satisfaction. The yamadutas of the Hindu Naraka formed out of fetid green effluvium, bearing whips and spears in their ashy-indigo hands. The iron snakes and fire-breathing dogs of the

Buddhist Avici ran across the battlefield on razor-sharp claws, leaving scarred, steaming earth in their wake. The many-winged Erkhil Khan, of the Mongolian Kasyrgan, flew above the fight, hacking at our enemies with his gleaming, golden sword while he dumped boiling oil over them from a massive cauldron. Last, but certainly not least, Hades himself appeared, his bare chest gleaming in the glow of his flaming hands. The monsters of the Greek Underworld took shape all around him.

"Boss!" Cerberus shouted from all three of his canine mouths at once. An eerily echoing sound. "You came! That's mighty fine of you!"

"Cerberus?" Hades looked confused for a second, but then the magic took hold of him again, and compelled him forward into the fray.

Sweet screaming sirens! I was pulling people across the Veil. Not just any people either, but gods and demons. The strongest, scariest sons of bitches in all the realms were being summoned here . . . to serve my will. And I was far from done.

"Alexandrite," I said to Hugh, and he nodded.

I held onto hell as I launched into the next song, a feat I wouldn't have previously thought possible. But the magic was growing, and it didn't want to let go of our creations. It rang out, driving the demons forward even as I sang a new song. "Last Resort" by Papa Roach.

I slashed my hand out with the stabbing vocals. Wherever I directed the magic, men fell, sliced to death as if by some gigantic blade. Every word seemed fatal, every riff filled with rage. Anger clenched my fists, and men choked to death, clawing at their throats. Blood gushed with the next line, and the fury of the fiction I sang threatened to overtake me.

The screaming climbed to an agonizing degree. If I hadn't been so lost to the power, consumed by the relic, I would have noticed that all of our troops had pulled back. They simply weren't needed any longer. The only magic in the air was mine; everything else was either nullified or hopelessly inadequate. The rival armies were throwing down their weapons, begging for mercy, but still I sang. And the song grew ever more vicious.

Soldiers began to slice their own throats. Their comrades shouted and tried to flee, but there was no escaping this dark energy. A part of me cried out in terror at the brutality, but it was trapped within the force of thousands of witches' worth of magic. My chest tightened, my lungs burning with silent screams, but my soul was drowning in fanaticism. The magic had lured me in, making me believe I was its master, when in actuality, I was nothing more than a slave. A tool for the relic to manipulate.

I waved a hand out, and a swath of soldiers went blind. Another slash, and a group of knights went insane, attacking their comrades. I started to shake as I sang with even more ferocity, my terror changing into zeal. The relic was wooing me again, luring me back into that blissful illusion that I was in control. I was so powerful. The armies of Tír na nÓg would bow before me. All of the worlds would bend knee to my will.

I watched smugly as King Galen came riding across the battlefield, waving a white flag, shouting his surrender, and still I sang. I loved it, every second of it, even though I knew this power was killing something inside me, something that very possibly *was* me. Who would be left when I finally stopped singing?

Hugh was down on the ground before me, begging me to stop. I ignored him, my gaze taking in the magnificence of the moment. The victory and honor I was bringing my ancestors. The protection I was providing to all of the worlds. Arrogance lifted its ugly head inside my chest, and smiled at me with shiny, celebrity teeth. *You're powerful, Elaria,* it whispered. *You are making them scream in fear!* The music faded into a new song, and I smiled into the narcissistic high. Hugh cringed away from me like I was one of the "Seven Devils" in Florence + the Machine's song.

319

The music slunk down into a sensual grind, but the words were pure peril. I lifted my chin as the music conveyed my personal feelings to King Galen. He didn't have anything I wanted, nothing to bargain with or offer me that would make me stop. Keep your jewels, keep your crown, keep your damn kingdom. It would be a wasteland by the time I was done. All I desired was his complete destruction. Vanquish. Conquer. Subdue. Whispers lurked just beneath my thoughts, like teeming fishes fluttering along the surface of a lake. They focused my intent for me.

Spread out below my vantage point, the denizens of the numerous hells roared in approval as the land around them slowly shifted into something they were more accustomed to. The sky darkened. The scent of blood and bile filled the air. Flames shot upward from the broken earth. Thunder cracked like a whip and lightning nipped at its heels in unnatural colors.

I sang on mercilessly, the hell of my previous performance merging with my current manifestation. Devils, demons, and dark gods ruled the war. But they were all there for me, eager to obey my every whim.

The Sapphire Castle shivered like a frightened feline, caught fire, and began to crumble. The crashes of its descent filled the air with the sound of doom, as fire filled it with oppressive smoke. The ground beneath my feet shook with earthquakes and the tread of monsters. Tír na nÓg was trembling in fear, and I rejoiced in it.

"Elaria!" Banning crested the hill, and came running to me. I couldn't hear his words, but I read his lips, the magic of the relic translating the motion so that I understood easily.

Hugh dropped his shields, and backed away from us both.

"Elaria!" Banning screamed into my face, shaking me. "Stop this! You're killing them all! This is pointless slaughter, Ellie. They've surrendered! Please stop!"

Banning yanked me against his chest and tried to kiss me, but I just tore my mouth away and continued to sing.

"Please," Banning begged me. "I know you're still in there. You can come back. Just believe in yourself."

"El, my girl." Cerberus was back in human form. He put a firm hand on my shoulder. "That's enough now."

Cer tore the iPod from me, the buds popping free of my ears. The cacophony of battle hit me hard as I lost my musical buffer. But I didn't need to hear the song anymore. It was inside me. I sang on, giving the lyrics life, helping their threats take shape. Ignoring Cer and Banning, I concentrated on the war.

Then a flicker of something crossed my vision. A flash of black and silver distracted my narrowed glare. Deep blue eyes, like the Pacific on a sunny day. Deep enough to dive into, clear enough to peer past fathoms. I smiled softly and something shook in my chest. An abrupt inhale. A startled gasp. Warm hands enveloped mine, and my stare lowered to a pair of sensual lips. They moved, empowering their words with resonance.

"Elaria, my love," Torin said gently, calmly. He had no need to shout. His voice became everything. "This is not who you are. You are stronger than the relic. Stronger than us all."

I sang on.

"It's no good," Banning groaned.

But then the lyrics became personal. Virulent. Something burned inside me, made me stumble and fall against Torin. The threat seemed directed against my lover, and that was not acceptable. I began to shudder, fighting the pull of violence, righteousness, and fury.

"Little bird"–Torin's lips brushed mine–"remember who you are and who you belong to. Come home to me."

321

Then he kissed me. The song strangled in my throat as emotion took over. Stronger than magic, stronger than revenge, even stronger than the relic. Love lifted inside me and burned away the collar's control. The light from the gems winked out as Torin's body surrounded mine. The taste of him revived me, his scent awakened me, his touch reminded me of who I was. This was real. This was me . . . and Torin. He was mine, and I was his. No masters here. Not even the relic.

A relieved cheering filtered up to us as Torin pulled away slowly.

"There you are." Torin stared into my eyes, revealing the barest flicker of relief inside his. "There's my little bird."

"Is it over?" I asked with a hoarse voice.

"As over as it could ever be," Cerberus answered before Torin could. "You demolished them, Song Queen."

"It's over," I sighed, and leaned into Torin.

With my words, the clasp at the back of my neck released, and the collar slid down my chest. I jerked back and tried to catch it, but the relic disappeared.

"What in the world?" I leaned back and laid my hand to my bare chest. "What happened to it?"

A rumbling shook the earth, and we braced ourselves. It went on for maybe five minutes, while people pointed into the distance and shouted. All of us on the little hill looked off to see Relic Mountain rising up to the heights it had previously held.

"The relic has returned to its slumber." Torin smiled broadly.

"Looks like our work here is done," Cerberus said to Banning.

322

"It appears so," Banning said softly, as he stared forlornly at me.

"Yes," I agreed, but then frowned at Cerberus. "Cer, why are you naked?"

The Relic War concluded with the booming laugh of the Hound of Hades.

Chapter Forty-Six

It had been a week since the Relic War, or the Sapphire Slaughter as some were calling it. King Galen had survived. His brother, Finbar, did not. Torin had kept his promise to me and found Finbar on the battlefield. Found him and killed him slowly. I've heard speculations that even with his grisly death, Finbar was still luckier than some of the men killed by my magic. I mean the relic's magic. It wasn't mine anymore, and it would hopefully stay that way.

Whenever memories of the battle surfaced, I sank into a dark place where I experienced it all over again. The savagery. The pull of power. The feeling of being both master and slave. The tightrope I had walked over complete destruction. Not of my body, but of my mind. I had been a step away from becoming the relic. Of losing everything that made me Elaria Tanager. Everything that made me a person, not some unfeeling, merciless weapon. At first, it took a while for me to shake off the horror, but it was slowly becoming easier to work through the anxiety. One thing was certain: I didn't miss the relic. All the power in the world wasn't worth losing your soul.

Still, the relic had been necessary, and it had done its job well. The sanctions imposed on Sapphire and its supporters were enough to discourage any fairy from ever looking covetously at Earth again. A collective of Shining One royals had stripped King Galen of his magic. Torin had led the collective. I thought it was kind of poetic. Galen had used his sister as an excuse to bring me to Tír na nÓg, when in actuality, he'd been the one to force Nila to flee. Now Galen found himself in her shoes, and by the hands of the very same king who had grounded Nila's magic.

Queen Ava's power was also drained, but not fully. She was left enough magic to assure her a place in a Jewel Court. Not nearly as bad a punishment as her husband received, but enough of one that she couldn't claim Sapphire in his place.

Humiliated and powerless, Galen left Tír na nÓg for the world he had wanted to conquer–Earth. I'm told that he asked Ava to join him, but she refused, withdrawing to a small property her parents had left her in Bloodstone. She took her dog with her. Galen was pretty broken up over his wife's rejection and went off to find his sister, hoping that Nila would give him comfort and sanctuary. Nila had laughed in his face, and slammed the door on her brother's pleas for help. Good for her.

Sapphire's castle had been reduced to rubble by the relic, and the rest of the kingdom became a sort of no-man's land–which Torin said will stay that way until someone rises up as the new monarch. He wanted me to claim the kingdom for myself, but I pointed out that without the relic, I wasn't actually a queen anymore. I couldn't control the stones. Not any of them. There was no way I could claim a Shining One kingdom. I couldn't even hear the damn walls anymore. Torin had grudgingly agreed.

The way home from Sapphire had been a strange journey. Our allies had headed immediately to their own kingdoms, and the Onyx army had once again been left with Cerberus, his shifter security force, the blooder soldiers, and Banning as travel companions. There was a general sense of satisfaction among the troops, but at the same time, they were traumatized. Very few of them would meet my eyes, and most skittered away from me when I got too near. I didn't blame them. How could I, when I had nightmares over it myself?

Thankfully, I was Elaria Tanager once more. Not Queen of Song or Warrior Witch. Just Elaria the Spellsinger, and that was good enough for me. Though I wasn't sure it was good enough for Torin.

The first night after the battle, we had made love with a wild abandon, relief and triumph heating our blood. The night after had been more sedate. We had come together slowly, sweetly, both of us glorying in the fact that we had survived. The third evening started to get awkward, and the sex felt strained to me. By the time we reached Onyx, I started to wonder if Cerberus had been right. Was the end of the war also the end of me and Torin?

The last few days at the Onyx Castle had been a rush of activity. Torin had to speak with several monarchs who hadn't allied with either side. After hearing of how we'd crushed Sapphire, they were afraid that their neutrality would cost them. So they'd come in person to feel Torin out, and see if they needed to make amends. They brought lavish gifts for him, and for me as well, the Queen of Song. No one told them that I didn't have my power anymore, but I was sure the gossip would spread eventually. Until then, I'd take the presents. I wasn't one to refuse a gift.

Torin seemed to be busy constantly, meeting with the monarchs and settling the mess that came in the aftermath of war. Each of our allied kingdoms had taken tributes from Sapphire and their allies; Malachite, Diamond, Jasper, Opal, Tiger's Eye, Carnelian, Selenite, Kyanite, and Blue Lace Agate. It was the spoils of war, but Torin said it was more than that. Basically, the loser paid the winner's expenses. Kind of like winning a legal case.

Anyway, the neutral kingdoms were coming to pay tribute after the fact, and their groveling was both tedious and satisfying for Torin. The Mongrel King had become more powerful than any of them, and I think it pleased Torin immensely to listen to their ass-kissing. But it also annoyed him, and by the end of each day, he was irritable. We hadn't been intimate since we'd returned from war. In fact, I'd taken to sleeping in my guest room.

I was exiting it, when I saw Oonagh coming out of Torin's bedroom.

I froze, staring at her with wide eyes. No way. She flinched when she saw me, then straightened her shoulders, and gave me a smug smile as she sauntered by. I grabbed her arm just after she made it past, and her smugness flashed to fear.

"What the fuck were you doing in Torin's bedroom?" I growled at her.

"Nothing." She yanked her arm out of my grip. "At least nothing that's any business of yours." She fled down the hallway as soon as she was free.

I turned my narrowed stare to Torin's door and strode over to it. I didn't bother to knock, just barged in, and there he was, in the process of pulling on a tunic. I gaped at him.

"Seriously?!" I shrieked as he settled his clothing in place.

"What?" Torin looked shocked. "You don't like my choice of tunic?" He looked down at it, as if he couldn't fathom how a piece of clothing could offend me so much.

"No, I don't like your choice of lover," I spat.

"You don't like yourself?" Torin looked baffled.

"Stop the bullshit, Torin," I stalked forward and got in his face. "I just ran into Oonagh... coming out of your bedroom."

"Yes." He shrugged. "She came by to ask me if she could have my portion of the tribute from Tiger's Eye in exchange for what she received from Kyanite."

"What?" I deflated.

"Oonagh said she's had trouble getting her hands on tiger's eye lately and needed a fresh supply of the stone for several of her people." Torin cocked his head at me, then he looked down to his tunic. "You thought that I had . . . what? Fucked Oonagh while you were right across the hall?"

327

"Maybe," I said in a little voice.

"Elaria . . ." He sighed, and ran a hand through his hair. "I know these past few days have been rough, but I'm trying to settle things among the kingdoms so we don't have another war stemming from this one. I'm busy with politics, not . . ."

"Pussy?" I finished with a chuckle.

"Not other women," he amended with a smile. "Come here." He pulled me against his chest. "You don't have to sleep in that guest room. I didn't ask you to do that."

"No, it's fine." I sighed and eased away from him. "I want you to be able to come and go without worrying about waking me."

"I appreciate that"–Torin leaned his forehead to mine,–but I've missed sleeping beside you. Why don't you sleep here tonight? I promise I won't schedule any late meetings."

"All right," I agreed.

"But for now, I must attend to the Topaz royals." He sighed, and then looked hopeful. "Would you care to join me?"

"Oh hell no." I laughed when he made a disgruntled face. I had opted out of all the ass-kissing. I just couldn't handle it. Diplomacy was not my strong suit. "You go ahead and have fun. I'll meet you back here later. Be sure and bring me my presents though."

"You're a heartless woman." He kissed my cheek, and then we headed out of the room together.

We parted ways in the hall, Torin going downstairs while I headed back into my guest room. Oonagh's deception had soured my sociability. I formed a new plan to hide out in my room and read all day. I'd borrowed a few books from Torin's study and they

328

looked promising. They were all works of fiction by Shining One authors, and several of them were set in the human world. I found it terribly amusing that fairy fiction would be about humans. I guess that was fantasy for them.

But just a few minutes after I'd settled on the bed, a knock came at my door. I debated not answering it, and then decided that was both immature and stupid. It could be important. So I got up and trudged over to the door. I wasn't entirely shocked to find Banning standing on the other side.

"Hello," he said in a low voice.

"Hey." I swung a hand in toward the room. "Come on in."

"Thank you." He looked nervous. "I won't be long. I just wanted to come by and tell you goodbye."

"You're leaving?"

"I have to make sure my gura gets home, and then I need to see to the soldiers the European Falca sent me," he said. "I'll have to make my report as well. There's a lot to be done."

"I understand," I sighed. It seemed like everyone was busy except for me.

"So, I . . ." He cleared his throat. "I'm not giving up on us, Elaria."

"Banning . . ." I shook my head, but he stopped me from saying anything further.

"No." He held up a hand. "I know that you're with Torin, but we're immortals, and things change. I just want you to know that should this relationship between you and Torin change, I will be waiting for you. I will *always* want you. It will never be too late for you to return to me."

I didn't know what to say to that, but he saved me from

replying by leaning forward and kissing my cheek.

"I want you to be happy, Elaria," Banning said sincerely. "If that happiness is without me, then I can accept that. But I will never love anyone as I love you, and no matter what happens in my world, there will always be a place for you in it. I need you to understand that before I leave." He pressed a card into my hand. "Just in case you lost the last one." He gave me a sexy wink. "Goodbye, Elaria."

"Goodbye, Banning." I clutched his business card. "I wish you happiness as well."

He didn't say anything to that, just smiled a little sadly and closed the door behind him.

Chapter Forty-Seven

Cerberus left shortly after Banning, and I suddenly felt very alone in the castle. Everyone was bustling about constantly, even Sara, who barely had time to help me dress in the mornings. She had a list of bustier orders to fill for several queens, including Queen Teagan, and most of her free time was spent sewing. I was happy for her, but lonely.

I had spent a sweet evening with Torin, but after that, things had gone back to the way they were. I had returned to sleeping in the guest room. I spent most of my days in there too. Either that or I'd sit in Torin's private garden. I had breakfast with him most mornings, but other than that, I rarely saw him.

Despite Torin's explanation for Oonagh's presence in his bedroom, I began to grow more and more suspicious. It seemed that whenever I wandered into a meeting I wasn't expected to attend, or a room I had entered by chance, I found Oonagh hanging on Torin. She'd be sitting next to him, leaning in to whisper to him, or gripping his arm conspiratorially. They always broke apart when they saw me, which made it seem even more fishy. I wasn't sure if I was just imagining things. If I was letting that first encounter screw with my head or if there really was something going on.

What I did know was that it was time for me to go home.

Whether or not our relationship was over, my staying would only make things worse. If Torin wanted someone else, I didn't want to stick around to watch him struggle over it. If he truly loved me, he'd be able to see that more clearly when I was gone. Plus, I needed to get back to my life on Earth, and touch base with my family so they knew I was okay. I couldn't stay in Tír na nÓg forever. This wasn't my home.

Now I just had to tell Torin that.

I walked through the halls, lost in my own thoughts, and almost collided with King Declan. A few of the monarchs who had allied with us had returned for a sort of post-war pow-wow/celebration. After seeing my self-imposed seclusion, Declan had made several attempts at coercing me to celebrate with him personally. You'd think I'd be annoyed, but the fact was, I liked Declan. He was never pushy, just very flattering, and he made me laugh. Plus, from interactions I witnessed between him and others, he seemed like a good guy. He was honest, nearly to the point of rudeness, which I appreciated. But he delivered his truths with such finesse that you failed to be offended. He'd simply smile and shrug, as if he couldn't change the facts. The perfect picture of poise.

At the moment, he looked panicked.

"Uh, Queen Elaria," Declan grabbed me by the upper arms, and started pushing me backward, away from the corner I was about to round. "I'd like to speak with you, if you don't mind."

"I can't right now, King Declan," I slipped out of his grasp. "I need to talk to Torin. I'll find you afterward."

I tried to go around him, but he snatched at me again, "He's not in that direction."

Declan was usually so honest that his lies had become vivid to me. I could see the falsehood painted across his mouth like red lipstick on a librarian. My eyes narrowed, and I jerked my arm away. I stalked to the corner, dread pooling in my belly, and peered around it. There was Torin, leaning against the wall, with Oonagh pressed tight against him. Her arms were around his neck, her mouth moving over his, and his hands were at her waist. I flinched away from the sight. Then I started walking back the way I'd come.

332

"Elaria." Declan followed me. "I'm so sorry. I had just seen them, and I wanted to spare you."

"You're sweet, Declan." I barely recognized my own voice. It was constricted, a breathy whisper. "But I needed to see that. It's good. Closure. All us girls like closure. Besides, I'm already packed. I knew something was up with Torin. Now it's confirmed. I have to admit though, it surprises me."

"It surprises me as well." Declan's jaw twitched. "Why bed an ice queen when you could make music with the Queen of Song?"

"That's lovely," I said. "Poetic. Thank you for being such a gentleman."

"You deserve better than that," Declan huffed. "Just because she's more powerful than you are now, you shouldn't be cast aside for her. What does magic have to do with love anyway?"

I stopped and stared at him. Magic. Love. Dear gods, had our bond broken when the relic returned to its hibernation? That spell we cast, those words, maybe it had faded along with everything else at the end of the battle. All the demons went home to their underworlds, the toxic radiation dissipated into harmless mist, and the insanity that had taken over the enemy ranks subsided. The warding spell I had cast over the Veil had disappeared. Maybe our vows had disappeared too.

That would explain so much. But I hadn't felt anything for Banning. No dreams, no tight sensation in my chest. Nothing. I had let the blooder walk away, and the only regret I'd felt was over hurting him. I actually liked Banning now. I counted him as a friend, and that was a miracle in my world. That I should think so highly of him, and yet remain unaffected by the removal of the spell separating us, seemed odd. Perhaps it would be a slower process with me, since I was the source of the spell. Torin's affection for Oonagh had obviously come back in full force.

333

Maybe my dreams of Banning would start again. Hell, maybe I should give him a shot. Or even Declan.

I looked at the Shining One with speculation.

"No." Declan held up a hand. "I see anger in your eyes, Elaria. Anger and betrayal. Please don't include me in it. I confess that I am half in love with you already, and I would allow it. Nay, I would *encourage* your ardor, and then I would regret it when you turned away from me."

"Who says I would turn away?" I lifted a brow.

"The humans call it a rebound, correct?" Declan asked. "What is a rebound, but a force compelling you away from something and into something else? If you are compelled hard enough, you bounce off that other surface as well. And we both know how hard you're being compelled right now."

"You really are a gentleman, aren't you?" I gave him a lopsided smile, liking him even more.

"I try to be," Declan sighed. "It's taking all of my control at the moment. But honestly, Elaria, this is not really about being proper with you. This is about the long game. My goal is your heart, and I won't get that if I take your body now. I'll wait and see this through. Now"–he held out his arm–"may I offer you my assistance, Your Majesty?"

"You know I'm no longer a queen."

"Once a queen, always a queen," he declared.

I took his arm. "I want to go home."

"I know, dearest." He tucked my hand into his arm. "And it would be my honor to escort you there. I happen to have a traveling stone with me."

"A traveling stone." I chuckled. "I should have

remembered. I have one too. A gift from Torin."

"Such a fool." Declan's amethyst eyes darkened to iolite. "Will you still allow me to see you home?"

"Of course." I pushed the door to my guest room open, and left his side in search of my traveling stone.

I found it on a desk. There were writing implements and paper there as well. I paused as I considered leaving Torin a letter. It shouldn't be too hard for him to figure out why I left, but it might be cathartic for me to get it down on paper. To let him know exactly why he didn't get a proper goodbye, and exactly what I thought of him.

So I did. I wrote him a brief, but clear, letter about catching him with Oonagh, and how he could have come to me, and simply told me it was over instead of being such a douche. He should have known that I wasn't the type to throw a fit like Nila. I had more class than that. I may have made the "class" comment seem ironic by adding some suggestions about where Torin could stick his penis next, since it was never getting near me again. But this was a fuck you letter after all. I signed my name at the bottom and smiled at it. It did feel good to get it out, and even better to leave the letter on my pillow for Sara to find. The entire castle would know I left before Torin did.

I scooped up my bag, and started yanking out the clothes Torin had bought me. I didn't want to take anything with Torin's taint on it. Then I came to the steel and onyx, magic-grounding bracelets, and paused. Those things could be useful, not just for pleasure, but for work. They went back into the bag. I may be sentimental about some things, but I wasn't a fool.

"All right; I'm ready." I held up the traveling stone and peered at it. "How do I work this?"

"Just focus on where you want to go," Declan pulled a similar stone out of his pocket. "As long as it's in another realm, there shouldn't be a problem. The stone can't travel within one plane of existence. It's made specifically to pierce the Veil."

"Okay." I closed my fist around it, and held my hand out to him.

"I'll just follow your lead." He took my hand, and I found myself admiring him.

Declan might not be as massive as Torin, but he wasn't exactly slim either. He was actually quite muscular, and I'd seen him use those muscles to his advantage on the battlefield. He was a powerful man and a handsome one–a deadly combination. Declan's features were regal, and his deep auburn hair complemented his eyes. Eyes so similar to my own.

"Elaria?" Declan cocked his head at me.

"Sorry." I blushed. "Yes, that's fine."

I closed my eyes and pulled a Dorothy. There's no place like home. The soothing monotony of waves on sand. The air thick with the scent of mangoes, guavas, and plumerias. A sharp base note of salt beneath the sweetness. Stone walls, such a rarity in Hawaiian homes, supported a series of sharply angled roofs. Beneath those angles, sunshine reflected off thick window panes, catching in faceted stained glass. Speckled patches of white and cream sand spotted the back lawn, tracked up from the nearby beach over the years. And around it all rose ponderous walls, heavy with age and covered in a spiderweb of vines–the perfect neighbors.

"Beautiful," Declan whispered, and I opened my eyes.

I hadn't even felt a pull. Nothing, no movement at all. Yet there we were, standing before the bleached wood gate that led out to my private slice of heaven. Huge boulders rose up to either side of my bit of beach, making it inaccessible to anyone else. I'd paid a fortune for the private access rights, which normally weren't sold in Hawaii, but it was worth it.

"Yes, I think so." I turned determinedly away from the ocean path. This wasn't the time for that. "Welcome to Hawaii, Your Majesty."

"Thank you." Declan offered to take my bag. "Do you think I could return sometime? Maybe you could show me more of your paradise?"

"I think I'd like that." I led him up to the back door, and then into my home. As soon as I crossed the threshold, I closed my eyes and breathed it in. Sanctuary. The sense of solace was so much stronger when I was wounded. "Just put the bag there, please." I gestured to a leather sofa. "How about some coffee?"

"Coffee?" Declan smiled. "That's the human drink with the drug in it, correct?"

"Ah . . ." I blinked. "I guess that's technically accurate, but it's just a minor stimulant. I think I may have some without caffeine in it, if you prefer."

"Oh no, I'd like the stimulant please." Declan followed me into the kitchen and took a seat at a dining set placed within the curves of a picture window. It gave him a clear view of the ocean, which he immediately praised. "Why do you ever leave this place?"

"That's a very good question." I busied myself with making coffee as I internally screamed.

I didn't want to hurry Declan out, but if I wasn't rebounding with him, I needed him to leave so I could have the necessary break-down. I had loved Torin, *still* loved him, and although I could put up a good front, I was falling apart inside. I had finally trusted a man enough to give him my heart, and he had used me, then tossed me aside. Torin's prophecy was fulfilled. I had lifted him up, stronger than he'd been before, and now he didn't need me anymore. That stung something fierce. I needed a good cry, then a nice swim, and then possibly a good cry while swimming.

"Damn the stones!" Declan growled from behind me. I looked up to find him standing very close to me, and before I could say anything, he grabbed me and swung me into his arms. "I can't sit here and watch you torment yourself. Just one kiss to remind you that there will be love in your life again. One kiss." He lowered his lips to mine.

Declan knew what he was doing. I had no idea how old the Shining One was, but he'd obviously had loads of practice kissing. I sighed into the delicious sensations his lips and tongue created with mine. I welcomed the heat of his hands sliding over my back, and released the rising pain of Torin's betrayal. Declan was right, this wasn't the end for me. There would be other men, other loves, and I wouldn't let Torin sour them. I would give my heart once more.

Chapter Forty-Eight

I did allow myself a good cry after Declan left. I had to. I couldn't just leave all that pent up inside me. Then I ate a lot of ice cream. I watched some romantic movies and cried some more. Then I watched some horror films to get over the romance. It took me about a week to work out my Torin issues, during which time, Cerberus came to visit.

"You look like shit, El," he said as soon as I opened the door.

"Thanks, asshole." I walked back into the house, letting him come in or not as he pleased.

I had been in the apathetic stage at that point. In my limited experience, heartbreak came in stages. You began with shock, then denial; no, he couldn't possibly have done this to me. Rage quickly followed this, which is why I'd left Tír na nÓg instead of confronting Torin. I have too much pride to show any man how much he'd hurt me. A fight may appear to be strength on the surface, but everyone knows that you wouldn't be so angry, if you didn't care so much. You'll wound a man deeper by acting unaffected.

After the anger, comes a good swim, preferably in the ocean, and for a minimum of half an hour. Though that may just be a siren thing. Then comes crying till you can't breathe because your nose is full of snot. When you're clear and dry again, the next stage was to consume vast amounts of food–anything premade or that someone was willing to bring to you. All this was done while watching movies that either made you hope, feel inadequate, or want to kill something male. Sprinkled into this consumption and couch potato stage, came mini-stages of apathy, a total lack of concern for anything or anyone. I think it's the body's way of coping with the emotional roller coaster. It needs to go numb or die.

Cerberus walked into my dark, dirty living room during one of those numb stages. He cringed at the chaos of discarded fast food containers, empty ice cream cartons, and piles of used tissues. His nose wrinkled at the stench of stale air mixed with even staler Elaria. Then he turned to me with a look of abject horror.

"What the fuck?"

"It's a process," I told him as I scratched my ass through my yoga pants.

"What happened between you and Torin?" Cerberus grabbed my upper arm, and escorted me roughly out of the living room. He found a fairly clean place to sit in my library, and plopped me down in it. He then crouched before me and growled, "Tell me what that fucker did. The length of his torture will depend upon the severity of his stupidity."

"He kissed Oonagh." I shrugged. "Probably much more than that by now."

"What?" Cerberus snarled. "That fairy fucker! I'll fucking kill him. That... that fuck! Slow it is then. I'll use claws instead of knives. Or maybe I'll just tap his forehead with my fist over and over, like water torture without the water. I'll keep going until his ugly face is flat."

"Don't bother; it's fine." I waved him down. "I'll get over it. I think it was the relic that kept us together anyway. When it went back to sleep, Torin and I went to sleep too. Or stopped sleeping together, rather."

"But this . . ." Cerberus waved his hand back toward the living room. "Elaria, this is fucking insane. I've never seen you like this."

"You've never seen me heartbroken," I said, and then I did something truly pathetic. I burst into tears. Farewell, numb stage.

"El . . ." Cerberus sat back as he yanked me into his lap. "Oh, Elaria, please stop. Gods damn that shiny son of a slut. He doesn't deserve you, and he definitely doesn't deserve your tears. Forget him."

Cerberus rocked me like a baby until I sniffled myself into silence.

"There you go," he murmured. Then he made a disgusted sound, "Damn, girl, when was the last time you showered?"

"I don't remember," I whispered.

"Shit." Cerberus sighed and stood. "Come on then."

He carried me upstairs to my bedroom, then into the master bath. Cerberus sat me on a vanity stool while he ran the bathwater. Then he searched through the army of bath products I had rallied around the tub's rim. He muttered to himself until he found a couple of options. Then he came over and stood me up. I finally overcame my stupor when he tried to take my top off.

"Hey." I slapped at his hands.

"Elaria," Cerberus grimaced, "I've known you since you were sixteen. Don't you think it's about time I saw you naked?"

"No."

"Fine." He sighed and turned around. "Get naked and get into the tub."

"You'll still be able to see me"

"Get into the water, El!"

341

"All right!" I shouted back and stripped.

I climbed in the massive tub, and pulled my legs up to my chin. Cerberus turned around and huffed. He pulled over the little stool I'd been sitting on and used it to loom like a gargoyle behind me. Then he pushed me under the water. I came up sputtering.

"What the hell, Cer?"

"I needed to wet your hair," he smirked.

Then he started washing my hair. I forgot all about being naked in front of my friend, and simply enjoyed the feeling of his massaging fingers on my scalp. The heat from the water soothed my tight muscles, and by the time Cer was done, I was ready to finish the rest of the bath by myself. I ordered him out, then scrubbed myself clean.

When I came out of the bathroom, I felt like a new woman. I got on the phone and called a cleaning crew. I wasn't up for dealing with the mess I'd made; I admit it, and I own my shortcomings. But hey, at least I could employ others and help the economy. After the call, I went downstairs to find Cerberus sitting at the dining table, eating a sandwich. He smiled brightly when he saw me.

"Much better," he nodded. "There's my girl."

"I *feel* better." I sat down across from him. "Thank you, Cer."

"Anytime," Cerberus grinned. "Hey, I wanted to tell you. I went to check on Hades. I thought he'd be pissed about you yanking him into our battle."

"And what did he say?"

"Didn't remember a damn thing." Cerberus chortled. "It's good I sort of hinted at it instead of saying outright what had

342

happened. He would have thought I'd lost my mind."

"He has no memory of it?" I gaped at Cer. "Holy shit, things really did go back to normal after the relic went to sleep."

"Well, not everything." Cerberus shrugged. "The damage we wrought is still there. Lots of Shining Ones are still dead."

"True," I whispered, then looked up and declared, "I need a job, Cerberus. What you got?"

"Seriously?"

"I can't stay here." I scowled at the pile of dishes in the kitchen sink. "I need to focus on something else."

"I hear ya. The stench alone would send a weaker man running," Cerberus said. "Believe it or not, I was in love once. She broke my heart too."

"What? Who? When?"

"Never mind all that." He swallowed hard, and looked out the window. "I threw myself into the job and got over her. You'll get over Torin too." He looked back at me steadily. "I know you, Elaria. You're like me. Nothing holds you down for long."

"Thanks, Cer."

"No problem." He stood and gave me a huge grin. "How does Switzerland sound?"

"Perfect." I grinned back. "I could use some neutrality and chocolate right about now."

"Pack for cold weather," Cerberus suggested.

"Yeah, maybe the cold will do me some good too."

Chapter Forty-Nine

I was on a job in Baltimore, Maryland, three weeks later. In a place called Angels Rock Bar. Up on their vibrantly painted stage, the glow of oval lights backlighting me and the band. A chandelier of pearl-colored beads spread out above me, and a matching beaded curtain shimmied on my right, caught in the vibration of the amps nearby. The promise of sex hung heavy in the air, a mix of perfume, Jose Cuervo, and sweat. It made the crowd anxious, as amped as my music, and I could practically taste the anticipation on my tongue. Or maybe that was the brandy.

The onyx cuffs Torin had charged to imprison me were actually liberating. I'd never been able to take a cover job as a singer before. It would have been too much work to infuse each song with benign magic while I waited for my target to appear. Now I could hold the magic back until I needed it. Which opened up options for my work and made it all so much easier. I simply went into a bar that I knew the person frequented, "auditioned" my way into a job, and then performed until my mark appeared. In theory, I could even kill someone that way, though I hadn't tried it yet. Crowds were best for coercion.

My target on this particular night was a loup, a werewolf who had pissed off a whole flock of harpies. Let's just say this hound liked chasing pretty birds. As a half-siren woman, I took personal offense at his behavior, and I had wholeheartedly accepted this job. Frankly, he was lucky that the ladies decided to give him a little magical neutering rather than performing the real deal on him with their claws.

I had my magic grounding cuffs on for most of the performance before I spotted Jack Armstrong walking in. One more song to warm him up, relax him, then I'd take off the bracelets. I turned to tell the hired band which song we'd be playing next, completely missing the entrance of another familiar face. The music had already begun, when I lifted my head to the mic, began to sing, and saw him.

Banning Dalca.

I blinked in surprise, almost fumbling the lyrics. As the music moaned and sobbed its way into a sexy thump, I noted how appropriate the song was for his appearance. It was suddenly personal, and I found myself singing to him, my stare colliding with his, and then latching on. He looked amazing, as usual, and completely at home in the luxury rock scene. Banning strode past thick couches clad in crimson velvet tapestry and around the more sparsely clothed patrons, all with that sexy air most blooders possessed. He came to a casual stop at the wall on my left, leaning against it to watch me avidly, as I sang Banks's "Waiting Game."

I undulated my hips and melted into the dark tempo, the erotically eerie music. The words came easily, but I couldn't focus on them. I was too intent on Banning. Oh gods, what was he doing there? How had he found me? And then the important question: how did I feel about it?

I swayed with the bass, my eyes closing as I felt the rise of emotions brought on by the sorrowful song. Heartbreak for Torin, regret that I hadn't given Banning a chance, fear that it would end badly if I tried to be with the blooder now, and an ache for causing him the same kind of pain Torin had saddled me with. The longing in the lyrics became my own; the apology in the words was my personal lament.

Banning's eyes sparked and brightened in the shadows. His chest was rising and falling steadily, but intensely, and his hands were clenching at his sides. A woman tried to approach him, and he waved her away without removing that mesmerizing stare from mine.

The lines lifted from self-blame into something hopeful, something pensive, and I felt like I was speaking my truths directly to Banning. Did we end with Fortune's death? Was that all there was for us? I felt my face shifting with the strength of my emotions, begging him to understand. What if we tried to be together, and it wasn't the same? Doubts had been bubbling up inside me since the moment I'd seen my own face tattooed upon his arm. Now they were surfacing in full force. Torin wasn't standing between us any longer. There was nothing to hide behind. So now I had to face those fears. Face Banning.

The music pulsed on, vibrating through my blood, as I made this strange, lilting appeal to a man I had loved in a previous life. When the song finally groaned its way into its conclusion, he slowly nodded, acknowledging everything that had passed between us. There was understanding in the tilt of his head, and smooth satisfaction in the twitch of his lips. He leaned back farther, crossed his arms, and settled in to wait for me. Yes, he'd waited a long time already, but he didn't care one whit.

I turned away from him determinedly, heading into a corner of the stage to secretly remove my steel and onyx bracelets. It was time to work, and I needed to push thoughts of Banning out of my head or I'd be swaying him as well as the loup. On my way back to the mic, I told the band what song was next: "Glory Box" by Portishead. It was a risky choice for the situation, a twisted sort of love song, but I wanted to do more than stop Jack from cheating on women. I wanted to make him see women as worthy of respect and love, and maybe show him how unworthy he was of them in his current state. I wanted to make him a better man.

Perhaps I was projecting my issues. But what the hell? If work helped bring me catharsis, then all the better.

I began to sing the cynical lines, letting them soak up the fury I felt on behalf of those scorned harpies. Magic lifted inside me, exultant in its sudden freedom, and it responded not only to my intentions, but to the intensity of my emotions. I may not have the relic anymore, but it had left a part of itself inside me. I was stronger than I'd been before, my magic exalted to a new level, and every time I sang, I discovered new facets of my enhanced abilities.

I directed the energy to Jack Armstrong alone, and saw him jerk in shock. His mouth softened, his eyes widening as he stared at me. As we connected through music. I spoke to him with my will as well as my words, showing him that women were more than sexual objects. That he was squandering the chance to have love in his life. To have something real. Something beyond the pleasure of flesh and the rush of blood.

I felt him succumbing to my spell, but more than that, I felt his anguish over his wasted life. The words made their own appeal, all on their own, enhancing my magic and forming a bond between me and Jack. I sensed the rise of his epiphany. His heart was a wasteland he had abandoned long ago. Jack Armstrong began to tremble as the jazzy sounds delivered my sweet, stuttering command straight into his subconscious.

I knew precisely when the spell solidified and cracked open that hard heart of his. Jack the womanizer bent over, covering his face with his hands, and wept.

I soothed him now that he'd submitted, ending the song with motivation instead of censure. Urging him to shift his thinking, and open himself up to deeper emotions. They were worth the risk. See more; *be* more. You do not have to limit yourself to this mask you wear. Let it go and you'll be rewarded. It will be all right, Jack. There's an endless supply of love; you just have to look for it.

The crowd cheered, and I hurried through accepting the accolades. My job was over, and I wouldn't be returning to the stage that night, nor would I likely sing there ever again. I'd collect our earnings and hand it all over to the band. Their pay would be nothing compared to mine, so it felt wrong to keep any of it. Not that I was in it for the money anymore. I just needed to keep moving, keep doing. I was trying to outrun the heartache. But maybe it was time to listen to my own music. I needed to stop running and start looking.

I jumped off the stage, making a quick stop to speak with Jack. I laid a hand on his shoulder as I pulled out my cellphone, surreptitiously hitting the Record button on my video screen.

"Hey, you all right?" I asked him.

The loup looked up at me with horrified eyes. "I've been such a complete asshole."

"Yes, you have." I angled the camera toward him. "But it's never too late to change. If you could speak to all the women you've hurt, what would you say to them?"

"I . . ." He blinked and sniffed. "I'd want to tell them that I understand. That I know what I did to them was wrong and I'm sorry. I'm going to change, I promise."

"I know you will, honey." I gave him a pat and walked away, hitting Stop on the video, then sending it to the harpies for confirmation. I would have my payment by morning.

I angled my way through the crowd, heading to Banning. When I reached him, I simply took his hand, and led him out of the bar. He didn't resist. In fact, he came up beside me and slid my arm around his, so it was more like he was escorting me than I was leading him. Subtle, but kind of sexy. I shot him a knowing look, and he smirked.

As soon as we rounded the bar's red-brick corner, I turned on him. "What are you doing here?"

"Cerberus told me I should come." Banning shrugged. "He said things had taken a bad turn with Torin, and that you might be looking for some comfort right about now. He thought I would be

348

better than some random stranger."

"First of all"–I pointed in his face–"thanks for the brutal honesty." I grimaced. "Second, I'm not seeking comfort from anyone. I'm fine. I'm a big girl, and I can handle my shit. That being said, I'm glad you're here."

"You are?"

"I am." I nodded. "I don't know if I want anything more than friendship from you, but I do want something. I want you in my life, Banning."

"I want that too," he said. "In any capacity. So how about spending some time with me before you run off to your next job?"

"What did you have in mind?"

"Walking"–he shrugged–"maybe sitting on a bench. The location and motions don't really concern me as long as we can talk."

"I need some dinner." I jerked my head in the direction I wanted to head.

As we walked, I pondered him and my response to him. I found him attractive, but that simmering emotional cauldron hadn't returned to my belly. I'd been waiting for it. When I saw Banning in the club, I'd been sure it would return. I may have even anticipated it a little. But I felt nothing, and there had been no dreams or flashes either. If the spell forged by the relic between me and Torin was broken, I should be seeing memories of my past life again. So where were they? Unless there had been no true memories. I looked sideways at Banning. Had a blooder somehow managed to trick me? Had I been under an enchantment? Or maybe his intensity had somehow influenced me, and my mind had fooled itself.

"What is it?" Banning asked.

349

He had his hands stuck into his pockets, looking like every other guy walking through the sea-scented night. Except he was gorgeous, his pale face shadowed mysteriously by the street-lamps we passed beneath, and his fit body evident, even through the layers of clothes he wore. I could smell the remnants of the bar on him, but his own dark aroma was lifting through it. Why didn't any of it affect me?

"Just thinking about our alleged past," I muttered.

"Alleged?" Banning looked surprised. "I thought you had accepted it as truth?"

"I'm not sure that what I saw was real." I narrowed my eyes on him.

I was raised to never trust a blooder. It wasn't just my bias either. Most of the paranormal community didn't like them. Blooders were viewed as parasites, no more than diseased humans. Except their infection turned them into leeches, and in most cases, murderers. They weren't even viewed as a true supernatural race. More like party crashers who had managed to slip in through the back. This existence, of killing or coercing their prey, along with centuries of hiding, had made them, in my mother's opinion, shrewd liars.

"It was real, Elaria." Banning sighed. "How would I have deceived you?"

"A spell." I shrugged.

"And the painting?" Banning asked. "My tattoo?" He angled me out of the way of the other pedestrians. "How did I fake those?"

"A really talented artist," I said. "On both accounts."

"And I just so happened to have them prepared for you to see, on the off chance that we met? An Elizabethan-style painting, and a matching, *healed* tattoo," Banning huffed. "I had no idea of your existence until Cerberus told me you could help me."

"Cerberus," I frowned, wondering if it had been a set up.

"Stop it!" Banning pushed me up against a wall. "You trusted someone, and they failed you. I get that. But you can't let it color all of your relationships from here forward. Don't let him break you, Elaria."

"I'm not broken," I pulled away from Banning, and started walking again.

"Then think without the taint of suspicion," Banning strode up beside me. "I have no reason to choose you to trick. I have nothing to gain but your affection, and I would hardly win that if I used foul means to seduce you. You're a magical being; you would eventually discover any deception, and then you'd hate me. That's not something I want, Elaria."

"All right," I whispered. "But the problem is, Banning, I don't know what *I* want anymore."

"You don't have to figure that out right this second." He eased his hand into mine. "Just be open to me as an option. That's all I ask."

I looked down at our joined hands and felt a glimmer of hope. Maybe there could be something between us.

"I think I can manage that," I said softly.

And I did. I let Banning ease into my heart. Just a little. Just enough to remind myself that there was still someone who loved me. Who wanted me desperately. Torin was not the last man I would love. I had talked a tough talk, saying all the things Banning had just reiterated to me. That I couldn't let Torin win. That I would have love again if I just opened myself to it. Now I needed to live the lines.

So I spent the night with Banning. Nothing naughty–I wasn't quite ready for that, but it was almost more intimate for the lack. We had dinner and talked. He told me more about our past together. I told him about my past in this life. Banning listened with gentle focus as I spoke of my parents, my childhood, and my friendship with Cerberus. Then I listened as he told me of his present. The European Falca had expunged all of his crimes, and he was free to grow his gura again. He explained the working of his various businesses to me–he had many more besides the country club–and what he hoped to achieve in the future.

We spoke long into the night, ending up lying beside each other in bed. I fell asleep, and he woke me shortly before dawn.

"I have to go, Ellie," Banning whispered as he pulled a blanket over me.

"What?" I murmured and blinked him into focus.

"Dawn is near." He smiled and kissed my forehead. "But I'll call you and we'll talk again."

"Okay," I said. "See you soon."

"Soon," he agreed.

Chapter Fifty

Declan found me in Venice.

I had just finished a job for a local ryū dread. They'd pooled their funds to hire me so I could run some blooders out of their territory. You'd think a bunch of dragon shifters could handle their own business, but these were of the Asian variety, and they're less inclined to violence than the Western, drachen dreads. And yes, there are Asian dragon-shifters in Italy. Don't be racist.

I was relaxing in a local cafe, sitting at an iron table near an only moderately odorous canal, when the Alexandrite king walked up, casual as can be. I nearly spewed expensive wine all over my new Valentino dress. I had been treating myself, okay? It wasn't like I didn't have money to blow.

"You look well," Declan observed, then waved a hand toward the empty chair before me. "Mind if I join you?"

"Sure." I patted at my mouth with a linen napkin, staining it pink. "How did you find me, King Declan?"

"Can't we dispense with the titles when we're in the human world?" Declan asked with a sensuous smile.

"If you like," I agreed. "How did you find me, Declan?"

"Bribery." He took my glass of wine and stole a sip. "Lovely." He looked up and motioned to a waiter. "Un altro, si prega."

The waiter nodded and ran off to fetch another glass.

"You speak Italian?" I looked over his sharp, but casual,

clothes: tailored pants and a white shirt, open at the collar. His cuffs were rolled back, and a gold watch glimmered on his wrist. The smell of expensive cigar smoke, and even more expensive cologne, wafted off him. "Hell, you *look* Italian."

"Thank you." He eased back into his seat, just as the waiter laid a glass before him. "How did it go with the blooders?"

"Cerberus." I shook my head.

"Cerberus was with the blooders?" Declan lifted a brow.

"No, Cerberus told you where to find me," I accused. "That's who you bribed."

"Yes, of course," he shrugged. "Who else would know your whereabouts?"

"No one," I sighed.

I'd been enjoying the string of new faces I'd met with every job Cerberus gave me. I hadn't been home since the day he sent me to Switzerland. And I hadn't seen a familiar face since my run-in with Banning. I was speaking to him regularly now, slowly warming to the idea of taking things further. But he didn't know where I was currently. Not even my parents knew that.

I had called them after I'd returned from Tír na nÓg. I wanted to check in and let them know I was all right. I told them about the relic and the Shining One war, but not about my catastrophic romance with the Onyx King. I had been too heartbroken then, and their pity wouldn't have helped. My mother had been horrified over my wielding an ancient weapon, but my father was thrilled. He ran off to tell all of his coven buddies about his daughter "the witch warrior." If not for all his enthusiasm over the relic, I would have gone for a visit. But I didn't want to have to talk about the war. So instead, I'd gone to Venice, thinking that I'd take a vacation there after I finished the job.

And now I was sitting across from Declan. First Banning and now the Alexandrite king. Maybe the Universe was trying to tell me something.

"So are you over the beastly King Torin yet?" Declan asked, right on cue.

"I think so," I lied.

I wasn't over Torin, but I did think I was at the point where I could perhaps date someone without it being a rebound. I probably should have considered Banning first, but I still wasn't feeling an attraction for him. I liked him more and more every time we talked. Yet there was no spark. I never felt the urge to take things further. Not even a twinge of the excitement Declan was currently inspiring.

"How long are you in Venice for?" I asked.

"However long you want me to be, Elaria." He smiled slowly. "Shall we start with dinner? That's traditional here, isn't it?"

"In Venice?" I smirked.

"In the human world." He chuckled.

"Dinner works"–I nodded–"but we're already having drinks together. You might as well stay."

"I might as well," Declan agreed. He looked around as if he were seeing the scenery for the first time. "I can't believe I chased you here."

"It's flattering," I said.

"I don't believe I've ever put such effort into wooing a woman," he said. "But you have my eyes."

"Is that it then?" I asked. "You know, there have actually

355

been studies done by humans that show that people are most attracted to those who resemble themselves. But with you, I think it's plain old narcissism."

"Oh, how you wound me." He held a hand to his chest dramatically. "That's not at all what I meant. You must know how rare this particular shade is." He waved his hand out from his chest to indicate my eyes. "When I first saw you, it startled me. I have never seen the color on anyone else. It was like a sign from the stones. As if they were drawing us together like they do with matching monarchs. Then I spoke with you, and I knew it for a certainty."

"You were so flippant at first." I frowned. "I didn't think you were truly interested in me until after the war."

"Well, you were always so entrenched with Torin," he shrugged. "If I had made my desires known, I think I would have received a polite, but stinging, rebuff."

"Valid," I said, then blinked my way through a realization. "Is that why I never saw you partaking in the . . . entertainments?"

"I fail to see how fornicating with Oonagh in front of you would be romantic," he smirked.

"I would have been disappointed in you," I agreed.

"Disappointed? And you noticed my absence." Declan tapped his wine-glass. "At least that's something."

"I noticed you," I admitted. "Of course I did. You know you're a beautiful man, and you're also funny. I like that. Torin could be so serious" I cut myself off with a groan. "Sorry, that just came out. I shouldn't have mentioned him."

"Actually, that's a perfect segue into something else I wanted to discuss with you." He grimaced. "Before we get into the possibility of us, I have to ask if you'd like to know about the

356

uproar you caused in Tír na nÓg?”

“Uproar?” I frowned. “What are you talking about? There was nothing left for me to do. The threat was eliminated, and the relic went back to hibernating on its mountain.”

“Yes,” Declan agreed, “but a certain king thought your departure was too abrupt. I ask again; would you like to hear about it?”

“What did he do?”

“Nothing too horrible, I suppose.” Declan shrugged and looked a little disappointed. I wasn't sure if his disappointment stemmed from Torin not doing anything horrible or from me wanting to know about it. “King Torin threw a few things. Some of them were cast out of his kingdom entirely, like Queen Oonagh.”

“What?” I gaped at him.

“I believe Torin came to his senses after you left.” Declan was watching me carefully. “He seems to have regrets over the way your relationship ended. Oonagh is said to have screeched obscenities at him while she rode away from the castle . . . after being escorted out by Torin's knights.”

“Holy shit,” I whispered.

“Yes, I was a little annoyed to have missed it.” Declan made a face.

“And then what?”

“And then?” Declan shrugged. “And then Torin became even more beastly. He snaps and snarls at his own people and hasn't been seen in public in months. I'm told that the onyx fey, who love their king to the point of absurdity, are actually relieved he's chosen to become a shut-in. That's how horrid his behavior has become.”

357

Something was fluttering inside my chest, some nasty little seed of hope. I tamped it down and hardened my heart against its questing roots.

"He shouldn't have kissed her," I said callously. "If he still cared about me, he shouldn't have kissed Oonagh."

"Indeed," Declan agreed. "But after telling you this, I feel inclined to ask you once more. Are you over Torin? I have no desire to compete with his memory."

"Torin made his choice." I sipped my wine pensively. "It may be petty of me, but I'm glad he regrets it. Beyond that, I refuse to allow him any kind of hold on my heart."

Something vibrated in my stomach, lower than that demon-seed hope. This felt harder, like a warning. A rung bell.

"Excellent." Declan's eyes flitted over me with unrestrained interest.

"Shall we see how much *you'll* be able to hold onto?" I gave Declan a hot look, despite the churning in my belly.

In fact, I knew I acted *because* of that feeling. I needed to do this: take immediate steps to relieve myself of the love I still bore Torin. Declan not only heated my blood; he came without baggage. That was the problem with Banning, and perhaps it was also the reason I hadn't felt aroused by him. Banning brought our past with him, and if I screwed things up between us, it would damage him doubly. I couldn't deal with that kind of responsibility right now.

Declan had none of those issues. The mere fact that he was a Shining One king prevented us from getting too serious. Declan would need a queen to marry eventually, which meant that anything between us would be temporary. I liked the idea of temporary. Forever was a mighty long time for an immortal.

358

His eyes widened. "Now?"

"Yes, now." I nodded my head toward the building behind me. "This is my hotel."

Declan pulled some money from his pocket and flung it on the table. He stood so swiftly, his chair rocked, and he had to steady it before he held his hand out to me. I looked at his elegant hand, the pale, long fingers, and then lifted my eyes to Declan's. I slowly stood, placing my hand in his.

"I think you'll find my grip to be very satisfactory," Declan purred as I led him up to my room.

Chapter Fifty-One

Declan's hands were on me as soon as the door was locked behind us. I turned into his arms, welcoming the fierce seduction. One strong hand went to the nape of my neck and held me still as his tongue lashed with mine. I moaned into the kiss. That's right–this was how it felt to want someone, to need to feel the press of their skin against yours. I had missed the feeling, and now that it was back, I wanted more. My hands tore blindly at his clothes, pushing his shirt from him and casting it to the floor. The smooth curves of hard muscles were revealed to my questing fingers as the sound of a zipper announced Declan's eagerness to undress me as well.

I stepped free of my dress, but as soon as I pressed my body to his, a horrible headache struck me, and I swayed on my feet. Declan caught me effortlessly, swung me up into his arms, and laid me on the bed. I groaned as he pushed the hair away from my face, and anxiously peered down at me.

"Elaria?" Declan eased onto the bed beside me. "What is it? Is something wrong?"

"I don't know." I was already recovering. "That was so strange. Never mind; come here." I reached for him.

Declan shimmied out of his pants first, so that we were both down to our underwear. Silk boxers on him and black lace on me. Then he slid over me, his narrow hips parting my thighs. I sighed in delight. There's nothing like wrapping yourself around a muscled, male body. But as soon as Declan was nestled against me, pain surged through my head again. This time, it came with an awful panic.

"No," I gasped. "Stop."

"Elaria."–Declan stared down at me in shock–"Are you enchanted?"

"Am I what?" I blinked.

"This has the feel of magic to it." Declan sat back and pondered me. "How do you feel now?"

"Fine," I scowled and sat up as well. "It's only when we start to get intimate . . ."

"That this illness overtakes you," Declan finished for me. "Yes, I see that."

"Fuck!" I swore and jumped up. "I thought it had worn off. It had to have. Torin wouldn't have been able to . . . oh shit." I laughed scornfully. "That's why he was so upset. He probably couldn't get any farther with Oonagh than we were able to go just now."

"Did you perform some kind of binding ritual with King Torin?" Declan's brows lifted.

"Yes."

"That doesn't make any sense."

"Why not?"

"I can't imagine why Torin would bond with you, if he intended on leaving you in the end." Declan shook his head.

"The relic started it; we just went along. Maybe he didn't want to seem like an ass by refusing it." I shrugged. "Whatever it was, it doesn't matter anymore. The relic is asleep. It can't defend its spell. I'm going to fix this right now."

"The relic cast the spell?" Declan stood. "Elaria, you may

not be able to remove it."

"Just watch me," I growled.

Then I began to sing. I'd be damned if I allowed Torin to hinder me after he betrayed me. Hell no, I was going to break this enchantment and move on. Nothing was going to stop me from getting my life back. I may not be the Queen of Song anymore, but I was still a spellsinger. A damn good one.

I had the perfect song for breaking the relic's hold on me. Clairity's "Exorcism." A subtle, slow burn of broken dreams transforming into a catharsis. An evolution of healing from the loss of love. The low hum of the lyrics surged up into a swirling cadence of freedom. Exorcism indeed. I needed to banish the ghost of my ex-lover. I closed my eyes to the power of the song, letting the magic fill my throat and rush out of my lips. It spiraled around my body, tingling over my skin before seeping back inside me. It was one of the few times I'd spellsung myself.

The words were full of righteous renewal, a woman remembering who she truly was and becoming herself again. I cast out the demons of a false affection and then sought to repair myself. There was denial in the music, a rebuke against the damage done, but also acceptance, and finally, release.

I saw Declan gaping at me as my skin began to glow. He stood in a sort of trance, then eased closer. His hand lifted slightly, as if he wanted to touch me but wasn't sure he should.

"Elaria," he whispered in wonder.

I let the magic multiply, let it manifest within me and climb to an apex of anguish. It was over at last, time to move on. Time to let him go. Goodbye, Torin.

The spell broke. I fell to my knees with a whimper, the words dying in my mouth. Their death left a bitter taste behind, hard to swallow. As I fell, I heard an anguished roar, echoing up to

362

my balcony from the street below. Declan was immediately beside me, cradling me. I blinked up at him in confusion.

"That sounded like..."

"Torin." Declan scowled, and helped me stand. "Impossible." He stepped out onto the balcony, and stared down to the plaza with widening eyes. "How did he find us?"

"No," I whispered, coming up behind him. "Not here. Not now."

I looked down, following Declan's gaze. Sure enough, there was Torin. He was just wobbling to his feet, as if he'd been struck down. There was a crowd around him, good Samaritans making sure Torin was all right. But he waved them off and looked unerringly up to me. I inhaled sharply at the fury in his eyes, and backed away from the balcony.

"Looks like we're about to have company," Declan slipped into his pants. "Allow me." He held out my dress for me.

"How can you be so calm?" I asked as I stepped into it.

"What else is there to be?" Declan zipped up the back, and then slid his shirt on. "In fact, I look forward to this. We can settle things between you two once and for all. I won't have to worry about him coming back into your life and"

"Elaria!" Torin's voice came from the other side of my door. "Open this door, or I'll break it down."

"Persephone poison you!" I swore as I headed to the door. "Stop making such a racket."

I swung it open and met his eyes. Torin's stunning, cerulean eyes. His stare was still furious, but the fury was replaced with something else as it flickered over me. Something even stronger than rage. Something I'd never thought to see in his eyes again.

363

"Why?" Torin growled as he slammed the door behind him. "Why would you leave like that? Without speaking to me first?"

"King Torin," Declan made his presence known.

"King Declan," Torin narrowed his eyes on Declan. "Get out before I kill you."

"Fuck you, Torin," I snapped at him. "Declan is here by my invitation. You are not."

"Get out!" Torin roared at Declan.

Declan looked at me calmly.

"Fine." I rolled my eyes. "You probably shouldn't be here for this anyway," I said to Declan. "Can I meet you down in the cafe after this is finished?"

"Of course. Take as long as you need." Declan gallantly kissed my hand and then left, closing the door quietly behind him.

"What the fuck are you doing with him?" Torin growled as soon as Declan was gone.

"You don't get to ask me that," I snarled.

"Elaria"–Torin took a deep breath and ran a hand through his wild hair–"I have been all over this human world searching for you. I've had spies everywhere. I tried to get that son of a bitch Cerberus to tell me where you were, but he refused. In fact, he threatened me with physical harm so ridiculous in nature, I'm fairly certain it's impossible to achieve. The only reason I found you today was because I had someone watching Declan. Now you say I don't get to ask you why he's here?"

"You don't." I lifted my chin. "You were the one who cheated on me."

"The hell I did!" Torin shouted.

"Oh?" I lifted my brows. "So that was someone else I saw kissing Oonagh?"

"No, that was *Oonagh* kissing *me*," he snapped. "I don't know what part of that moment you witnessed, but if you had watched a little longer, you would have seen me push her away. Violently."

"Declan saw you first." I narrowed my eyes on him. "Then I saw you. That would have given you plenty of time to remove her from your person."

"You've obviously never been attacked by Oonagh." He rolled his eyes, then suddenly deflated, as if all of his energy had been sapped away by his rant. He dropped onto the edge of the bed and stared at me mournfully. "All of this because you saw something that meant *nothing*."

"It wasn't just the kiss," I tried to hold onto the anger, but part of me was beginning to doubt my interpretation of the event. I replayed it in my head. Torin's hands had been at Oonagh's waist, but had they been holding her or pushing her away? I wasn't sure anymore. "You withdrew from me. We hadn't slept together in days. And Oonagh was always there, always touching you, looking at you like you were hers."

"I was trying to set things right in Tír na nÓg," he huffed. "And part of it was a settlement for you. As far as Oonagh, she's always acted like this. Why would you suddenly be suspicious over her?"

"What?" I eased forward a little.

"Which part?"

"The settlement."

"I was negotiating tribute for you," Torin explained. "It was rough going and I was exhausted. Then you started sleeping in the guest room. I thought you didn't want to be bothered with my attentions. That maybe you were tired too."

"The fight you had with Oonagh," I whispered. "When she left Onyx . . ."

"How do you know about that?" Torin scowled.

"Declan told me," I shrugged. "Just before you arrived."

"I cast Oonagh out of my kingdom after I found your letter." His jaw clenched. "I couldn't stand to look at her. Then I began to search for you. I finally found your home in Hawaii, but you weren't there. It was empty, just as you left me. Damn it all, Elaria." Torin shook his head. "How could leave me like that? After everything we went through, how could you think I would cast you aside for Oonagh? *Oonagh!*" He spat the name like it was a curse.

"I . . ." I blinked in shock. "I thought the relic's spell was broken when it went back into hibernation. I thought your desire for Oonagh had returned."

"No, it wasn't broken, not that it would have mattered if it had been," he sighed. "You broke it just now."

"Yes, I know," I whispered.

"That hurt, little bird."

"Yeah, it did," I agreed. "I'm sorry."

"I'm not." He stood, a hard expression settling over his face.

"You're not?" I felt my stomach drop.

Damn him. I had just begun to think we had a chance again, and there he went, dashing it all to pieces.

366

"No." Torin brought us together with a single step. "Because now you'll know that what I feel for you has nothing to do with a spell. You'll know that we're together because we want to be, not because of some bond the relic has forged between us. You'll know that the reason I don't look at other women is because I think you're the most beautiful thing I've ever seen. And you'll know that this is real." He pulled me against his chest and kissed me.

It was a slashing, punishing kiss, but it quickly morphed into pure passion. My arms fell limply to my sides in shock as the taste of him brought memories exploding to life within me. My heart started pounding and tears filled my eyes. Internally, I shouted at myself, "Kiss him back you fool!" And I did. I wrapped my arms around his wide shoulders, and clung to him like he was the last real thing in my world. And I kissed him. I kissed him with every ounce of emotion I had. All those nights of pain, those numb days, and those screaming fits of fury. And the love, the deep well of love that was somehow still overflowing inside me.

When Torin and I finally pulled away from each other, my cheeks were drenched with tears, but so were his. I blinked at that, swiping at my eyes to see him more clearly. Yep, Torin was crying. His long lashes were spiked wet, and his eyes were bluer than ever with that shine over them. Of course the man looked amazing, even when he wept.

"Don't ever scare me like that again," he whispered, and pulled me back into his embrace. "Do you know what you've put me through? How did you expect me to live without your song in my heart?"

"You?" I teased. "I stopped bathing."

"You *what*?" Torin pulled back in mock horror.

"Shut up," I huffed.

"If you ever suspect me of wrongdoing again, speak to me

first." Torin bracketed my face with his palms. "Don't just pack your things and leave, Elaria. That was cruel and cowardly. Behavior unfitting of a queen. I never expected it from you."

"I'm not a queen anymore," I whispered to him. "I thought that might be one of the reasons you didn't want me."

"Because you weren't a queen?" Torin's eyes widened. "Do you think I'm somehow restricted by my status? That a king can only marry a queen?"

"I . . . yeah," I frowned, trying to remember all I'd heard about fey monarchy. "That's how it sounded."

"You met Duchess Branna." He shook his head.

"Duchess Branna . . . yeah. And?"

"Branna is Parthalon's wife." Torin wiped at my wet cheeks. "A ruler can marry whomever they wish. If that person happens to be another ruler, it works out to their benefit. But it's not necessary. I could marry a woman with no magic at all, if I chose to. She would be my wife, but she wouldn't hold the title of queen. That title is earned through magic; it can't be gained through marriage."

"So Branna . . ."

"Has the magic of a duchess." Torin nodded. "Just a step down from queen. Not that Parthalon cares."

"So the loss of the relic doesn't concern you?"

"It's kind of a relief," he admitted. "The relic seemed to have its own agenda. I was constantly worried over what it might do to you. To us."

"Like bind us together?" I lifted my brows at him.

"That was something I started, if you'll recall." Torin

smiled. "And another reason your departure baffled me. I made a vow to you, Elaria. It may not have been a vow of marriage, but it was a considerable one. With or without the power of the relic behind it, it meant a lot to me. I can't conceive of you walking away from that. Or of you thinking that *I* would walk away from it."

"The heart can be silly sometimes," I shrugged.

"Evidently your heart can be down-right dumb," he grimaced.

"Hey now," I growled. "I did see you kissing Oonagh."

"Stones, I hate that woman." Torin groaned, and hung his head back in agony.

"Me too," I huffed.

"Our hearts are caged together, even without the relic's spell." Torin laid his palm over my chest. "Fly away, and you'll only take me with you. You're mine, remember?"

"And you're mine," I nodded.

"I love you, Elaria." Torin lifted his palm to my cheek.

"I love you too." I covered his hand with my own. "But if I ever catch you with another woman, I'll sing you both one last lullaby."

"Agreed." He smiled brilliantly. "And speaking of other lovers"–his grin turned into a grimace–"let's go down and have a few words with yours."

"We aren't lovers." I rolled my eyes.

"That's not what it looked like when I saw you on the balcony." Torin's eyes narrowed.

"Okay, yes," I huffed. "I brought him up here to have sex with him. I needed to try and get over you," I added when Torin started to growl. "But I got a damn headache every time we attempted to take it beyond kissing."

"The spell," he smirked. "You weren't able to go further?"

"No," I admitted, "and that's why I broke the enchantment. I assumed that you sent Oonagh away because you were frustrated over the spell."

"Hardly," he grumbled. "It was never pushed far enough for me to know it would have that kind of effect."

"Oh."

"Yes, 'oh.'" Torin glowered at me. "How many times did you kiss Declan?"

"A couple," I shrugged.

Torin glowered more.

"Maybe three?"

"You're asking me?

"No, I'm just not sure."

"So they weren't very memorable then?" Torin mused.

"No, they were good." I flinched when his hands clenched around me. "I mean, no, I can hardly recall them now."

"Sweet stones." Torin shook his head. "I'm going to have to murder the Alexandrite king in Venice. Maybe I can dump his body into the canal."

"Leave Declan alone," I sighed as I followed Torin out of the room. "He's been a total gentleman."

"Yes, he looked like a gentleman, standing on your balcony in his shiny sex clothes."

"Shiny . . ." I gaped at him. "You mean his silk boxers? Those are what human men wear. Maybe not always in silk, but it's not an unheard of choice."

"They look like women's clothing."

"They do not," I said. "I think they're kind of sexy."

"See?" Torin pointed his finger at me. "Sex clothes."

"You're impossible." I rolled my eyes. "Just don't be mean to Declan."

"I will be firm, but not mean." Torin lifted his chin. "I have won the fair maiden after all. I can afford to be gracious."

"You're such an ass," I muttered.

"What's that?" Torin lifted a brow.

"I said your ass would look good in silk boxers," I replied with a straight face.

"You like those shiny men's undergarments?" Torin lifted a brow.

"Yeah."

"All right." He sighed dramatically. "We shall purchase some before we leave Earth."

"What kind of underwear do you have on now?" I asked, suddenly curious. Torin was dressed in a fashion similar to Declan: slacks, buttoned shirt, and dress shoes. All human-made.

"What I always wear," he smirked.

"So, nothing then?" I smirked back, and slid my hand over

his rear. Yep, just one layer of fabric between us.

"That's right." Torin sucked in his breath as my hand roamed. "I believe we'll need to make this conversation with Declan a quick one."

"That sounds like a wise decision, Your Majesty." I winked at him, and slipped ahead to find Declan.

Torin hurried after me.

Poor Declan, he was about to be very disappointed. But at least I had saved him from being murdered and thrown into a canal.

Chapter Fifty-Two

We didn't go back to Tír na nÓg right away. Instead, Torin and I headed to Hawaii and had the vacation I'd been planning to have in Venice. During the day, we lay out in the sun and swam together in the sea. Then we made love in the hot Hawaiian nights. The scent of coconut oil and sun-warmed man would forever bring back those memories for me.

Banning called, and I was put in the awkward position of telling him what had happened with Torin. He was upset of course, but gave me the same line he had in Tír na nÓg. He would always be there if I changed my mind. Declan's response had been similar, but much more succinct. With a regal air, he'd informed me that I knew where to find him. Immortality gave a man the option of being patient, I suppose.

Cerberus was the hardest to deal with. He just couldn't get over the fact that Torin hadn't done anything wrong. Once Cerberus has scented blood, he hates giving up the hunt. It took me weeks to convince him that Torin wasn't to blame. He did finally come around, though it took several shots of Tequila for him to grasp the concept of Torin's innocence.

I finally told my parents about Torin, and they came to Hawaii to meet him. Torin's witch blood eased him into my father's good graces nearly immediately, but my mother took a little longer to win over. She lasted through the appetizers before she succumbed to his Shining One charm. At which point she declared that she didn't care if he was a pervert; he was a lovely man. The look on Torin's face was one I'll cherish forever.

So now we're back in Tír na nÓg, building a tremulous plan

to live our lives together. Torin can't stay away from his kingdom for long stretches, but he promised he'd visit Earth with me as often as he could. The remainder of our free time would be spent together in Tír na nÓg. But the key word there is "free." He had kingly duties, and I still wanted to take the occasional job to keep my reputation solid and my magic in tip-top shape. There would be spaces of time we'd have to spend apart. But I think that's good for a relationship. How can you miss someone who never leaves?

Besides, our hearts were caged together. When I flew away, I took him with me.

Keep reading for a sneak peek into the next book in the Spellsinger
Series:

A Symphony of Sirens

Chapter One

"El?" Cerberus rapped on my picture window, startling me enough to spill my coffee. He chuckled.

"Gods damn it, Cer." I swiped at the mess with a napkin. "Can't you come to the front door like a normal person?"

"It's much more fun this way." He came in the back door and started rooting around my kitchen. "You got anymore of that."

"You mean, so you can replace what you made me spill?

"Yeah sure." He got himself a mug and filled it, then brought the pot over to me. "I've had some unsettling news."

"No." I shook my head adamantly. "I just finished that crazy job for the nagas. I'm tired and I intend on heading back to Tír na nÓg as soon as I finish this coffee."

"Still with Torin, eh?" Cerberus took the seat across from me.

"Yes, I'm still with Torin," I huffed. "Things are going really well actually."

"Things are going really well actually," Cerberus mocked me.

"I don't sound like that," I grimaced.

"It's not a job." He ignored me. "It's straight up news. Siren news."

"If it's siren news, why hasn't my mother called?"

"She may not want to bring you into it." Cerberus sighed. "It's bad."

"The last time you used those words, I had to kill an entire army of blooders."

"Uh-huh."

"Sweet stones, Cerberus, just tell me."

"Since when have you started using their expressions?" Cerberus scowled.

By "their" he meant the Shining Ones, of which my boyfriend happened to be a king. I'd been spending most of my time in fairy central, aka Tír na nÓg. It was possible that Cerberus, who was not only the ex-Hound of Hades but also my best friend, was jealous. It looked as if I needed to make some more time for him.

"You know you can always come for a visit," I offered. "I'll get you a traveling stone."

"Torin already gave me one," he admitted.

"What? Then why don't you come to see us in Tír na nÓg?"

"I don't know," he sighed. "Do you want to hear about the sirens or not?"

"Go on then."

"They're disappearing."

"Disappearing how?"

Cerberus gave me a look that clearly said I was an idiot.

"There are several ways a supernatural of the Beneath could disappear," I chided him. "They could fade out of existence, they could go invisible from a spell, they"

"Someone is abducting sirens," Cerberus growled.

"Oh," I blinked. "I'd better call my mother."

"Yeah, you might want to do that." He rolled his eyes.

I left the dining table in search of my cell. My mother answered on the second ring.

"Praise Persephone," my mother exclaimed. "I need you, Elaria."

"I've just heard about the disappearances," I told her. "Why didn't you call me?"

"I've just heard as well." Her voice dipped into an angry mutter. "Cerberus is evidently more informed than I. And about my own people no less."

"Well, he makes it his business to know everyone else's," I said. "Do I need to get on a plane?"

"Yes," she said immediately. "Come home, honey."

"How many have gone missing, Mom?"

"Eight, including your Aunt Aoide."

"Aunty Aoide is gone?" I felt my knees go weak.

She was my favorite. Aunty Aoide had often come to visit me when I was a child. Being raised on an island with only my parents for company made me appreciative of consistent visitors.

"Yes." Mom's voice quivered. "Your father is upset. He's already started five fires by accident."

"I'm on my way." I hung up the phone and looked at Cerberus. "You coming along?"

"To siren central?" Cerberus smirked. "I wouldn't miss it for all the worlds."

About the Author

Amy Sumida is the Internationally Acclaimed author of the Award-Winning Godhunter Series, the fantasy paranormal Twilight Court Series, the Beyond the Godhunter Series, the music-oriented paranormal Spellsinger Series, and several short stories. Her books have been translated into several languages, have made it to the top seller's list on Amazon numerous times, and the first book in her Spellsinger Series won a publishing contract with Kindle Press.

She was born and raised in Hawaii and brings her unique island perspective to all of her books. She doesn't believe in using pen names, saving the fiction for her stories. She's known for her kick-ass heroines who always have a witty comeback ready, and her strong, supporting male characters who manage to be sensitive and alpha all at once.

All she's ever wanted to do since she was a little girl, was to write novels. To be able to do so for a living is a blessing which she wakes up thankful for every day. Beyond her books, she enjoys collecting toys, to keep herself young, and cats, to keep herself loved.

For information on new releases, detailed character descriptions, and an in-depth look into the worlds of Godhunter and the Twilight Court, check out Amy's website;

http://www.amysumida.com/

You can also find her on facebook at:

https://www.facebook.com/AmySumidaAuthor/

On Twitter under @Ashstarte

On Goodreads:

https://www.goodreads.com/author/show/7200339.Amy_Sumida

On Tumblr: http://vervainlavine.tumblr.com/

And you can find her entire collection of books, along with some personal recommendations, on her Amazon store:

https://sites.google.com/site/authoramysumida/home?pli=1

Made in the USA
Coppell, TX
11 July 2020